REVEREND MOTHER MARY CHRISTOPH
ASKED ALL THE NEW GIRLS:

"Why do you want to be a nun?"
"I don't know," said Kat. She was twenty-four,
cially independent, ex-student, ex-traveler, ex-lov
tell myself I'm crazy and I keep coming back to
think I'm a raving lunatic."

"Why do you want to be a nun?"
Jane couldn't answer. There was such a thing as fanaticism. They didn't like it any more here than her
mother liked it at home. She said, "I want to give my
whole life, body and mind, to God. I don't know if I
have a vocation. I think I do. I want to find out for
sure."

"Why do you want to be a nun?"
All Annie could think of was her mother's small
cramped living room, the worn furniture, the knickknacks, and her mother's complaint, *who do you think
you are?* Annie looked at the tall nun, trying to decide
what she was supposed to do, what she was supposed to
say.

"Why do you want to be a nun?"
Kat and Jane and Annie didn't know the answer. Before
they found it, they were trapped in the growing horror
of unhallowed evil.

Sanctity

A NOVEL BY

ORANIA PAPAZOGLOU

IVY BOOKS • NEW YORK

Ivy Books
Published by Ballantine Books
Copyright © 1986 by Orania Papazoglou

Library of Congress Catalog Card Number: 86-1009

ISBN: 0-8041-0115-9

This edition published by arrangement with Crown Publishers, Inc.

Printed in Canada

First Ivy Books Edition: June 1987

A vocation is God's call: "What would God prefer me to be?" —Not "What would I prefer to be?"
> ——THE NEW SAINT JOSEPH BALTIMORE CATECHISM

Why do you want to be a nun?
> ——REVEREND MOTHER MARY CHRISTOPHER

"*They're going to say it was the crisis in vocations, you see. They're going to say we never would have—*"

"*Crisis in vocations?*"

"*Crisis in vocations, yes. That was because of the sixties, you see, and Vatican II and changes in the Orders and, oh, a lot of things started to be different. All of a sudden everybody wanted to be a nun. We turned down two thirds of them and we still took more than we ever had before. Then all the changes started and there were fewer and fewer applicants and fewer and fewer postulants and some of our younger Sisters left. Many of our younger Sisters left. Do you know what the average age of American nuns is today? Fifty-five. Fifty-five.*"

"*I see.*"

"*No, you don't. That's what people are going to say. They're going to say because of the crisis in vocations and not having enough applicants we took someone we never would have before. But that isn't true. It didn't happen that way.*"

"*No?*"

"*No. We've taken some risks and some of them have worked out and some haven't, but she wasn't one of them. She wasn't a risk, you see. We'd have taken her anytime, even in the old days. She was perfect, you see. She was exactly what we were looking for.*"

"*Dear sweet Jesus Christ—*"

"*We can only know what we know. I realize that doesn't sound like sense, but it is. We had the recommendation of her sponsor and a letter from her priest and we interviewed her. And it was all perfect. We couldn't know what was going on in her mind.*"

"*No.*"

"*Maybe nothing was going on, not then.*"

"*Maybe not.*"

"*There were things, but everyone who comes here has . . .*

1

things. Redemption is the point, Lieutenant. Are you a lieutenant?"

"Yes."

"Redemption and salvation. That's what we're doing here. So there were things, but that was normal."

"Normal? Normal?"

"Normal. In the beginning, as far as we could know. Normal."

"Normal. Dear sweet Jesus. There's two pints of blood on this floor and you talk about normal."

"Please—"

"Please what, Sister?"

"Please listen."

INTERVIEWS

1

"Why do you want to be a nun?"

The room was oddly shaped, misproportioned for the people in it. It put Kat off balance. The older nun—the important one, Kat thought—was a monster. She was over five feet ten and topped four hundred pounds. Her long gray robes were a layered tent. Her eyes were very old. Her face was as smooth and soft as an infant's. Kat had seen girls of twenty whose skin was not as clear and tight as the Reverend Mother Christopher's.

The other nun was more of a type. Small and round and rosy-faced, she could have been the female support in a Barry Fitzgerald marzipan epic. The white wimple made her eyes seem very large and very bright. Looking at her freed Kat's throat for the endless tea-talk that seemed to be the only content of this interview. It was like being lulled to sleep by water. Kat had always been able to sleep on boats, even when she'd seen the wormholes in the hull, even when she knew they were loaded double capacity and no one cared if they sank. She was slipping into a memory of it, the good memory, when the question came.

Why do you want to be a nun?

The question should have been, why do you *think* you want to be a nun?

Four weeks of fevered preparation, and it was useless. This was the one question she had been sure she'd be asked. She had a hundred answers to it, a thousand reasons why Katherine Mary O'Brien, aged twenty-four, financially independent (though barely), ex-student, ex-lover, ex-traveler, ex-(mild) political radical (three Greenpeace demonstrations and a march on the Indian Point nuclear power plant), should want to spend the rest of her life in the most traditional active Order of nuns still operating in the United States. She had drunk a million cups of coffee and paced her mother's bare-wood Massachusetts floor, talking to herself, drilling herself. She thought of it as an essay contest. Complete the following in a hundred words or less: I, Katherine Mary O'Brien, want to be a nun because...

Now she couldn't say any of it. She was uncomfortably aware that her dress was too bright, too expensive, too sophisticated for this room. What was the message here? What was the point of wearing red silk to an interview in a convent?

She opened her mouth and told the truth.

"I don't know," she said. She sounded very clear and sure of herself.

"You don't know." The Reverend Mother Christopher didn't sound surprised, didn't seem to be questioning. The other nun—Sister Clare Marie, Mistress of Postulants—looked pleased. If they admitted her, Kat thought, she would spend the next year with Sister Clare Marie.

"It keeps coming up," Kat said. This time she sounded lame. "I tell myself I'm crazy and I keep coming back to it. I can't get rid of it."

"And you think you're crazy, for wanting to be a nun?"

Kat wished the other one would talk. The Reverend Mother Christopher had a spirit voice, like the Ghostly Presence at a séance.

"I think I'm a raving lunatic," Kat said. "Every time I bring this up, my mother threatens to have me committed, and I'm not sure she's wrong."

"Why do you want to be a nun? Jane? Why—"

The words were in the air, cold, separate, and she thought: all the rooms in this house are empty. She had to bite the inside of her cheek to keep herself from giggling. It had been like that all morning. She'd sat before these two women—the small, round, smiling one and the huge, round, glowering one—telling herself over and over this was a Solemn Occasion. Sister Mathilde back in West Haven had stressed that. The interview was a Solemn Occasion because it determined the decision of the Motherhouse, and only if that decision was favorable could you be said to have a vocation. What you felt in your heart didn't matter. That could be a trick of the devil. That could be gas.

What did she feel in her heart? *All the rooms in this house are empty.* She wasn't thinking of the convent, of course. The convent was full. She could feel it. It shifted and sighed, like an arthritic, overweight old woman turning in bed. She was thinking of the house in West Haven, with its twelve rooms and the name "Galloway" on the mailbox in black letters on a gold background. The letters slanted.

She looked at the Reverend Mother Christopher and almost said: All the rooms in this house are empty. Let me be filled with the Lord. She held herself back. There was such a thing as fanaticism. They didn't like it here any more than her mother liked it at home. "Everyone wants to be a nun at your age," her mother said. "It doesn't mean anything." Here they thought it did mean something, but you had to be careful. You couldn't admit to fear. You couldn't show desperation.

She said, "I want to give my whole life body and mind, to God."

The Reverend Mother Christopher inclined her head. It was the right answer, the practiced answer. Jane was suddenly sure it meant nothing. She could see herself going to the mailbox and opening the rejection letter. She could feel her mother's hand on her arm, leading her down the crushed gravel path to the driveway, steering her to a psychiatrist the way a pilot steers a boat into a safe port. "You don't have a vocation, you have an obsession."

Her mother and her father. Her father was gone now, married for the third time, living in Florida. "A phase," her mother said, hanging on to the house and the alimony (when it came) and her status in the Church. "He'll end a suicide," her mother said. Suicide was destiny, humiliation, damnation. They would all end suicides, everyone her mother didn't like, or didn't approve of.

"I don't know if I have a vocation," she told the Reverend Mother Christopher. "I think I do. I want to find out for sure."

The Reverend Mother Christopher inclined her head again. Stock answers to stock questions, examination and response. That was the Church they all grew up with, the Church that was supposed to be fading away. But it wasn't fading away. The outward and visible signs had disappeared, but the inward and spiritual—she wouldn't call it grace—the inward and spiritual were still there. Original and venial and mortal, the sins piled one on top of the other. They made a tower twice as high as Babel and half as sturdy. Put one more sin on that pile and it would fall on you, crush you, obliterate you. Not send you to hell, obliterate you. As if you'd never been.

Somewhere in the towers overhead, bells started ringing. The two nuns stood up, smoothing their long gray skirts.

"You must come on the twelfth of September," Reverend Mother Christopher said. "Sister Clare Marie"—the other nun bobbed, a happy child making a curtsy at a tea party—"will be your Postulant Mistress."

"Yes," Jane said. "Yes."

"There is a list of things to bring," Reverend Mother Christopher said. "You can pick it up in the office on the first floor."

"Yes," Jane said again. She stood watching the nuns leave, wondering what was behind the heavy wooden door at the back of the room. A hallway, perhaps. A refectory.

She felt nothing.

5

"Why do you want to be a nun?"

Annie Bliss looked down at her skirt—her uniform skirt, from Precious Blood; there hadn't been time to go home to change—and wondered what the two women sitting on the couch thought of her. The question had come and gone. The answer had come and gone. Had they listened to any of it? Had they decided to accept her before she ever stepped into this room?

They had accepted her. Annie was sure of that. The tall one—the angry one, Annie would have said, under other circumstances—was talking about equipment lists and arrival times and the things Annie shouldn't bring. Annie wanted to feel relieved, but she couldn't. She couldn't even feel triumphant. She would go back now, to her mother waiting in the rented Lincoln Continental, and it wouldn't matter. She would get in the passenger side and not even hate her mother for insisting on the car.

Why do you want to be a nun?

"You can go to secretarial school," her mother said, and "ask them what the dowry is, ask them that. If it's too high, we can't pay it." There hadn't been a dowry. Her grades were good—college-course grades all of them, in spite of what her mother wanted, what her mother thought proper. The letter from Father Keenan was lying on the coffee table, glowing like one of those phosphorescent necklaces they sold at the street fairs in New Haven. When she went out to the car, she would have won.

Why do you want to be a nun?

The smaller of the two, the happy one, leaned forward and tapped Annie's knee.

"I think the poor girl's in shock, Reverend Mother."

The larger one smiled. She was much more human when she smiled. "If she's in shock now, what will she be like by the end of the year?"

The smaller one rose and took Annie's arm, forcing Annie to stand. "I'm Sister Clare Marie," she said, in a tone that indicated she'd repeated this information more than once in Annie's hearing. "If you'll come with me, I'll get you the papers you need."

Annie looked at the taller one, trying to decide what she was supposed to do, what she was supposed to say. She couldn't just turn her back and walk out. She couldn't genuflect.

Why do you want to be a nun?

All she could think of was her mother's small, cramped living room, the overstuffed furniture, the knickknacks, the worn place in the carpet, and the complaint—who do you think you are who do you think you are who do you think you are—that assumed that some people were magically born to interesting lives and others (themselves and everyone they knew) to knowing what to expect. Sharon O'Shaughnessy went off to Wellesley, but that was a sin. That meant the O'Shaughnessys were forgetting where they came from. Mary Tyler took a job in Paris, and that was a sin, too. She would only get pregnant and never be married, or else have one of those French abortions and lose her faith. Bobby Carney seemed to have made a lot of money, but you couldn't trust appearances. He could be in debt up to his ears and it would all come down on his head someday; the bankruptcy would be in the paper and everyone would know.

Jealousy and malice, Annie thought, were the passports. Say the secret word and win a hundred dollars.

Why do you want to be a nun?

Sister Clare Marie opened a door at the far end of the room, a door Annie hadn't noticed before. The Reverend Mother Christopher stood, bending at the waist in some kind of final salute, holding out her hand.

"Thank you, Reverend Mother," Annie said. She took the offered hand and curtsied.

"This way," Sister Clare Marie said.

Annie wondered how many doors she'd passed and not seen, how many they'd kept hidden from her. Doors and windows and walls, she thought. Then, realizing she wasn't making sense, she tried to hurry without seeming as if she were hurrying to the door Sister Clare Marie was holding open. The little nun was beaming at her.

Why do you want to be a nun?

"Please listen."

"I am listening, Sister. It's—what?—four o'clock in the morning? I've been listening for almost an hour."

"It must all sound so beside the point, but it isn't. We're a very old Order. The only Order older than ours is the Benedictine, and the Benedictines started cloistered and stayed that way. We have some cloistered Sisters in each of the Motherhouses, but most of us go out into the world—"

"She was very active, Sister."

"Lieutenant—"

"It obviously isn't necessary to go out into the world to be active, Sister."

"I told you it sounded beside the point. I told you it wasn't."

"Why isn't it?"

"Because it explains why things were the way they were. Why we didn't notice sooner. The great teaching Orders are communities. They put a lot of emphasis on the group. We still think of ourselves as a contemplative Order. We live in community, but we come here to find a personal salvation, an individual salvation. We come to speak privately with God. When we train our Sisters, we emphasize introspection. We build interior silence. No Sister may intrude on the interior silence of another Sister. No Sister may cause a distraction or seek one. No Sister may invade the privacy of another Sister by asking personal questions. No Sister may break silence except for reasons of courtesy or necessity."

"Courtesy or necessity."

"No human system is perfect, Lieutenant. We watch them for infractions of the Rule. We can't hear everything, see everything. And they talk at dinner. We dropped the rule of silence at dinner twenty years ago."

"Sister—"

"They're supposed to report on each other, as an exercise

*in charity. It's an exercise in charity to report the failings of
your Sisters because only in that way can failings be corrected."*

"Good Lord—"

*"Don't look like that, Lieutenant. They don't do it. The
good ones don't, anyway. The ones who come telling tales are
never the ones you want to stay in. But that's the problem,
you see. You can't trust the ones who come to you, and the
ones you trust won't talk. You don't know how much to believe."*

"Are you trying to tell me someone told you—"

*"No one told me anything, Lieutenant. Maybe they told
each other, maybe they didn't. We'll never know. What we do
know is that* they *knew."*

"Knew what?"

*"Knew something was wrong. They knew the very first
day."*

ARRIVALS

1

Going from Framingham to Northton they took 91 South
just past Hartford, then got off and shot into a farmer's maze
of back roads, heading for the sea. That's where the trouble
started: something in that country had turned back on itself.
Something in that country had buried itself in sand, protecting itself against the fifties and the sixties and even the Second World War. What was left was a preserved-in-stripwood
skeleton of the Great Depression, complete with greasy-
spoon roadhouses, each called Dew Drop Inn, and family-
run convenience stores with cobwebs across the torn screen
doors. Kat could have accepted a fast-food Miracle Mile,
one of the space-story lunar-landing colonies where white
tile and mock brick replicas of Roy Rogers and the Burger
King have been set down in the middle of vacant, open
country. That was normal. That was suburban blight, a subject she had discussed endlessly (as she had discussed What
the Sixties Really Meant and Where to Get the Pill) with the

six women closest to her in the Vassar class of 1981. The back country between Hartford and Northton was not normal. The buildings were made of wood and set down without foundations, listing in the wind like low-rent Towers of Pisa. A (very) local country station played uninterrupted half hours of suicidal music. The words got into her lungs and around her muscles, making her feel already dead.

What I feel is buried alive.

She shifted in her seat, not wanting to look out at decaying hay barns, not wanting to watch her mother's black-gloved hands sliding over the steering wheel. Her mother looked exactly what she was: a suburban Massachusetts matron (good suburb, houses in the four-hundred-thousand-dollar range), overeducated and overcritical, committed to practicality. Vassar was practical. If you were going to college, you might as well go to a good one. A degree from a half-assed state school wasn't worth the paper it was printed on. Northton was not practical. Girls thought about becoming nuns, but they didn't really do it. That was the kind of dream you had when you were still young enough to think nurses and teachers were important.

"It won't last," Kat's mother said. "You like the way you think you'll look in that habit, but it won't last. They're all wearing short skirts now."

"Most of them wear short habits outside," Kat said. "They use traditional habit at the Motherhouse."

"They'll make you change your name. They'll make you take a man's name."

"After Epiphany, I'll take a name in religion. My choice. As long as no one else has it."

"Not my religion," Mrs. O'Brien said. "Don't forget that, Katherine. Not *my* religion."

There was a pack of cigarettes in the glove compartment. Kat got it out. She could see her mother starting—*they won't let you do that in there*—but the words never came. Kat lit her cigarette and threw the match (where had her mother got Ma Maison matches?) into the ashtray under the radio.

"It was your idea to come with me," Kat said. "You were the one who didn't want David—"

10

"David," Mrs. O'Brien said. "I don't see how you can even think of David. In this context."

It isn't a context, Kat thought. She stayed silent, the better part of valor. This argument had started in April and never recessed since—David, Agnus Dei, A Mother's Hopes for her Children. Kat's mother expected things: seven-sisters college, job in a New York publishing house, marriage. Maybe the trouble started right after Kat graduated, when instead of looking for a job she decided (she had money of her own, didn't she?) to travel. Even travel would have been all right if she had stuck to Paris, or Rome, or Casablanca. Her mother remembered every movie romance of the forties, dreamed about intrigue and champagne in crystal glasses with a man who didn't ask questions. It was Asia that bothered Mary Connor O'Brien, Kat going off to "learn the truth about the poor" like some lower-middle-class hippie with even less brains than money. Kat supposed her mother was right, to a point. She hadn't learned much about the poor. She found something unreal about people who sat all day in the street, making marks with sticks on the surface of an unpaved road. They covered the ground like a writhing carpet in every city she visited. Calcutta, Bangkok, Kuala Lampur. It was all the same.

"David," Mrs. O'Brien said. "David started all this. What did he *do* to you? That's what I want to know. What did he *do* to you?"

Gave me some of the best sex I ever had, Kat thought. She didn't say it. Not that her mother would care about the sex. In fact, she'd probably welcome it. In the beginning, Mary had tried a few arguments that depended on an assumption of Kat's virginity. ("You don't know what it means to be a woman. You don't know the kind of things you have to have. You think it's going to be easy.") The arguments went on and on, filling the heavy-beamed, high-ceilinged living room. Sometimes they took a tangent. ("Aren't you normal? Don't you feel things? Don't you want David to do things to you?") All the answers Kat had were contradictory. Yes, she felt things with David. No, there wasn't anything she wanted him to do. Nothing sexual. She wanted to drive up to Agnus Dei and find him on the steps, waiting for her—but that was different. The sexual part had been resolved months ago. She was still attracted to him, but there was something... detached... about the feeling. He was a good-looking man with a strong, high-cheekboned face and a broad back and the long, tight-muscled legs of a distance runner. He was a man other women envied her for. Women on the street studied her, calculating his commitment to her. Waitresses and stewardesses turned their backs to her, pretending she wasn't there.

When they made love, it was like listening to music underwater, very clear, very slow. He slid up inside her with a kind of effortless glide. She had always thought of herself as "tight." She had always considered herself "too small." It would always be painful because she was "too small." He was the largest man she had ever known—largest in that way—but she was not too small for him. She was liquid when he needed her liquid, and stiff, hard, arching when he needed that. Even at the end, when she had started to float, when it seemed her soul had separated from her body and sat down on the sidelines to watch, they were synchronized.

Eventually, she had resolved the sexual part; he had not. Or rather, he had half resolved it. He accepted her abstinence just enough: just enough to be happy for her if Agnus Dei was what she wanted; just enough to catch and reclaim her if she ran screaming from its halls. He tried to talk her out of it only once. He didn't attack the "problem" like a pro quarterback fighting for a (decisive) eleventh-hour touchdown. He bought her a book, *The Penguin Dictionary of Saints*, and read her pieces of it.

"Saint Lucy," he said, "died with a sword in her throat. Saint Barbara, beheaded by her own father. Saint Pelagia, roasted alive—"

"Virgin martyrs," Kat said.

"Saints," David said. "It takes a lot to be a saint."

"I'm not a saint," Kat said. "And I wouldn't be a virgin martyr."

"That's the turnoff," Mrs. O'Brien said. She slowed the car, inching under the high, arching canopy of trees. Northton was farther south than Framingham, but the trees here had already started to turn. Kat thought of the ancient

12

maple on their front lawn, still heavy with end-of-summer green. Something poisonous in the air, Kat thought, and then: industrial waste, atomic spill, acid rain. They were in rural Connecticut. There was no industry here and no atomic power plant. If acid rain had fallen this close to Hartford, she would have heard about it. There was nothing here but rock hills and decaying farmland and the fairy-tale replica of a Gothic castle that was now Agnus Dei, Motherhouse, Province of North America, Society of Mary.

"Listen," Mary O'Brien said. "You don't know what bastards they were. What bastards they *are*. You think it's *The Bells of Saint Mary's*. You think it doesn't *matter*."

"All right."

"You call yourself a feminist. How can you call yourself a feminist and do something like this? How can you join up with them?"

"Mother—"

"You can still change your mind," Mary said. "I can turn the car around and drive us both right back to Framingham. I wouldn't even mind."

Kat took another cigarette from the pack, lit it with another Ma Maison match. *I feel buried alive.* If she had any sense, she would give it up, go back to living in Framingham or Boston or New York, in a world she understood. She'd do it if it weren't for a single, niggling premonition: if she turned back now, she'd turn again when she got home. She'd turn and turn until she found herself somewhere with a veil on her head and a rosary in her hands. She'd been dreaming of it off and on since she was seven years old, since she first saw a nun. She was dreaming of it now. There was a still, quiet place, very dark, very cool, somewhere inside her. She was not religious, she often hated the politics of the Catholic Church, but she wanted that cool, dark place. She wanted to drown herself in that silence. Forever.

Maybe.

Mary Connor O'Brien popped the clutch into second gear.

"They steal it all from you," she said. "In the end, they steal it all from you. Even your self-respect."

13

2

Her mother walked into the great front room, took one look at David standing nervously by the door, turned on her heel and walked out. Kat watched her go, half irritated, half amused.

David was running his palms against the sides of his jeans, shifting from foot to foot. He was hunched over, as if protecting himself against a particularly vicious rain. Kat looked at the cavernous room and found a small "conversational grouping" of backless, low-riding couches, empty. She made a vague gesture in their direction. David nodded.

"Vows of poverty," he said. "I've been looking at the walls. There's a Raphael madonna. A cartoon, mind you, but a Raphael madonna nonetheless."

"It's a very old Order."

"And old Orders are rich?"

"What did you expect? I was going to join the Little Sisters of Our Lady of the Rock Springs in Panharduck, Illinois?"

"I've been telling everybody I'm your brother," David said. "Everybody. Even if they didn't ask."

Kat sat down on one of the low couches, careful to keep her feet flat on the floor, her legs close together. There was an ashtray on the coffee table beside her, but none of the other postulants was smoking. You could tell the postulants by their long, tight-sleeved gray dresses. They all wore the same expression: eyes a hairline away from being wild with panic, mouths tight, jaws working. They sat or stood in the center of small family groups, wondering what to do with their hands, and their legs, and their fear. They were all hanging on, sitting still, by an effort of will. Kat felt the urge for a cigarette again — a sharp tug of irritableness, a swelling of irrational anger. Her mother should have said it. They wouldn't let her do *that* in here. If she was going to quit, she might as well start now.

She hated the idea of quitting.

David took a pack of Camels out of his back pocket and offered her one.

"I thought you gave those up," she said.

"I tend to revert in times of stress," he said. "Jesus Christ, Kat. What am I doing here?"

"Wishing me well."

"Am I?"

"Somebody has to. You should have heard my mother on the trip down."

He lit his cigarette with a green plastic Bic lighter and sat with his arms across his knees, miserable. Kat looked around the big room and tried to size up the . . . what? Competition?

Directly across the room, two postulants sat together, flanked by women Kat supposed were their mothers. The fair, blond one had a fair, blond mother. The girl's face was open, impatient and excited. The mother's was pinched, angry, disapproving. The mother held herself in, touching as little as possible. *This room is diseased*, she seemed to say, *it's diseased and contagious and I'm not going to be contaminated*. The mousy girl's mother also held herself in, but it was with the containment of a zookeeper surrounded by live exhibits. She was friendly. She was determined to look interested. She knew none of this was of any importance whatsoever.

David tugged at Kat's sleeve. "I was talking to them," he said. "The two of them over there. The mothers, too, later."

"Telling them you were my brother?" Kat smiled. She put her hand over his and felt the fine-boned ridges. She liked men's hands, hard, well-developed hands. She liked touching them.

David took his hand away and started fiddling with his pack of cigarettes. "The mothers make Mary Connor O'Brien look like an angel of light."

Kat raised her eyebrows—the old Kat, sardonic, bright. It felt phony, but she didn't care. She tapped David on the knees, unthinking. He flinched. She took her hand away. "Tell me about the mothers," she said. "What could they do?"

David lit another cigarette. "The blond one's named Annie Bliss," he said. "Anne Fairchild Bliss, her mother says, very stiff, like that. The mother's got a rented Lincoln in the driveway—I saw it drive up, with the rental plates, you know—and she's wearing a set of pearls must have be-

15

longed to Annie's grandmother. The theory there is this place is too high-class for her or her daughter and her daughter ought to have the good sense to realize it. Also, everybody here is out to snub Mrs. Bliss first chance they get and she isn't having any."

"Oh," Kat said. "Oh."

"The other one . . ." David stopped. He looked across the room at the mousy one and her ferociously well-put-together mother. The woman was a hawk. Her eyes were laser beams. She stared straight ahead. She didn't see things, but what was beneath the surface of things.

"The other one," David said, "thinks her daughter is psychotic."

"What?"

"She thinks her daughter is psychotic," David repeated. "I tried to work it out. It's a schtick, I think. It's the way they are with each other."

The mousy girl had dreamy, opaque eyes that looked at nothing. She was holding a rosary and a prayer book—the Little Office, Kat knew, because she had a Little Office of her own in her right pocket. It was a regulation gear, like thick black stockings and black shoes with rubber soles. The mousy girl's lips were moving, saying something over and over. Kat didn't think she was speaking aloud. The others were talking around her, paying no attention.

"Her name's Jane Galloway," David said.

"Did she just graduate from high school?"

"They both just graduated from high school," David said. "Different high schools, but both in New Haven and both all female. Miss Galloway had Society of Mary nuns. Miss Bliss didn't, but—"

"But Miss Bliss doesn't hold the same theories as her mother?"

"Exactly," David said. He stretched, took another cigarette, offered the pack again to Kat. When she refused, he shrugged and lit his own, still staring across the room at Annie Bliss. Was Annie Bliss really that pretty? She had the round, unformed face so many girls have at seventeen—pretty enough, but not striking. No bone structure, unclean lines, unclear features.

"What's the matter?" David said.

16

Kat took the cigarette out of his hands and sucked on it. The smoke filled her lungs and cleared her head. There was nothing wrong with her but nicotine deprivation.

"I was just watching you and thinking I'm much better-looking than Annie Bliss."

David laughed. "I always thought you were the one woman in the world who wasn't neurotic about her looks."

"I'm neurotic about my looks. Am I prettier than Annie Bliss?"

"No," David said. "Annie Bliss is pretty. You're beautiful. That's a difference in kind, not of degree."

"Ah," Kat said. The way David was looking at her satisfied her, and that was—(*over*)—uncomfortable and a little shameful. She took another drag on his cigarette. Nicotine deprivation and nerves. That explained everything. The room was not expanding and contracting. Her skin was not shrinking, squeezing the liquid out of her body onto the cool rough linen of her dress. She did not want David that way anymore. She did not want him to want her if she could not return the feeling. She was sure of that.

This time, when David offered her the cigarette pack, she took it. She found her mother's Ma Maison matches in her pocket and lit up. Was she nervous about going in, or nervous about David, looking at Annie Bliss?

"Still," she said. "There's something about Annie Bliss."

David smiled. "I like Annie Bliss," he said. "She's an infant, but she's a good infant. I think. Mama hasn't ruined her. And . . ."

"And?"

"She's as much put off by Jane Galloway as I am."

Kat wanted to ask what that meant and why it should matter, but at the far end of the room someone started sounding a wooden clapper. Kat crushed the cigarette in the ashtray, but didn't manage to put it out. She stood, wavered, nearly toppled. When she wiped her hands against her skirt, they left sweat stains.

David put a hand under her elbow, steadying her. He wore a look of surprised sadness.

"Nervous, Kat?"

"It's like jumping out of an airplane," Kat said.

17

"You've got a parachute, Kat. You'll always have a parachute."

Kat looked at the nun at the other end of the room—the nun in her gray robes and white wimple and black veil. Audrey Hepburn in *The Nun's Story*, Glenda Jackson in *In This House of Brede*, Ingrid Bergman in *The Bells of Saint Mary's*. Her mother was right. She did think of it as a movie, believe in it the way she believed in movies.

They would censor her letters. They wouldn't let her write to David.

David was standing over her, his mouth set in a downward curve, his forehead creased. She started to put her hand out, saw the look on his face, took it back again. She grabbed his arm and pulled him toward her, making the kiss quick, light, almost imaginary. It was a kiss, even so. She had kissed him in the main reception room of Agnus Dei, kissed him while wearing her postulant's dress.

3

Kat was in the anteroom when Jane Galloway first spoke to her. She had put her small, square, black cardboard suitcase with all the other small, square, black cardboard suitcases on the rack. She had taken her short white postulant's veil from the pile on the table. She had taken her place against the wall.

Sister Clare Marie paced, worrying, murmuring instructions. Annie Bliss fumbled with her veil, dropped it, picked it up, dropped it again. Clare Marie stationed herself at Annie's side, giving instructions. They all looked strained.

Jane Galloway tugged at Kat's sleeve. Jane's eyes still looked at nothing, but now they were shining and oddly secretive. Like the black lagoon right before the creature comes out of it, Kat thought.

"You're wearing jewelry," Jane Galloway said. She pointed to Kat's ring—Kat's grandmother's ring, the only thing she had from her father's side of the family. Jane Galloway had a smile like Olivia De Havilland playing Melanie Wilkes and a voice like hot treacle. "You shouldn't wear jewelry in the convent. It's a worldy vanity. It's abominable in the eyes of God."

18

Jane pulled at the ring. It came easily, too large for the finger Kat wore it on. Jane looked at the three small pearls and smiled. She put the ring in Kat's palm.

"We must always try to follow the perfect example of Christ," Jane said.

Kat watched her turn and walk away, searching for her own place in line. She waited until Jane was settled against the wall and looking at her. Then she took the ring and jammed it onto her finger, cutting the top of her knuckle.

Kat had always *hated* Melanie Wilkes.

DINNER

1

Annie Bliss had always wondered about the stories of nuns walled up alive—stories, according to her mother, invented and promulgated by the Protestant Antichrist as a weapon in his unceasing war against Holy Mother Church. Annie wasn't sure. She had grown up in the kind of Catholic family that kept a splinter of the True Cross (mail-ordered from an ad in one of the newsprint missionary monthlies) on the living-room mantel. The splinter was sealed in hard plastic and surrounded by holy pictures. Annie remembered the holy pictures (Sacred Heart, Miraculous Medal, Our Lady of Fatima) the way she remembered her mother's backyard rock grotto with its plaster Blessed Virgin and red glass devotional oil lamp buried in the lichen at the statue's feet.

Annie's mother was confounded by nuns. Nuns got the front pews at church. Nuns walked wherever they wanted on the sidewalk. Ordinary people got out of their way. Nuns were the direct descendants, the spiritual heiresses, of the virgin martyrs.

It was all the talk about virgin martyrs that made Annie think of nuns walled up alive. She suspected the stories had been invented not by the Protestant Antichrist, but by conscientious Catholics with a dozen years of parochial school behind them. Holy Mother Church had a nearly pathological obsession with virgins and the deaths of virgins.

19

Agnus Dei was obsessed with the glory of resurrection. On the North Wing fourth-floor landing, just outside the carved wood door leading to postulant corridor, was a painting of Saint Joan rising from the flames. The phoenix ascends into Heaven, Annie thought. She turned away. Clare Marie opened the door and propped it back with a wooden doorstop. She stood to the side, waiting for them to enter.

Annie moved forward with the rest of the double line, nervously out of sync. Postulant corridor was a single long, dark room partitioned into cells by muslin curtains hung on hollow metal rods. The curtains were pulled open. The cells on the right each had a window overlooking North Lawn. The cells on the left were dark. Clare Marie waited until they were all in the room. She shut the door and walked between them.

"In this house, privacy is an inner state," she said. "Muslin walls will not contain sound. Your Sisters can hear you and you can hear them. If your attention is on your Sisters and not on God, you will never have peace."

She folded her hands under her short cape and nodded. The lines hesitated.

"The schedules for this evening and tomorrow are on your bureaus," she said.

The lines broke. Annie ran into the nearest cell, a dark one on the left side. Her black cardboard suitcase was lying flat on the only chair, "Anne Fairchild Bliss" written across the black-edged identification tag.

Annie took the mimeographed schedule from the bureau and sat on the edge of the bed to read it. 5:00, dinner. 6:00, evening prayer (Vespers). 9:00, night prayer (Compline). 9:30, Grand Silence. 10:00, retirement. What happened between Vespers and Compline? Would they be allowed alone in their cells? She put her hand in her pocket and touched Stephen's unopened letter. She had taken it out of the mail box this morning on her way to the car. There hadn't been time to lock herself in the bathroom. She could have opened it in the car, committed an act of defiance, but that would have started another social-order litany. Who do you think you are who do you think you are who do you think . . .

"We don't sit on the edge of the bed," Clare Marie said. "Sitting on the edge of the bed wears down the mattress."

Annie jumped up, guilty, panicked, awkward. She came down on the wrong ankle—the one she'd injured playing volleyball—and fell against the bureau. Clare Marie reached out to steady her, smiling.

"You mustn't take things so to heart," Clare Marie said. "You're not expected to know. You're only expected to learn."

Annie tried to smile an answer. She felt sweat-clammy sick, as if she'd eaten bad tuna fish. One minute she was anonymous and terrified of being anonymous. Then she was singled out and knew, the way she knew she had blond hair and green eyes, that her every movement was being watched, her every thought screened. Clare Marie went into the corridor between the cells. Annie took her suitcase off the chair and sat down. If she had time, she would read Stephen's letter and tear it to pieces. She would keep the pieces in her pocket and get rid of them a piece at a time. If she made the pieces small enough and put each in a different wastebasket, no one would be able to read them.

She wasn't making sense. Stephen would write her here —he had promised—and Clare Marie would read the letters. Clare Marie would read every letter any of them received. She would weed out the blasphemous and illegitimate.

There was a pain like a wasp sting behind her eyes. Annie rubbed her forehead with the back of her hand, waiting it out. She wanted to feel exhilarated, or pious, or triumphant. "In my day," her mother said, "only college girls went to Agnus Dei." "You don't have anything in common with those girls," her mother said. "You won't be able to talk to them." (Pictures at an Exhibition: Christmas, 1973. Annie sits on the floor beside a sparsely decorated, anemic pine, fine blond hair braided into stiff pigtails. Stephen hangs against the front door frame, his hands contorted against the warped wood. Their mother wields a blue glass unicorn, a piece badly cast from a mold, with a visible seam. "Are you going to believe such a thing about your father? About your father? About your father?" Everything in this conversation

21

echoes. Only the mute sequence is final: Stephen slamming the door, pounding down the porch steps, starting the car. Stephen leaving. As far as Annie is concerned—seven-year-old-Annie, Annie who, according to their mother, doesn't understand things—Stephen's exit is better than their father's. Stephen says good-bye, in his fashion. Their father just disappeared.)

"I think we can talk now," somebody said. "Are you all right?"

Annie opened her eyes. The wasp sting became a hostile darning needle. The memories were a flood. Her father committed suicide. She knew that. She knew it even before Stephen left. She didn't talk about it, but she knew. The Church said her father died "while of unsound mind due to severe illness." Her mother said her father died of cancer. Stephen said "he committed suicide" as if saying it would cure cerebral palsy and render all atomic weapons impotent. Then he walked out the door and never came back. She remembered her father the day before he died. His eyes were dull and his face was gray and he couldn't look at their mother without hating himself.

"Are you all right?" somebody said again.

It was the beautiful one. The beautiful one had black hair and violet eyes and the kind of posture Sister Benedict would have awarded a gold cross. Her spine was so straight you could use it for a ruler.

Annie tried to sit up. Tiredness pulled at her shoulders. The unaccustomed strain made her stomach muscles hurt.

"I'm very tired," she said. "I don't think I got much sleep last night."

"I'm Kat O'Brien," the beautiful one said. "Nobody got much sleep last night."

Annie forced a smile. She was tired and a little crazy. She wanted to be alone. She did not want to anger Kat O'Brien.

"There's a girl called Martha," Kat said.

Martha appeared in the opening to Annie's cell, a short, round girl with a cherubic face, a Clare Marie in training.

"Martha has a cat," Kat said.

"It isn't my cat," Martha said. "It came into my cell." She

22

had the cat in her arms, a bland-faced tabby with a swollen belly. She held it out for Annie.

"At least one of the clichés about convent life is true," Kat said.

"Kat and the legend of the convent cat," Martha said.

Kat sat on the edge of Annie's bed. "You were talking to David Marsh," she said. "David Marsh, by the way, is not my brother. He doesn't even want to be my brother."

"Oh," Annie said.

"She has an entire pack of cigarettes with her, too," Martha said. "Why do I have this feeling her knees are going to have calluses by the time the year is over?"

"You can knit me kneepads," Kat said.

Martha hoisted the cat onto her shoulder and shook her head. "You're Annie Bliss and I'm Martha Kowalski," she said. "I'm from Paoli, outside Philadelphia. I always wanted to be a nun."

Annie started to say something amusing. What came out was "We're not supposed to sit on the edge of the bed. We're not supposed to talk about our private lives."

Kat's eyebrows climbed halfway up her forehead. Annie blushed. She didn't want to be a goody-goody, one of the girls she thought of as "The Sodality Set." She hated goody-goodies. *She* hadn't spent high school with her head in a confessional. *She* hadn't smiled with unbearable tolerance when somebody said "hell" at lunch. She was in the boiler room with the rest of them, drinking gin from Listerine bottles and smoking cigarettes and even passing a single, furtive (ineffectual) joint and eating the roach.

Martha patted her shoulder. "Clare Marie's gone off somewhere," she said. "We won't get caught."

"We can't even tell on each other," Kat said. "Not until next week. Or next month. That doesn't start until later, anyway."

Annie relaxed. It was going to be all right. She wasn't going to be labeled a hopeless prude. She hadn't ruined herself forever.

Kat O'Brien was smiling at her.

Why do you want to be a nun?

23

Stephen's first letter came on a cold day in late October, three weeks and four days after Annie told her mother she was applying to Agnus Dei.

"They won't take you there," her mother said. "They don't want anything to do with people like us."

Annie thought of answering that, but didn't. It wasn't a question. Her mother's world was as precisely ordered as a Japanese Noh play, as petrified in ritual as the old Tridentine Mass. Her mother was happy to see her become a nun (Annie had expected that), not happy to see her in the Society of Mary. Annie had expected that, too. She told her mother about Agnus Dei and thought about the picture on the Society of Mary brochure, the great Gothic castle with windows and doors tortured into pointed arches. There were other things in the brochure—the professional program, for instance, which sent Sisters to law and medical school—but none of it seemed to matter.

"You could apply to the Paulines," her mother said. "You could teach in a parish school."

Stephen's first letter came the day Annie talked to Mary Haughey, who was applying to enter a small Dominican Order based in Ohio.

"My father thinks I really want to be a priest," Mary said. "He thinks I'm going to get in there and agitate."

"Are you?"

"Hell, no. I wouldn't want the responsibility. I wouldn't want the hassle." Annie got off the bus at Ellery Street, leaving Mary to ride to the end of the line. It was overcast, on the edge of rain. The trees encroaching on the cracking sidewalks were nearly bre. There was something unsatisfactory about what was happening to her. She had expected to be exhilarated, maybe even happy. She didn't think it was possible to be happy in her mother's house—she'd seen funeral parlors more brightly lit, deathbeds more determinedly cheerful—but she had expected to be happy in anticipation. Instead, she was weighed down with forms and admonishments. Her mother radiated dark prophetic gloom. The nuns talked like popular-psychology books: support, nurturance, goal orientation. Becoming a nun was a risk, a dare, a grand gesture. The danger needed acknowledgment, or encouragement, or both.

She reached the porch of their half of the small two-family house just as it started to rain. Through the window she could see white net curtains and heavy green drapes. She opened the door with her key, went into the living room, and pulled back the drapes and curtains. It didn't matter that there was little light. Opening the drapes was her revenge. She wasn't going to live like this forever.

She went back to the porch and took the mail out of the wooden box. Her mother had a letter from Connecticut Light and Power, where she worked. At the bottom of the letterhead were the words "The Employee Committee." The Employee Committee was always sending her mother information about group tours to Europe at special low prices. Her mother had never been to Europe and wouldn't go. *People like us.*

Stephen's letter was the last in the pile. It had been addressed to Annie Bliss, crossed out, readdressed to Anne Fairchild Bliss. Annie looked at the "S. B. Bliss" on the back flap. Stephen. Stephen lost, and, according to her mother, spiritually dead. Stephen home.

In his fashion.

She took the letter upstairs to her bedroom and locked herself in. Her mother had replaced the dark blue spun plastic drapes that matched the dark blue walls. Annie took them down, dismantling the copper-look tin curtain rods, and threw the whole mess onto her closet floor. That was her customary after-school ritual. "You can't dress in front of bare glass," her mother always said. "It isn't modest."

Stephen's letter was typed on onionskin paper.

> *Dear Annie,*
> *It's been a long time and I'm not writing for any reason, just to say hello. Right after I left I went out to California, and since then I've been around, but I'm back East. I'm working for the American Automobile Association and doing okay. I just wanted to know how you were and what you were up to. Also*

how Mother is. I think about you often. Do you know what happened, when I left?
Write to me.

Stephen

The "Stephen" was handwritten, in large, swirling letters with missing pieces. The "h" was half an "h." The "t" was uncrossed. Annie put the letter between her mattress and box spring and sat down to think.

"He said terrible things about your father," her mother said, when Annie told her Stephen had written. "Terrible, blasphemous things."

"He didn't say anything about Daddy in the letter," Annie said. "He just wanted to know how we were."

"I know how *he* is," Annie's mother said. "The way he's always been."

They were sitting in the kitchen, eating dinner from cracked stoneware plates gone gray from use. The meat loaf was pale brown and as textureless as baby food. The cabbage had disintegrated. Cooking was something Annie did well, but her mother wouldn't allow it. "It's a mother's duty to cook for her children," her mother would say. Annie would close her eyes, nauseated by anger. It was one thing not to be able to afford luxuries, another to ruin what you could afford. It was one thing . . .

Her mother always made her angry. Always. Their lives were an unnecessary penance for an unspecified sin, and would be unto the Day of Judgment. *People like us.*

"You didn't know your brother," her mother said. "You were too young. I knew him. It wasn't just the things he said about your father."

"It's been ten years," Annie said.

"He was always a very handsome boy," her mother said. "You looked up to him. Little sisters look up to big brothers. I *knew* him."

Annie wrote to Stephen, partly because she wanted to, partly because her mother didn't want her to. She called it "adolescent rebellion" and was a little proud of herself.

Their correspondence had two topics, each as self-suffi-

26

cient as a Host in a chalice. They talked about death and money. Stephen had been sixteen when he left. Annie remembered him as thin and nervous and loud, with thick undisciplined hair. Death was another name for their father, a dead subject centering on a corpse. Money was the chronic illness of their childhood.

He killed himself with a .38 Colt automatic, Stephen wrote. *It was a stolen gun and he'd bought it from Kelleher's pawnshop in New Haven. He came home with it in the pocket of his brown suit. He locked himself in the room he shared with Mother and put the barrel in his mouth and blew off the back of his head.*

Money is the only safety, Stephen wrote. *If you have money you can protect yourself. If you don't have money you keep getting slapped down. I've taken a lot of pain, but someday I'm going to get through the crack in the wormwood and out into the air.*

Annie was fascinated by money, but only in the guise of fame and fortune, and only as presented in novels with one-word titles and pictures of jewelry on the covers. Their heroines started poor and clawed their way to expensive unhappiness. Annie ignored the tragedies and concentrated on fantasies of long, low cars with uniformed young men in the drivers' seats, on clothes and jewels and airplane tickets, on dinners in amber-lit restaurants where half a dozen waiters appeared and disappeared at will, like ghosts in a sentimental Christmas story. She believed in this world with the simplicity with which she believed in the Holy Ghost, but she thought of it as a locked room in an ancient house, a room to which she would never have the key. Stephen's money letters disturbed her. Stephen saw that world as possible. He thought he knew where to find the key and only wanted a chance to look.

All it takes is a single break, Stephen wrote.

She was more comfortable, and more compulsive, about the story of their father. She thought of their father as pieces of blood and skin and bone, ground into the cracks in the plaster walls of her mother's bedroom. She tried to think of him in Heaven, or Hell, but the image wouldn't hold.

I don't know where you were, Stephen wrote. *I was at*

school. She was in the kitchen. After they took him away, she cleaned up the room and went on using it.

At Easter, Annie asked Stephen to come home. *At least meet me somewhere,* she wrote. She had been accepted at Agnus Dei and named Honor President of her class. Time felt compressed and endless at once. The nuns at school refused to be specific. Her mother hinted at webs of social intrigue, spiders of snobbery, lying in wait. Annie didn't think she'd ever been so tired. Her friends were shy and standoffish. She was Taking the Veil. They watched their language at lunch and asked what the call of God *sounded* like. Did she hear voices in her head? Did the Host light up when she looked at it? The sincerity of these questions terrified her. The call of God didn't sound like anything. She didn't hear voices or see the Host light up. She just wanted to be a nun.

In this country, it's a crime to be poor, Stephen wrote, answering his Easter letter. *It means you haven't worked hard enough, you haven't realized your potential, you haven't lived soberly and saved. Those are the American virtues and they are good virtues and poverty is impossible if you practice them.*

He didn't say anything about her request to see him. She almost didn't answer. Everyone was pulling at her. She was beginning to get needle-sharp headaches. Agnus Dei reduced itself to logic puzzles. All she knew was that the convent was a strange, eternal place and she had to have an anchor before she launched herself into it.

She wrote Stephen about Agnus Dei. He did not write back for six weeks. By the time the letter came, she thought he'd abandoned her.

I've been thinking it over, he wrote. *Maybe I've been a little afraid to write. It's such a wonderful thing for you to do. You have to be really brave to trust God so much you'd give your whole life to Him. I won't tell you what a saint I think you are. You know if you are or aren't, and you don't need to be a saint anyway. Just brave. I'm proud of you.*

It was better than a tranquilizer. Annie read it once a day. He was proud of her. She was brave. He understood. Before that letter, she had been *interested* in Stephen, because he was her brother and knew things about their father's death.

28

After that letter, she was committed to him. Her loyalty to him was as absolute as her loyalty to the Church. Her picture of him was painted in light. She imagined him tall and strong and sure, like the hero of a paperback romance

3

"When you go into refectory tonight," Clare Marie said, "you will find a small wooden tag under your plate. At the end of dinner, bring this tag to me. It will tell me where you sat, and with whom. You will keep your place at table for one week. Then you will be assigned a new place. Your place will change each week and you will sit at table with every member of your class at least once before the year is over."

Clare Marie looked over their heads, as if that would tell her if they'd understood. Then she turned her back on them. Annie's breath came up in a whistle. She jumped, surprised at herself. She hadn't realized she'd been holding it in. She looked around to see if anyone had heard her. Four rows ahead, Kat turned, smiled, winked. Annie relaxed.

They were waiting against the wall outside the open double doors of the refectory. Nuns filed past them: first the fully professed, then the tertiary professed, then the senior novices. The junior novices, who were "in enclosure" for this one year, ate with the cloistered nuns and used the entrance on the other side of the wing. The cloistered nuns ate in a part of the refectory shielded by a grille. They lived behind a grille, too. The West Wing had been partitioned off for them.

Annie looked at the lines of gray and black and white. They made her cold. They had nothing to do with teaching parish school or doing social work in Appalachia. They bore no relation to the bland lectures on Service to God, the Church, and Your Community that comprised high-school vocation talks. The nuns were straight and black and set each in her particular halo. They glowed in the dimness of the corridor. Their faces shone with inner light. *Shone with inner light*. That was the kind of phrase that plagued books like *Song of Bernadette*, mindless apologias for superstitious

Catholicism. If you receive Holy Communion with a mortal sin on your soul, the Host will burn your tongue and make you run screaming from the church. If a suicide is buried in consecrated ground, the earth will spit up his body. If you are called by God and spurn your vocation and marry, your husband will die a horrible death. In grammar school, they speculated endlessly on the horrible deaths that befell Catholics who persisted in a life of sin. Falling into a nest of razor blades. Drowning in honey.

Dear God.

Annie wanted to put her hands to her face, to massage away the headache. There were too many nuns. They made her feel like running.

She held her hands more firmly under her short gray cape. She was going to have to do something soon—about the headaches, about the panic. If she didn't, she was going to find herself on her mother's doorstep, and that would be a failure. Her mother would love to celebrate that particular failure.

Clare Marie turned to them, nodded, turned again. They began moving into the refectory, two by two in silent procession, a parade of Noah's ark animals struck dumb. Annie wondered if they were objects of curiosity. Were the nuns looking at them? The nuns didn't look interested in anything.

There were two tables at the back, empty except for four novices each in the anchor chairs. Annie took her place behind a chair at the first table, between Kat and a sharpboned novice with a face like a cadaver. She folded her hands over the chair back and bowed her head.

At the front of the room, someone made the sign of the cross. The novice at the head of Annie's table said, "We thank You, O Lord, for these Your gifts, which we are about to receive from Your bounty. Through Christ Our Lord. Amen."

Somebody at the front of the room made the sign of the cross again.

"You can take your seats," the novice at the head of their table said. "You put your napkin under your chin and tie it behind your neck. Like a bib."

Annie pulled out her chair and sat down. The white linen

30

table napkin folded in thirds on her plate was as large as a car blanket.

Kat touched her arm. "Just like nursery school," she whispered.

Annie tied her napkin under her chin. It fell to her lap. The novice at the head of the table had a round, doughy face with a string of pimples along the jaw. She stared at Kat, ignoring Martha, who had tied her bib on sideways and was now disassembling it; ignoring Jane Galloway, who was transfixed by her flatware. Annie wished Jane Galloway away. Without her, their end of the table was a perfect mix. Kat and an intelligent-eyed black girl and herself on one side. Martha and a girl named Geraldine on the other. Geraldine came from Boston. She wore a green silk garter under her postulant dress, high on her left leg.

Jane Galloway was strange. Annie had spent half an hour talking to her—if you could call it talking—and she would just as soon never do it again. The girl oozed. When she smiled, her eyes were snake eyes.

"Wearing your napkin as a bib saves your habit from food stains," the novice at the head of the table said. "When there are food stains on your habit, it must be washed. Washing wears the material. Wearing your napkin as a bib is a practice of poverty."

They contemplated wearing their napkins as bibs as a practice of poverty. Geraldine looked ready to laugh. Kat *was* laughing, silently but helplessly. Annie could feel her holding herself in.

The novice at the head of the table said, "My name is Sister Angela Louise. Facing me at the far end of the table is Sister Daniella. To my right is Sister Lucy. To my left is Sister Marie Bernadette."

Annie looked at Marie Bernadette. They all did. Marie Bernadette looked dead. Her bones were sharp and poled against the thin paper of her skin. Her eyes were sunk in dark hollows. Her fingers were restless, jointed bones poking out of large oversleeves of her habit.

Kat said, "My God," into Annie's ear.

Annie nodded vigorously and looked away. She did not want to contemplate Marie Bernadette while she was eating.

Two novices, veils and oversleeves pinned back, came to

the table with trays. Annie felt better. The food was wonderful. The roast beef was pink at the center and dark at the edges and piled high on its stainless-steel platter. The potatoes were boiled but still firm. The zucchini had been lightly sautéed.

"You are required, as a practice of poverty and obedience, to take at least one spoonful of everything offered you," Sister Angela Louise said. "You must take it whether you like it or not. If you are dangerously allergic to any food, you will be excused from eating it."

Annie smiled at the novice who offered her the meat platter and took three large pieces. She smiled at the novice who offered her the vegetables and took four spoonfuls of everything.

Marie Bernadette took one spoonful of everything.

"As a practice of obedience," Angela Louise said, "you may be required to take up to five spoonfuls of everything. This is at the discretion of the Reverend Mother Christopher, or the Novice and Postulant Mistress." Angela Louise looked down the table to Marie Bernadette. "Sister," she said.

Marie Bernadette took four more spoonfuls of everything.

"Anorexia nervosa," Kat said in Annie's ear.

"What?" Annie said. Marie Bernadette had her hands folded in her lap. She stared across the refectory, refusing to look at her food.

"Anorexia nervosa," Kat said again. "It's a psychological problem. They try to starve themselves to death."

Annie didn't believe a word of it. She had been waiting a lifetime for food that tasted like food. She had prayed for it.

Angela Louise picked up her fork. Everyone relaxed. The instructional part of the meal was over. Annie was suddenly aware of a buzz all around them. Nuns were talking, laughing, arguing over trivialities—behaving like ordinary women. It was a peculiarly comforting thought.

Annie speared a potato. Lucy wagged her fork across the table. "Don't fill yourself up," Lucy said. "Antoinette made chocolate cakes. Twenty-two of them."

"Don't tell me," Antoinette said. "The Red Sox won a game. Or Mahalia Jackson is coming to Hartford."

"I think Mahalia Jackson's dead," Lucy said. She smiled at the table at large. "I work with Antoinette in the kitchen," she said. "Antoinette does things like sing 'Amazing Grace' at the top of her lungs when she kneads bread."

"And 'Swing Low, Sweet Chariot,'" Daniella said.

Miriam, the black girl, sang out in a loud voice, "Looked over Jordan, what do I see, coming forth to carry me home." She shrugged at the stares. "Born and raised Baptist. Church choir fourteen years. Drove my mother crazy."

"Your mother didn't want you to sing in the church choir?" Annie said. She'd known parents indifferent to the Church, but never any opposed to it. Or to any church.

Miriam tapped her plate with her fork. "My mother's a medical doctor. My father's a lawyer. Gospel is—"

Across the table, Martha was nodding. "The old country," she said.

Miriam smiled. "In more ways than one."

Beside Martha, Jane Galloway stirred. She frowned at her food, then at Martha, then at Miriam. "It's a heathen song," she said. "You shouldn't sing heathen songs in the convent."

Annie felt the roast beef turn to cardboard in her mouth. Jane Galloway is strange, she thought, and then: she's a vicious, bigoted little asshole. She felt her stomach knotting up, and willed herself to relax. The others were feeling it, too. Martha was edging her chair away from Jane's. Miriam's eyes had gone from intelligent to hostile. Kat looked murderous.

Annie cut a perfectly square piece of meat and put it in her mouth. They won't let her stay, she told herself. She's obnoxious and ungenerous and she'll be a bad nun. They won't let her stay.

At the head of the table, Angela Louise seemed inordinately interested in a blue china saltshaker. She put it down and looked at Jane.

"It's an ecumenical year," she said.

Jane stared at Angela Louise, her expression guarded, her eyes quick and sharp and looking for a way in. Annie shifted in her seat, feeling a crazy need to be *ready*.

Angela Louise picked up the blue china pepper shaker, twin to the blue china salt. "The Pope has decreed us," she said, "to remember that sincere worship of Christ in every form is worthy of our respect."

At the far end of the table, Daniella dropped her butter knife. "Give it up," she said. "For Heaven's sake, Angela, give it up. Let it go. Talk about the weather."

FEEDING THE BIRDS

Jane had to wait for midnight before she was safe. Until then, postulant corridor was a perpetual-motion machine of rustles. Postulants coughed, postulants hummed to themselves, postulants tossed in bed. In the next cell, Kat O'Brien lit cigarette after cigarette, the sudden flames of sulfur matches looking like jerky flares behind the muslin curtains.

Bed at ten, morning bell at five forty-five. They'd be shell-shocked in the morning. They'd stumble through the Angelus, doze through Mass.

The midnight bells rang in the chapel tower, two hundred feet away across North Lawn, in a separate building. Agnus Dei had four bell towers—one over each wing—but they rang only the daylight hours. There were no bells in North Tower at all. Someone had killed herself there, strung herself from a rafter with a bell rope, and the bells had been taken down and the ropes put away in the tool cellar. That was twenty years ago, but the ropes were still in the tool cellar.

Jane sat up, swung her legs over the side of the bed, waited. She had the corner cell on the window side. She could hear Kat beside her and Martha across the hall, but no one else. Kat was kicking restlessly at her covers. Martha was snoring a gentle, ladylike snore.

Somewhere outside a car came to life, ground gears, whined on bald tires. It sounded close.

Jane got out of bed, considered putting on slippers, rejected the idea. Regulation slippers were flat-heeled mules. They would flap against the polished wood floors. She took

34

her robe from the hook by the bed and wrapped it around her. She would walk slowly to the end of the corridor, listening. If anyone was awake, she would go to the bathroom, make the appropriate noises, come back. She would risk nothing else.

She felt in the pocket of her robe for the piece of bread she'd brought up from dinner. It had reduced itself to crumbs. She would have to be more careful. She didn't want crumbs in the pocket of her robe. She would have to steal a Baggie from Antoinette's kitchen and keep her bread in that.

Her bread to feed the birds.

At the far end of the corridor, someone groaned. Jane stopped, listened, made herself wait a full count of sixty before she relaxed. Someone was having a nightmare. They were all having nightmares. She'd have a nightmare herself, when she finally got to sleep.

After she fed the birds.

This was what Jane Galloway knew, one minute past midnight, September 13, 1983: everything the Church taught, everything her mother promised, every moral in every story in every magazine for young adults, was a lie. Of all the things she had ever heard about living, or morality, she believed only one. There *was* original sin. The Church, however, had it wrong. Everyone was not born with original sin. Only some people were.

Baptism didn't wash it away. Confession was spiritual masturbation. Contrition was useless.

If you were born with original sin, other sins piled up on top of it. When the pile got high enough, you disappeared.

Jane paused outside Kat's cell, listening. The cigarette smell was very strong. It was cold, which meant Kat had opened her window, but the air was still and heavy and cigarette smoke drifted into the corridor, looking like fog. Kat, Jane's mother would have said, was "the kind of girl boys date, but don't marry." That was the heart of the lie: the beautiful always failed, the rich always faltered, the intelligent always found themselves unable to put anything into action. God loved the poor and the meek, the ugly and the lame.

Jane almost laughed, almost said out loud: I'm crazy but

35

I'm not stupid. For a single, slithering minute, she wanted to part the curtain of Kat's cell, enter it, walk up to the bed, and . . . what? She thought of the birds in the bell tower. She had heard them when she first came onto postulant corridor. They were nesting up there, in the dark.

Kat was *exactly* the kind of girl boys wanted to marry. She could screw her way from here to Tahiti and still be a virgin.

Jane backed away, turned, headed for the door. Sex was not the problem. When she dreamed of herself with boys, what she saw was not hands and nipples and bellies arranging themselves on sheets. What she saw was a light in their eyes, a recognition. Boys saw nothing unless there was something to see. Kat O'Brien was something to see. Jane never was.

Even so, boys weren't the problem. Jane rarely thought of herself with boys. Her world was full of women. And birds.

Birds were the best. Mice were too fast. Cats, unless very small kittens, were too large. Her world was full of small animals awake in the night.

She came to the end of the corridor and stopped. They were all asleep now, the girls who would close the circle against her. If they noticed her at all. They had noticed her at dinner, but that was a fluke, maybe a mistake. It might have been a dangerous mistake.

Geraldine wore a garter under her postulant dress. Martha stole matches from the silver bowl in the reception room to light Kat's cigarettes. Miriam sang coon songs at dinner. It didn't matter. They would succeed and she would fail, just as Marie Bernadette was failing. They were identical twins. They were ambassadors from the world of original sin.

When she was gone, they wouldn't remember her. Twenty years from now, they would sit in convent parlors, surrounded by overstuffed furniture and the claustrophobic airlessness of enforced gentility, unable to remember her name.

Maybe.

It was odd how easily she surrendered, when she let herself think. The convent was supposed to be her escape, the other world where she would be granted distinction, desirability, place. She had thought it all out. Even in short habits, nuns were set apart, women released from the world of women. Standards of beauty and ugliness didn't apply to them. Nuns needed no individual virtues. They were recognized as virtuous because they were nuns.

Jane lifted the bolt on the corridor door and slipped onto the landing. She was not—no matter what Sister Marian implied in red-inked comments in the margins of term papers—stupid. Theories didn't matter. Thinking didn't matter. Even faith, which was supposed to be above thought but was just another kind of thought, didn't matter. What mattered was Kat with her black hair and violet eyes, Geraldine with her garter, Martha with her easy conviction that in any game of us-against-them, she was part of the "us."

What mattered was feeding the birds.

She closed the door to the corridor and started up the stairs. There was a dim light on the landing, none over the staircase. The stairs didn't creak. They hadn't been abandoned to spiderwebs and dust. Twenty years ago, a young girl had climbed these stairs to wrap a rope around her neck. They didn't remember her name.

Marie Bernadette had spent most of recreation telling the story of the girl in the tower. "In the North Tower," she had said. "At the feet of Christ. Imagine." The story had been so jumbled, Jane had thought at first that Marie Bernadette had made it all up. It was only four or five versions later, after Angela Louise and Lucy and Daniella had each told it her way, that she realized there was some truth to it. Sometime in the winter of 1960, a senior novice had gone to the North Wing bell tower at night, made a noose out of a bell rope, and hanged herself. That much everybody knew. The rest of it—ghost screams for Marie Bernadette, ghost footsteps for Daniella—was a kind of game. They were like Girl Scouts telling maniac stories around a campfire at night. They loved scaring themselves silly.

Only Annie had been badly affected. Jane thought Annie was going to hit somebody, or throw a cup of coffee on Marie Bernadette, or storm out of the room. Except, of course, Annie couldn't have stormed out of the room. She had nowhere to go. They were sitting in the reception room having coffee after dinner. It was their first "recreation." They were supposed to adhere to the group and make general conversation, or darn socks and smile at the others. The others let Marie Bernadette talk.

Kat and Martha. Geraldine and Miriam and Annie. The core.

She reached the top of the steps and sat down to catch her breath. Kat and Martha. Geraldine and Miriam and Annie. This was the part she was never able to control. Left to herself, she was calm, her actions considered. Faced with *them*, she was crazy. She had smiled at hypocrites, poured treacle on sour-voiced old maids. She had eaten a pile of horse dung—all to get here, to escape *them*, to have a place of her own at last. But they were here, too. They were going to take this away from her.

Maybe.

She couldn't think. She hated them and loved them. She was afraid of them and knew she belonged with them. She wanted to go to Annie Bliss and say, "We are very much alike. We could be friends." It made her crazy with hope.

And hope made her stupid.

She stood up and brushed off the back of her robe. There was a lock on the tower-room door, but it was ancient, useless. It snapped at a push. The bell tower itself was a small octagonal room. The birds were in the rafters, hushed and waiting. She stumbled through the darkness until she thought she was at the center and began laying down crumbs. She backed up slowly until she touched the wall. She took off her robe and nightgown—robe in regulation gray, nightgown in regulation white—and folded them in a pile. She sat down on them to wait.

It could take ten minutes, or half an hour. It could take all night and be useless.

Above her head, birds began to flutter and dip. She wondered what kind they were.

She wondered why they had been allowed to stay, unmolested, in this antiseptic holy place.

It took over an hour. When the first one came close, she was nearly asleep. She was dreaming. There was an awards ceremony in the auditorium. She had won the Medallion of Honor, the prize given to the senior girl who had done most for the school. She was walking through the bleachers, stepping unafraid from riser to riser, her hands behind her back. Sun glinted off the Honor Society pin on the pocket of her blazer. Girls looked up at her and smiled. They tugged at the pleats in her uniform skirt, begging recognition.

The bird darted at her, hovered, darted away. It made a high, keening screech in the air. She sat frozen, holding her breath. If she didn't move, it would come back.

Except it wasn't a bird. It was a bat.

She listened to them in the air over her head. Bats were rabid. She would have to catch it in her robe.

She slid the robe from under her and held it in her hands. She would have to bring something with her next time, a towel she could throw away or a plastic garbage bag. She would get the robe dirty. It would hang from the hook behind her bed, waiting to be discovered.

In the chapel, bells rang half past one. She wondered if they were asleep on postulant corridor. She wondered what Kat O'Brien dreamed of, the man who had been with her in the reception room? The way she would look in a habit? Maybe Kat O'Brien didn't need to dream.

She looked at the crumbs littering the floor. They were untouched. The bats would have no use for them.

She would have to clean them up before she left.

A second one came close, fluttered, darted away. She held the robe like a bullfighter's cape, waiting.

Annie Bliss dreamed. Annie was hungry, watchful—starving, maybe, for something just beyond what she had. Jane knew about starvation. She could see it in other people, even if she couldn't imagine what they wanted. Annie Bliss sat in the reception room, looking at the china, looking at the crystal, feeling the plush upholstery of the couches. Annie Bliss dreamed, and when she dreamed she was complete.

It was, Jane thought, a bond between them. It was something that might be built on.

The third one came closest, hovered longest. She got it just in time. She wrapped the robe around it the way boys twisted wet towels in high-school locker rooms.

The bat jerked and squeaked and clawed inside the robe, making the gray terry cloth jump in the dark. She held both ends in one hand and anchored the robe to the floor. Then she used her feet against it.

She had never had a bat before. Bats were small and fragile. They would be easy to kill.

When it was dead, she would put out its eyes.

It had Annie Bliss's eyes.

"Sex is nothing."

"Sister?"

"Sex is nothing. Somebody's going to write about this—"

"A lot of people are going to write about this, Sister."

"They'll say it's sex. Or lack of sex. They think we sit by ourselves and think about sex. Because they think about sex. But sex is nothing."

"Are you trying to tell me something? I don't care if she was a lesbian."

"She wasn't a lesbian. I've been in this Order forty years and I've met only one lesbian. She left. It isn't congenial for them here."

"Sex was something to her."

"The woman who left? Maybe. I don't think so. Sex is not as strong as you think, Lieutenant. Death is stronger. Martyrdom is stronger. If you don't have sex you don't miss it. The desire for motherhood is very strong. When we lose them and they're thirty-five, it's usually that."

"She wasn't thirty-five."

"She wasn't sane."

"She wasn't sane? Which one are you talking about, Sister?"

"I'm trying to tell you how it happened. How it really happened. Not the way the newspapers will say it happened. Not the way it will be explained in court. I want to tell you how it happened."

"And for that you have to tell me sex is nothing."

"I didn't believe it was nothing, not then."

"Sister?"

"The important things don't always make the most noise. And the things that make the most noise—well, Lieutenant. Sex makes a lot of noise. Most of us here are not cloistered. We see the books and the magazines and the posters for movies. Everyone takes it so seriously, don't they?"

"I take it seriously, Sister."

"I took it seriously, Lieutenant. I took it so seriously, I concentrated on it. I ignored the other. You see, the sex made a lot of noise. The threat of sex. The danger of sex. The really important thing made no noise at all."

"Sister—"

"The really important thing, Lieutenant."

DAVID

1

When the doorbell rang, David was lying on his bed, eyes wide open, staring at the ceiling, seeing Kat. He had been seeing Kat ever since she disappeared behind the door to the anteroom at Agnus Dei.

That had been the beginning of it. He had left Agnus Dei, walked to his car, slid behind the wheel, put his keys in the ignition. That was as far as he got for the next eight and a half hours. He sat behind the wheel and watched the lights go on, watched the start of a late summer rain, watched the lights go off. He felt dizzy and groggy at once—half high, the way he got on second-rate marijuana. Within the walls of Agnus Dei, nuns moved in concert, drifting from one corner of the building to another, dancing to bells. He wondered what Kat was doing in there. Did they make her keep silence? Did she walk with hands folded and head bent, anonymous in a gray-and-black line? He couldn't imagine Kat anonymous—especially in that crowd of children—but for all he knew there were a hundred Kats locked away in Agnus Dei. Maybe that was what happened to women like Kat. Maybe they shut themselves up in convents, away from men.

Away from me, David thought. He had a sudden vision of Kat in her postulant's dress, and wished he hadn't. It had been bad enough in the reception room—that dress with its high collar, its line of wooden buttons at the throat. The buttons were small and close together. He saw them slipping out of their buttonholes, the skin appearing under the cloth, the hollow at the base of Kat's throat where his tongue traced jungle tattoos in the morning. Just below that line her breasts began to rise, curving up and out to the uneven surface of her nipples. The fantasy was almost irresistible: he and Kat in the reception room, surrounded by postulants and their families, watched by nuns. He put the palms of his hands against the bare skin of her shoulders and pushed the top of the dress over her arms. He ran his fingers over the bland, concealing, formal construction of her nun's bra until he found the clasp at the back and could release it. Her nipples were hard and red. He ran the tips of his fingers over her waist and touched the high cotton underwear. Her clothes fell away in a rushing sigh. Her shoes and stockings disappeared. He put his hands between her legs, ran his fingers along the impossibly soft skin of her inner thighs. Fine, stiff hair escaped the underwear. He followed it, looking for a deep place. Her clitoris was swollen and painful, thick and logy against the pad of his thumb. He rubbed slowly, patiently against it. All he had to do was step closer, push aside the cloth. His penis was raw and hard. He would take her standing, pull her up to him, position the slight curve of her hips against the flatness of his own. He felt the wetness of the mouth of her vagina. He slid his finger into the fold and thought: one inch. All I have to do is move a single inch.

From the moment he first saw Kat walking into the reception room to the moment the doorbell rang, he did nothing but stumble through a nonstop triple feature of lewd memories, obscene fantasies, and explicit daydreams. He could not get his mind away from Kat—the body of Kat, the sexual proclivities of Kat, the *possibility* of Kat.

The possibility she would give it up.

What did she do in there? She wanted to be a nun. The *differentness* of nuns attracted her. He understood as much about her as she failed to understand about him. It was her

42

mother who saw the convent as a medieval dungeon where young girls were buried alive. He could see it as a way of life, acceptable and even admirable. His objection was not to nuns, but to Kat-as-nun. They would never let him walk through the door to the anteroom and up the stairs (were there stairs?). He would never again have access to her.

He thought of the kind of access he had had to her, in the beginning, before things got confused. He saw her in the shower, breasts full and high and just out of reach behind the white plastic curtain. He saw her with a forest-green towel wrapped under her arms—movie-starlet-emerging-from-bath—crossing the industrial gray carpet in the hotel in Hong Kong. He parted her legs and put his tongue there, on the rim and on the triangle and deep inside her. He held the splayed bones of her hips until her skin was sweating under his palm. He turned her until they lay head to heel. What he liked best was tipping into her, feeling the muscles in her vaginal wall tightening against him, sucking him in. She could do it at will, that tightening and sucking. It made him swell in seconds. Sometimes it made him lose control. He exploded, pumping into her, while she was cool and still beneath him. Sometimes he started her on top of him, because while she was there he could last forever. He put his hands on her breasts, his fingers on her nipples, and let her rock him. When he wanted his own release, he swung her around, laid her out, pushed in as deeply as he could go. She liked her ordinary intercourse rough. She wanted him fast and hard and unrelenting.

She still wanted him. He could smell it on her. They sat knee to knee in the reception room at Agnus Dei, aware of each other. It would have been easier if she were no longer attracted to him. He could have accepted that. It was Kat wanting and giving up, Kat in an orgy of self-denial, he couldn't stomach.

The other part of the problem was himself. He was doing nothing. He was wallowing. Kat was walking the corridors of her convent, finding a new world. He was as addicted to the loss-of-Kat as he ever could have been to cocaine. He drifted in and out of the things he was supposed to forget he knew about her. Her breasts were much fuller than they looked in clothes. The nipples were almost red. If he rubbed his hands

43

against them too long, she would turn away, saying they chafed. She had long, lean thighs, very white on the inside. She liked to lift her legs and wrap them around his back. When she came, she laughed.

Since he had left her at Agnus Dei, he woke thinking they were still in London, making what she called "small love." Her fingers began to move over the soft-haired skin of his testicles. He felt his back arch and his chest tighten. It was hard to breathe. She began to rock, forcing him in and out of her, establishing a rhythm. When she had him completely inside her mouth, her tongue traced zigzag helices against the skin.

The rhythm became faster, harder, almost driving. His hands clutched at the mattress. His legs went stiff. He felt himself bucking, arching into blackness.

He was slipping into the blackness when the doorbell rang, six days, seven hours, and forty-four minutes after she was gone.

2

When he first saw her through the screen door, he thought it was Kat. He felt as if someone had rammed a baseball down his throat. Then she turned her head under the porch light, and he saw the fine net of wrinkles around the eyes, the blurring slackness along the jaw. Not Kat. *Mary.* What in the name of God was Mary doing here at quarter to eleven on a Sunday night?

He opened the door for her. She waved small bugs away from the top of her head and walked in past him, her hands jammed into the pockets of an ancient Burberry trench coat. Kat had been fond of Burberry trench coats. It was the kind of thing he rarely remembered about Kat.

He waited until he heard Mary sit down on the living-room couch, then pulled the screen door to and shut the storm door after it

He went into the living room and took a chair at the side of the couch. Mary shrugged off the trench coat and tugged at the sleeves of her golf jersey. She looked like some college student's well-heeled mother, come to inspect life off-

44

campus. She lit a cigarette with a sulfur match and dropped the match on the floor.

"Let's start with this," she said. "I don't like you and you don't like me. We can agree on that."

David took a deep breath. "Right," he said.

Mary waved her cigarette in the air, eyes darting around the room, looking for an ashtray. David got up and found her one. He put it on the arm of the couch and went back to his chair.

"Neither of us wants Kat in that *place*," Mary said.

"Ah," David said.

"Don't say 'ah,'" Mary said. "I've been thinking about it all week. We both want her out of there. I can't get her out of there. You can. So I'm here."

He got up. He wanted an ashtray himself. He wanted a drink. He had a meager collection of bottles on one of the bookshelves. He headed for it.

"I can't make you a gin and tonic," he said. "I don't have tonic. I've got some sherry. And Drambuie."

"I never understood how Kat drank that stuff," Mary said.

"Straight whiskey," David said.

"Straight Scotch," Mary said.

David poured two glasses of undiluted Scotch and brought her one. She put it on the floor at her feet.

"How long have you had this house?" she asked him. "Since May?"

"That's not fair."

"Why not? For God's sake. Don't you think I've been doing crazy things since May? Ever since I heard they let her into that place. I've got a house full of chocolate bars. Every time she came home, she wanted chocolate bars."

"She'll come home again," David said. "That's one of the rules they changed. After she's through the novitiate, she can come home whenever she wants."

"If she isn't posted to Seattle."

"All right."

Mary looked into her Scotch. "I thought you'd be more cooperative. I thought you wanted her out of there. I thought I'd get a little help from you of all people."

This woman thought of Kat as her property. She thought

45

nothing of walking into his house unannounced in the middle of the night, demanding things of him. David wanted to break her neck.

"Look," she said. "It's a four-hour drive from Framingham. I wouldn't be here if I wasn't desperate."

"I don't know what you're doing here," David said. "I don't know what you think I'm going to do now that you *are* here."

"This place is less than half an hour from Northton."

"So?"

"I knew it was close. I've been thinking about it all week. You're close and she listens to you. You can go up and get her out."

"Get her out *how*?" he exploded. "What do you expect me to do, walk in there with a winch and a hook and a Gatling gun and take her hostage? All right, all right. I don't like this any better than you do. But it's what she wants."

"She doesn't know what she wants."

"She did the last time I talked to her."

"I tried to get one of those deprogrammers," Mary said. "They won't touch it. The Catholic Church is not a cult." For a moment, David thought she was going to spit on the floor. "God, what some people don't know about the Catholic Church."

She took a long swallow of her Scotch, closing her eyes like a movie-stereotype drunk as it was going down. David found himself admiring her. A deprogrammer. Would anyone else have the balls to hire a deprogrammer to get her (twenty-four-year-old) child out of an established Roman Catholic convent?

Mary put her glass back on the floor. "We can't just let it ride," she said. "If we let it ride, we'll lose her." She got to her feet and started pacing. "If you're going to say maybe we've lost her already, I don't want to hear it. We can do something about it. We can if you go up there."

Another cigarette, another swallow of Scotch. He was beginning to cool out. She was a fine shadow-Kat. He liked looking at her. She no longer made him angry. No matter what she wanted of him, no matter what master plan she'd hatched in the bowels of suburban Massachusetts, there was nothing he could do.

"I was asleep when you rang the bell," he said. It was half true. He didn't need to be more honest than that. "I come down and you start lecturing me. Let me get acclimated."

"Acclimated to what? What else do we have to talk about? What was I supposed to do, come in and admire your clematis?"

"My clematis is dead."

"Your yard looks like a junk pile. I don't give a shit."

"Right," he said.

"We've got one thing to talk about. Are you going to listen to me?"

She sat with her elbows on her knees, pulling herself close to him. She had Kat's taste in more than Burberry trench coats. He wouldn't even have to seduce her. All he had to do was put his hand on her arm, steer her to the stairs and the upstairs hall. He could lay her out on the narrow bed where he dreamed of Kat. They could have Kat by proxy.

She was looking at him, searching his face, holding her body very still. It was a good body, well tended and conditioned. She was handsomer at fifty-four than most girls were at twenty. In another time and place, he might have wanted her.

He turned away. He did want her. She knew what he was feeling, what he was thinking, what he would do in the next ten minutes. He felt manipulated—by Kat, by Mary, by nebulous beautiful women in his future. Women who knew what they wanted and how to get it. Women who could not be replaced.

Mary pulled away from him, leaning back on the soft cotton couch cover. "I've got a plan," she said. "You could at least listen to the plan."

Now what? What was he supposed to do? Run at her, tear her clothes off, drag her down? Kidnap Kat and bring her to Eagleville for a little *ménage à trois*? That would be a sex orgy of the first water, truly. That would be one of the great bedroom farces of all time.

"It's just a plan," Mary said.

"Right," he said. "It's just a plan."

She patted his knee. He thought of Kat patting his knee, in the reception room at Agnus Dei. This time he did not jump away. He took a long pull on his Scotch and considered what he might or might not be talked into doing. Mary leaned away from him again, flicking her skirt over her knees. Her moves were out of date. He didn't care.

"You'll see," she said. "We'll get her out of there."

He nodded. He was getting a little drunk. He wanted to drive up to Agnus Dei with a Gatling gun, storm the wall, rescue a damsel in distress. He wanted to believe Kat was a damsel who wanted to be rescued.

What he did not want to do was go to bed with Mary Connor O'Brien.

He finished his Scotch and put his glass on the floor.

"If you want to go up to Agnus Dei, you should go," he said.

"I want you to go," she said.

He smiled.

3

It was after two when she left. She walked off his porch reluctantly, expecting him to ask her to stay. He stood under the porch light, watching as she got into her car.

When she started backing out of the drive, he went inside. He shut and locked the screen and storm doors. He went into the living room and lay down on the couch.

Three hours of Mary Connor O'Brien would exhaust anyone.

He had had two victories. He had not agreed to her plan. He had not made love to her. Her plan wasn't worth much. Making love to her would have been too great a risk. If she wanted to hurt Kat, she would have to think of another way.

He had to see Kat, talk to her, convince her. Or maybe not convince her. He had always prided himself on his unselfishness, his generosity, his charity. He didn't think he wanted Kat out of Agnus Dei if she didn't want to leave. He wanted to handle this the way he handled almost everything else in his life—rich-boy-dilettantism though his efforts might be—with measured tolerance, good humor, self-respect. That was how he saw himself. Except right now, if he didn't do something, he was going to crack up.

He had to give it time.

He felt himself drift into a dream of Kat in ice-blue silk

48

and white lace, another pornographic nightmare in a concatenation of pornographic nightmares. In a few minutes he would see her stretched naked and willing across the couch, against a wall, on a coffee table. He would taste dry sweat salt on the inside of her arm. He would feel her hands reaching for him under the stiff quilting of a down sleeping bag.

He told himself he wanted only the best for Kat. He told himself he wanted her to be happy. He thought of her turning to him in the faint light of a London dawn. He thought of writing to her, of driving to Northton, of meeting her in an empty field bordered by pines.

Not yet.

But soon.

"You can close the window, Sister. You don't have to freeze to death."

"You said nothing was to be touched."

"I know the window was open when it happened, Sister."

"Do you?"

"I know it was open when we got here."

"Better. You see how hard it is? And you know what you're supposed to do. How would you feel if you walked into this, still the officer in charge, with no idea whatsoever what the procedures were?"

"It couldn't happen. Before they put me in charge of a case, they'd put me out as an assistant for a few hundred years."

"Of course they would. They wouldn't have expected you to be what you hadn't learned to be. We don't have that luxury here. We bend the rules as far as possible. We let them talk more often than the rest of us. We look the other way at some of the more ordinary kinds of rebellion. We postpone some of the penances, some of the practices, of this life. But there's only so much we can do, so much room we can give them. We have to consider the professed Sisters, the way their spiritual

49

lives might be affected by too much noise, too many distractions. We bring these girls into a world where almost everything they have ever known is gone. Even things they expect to be familiar, like how they make their beds or when they take their showers or the way they walk, must be changed. The rules are all new and unfamiliar and cover almost everything. They don't know the rules, Lieutenant, but they have to follow them. Or try to. And day by day, we add more rules, more customs, more practices. Day by day."

"You're telling me this happened because somebody got confused about the rules? What rules, Sister? Since when have the ten commandments become confusing?"

"I'm telling you the first few weeks in a traditional novitiate, and this is a traditional novitiate, no matter how many changes we've made since Vatican II—those first few weeks are like having your head in a vise. A constantly contracting vise."

"Sister—"

"It creates pressure, Lieutenant. It creates almost unbelievable pressure."

A N G E L U S

1

On the day they were first admitted to choir, Kat woke to find the hall curtain of her cell pulled all the way open on its rod, exposing her to the corridor.

She would have worried about it if she'd had the time. Instead, she leaped out of bed at the first sound of the electric bell going off in the stairwell, drew the curtain shut, and made it to her knees by the time Clare Marie started her long walk between the cells.

"Grant me, O Lord, the grace to love You without reservation, with my heart and my body and my soul," Clare Marie said.

"And the grace to persevere in Your service, all the days of my life," they sang back. Even after a week, they were ragged. Kat could hear the missed beats, the fuzziness, the stuttering as words were forgotten and sequences missed.

The row of harsh overhead fluorescent lights went on, triggered by Clare Marie's "small key" in the lock switch. Kat pulled the flat, unfitted sheets tightly across her bed and made hospital corners. She pulled the gray-and-white quilt over the sheets and arranged it so that the edges fell exactly one quarter inch over the top of the metal bed frame on either side. Clare Marie's voice slid into the Our Father, the Apostles' Creed. Kat struggled into shoes and stockings and a clean postulant's dress, took a clean veil from the second drawer of her dresser, and headed toward the lavatory.

Half a dozen postulants were going in the same direction. Jane was moving against them, washing up done, hands folded under her cape, eyes cast down, forehead wrinkled in a parody of concentration. Kat brushed past her, wondering how she always managed to be first—first dressed, first washed, first against the wall of the corridor, waiting for the line. Did she sleep at all? Had she waited until Kat was asleep and then drawn the curtain back slowly on its metal rod, quietly, so no one would hear? Whatever for?

Jane walked the corridor at night. Kat heard her get out of bed and go through the stairwell door, toward the lavatory. North Wing was locked at night. Jane walking had the choice of corridor or lavatory or bell tower—or the novice corridors beneath them. Did she shut herself in the bathroom and write letters to her mother? *Had* she pulled the curtain open? Whatever for?

But Jane kept rules Kat knew they were expected to break, rules instituted by Reverend Mother Christopher or Clare Marie to provide safe avenues of rebellion. How could such a personally objectionable, socially obnoxious child make such a perfect postulant?

Sometimes Kat woke in the dark reaching for David beside her. Sometimes she lay awake, seeing movies of them together on an otherwise vacant ceiling.

She took her toothbrush and soap and towel from her cubicle and went to one of the basins along the east wall to wash, reminding herself that she was not to think of these things as "hers." It was *our* cell, *our* toothbrush, *our* dinner, *our* work charge, *our* English essay. "You must begin to

51

think of yourself as part of the Mystical Body of Christ," Clare Marie said, "as functioning organs in a living entity made up of the Church Triumphant in Heaven, the Church Militant on Earth, and the Church Suffering in purgatory, with Christ Himself as the head." Kat put *our* toothbrush back in its case and splashed water on her eyes, trying to make them less raw and red and dark-circled. There were no mirrors, but she could feel the dry skin around her eye sockets, the burning under her lids.

They had spent the past week being "prepared for community." Clare Marie's lecture on the Mystical Body of Christ was the only theology they heard. It was as if religious life consisted not of faith and virtue, but of a thousand small habits for a thousand everyday operations, each devised in opposition to the dictates of common sense and the customs of the world. Clare Marie demonstrated the proper way to make beds and dress during morning prayers, to enter and leave chapel, to walk without making a sound, to deliver clothing to the laundry. Kat woke every morning to the struggle to become part of a machine, to function flawlessly, efficiently, obediently. She went to sleep at night wondering if she had put the things she was allowed to carry in her pockets in their correct sequence on top of the bureau. She was told when to get up and when to go to sleep, when to pray and eat, what to wear and what to say when answering the door.

She put *our* things back in *our* cubicle and headed for the door, passing Annie coming from the other direction. Annie looked sleepy and disheveled. Her cape was uneven. Her veil was balled into her hand, threatening to wrinkle. Kat tugged the cap into place and unwound the veil from Annie's fingers. Annie smiled and shook her head, mouthing "Klutz" in the silence.

Half the postulants were already standing next to the now open curtains of their cells, waiting for the procession to chapel. Today they would be led out of the balcony where they had been hidden for the past week and into the main body of the choir. They would be "admitted"—absorbed into the body of the Sisterhood, given work charges, allowed to live ordinary convent life. Only after today would they actually, technically, be postulants. They were supposed to be excited. Kat thought she wasn't the only one who was scared to death.

Annie drifted into place, second to last, veil on sideways. Clare Marie came down the corridor to straighten it.

The only problem with the machine, Kat thought, was that it didn't stop her from thinking, or dreaming, or daydreaming. Would she be at Agnus Dei if it hadn't been for David? Could the sexual love of a man lead a woman to want to become a nun? She thought about it constantly. What would Reverend Mother and Clare Marie have thought if she'd answered their stock questions—why do you want to become a nun?—with "because I fell in love with a man and he loved me back"?

They swung out of North Wing, then through the South Wing doors. The trees of South Yard made a wind tunnel. The wet cold went through her dress, pricking her skin. In the half dark, not quite dawn, the flames of the tall candles on either side of the chapel door looked like ice sculptures reddened with food coloring.

What would David say if she told him it was he who'd brought her here?

2

They had gone to Paris to "work things out." David thought they needed "time away from the day-to-day pressures of the relationship," that a week in Paris would be "good for us." Kat went because she liked Paris, and because the restlessness she'd been feeling since they left Greece—and before—had been getting worse. David thought she was sexually and emotionally bored. David thought she was "getting an itch."

It hadn't been like that. Kat knelt at the balcony rail and thought about how not-like-that it had been. She could see David hefting their bags out of the railway car at the Gare du Nord, the muscles tensing in his back and neck and across the flat expanse of his belly. She could feel him without touching him, catch his rhythms when he wasn't in the room. Sometimes she felt that if she spent the rest of her life in this Order, if she came to her end in a Motherhouse infirmary bed, she would still wake every morning feeling the lightly haired surface of his skin against the palms of her hands.

"We can work this out if you want to," he had said. "We can figure out what's wrong and what to do about it and go on from there."

They couldn't go on from there. She had known that in the Gare du Nord. She never talked to him about God. He associated God with demagogues and tyrants, with small, malicious men who itched to burn the books in libraries. He looked at the people who most loudly proclaimed themselves Christians and wanted no part of them. She thought she saw beyond them. She wanted to tell him: God is a *place.*

Instead, she followed him onto the platform, hands stuffed deep into the pockets of her sweater coat. He took a suitcase and headed toward the barrier.

"It would be easier if you told me what was going on," he said. "If you're just sick of it, there's nothing I can do. But at least I'd know."

"I'm not sick of it."

"You're just sick of sex."

"David—"

He pulled up to the cab rank and threw the suitcases on the ground. "We haven't had a decent night since before we left Greece," he said. "You don't respond anymore. You won't tell me why not. You won't tell me to fuck off. You won't admit that anything's wrong. What the hell am I supposed to do, O'Brien? Jerk off in the bathroom and pretend everything's hunky-dory until you get your act together and tell me to take a walk?"

She got out a cigarette and lit it, even though she knew nice women didn't smoke on the street in Paris. A cab pulled up and she put the cigarette out, levering herself into the inadequate back seat. David helped the driver put the bags in the trunk and got in beside her.

"Just tell me one thing," he said. "Is there someone else?"

Their hotel room overlooked San Sulpice, the square and the church. They checked in, took showers, made love. They went out to dinner, came back, took showers, made love. They made love the way their brushed their teeth, as if

54

it was a ritual for the beginning and end of days. The urgency remained, but it was tinged with panic.

In the morning, she got up and left him sleeping while she went to Mass.

San Sulpice was an ancient church, built when a congregation was expected to stand and kneel but not to sit. Instead of pews, it had only makeshift collapsible rows of cane chairs with unpadded kneelers. The seats looked unworthy of the church, small and badly made.

She took a seat in the center of the fourth row. The first was taken up by a thin line of nuns in navy blue habits, their hair concealed under white helmets ending at their ears and covered by long blue veils. There were a lot of nuns in Paris. She had seen them on her last trip, riding in groups of ten or twelve in Métro cars. They all wore habits. They all concealed their hair. Maybe what she needed was a French convent. Maybe French convents were still convents, instead of whatever American convents had become.

She sat back in the narrow chair. She couldn't say she had never before considered becoming a nun. She had considered it the way she sometimes considered being the first civilian passenger on a moon flight. It wasn't that the project was impossible. *Somebody* had to be the first civilian passenger on a moon flight. Possibility, however, was not probability. People did not go along for the ride on moon flights. People did not become nuns.

She looked at the line of nuns again. It was ridiculous. She had David. She had a need, picked up God only knew where, to find out what God meant, what Christ meant. The two things canceled each other out. Surely her need for David disqualified her from "having a vocation." Even her new religiosity was suspect. She had begun going into churches out of curiosity, to look at the statuary and the stained-glass windows. In London she went to Westminster Cathedral and wandered from one Station of the Cross to another, reading words carved into stone. She returned for Mass, first sporadically, then almost every day. Something inside her was comforted by the candles and the incense and the Presence of the Host on the altar. She was slightly appalled to find she believed it all. Christ has died, Christ has risen, Christ will come again. Oh, yes, she believed that. She believed the Virgin Mary had been taken body and soul into Heaven. She believed in Heaven. She told herself these were things neither she nor anyone else could prove. She told herself the history of the One True Church (and she believed it was the One True Church) was a savage chronicle of wars and persecutions, even now unended. She believed that, too. It was beside the point. Kneeling in church, looking at the light on the altar that told her the Host was in the monstrance, she was free of restlessness. She was not "at peace." She was *home*.

The priest appeared, trailing altar boys and deacons. She stood and made the sign of the cross, letting her voice fall muffled at the back of her throat so no one would realize she couldn't speak French. She had to find a way to put her need for David and this other need together. She had to find a way to keep her relationship with David solid, while she found out what kind of relationship she was supposed to have with God.

Was it crazy, thinking you could have a relationship with God? Thinking there was a God to have a relationship with?

Suddenly, she was angry with David, furious with him. He had taken her out of herself, taught her to trust herself. And when she trusted herself, what did she find? This half-crazed compulsion to move toward that place she thought was God, It embarrassed her to think words like "God." She was a grown woman with a man who loved her. She was not distorting a need for sex into a delusion of Mystical Rapture. She wasn't even sure what "Mystical Rapture" meant. So what was wrong with her?

The priest started the Sanctus. The nuns took up the chant. Kat repeated the prayer under her breath, in Latin, dredging the words from some childhood memory. In a few moments, she would be the only one in church not going up for Communion. It felt like a deprivation.

To receive, she had to somehow give up David.

She let her eyes wander around the church, to a statue of the Virgin in a niche. According to Saint Teresa of Avila, when you pray you should try to see Christ beside you at the rail, the Holy Mother leading you along the Stations of the Cross. Kat stared at the statue and tried to imagine the Holy

56

Mother doing anything, even just standing there, cold in the stony draftiness of San Sulpice.

Her imagination failed. She saw nothing, heard nothing. Then, just for a moment, the barriers came down.

There was nothing between herself and that *place*. She could feel the width and depth and thickness of it. It didn't swallow her up. It didn't overwhelm her. It didn't feel like joy or gladness or peace or any of the things she had been told to expect. It did not feel like pleasure. She didn't hear voices or see the Virgin on a white cloud. She was simply in that place. It had not been her imagination. It really existed. It was home.

She knew she was looking at something inside herself. Bernadette might have seen the Virgin in a grotto. Saint Francis might have had a vision of the triumphant Christ. She had only a sudden, nearly crushing self-knowledge. She was not transported, only shocked. David had taught her to recognize what she believed, but she had kept this from herself. There was such a thing as the soul. The soul was eternal. The soul wanted—could want—only one thing. Union.

She felt the giddiness like champagne bubbles inside her head. Union. What in God's name was that supposed to mean? Union with what? And how? How did you effect union with something so remote, so unimaginable, as the Judeo-Christian God? If you *could* find a way to union, would you exist after the uniting? Would you want to?

The feeling of that place washed over her again, deep and dark and sure. When she abandoned herself to it, the questions disappeared. It was only when she fought it that things become confused, that she felt an aching sense of loss, a yearning after David.

A moment later, it was over. She was standing in the fourth row from the altar of San Sulpice. The nuns were kneeling at their seats, heads bent over folded hands. She felt the undeniable wanting come up in her, the kind of wanting she had felt when she first knew she had to have David. There was nothing different about this, except the intensity. She had always been ruthless about going after what she wanted, but this time she meant it literally. She would do *anything* to get back to that place.

The priest muttered something that must have been "The

Mass is ended. Go in peace." The nuns got out of their seats and walked down the center aisle in a line. Kat stumbled to her feet, groping against the chairs as if she'd been blinded by a flashbulb going off in her face.

It would have been easier if she'd had a religious childhood. Then she could have accepted this as the voice of God, calling her. Instead, she knew too much and too little. She knew she wanted to drown in that deep motionless well, but not how it was done.

She watched the disciplined serenity of the nuns filing out. At the door there was another nun, this one dressed in full habit to the floor, collecting for a Christmas charity. Did nuns know how it was done? Could they teach the method? If she decided to do something—drastic—like enter a convent, how would she explain it? She had not been converted. Her faith had been strong all along, only buried, denied. She had not had a vision, in the accepted sense. What would David say? Her mother? Her best friend from Vassar, who had gone to work for Morgan Stanley?

She had to get back to that place.

When she came out of the church, David was in the square, sitting on a bench with his arms thrown out over the backrest. She suddenly felt like a fool. He was a beautiful man. He loved her. *She* loved *him*.

But not as much as she wanted that place.

He stopped her when she was a foot away from him. He looked tired.

"You don't have to explain," he said. "I used to follow you in London, when you went to Westminster."

"Why?"

"Because I thought it had something to do with it. It does, doesn't it?"

The fine mist that had been falling all morning was turning to rain. Kat could feel thick, slow drops against her face.

"It's going to be hard to explain," she said. "It's going to sound crazy."

He put his hand on her throat, feeling the pulse at the base. She felt it as sympathy—sympathy extended to someone else, on another planet.

"I've been deciding I love you," he said. "Not just that

58

I'm in love with you, but that I love you. Do you know what I mean?"

"No," Kat said. *"No."*

"I don't think it matters." He took off his jacket and handed it to her, giving her something to cover her hair in the rain. She always caught cold when she got her hair wet in the rain.

"Kat?" he said. "Just one thing. You're terrifying me."

3

In the choir, the Sisters got off their knees and sat back in their prie-dieux, waiting. In the balcony, Clare Marie motioned them up. Kat felt Annie tug her sleeve, pulling her out of memory. She got to her feet and tried not to be too obvious flexing her back. This was ritual. She was not supposed to break the line.

Clare Marie stood at the balcony door until they formed their lines, then turned and led the way downstairs. By the time they got there, Reverend Mother would be ensconced in the center chair on the dais, flanked by her council. Then Clare Marie would take her place and they would take theirs, and it would all become real.

Kat kept her eyes trained on Constance's heels. What was about to happen was horrible, in a way. It was a medievalism, something that should probably have been swept away by renewal. Kat remembered Annie's eyes growing wide when Clare Marie explained it to them. She almost laughed. Everything was so new to Annie, exciting and singular.

They slipped into the choir, passed the pews, and fanned out, making two horizontal rows facing the dais. Kat felt her breath catch.

There had been no certainty since that day in San Sulpice. She bounced back and forth, wanting and not wanting, going in one direction and turning back to run the other way. She craved David's hands on her throat and arms and breasts, cigarette smoke in her lungs, Drambuie in a dark bar with Frank Sinatra on the jukebox. She craved the place, and the unvarying security of faith.

There was a sound of wood clapping against wood. Kat

felt herself sink to her knees, bend at the waist, touch her forehead to the floor.

They were supposed to make their promises this morning as if they were making them for life. Kat couldn't do it. Maybe someone like Martha, from a family full of staunch, churchgoing Catholics, who had never wanted or known anything else, could enter a convent without conflict. Kat was keeping her confusion at bay with a sledgehammer.

Someone on the dais made the sign of the cross, echoed by the rows of nuns in choir. Kat tried to give herself up to it just once more. She tried to put David's body out of her mind and concentrate on his soul, which she was still allowed to love.

"Children," Reverend Mother Christopher said, "why have you come?"

"We have come," Kat heard herself say, "to beg permission to try our vocations to live in the Lord in this community."

Her voice was strong among the high-school voices, steady among the tremolos.

ATTENTION TO DETAIL

1

There was a letter from Stephen on the hall table when they came out of breakfast. Annie almost didn't see it. She was thinking of Reverend Mother's eerily inhuman voice, sounding deep and hollow in the stone-walled chapel. Do you put away wordly things, and worldly loves, to have and to hold only the love of Our Lord Jesus Christ? Do you offer up your heart, your soul, and your will, that His will may work in you? Do you offer up your life, and die to yourself, that He may live in you? Annie had been ready to die then and there. It was all so perfect, so beautiful. They would abandon themselves completely, become hollow shells.

Christ would come and fill them up. They would be taken into Heaven, to live in the sight of God forever.

Later, she had begun to feel a little uneasy. Nuns always talked like that. What was it supposed to mean? It couldn't mean what it sounded like it meant. It sounded like death. If she did exactly what she'd just promised to do, she would blot herself out. Obviously she was getting it wrong. Reverend Mother was not a cipher. Clare Marie hadn't blotted herself out.

She was thinking about Jane when she passed the hall table. Jane was small-minded and petty, but that was no longer what Annie hated about her most. Jane was always *perfect*. She glided instead of walked, kept silence when the rest of them couldn't help speaking. Jane never made a slip, never revealed anything personal. She never looked listless or unhappy or afraid. Sometimes Annie thought Jane had been born a nun, detached and cool, so enveloped by the love of God no human emotion could touch her.

Could someone enveloped by the love of God be so—so distasteful?

She saw her name on the board. She stopped, surprised. Her mother wrote every day, though she knew Annie could write only once a week, but those letters came in the afternoon delivery. Annie pulled up behind Martha and Constance and ran her finger along the edges of the envelopes until she found one addressed to her. She turned it over and looked at the "S. B. Bliss" on the flap. Stephen. How like Stephen to write the return address on the flap, when people had stopped doing that years ago.

She put the letter in her pocket and reminded herself that she did not know Stephen. She did not know what was "like him." She was making him up.

She went into the instruction room and took her place on the long wooden bench. Her place in line, her "age in religion," had put her against the rough brick wall. She turned in her seat and leaned over the bench.

"What do you think?" she said. "Are they really going to change everything today?"

"They can't change everything," Constance said. "Why would they teach us all those things and then change them?"

"So we don't get too attached to custom," Geraldine said.

61

Geraldine sneered at everything. She tugged and pulled and fought. She asked questions that had no answers, refused to do anything that did not make "common sense." Annie didn't know if Geraldine's diatribes were "common sense" or not, but she was tired of listening to them.

"I think they're going to change the work schedule," Kat said. "We're going to get work charges in the morning, like the novices. And instruction after noon."

"Real work?" Constance said. "Like in Children's House?"

"Like in the laundry," Kat said. "And the kitchen."

"I don't see why we have to do all this housework," Geraldine said. "Other Orders start you right off in college when you're a postulant."

Annie shrugged. Most of Geraldine's most annoying statements started with the words "other Orders." "We'd only have to stop next year for enclosure," she said. "And then what?"

"Other Orders have gotten rid of the enclosure year," Geraldine said. "And they've gotten rid of all this stuff, too. Not talking. Walking in line everywhere. Making your schedule so tight you hardly have time to breathe. Getting up at some God-awful hour of the morning, to a bell."

"Some Orders don't live like nuns at all," Kat said. "What's the point?"

"What's the point of this?" Geraldine said.

Annie turned to face front. Stephen would have something bright and funny to say. It was odd how easily she got depressed at Agnus Dei. At home, even her mother couldn't get her down most of the time. Here, anything at all—Geraldine's griping, the bare, unfinished walls of the instruction room, the mere sight of Jane—could make her listless and sad.

She looked up to find Jane leaning over the bench in front of her, smiling. Annie shifted in her seat. She didn't want to talk to Jane.

"I heard you talking before," Jane said. "You got it wrong, you know."

Annie fidgeted. When Jane said, "you got it wrong," she always made it sound as if the mistake were deliberate. It

62

wouldn't have been so bad if Jane got it wrong sometimes herself, but she never did. What was worse, there was a lot to get right and wrong.

"I'm doing the best I can," Annie said. "Leave me alone."

Jane smiled. Patiently. Jane always smiled Patiently, or Sympathetically, or Charitably. "It wasn't just you," she said. "You all got it wrong."

"We weren't all saying the same things," Annie said.

"You aren't supposed to want one kind of work charge or another," Jane said. "You're supposed to thank Jesus for the one you're given. It's God's grace if you don't like what you get. It helps teach you perfect obedience."

"Letter and spirit of the law," Kat said, from somewhere behind Annie's shoulder. "You ought to learn the difference."

Annie turned and made a face. Kat was staring at Jane, something hidden and evaluative in her expression.

Jane was looking at Kat as if no one were there. "A nun speaks only for reasons of courtesy, charity, or necessity," Jane said. "We shouldn't be speaking now."

Annie was shocked. "You got hold of a copy of the Rule. We're not even supposed to look at that until next year."

"She should have got hold of the Postulant Regulations," Kat said. "We don't keep Minor Silence yet. If we want to talk before instruction, we can talk before instruction."

Jane smoothed her skirt with the palm of her hand. "I didn't need to get a copy of the Rule," she said. "I just pay attention to what I see around me. You can work out Minor Silence from the novices if you watch them."

"Whatever for?" Kat said. Annie could feel Kat's hostility flowing out to Jane, a one-way hostility that missed its target. Jane was oblivious.

"What we do here is try to become perfect for God," Jane said. "It's not the Rule that matters, it's our own will to perfection. To self-abnegation. To sanctity."

"Start with charity," Kat said. "Charity begins at home."

"Sanctity begins in Heaven," Jane said. Her smile was triumphant.

Behind them, Clare Marie pushed the door open on its

creaking hinge, pushed it back, started coming up the aisle.
Jane turned to face front. Annie slid forward onto the
kneeler, getting ready for prayers. Then she felt Kat's nose,
pushing against her hair.

"Don't let the little idiot get you down," Kat said.

2

It wasn't Jane who was getting Annie down. She made
the final sign of the cross and straightened on the kneeler.
They were supposed to kneel all through instruction, as a
gesture of respect for the Christ in their superiors and in the
Rule that revealed the will of God in their lives. Being smal-
lish and in the second row, her view of the instruction room
was obstructed by Constance and Jane. That was what really
depressed her—not Clare Marie or Jane or rules or poached
eggs for breakfast, but the physical reality of Agnus Dei.
The reception room with its Raphael and Royal Doulton
was an anomaly. Most of the Motherhouse was bare wood
and white-washed plaster, relieved in too few places by large
wooden crucifixes hanging from bare nails. The silver and
china were for guests. In the refectory they ate off stoneware
with tin utensils so painfully cheap, Annie's mother wouldn't
have had them in the house. Passing through the reception
room on her way to chapel or lunch, Annie couldn't keep
her eyes on the heels of the postulant in front of her. She
had to look at the pictures, at the cups and saucers in the
cabinets, at the figurines in the niches, at the things that
spoke of wealth and grace.

She rubbed her hands over her eyes. She was being a
fool. People didn't pile up great fortunes anymore. People
didn't start from nothing these days and end up with yachts
and accounts at Harry Winston. You had to be born with
money, or be some kind of genius. She rubbed her eyes
again. She hated thinking about these things, hated the
crack in the wall next to her, the drab barrenness of North
Wing. She wanted something.

She folded her hands over the back of the bench in front
of her and tried to look bright and happy and alert for Clare
Marie. They sent you home if they thought you were too

64

miserable. Being sent home from Agnus Dei was the only thing Annie could think of worse than spending her life there.

She had no illusions about herself. She wasn't a genius. She wasn't an "exceptional person." She was just Annie Bliss from Ellery Street. If she went back to her mother's house, or if they sent her back, she would never escape again.

Clare Marie rapped the lectern and looked out over their heads. "We will talk today about particular Examen of Conscience," she said. She nodded toward the back of the room. Two novices appeared, carrying a large cardboard box. They set the box at Clare Marie's feet.

Annie felt the ache in her back, her legs, her arms, a saturation assault of pain. They were supposed to kneel erect, unmoving, through the hour. It was impossible when you knew they were going to throw something outrageous at you.

Clare Marie took a black, leather-covered book from the box at her feet. She looked up and down the rows of postulants, seeming to nod to each in turn. Then she held the book over her head.

"This is an examen book," she said. "Beginning tomorrow morning, and continuing the rest of your life in this Order, you will write in this book every morning after Lauds and every evening after Compline, before meditation. In the morning, you will write what you wish to attempt for the day. You may work on the Ecumenical Counsels—poverty, chastity, obedience. You may work on humility and charity. These five are the chief virtues necessary for perfection in the religious life. Each morning, you will choose one and write it at the top of the day's page." She held the book up, showing the pages. The book was hardly larger than Clare Marie's hand, but each page had to have a hundred lines on it.

Clare Marie took a handful of books and handed them to the postulant in the aisle seat of the first bench. "In the evening," she said, "you will return to your books and list the ways in which you have failed to practice the virtue of the day. You will be specific. If you are working on poverty and you waste a paper towel, you will write exactly that in your book, and how many times that day you committed that particular fault. In the morning, you will say a prayer for your intention. In the evening, you will make an act of contrition for your faults. Do you understand?"

Annie understood she was to make a record of the worst part of herself. She saw the black book filling up, day by day, with the stupidities and meannesses of ordinary life. It was repulsive. If you filled a book with nothing but your faults, anyone reading it would think you were a monster.

"You mean our sins?" she blurted out. "We're supposed to write down our sins?" She blushed. She had it wrong again. Everyone was looking at her.

"Don't be embarrassed," Clare Marie said. "Come to the front of the room."

Annie got up and moved along the row, murmuring apologies first to Constance, then to two quiet Italian girls she hardly knew. She stumbled into the aisle and across the last few inches to Clare Marie. She hated standing in front of everyone.

"This, too, was something we were going to discuss today," Clare Marie said. "From now on, you will be responsible to your Sisters for your behavior. Interrupting someone can be a fault against charity, because you may hurt that person's feelings. In this case, it was a fault against obedience. You have been instructed to stand and wait to be called on before you speak in this class. When called on, you say, 'Sister, I ask permission to speak.'" Clare Marie nodded to Annie. "Did you remember that, Anne?"

"Yes, Sister," Annie said. She blushed again.

"Even in the world, when you commit such a fault you apologize for it. Here, you apologize not to the Sister against whom you have committed the fault, but to the entire community." Clare Marie rapped her palm on the side of the lectern. "There are no individual failings here. Everything you do, everything you say, everything you think affects your Sisters. We are a single living, breathing entity dedicated to the service of Our Lord Jesus Christ."

Clare Marie came out from behind the lectern. She was smiling, but Annie didn't like the smile. It was too gentle

66

and pitying, too full of secrets. Annie wanted to lick her lips, but didn't dare. It might be against the rules. It might be useless. The roof of her mouth felt dry and cracked. Her tongue felt like a clod of dirt.

"Now," Clare Marie said, "you will go to your knees, kiss each of my shoes in turn, and say, 'I beg the forgiveness of this community and of my Sister Superior Clare Marie, for having committed a fault against obedience in having interrupted instruction.'"

Annie felt a hiss rising behind her like a wave. They didn't like this any better than she did. She clamped her teeth together, sending a needle of pain through her jaw.

The hissing became a rustling. They were moving on the benches, uncomfortable for themselves and for her. Annie prayed Kat was angry at Clare Marie. She needed someone angry for her.

She got slowly to her knees and stared at the tops of Clare Marie's shoes. They were clean and polished, a model of nunly perfection. Clare Marie was a model of nunly perfection, a Living Rule. That was why she was Postulant Mistress. Her shoelaces lay flat against the soft black leather. They made Annie ill.

She bent over and kissed each one of them, forcing herself to brush her lips against the stiff edges of the seams. Dirty, she thought. She had to swallow a heave. Shoes were dirty, moving all day over the floor.

She said, "I beg the pardon of this community and of my Sister Superior Clare Marie for having committed a fault against obedience in having interrupted instruction."

"Forgiveness," Clare Marie said. "I beg the forgiveness of this community."

Annie took a deep breath. She imagined she could smell Clare Marie's feet, sweaty and foul in the trap of her stockings. This time the heave came up, but dry.

She was not going to kiss those feet again. Unless she was told to.

She said, "I beg the *forgiveness* of this community and of my Sister Superior Clare Marie for having committed a fault against obedience in having interrupted instruction."

Clare Marie said, "In charity, I pronounce myself not without fault and unworthy to judge."

Annie felt Clare Marie's hand on her shoulder. "You can get up now," Clare Marie said. "Get up and go back to your seat."

Annie's arms and knees were locked. She had gone rigid. She was frozen to the floor, bound to Clare Marie's shoes. She would never be able to get up.

"It's all right, Anne," Clare Marie said. "You can stand up. You can go back to your seat."

Annie jerked upright, surfacing much too fast, reeling off-balance. Behind her, the rustling turned to laughter, helpless and panicked. The blood rushed to her face, making her hot and stupid.

Her embarrassment became thick, solid anger, covering everything. She hated them all, the other postulants for laughing, Clare Marie for humiliating her. She had been made a fool, *degraded*, for what had been nothing but a mistake.

She spun away from Clare Marie and plunged into the aisle, looking neither right nor left. She didn't want to see any of them. She didn't want to know how they were looking at her. Their pity would be worse than their amusement.

She stumbled over the feet of the other postulants in her row and sank to her knees at her place, refusing to correct herself for the possessive. It hadn't been *our* humiliation. It had been hers. It could damn well be *her* place.

She stared at the back of Jane's head. She knew Jane was smiling. Clare Marie might see a solemn frown, but anyone looking at the back of Jane's head would know she was smiling.

"If Anne is a normal postulant," Clare Marie said, "what she feels now is anger, not only against me, but against the Order, her Sisters, you. That anger is important. That anger is her will. The strength of it is the strength of her will. What Anne and all of you must learn in the postulancy and novitiate is to subject your will to the will of God spoken through your superiors. To subjugate your pride to the humility of Christ and the meekness of Mary. To die to yourselves and live in Him . . ."

When the bell rang the end of instruction, Annie kept her place in line just long enough to get out the door. Then she ducked into the side hall and headed for the only privacy at Agnus Dei—the lavatory. She locked herself in a stall and sat on the toilet-seat cover. She liked Miriam and Martha and Kat, but it hadn't happened to them. It had happened to her.

Would she look back on this and smile, pitying the naïve little postulant she'd been, so attached to her self-deluding pride? Would she thank God for teaching her humility? Did she want to be humble and without pride?

What would she do if she did not have a vocation? She thought of the shoes, the nervous laughter, the crack in the instruction-room wall. In her mother's house, there were cracks in the ceilings, spreading like bolts of lightning from the bases of overhead light fixtures. Her mother had died and petrified in that house.

She put her hands in her pockets and came up with Stephen's letter, the envelope slit carefully at the top. She took the letter out and laid it across her knees, thumbing through the pages to find something light and unconnected to convent life. Stephen wrote a lot about her vocation. Right now, it would only embarrass her. Stephen wrote a lot about their father, too, but she was beginning to realize it wasn't safe to think about that when she was depressed. It got under her skin, somehow. It made her nervous.

She found what she was looking for on the fifth page.

"I have to tell you about a trip I made Thursday," Stephen wrote, "to a house out in Orange. You wouldn't believe it if you saw it. I didn't. To start with, this place had thirty-five rooms . . ."

Annie settled in over the letter. A house with thirty-five rooms. A mansion. Before, whenever she'd thought about money, she'd thought about getting it, or having it. It had never occurred to her that wealth could be *observed*. Stephen might not have money, but he had been inside a mansion. It made her feel the way she felt when she looked at the silver and china in the reception room. It made the world seem very bright and wide.

She thumbed through the pages again. Stephen had written a very detailed description. She wondered what kind of work he did to get himself admitted to houses like this. She wondered what he looked like.

She would write and ask him to visit her. He would tell her about the house with thirty-five rooms, and the furniture and the carpets, and the way people lived there.

GUIDANCE

1

They were sitting on benches in the first-floor North Wing hall, novices on one side, postulants on the other, waiting for their turn at Guidance. Jane bent over her copy of the *Summa Theologia* and tried to look as strictly preoccupied as Angela Louise across the hall. The first few days, she had imitated Marie Bernadette, but she'd finally realized it was a mistake. They were suspicious of Marie Bernadette. They thought her ardor was psychotic. What they wanted was a good girl who would not go to extremes.

Annie was sitting in Clare Marie's office, probably still upset. The fact of it hit a wall in Jane's mind. What in God's name was Annie upset about? Nothing had happened to Annie that hadn't happened to Jane a hundred times. She'd never kissed anyone's shoes, but there were many methods of public humiliation. Back in West Haven, the nuns had heaped them on her head. She had smiled and nodded and learned how little they meant. You could not be humiliated if you did not want to be. You did not have to take it seriously.

They couldn't catch you with public penance. That's what Annie should have realized. Public penance was nothing but a formula. Anyone could learn to repeat it. Guidance was the real danger. Guidance gave Clare Marie a chance to poke and probe at you. You could make a mistake.

70

"All anyone has to do is talk to you," her mother said. "As soon as they talk to you, they know."

Jane ran her fingers over the first page of the *Summa Theologia*. She would have to remember to turn pages once in a while. She wasn't supposed to be meditating on Thomas Aquinas, just reading him.

She wondered how her mother would define whatever it was everyone "knew" as soon as they spoke to her. Craziness? Viciousness? Her mother was worse than a bitch. Her mother was a *cunt*.

"I've heard all about the novitiate," her mother said. "It's worse than a mental hospital. They dig into you there. They find out everything."

She had half expected her mother to tell them. She had walked around half paralyzed for a week, waiting to be called into Reverend Mother's office and presented with dear Mama's letter, "explaining the situation." It was only last night she'd realized it wasn't going to happen. That was what was so wonderful about feeding the birds. It cleared her head. Her mother couldn't tell them even the little she knew. She couldn't risk exposing herself. Jane rocked in her seat, caught herself, stopped. Rocking was a sign of madness. Her mother had told her that. She couldn't trust her mother for much, but she could trust her to know the signs of madness.

"You'll be a fake," her mother said. "You don't care about that, do you, dear? You've always been a fake."

"I can make you disappear," her mother said. "Don't you believe me? Watch."

The week her mother had made her disappear, she killed a cat. A real cat, not a kitten or a half-dead stray from the garbage dump on Holt Street. "I can make you disappear," her mother said—and did. Jane could remember the silent, summer-stifled rooms of their house, empty room after empty room, empty hallway after empty hallway. She was fourteen. She had just returned from visiting her father in Florida. She had said something—she was never sure what—and her mother had dematerialized her. For a week. Her mother had looked through her, walked around her, gone on doing crossword puzzles while Jane shouted in her ear. Once, when Jane found her mother eating breakfast in the

71

kitchen, she picked up the bowl of cereal and milk and dumped it over her mother's head. Her mother let the milk and cereal drip over her hair and onto her shoulders and down the front of her blouse, reaching all the while for a jar of Cremora for her coffee.

The cat belonged to Mrs. O'Bannion next door. The night after the cereal incident, she put out a plate of milk for it. She sat on the porch, huddled on the damp concrete, waiting. Her mother went to bed, turning out all the lights, as if there was no one who might come in and have to stumble through the dark. Jane held a piece of cheese in her hand and sang to herself. She could hear thunder in the distance, feel damp wind in her hair. She hated electrical storms. When it started to thunder and lightning, she always panicked.

The cat came finally to get out of the rain. The O'Bannions had only closed porches. There was nowhere there for it to hide. It drank the milk Jane had left out for it and climbed into her lap to gnaw the cheese in her hand.

Jane put her hands on the cat's fur, feeling the muscles beneath the skin, the warmth in the belly. If she did that to her mother, her mother would never notice, but if she went further... She wrapped her hands around the cat's neck, leaving one finger free to stroke its throat. The cat was lying against her stomach, purring, condescending. Her mother was a cat, self-sufficient, iron-whimmed.

She shifted her hands so that her fingers were still around the cat's neck, but her palms were against its head. It squirmed, uncomfortable.

What would they say if she told them about the night of the cat—not about the cat itself, but about being locked out in the thunderstorm? She could still hear herself, screaming and screaming, pounding against the storm door until she tore the mesh, kicking at the wooden door that wouldn't budge. Would they think she was making it up? Her mother always said she had the look of a pathological liar. That it wouldn't matter even if she told the truth. No one would believe her.

Somehow, she thought Annie would believe her. Annie didn't know it, but they were kindred spirits. There was a bond between them. If she could find a way to get close to Annie, she could make it clear to her.

Lacking Annie, she closed her eyes again and thought about birds. She imagined drawing the robe around a bird's head, slamming the heel of her palm over and over into its neck. She could feel the thin hollow bones cracking, the wet idiocy of the eyes under her thumb.

2

Clare Marie's office had a desk, two chairs, a wall of bookcases filled with biographies of the saints. Jane took the smaller chair and positioned it so that the bookshelves were at her back. She kept her hands folded on her lap and her feet flat on the floor.

Clare Marie took a seat behind the desk. "Well," she said, "you're finally a real postulant. How do you feel about it?"

Jane nearly panicked. She hated questions about how she felt about things. She never felt the right way. What would Annie say? What would Annie have said if she hadn't been through that scene in instruction?

"Nervous," Jane said. "Excited but nervous. Like I'm in a race, you know, where I want very badly to finish but don't know if I can, because I'm really surprised to be allowed in the race at all."

Clare Marie nodded, pleased. "That's very well put. Very well put. Maybe I'll do an introductory lecture next year, comparing the novitiate to trying out for an Olympic team. It might go over very well."

"I think it will go over *very* well," Jane said. She almost wasn't able to get the words out. Good Lord, what sort of idiot was this woman? Even the nuns back in West Haven had been less saccharine than this. Clare Marie could be tricking her, ridiculing her. How could she know?

Clare Marie's eyes were bright and friendly, although, like the eyes of most nuns, they didn't seem to be looking at anything in particular. "You weren't upset by what happened in instruction this morning?" she said. "It didn't throw you off-balance?"

"No," Jane said. "I'd heard about things like that."

"So it lacked surprise," Clare Marie said. "Yes, I could see it might be less disturbing if you expected something of the sort. And, of course, a lot of people think the Orders have done away with all that. As some have."

"I wanted a conservative Order," Jane said.

Clare Marie nodded again. Jane relaxed. Clare Marie wasn't trying to trick her. She was merely a very stupid woman, stupid and blind. That odd gaze, meant to look so penetrating, was just another nun habit. Jane concentrated on looking bright and eager, the way she thought Annie must have looked once she'd calmed down and been comforted.

"Now we have goal projection," Clare Marie said. "That's a very new term for us, since renewal. We want you to be the most perfect nun you can be. Think over the Ecumenical Counsels, the vows you hope to make, the cardinal virtues. Where do you feel you fall short? What do you want us to help you with?"

Jane nearly jumped out of her chair. It was the worst kind of trap. If she said "obedience," they would watch her much too closely. They would cut her off from the birds. If she said "poverty," they would probably make her walk around in rags, or cut her off from secular books and magazines. If she said "chastity," they would paste a Freudian interpretation on everything she did.

The trick was to present the maximum amount of piety for the minimum of restriction. She had to find something that required them to scrutinize her soul without monitoring her movements.

When it hit her, she was surprised she hadn't thought of it before. It was the most natural thing. It would get her everything she wanted.

She plucked against her skirt, only half feigning nervousness. Nun-habit or not, the way Clare Marie was looking at her was unnerving. Jane wanted to turn away, or close her eyes. Clare Marie was always saying the eyes were "the windows of the soul." Jane wanted no windows on her soul.

She had been worried she wouldn't be able to present the right mixture of tentativeness and humility. Her nervousness provided a substitute. Her throat was tight. Her body trembled. She looked the picture of bashful contrition.

She said, "Charity," in a voice like a dying frog's.

"Charity," Clare Marie repeated.

Careful, Jane told herself. It all depends on this. Her voice had to be hurried and hushed. Her face had to be creased with embarrassment.

"I know we're supposed to like all the Sisters equally," she said, "and I really try, but you see, I can't like her. I can't stand her, no matter what I do. It's all for such silly superficial reasons. I don't like her voice. I don't like her hair. Silly, worldly reasons."

Clare Marie sat back in her chair. Jane didn't think she was seeing anything at all. Her face was dark. Her eyes were hooded.

"Who?" Clare Marie said.

Jane pushed her veil off her forehead. It had fallen forward in her exertions. The linen edge was damp with sweat. She could feel sweat all over her body, as if she'd taken a bath in dirty water.

Clare Marie was waiting, sitting slightly forward in her chair. Jane nearly choked on her exhilaration.

She leaned closer to Clare Marie, her voice low, soft, penitent.

"It's Annie," she said. "Annie Bliss."

ROSARY

1

Martha's cat had killed a bird. It had sat hunched over the corpse near the North Wing–North Lawn wall, pawing at the bloody feathers. Annie prodded the cat's rump, making it jump. She didn't look at the bird. She didn't like seeing animals accidentally killed in the road, never mind evidence that the domestic feline was less domestic than she'd like to think. Besides, the mere idea of it lying there dead in the grass threatened to break the mood she'd been building so carefully since Guidance.

"The Rule is not the ten commandments," Clare Marie had told her. "Here you have nothing to do but keep the

Rule, so we stress observance. But in a few years, you'll be out on apostolate, in college or on mission, and if you have to deliver a baby, the baby isn't going to wait—or the mother be comforted in silence—just because the Rule says you're supposed to keep your mouth shut from ten-thirty to eight."

Pour forth, we beesech You . . .

Annie looked at the nuns in the arbor, spaced out on stone benches facing a marble statue of the Virgin. Did Clare Marie know she'd had a nightmare in the early hours of Wednesday morning? If she did, all that circumlocution would at least make sense. The whole mess had been the result of her own stupidity. She had known from the first night that she couldn't listen to the "tower stories," no matter how much of a tradition they seemed to be. She didn't like Marie Bernadette's voice, or Jane's. She didn't like stories about suicide. Or ghosts. They hit too close to something raw in her. On Tuesday, she decided she liked being left out even less. She wedged herself between Kat and Miriam, prepared to hear Jane's bloody morality tale about loss of faith and the wrath of God.

It was ridiculous. She didn't believe in ghosts, or the wrath of God appearing as a specter in chains. None of them did. If they had, Clare Marie would have put a stop to the whole business with no further discussion. If Jane hadn't had such an eerie, insinuating voice, a voice that made Annie's spine tingle and head ache, Annie would have stood up in the middle of all that folderol and said, "Oh, come now."

Which made what happened later all the more embarrassing. First the dream, something she couldn't remember, except that her mother had been in it. Then the crying out. She'd awoken herself, and probably half postulant corridor, yelling at herself in her sleep. The next thing she knew, she was sitting up in bed and Kat was sticking her head through the muslin curtains, frowning. The last thing Annie had wanted was talk. It mortified her to have called out in the first place.

She moved carefully down the slope to the arbor, the statue of the Virgin, the nuns on the benches. There really had been a death in the tower. That was what made the ghost stories so hard to handle. A girl had hanged herself

76

from a rafter. Now postulants amused themselves by making up scare stories about her ghost. Thinking about it made Annie even sicker than thinking about kissing Clare Marie's shoes.

She found a place on an empty arbor bench in the last row. The nuns on the other benches were all old, bent at the waist, encapsulated. Annie wondered what it was like for them, coming home to Agnus Dei the way other old people went off to nursing homes, to a place that would indulge their feebleness and someday let them die.

2

"I'm glad you came," Angela Louise said, sitting on the other end of the bench. "You're the first."

Annie moved away, partially to give Angela Louise room, partially to bring herself back to the present. Sitting in the arbor, looking across the great lawns at the hulking Gothic magnificence of Agnus Dei, it was easy to remember why she wanted to be a nun. Even Stephen's thirty-five-room mansion could not be as large and imposing as Agnus Dei. The pinched bitterness of her mother's house could never take hold on North Lawn. The place was a stage set for an enchanted princess.

"You've got to at least look like you're talking to me," Angela Louise said. "Otherwise, it won't work."

"What won't work?"

"In front of us." Angela Louise nodded.

Annie looked at the benches. Each of the old nuns was sitting just a little sideways, looking at them and pretending not to. Annie felt a wave of nervousness.

"Now, don't get jumpy," Angela Louise said. "We've got five minutes before the rosary bell rings and they want to come over to talk. If I'm here, they have an excuse. They'll see us talking and decide it's because you're lonely and need to be comforted. Homesick."

"I am lonely sometimes," Annie said, leaving out any explanation as to why she wasn't in the least homesick.

"Good," Angela Louise said.

Two old nuns got to their feet and started back through the benches. The rest rose as at a signal, staying close together, bobbing their heads in the bright afternoon sunlight. Annie was suddenly looking at a wall of ancient, gentle faces, framed in black and white and gray.

"I'm Sister Mary Perpetua," the first one said. She nodded at the nun beside her. They were going down the line like a postulant class answering a roll. "Sister Mary Jacob." "Sister Mary Thaddeus." "Sister Mary Vianney." "Sister Mary Bonaventure." "Sister Mary Canisius." The out-of-fashion names spread like mist into the hard modern air, making it softer. Sister Perpetua nodded to Annie, encouraging.

"Oh," Annie said. "I'm Annie. Annie Bliss."

"They keep their names now," Bonaventure said, "until Epiphany, when they receive the rosary."

"*Much* more sensible," Jacob said. "Silly to get your name changed before you even know if you're supposed to be here. Ridiculous to go to all that trouble just to find out you're miserable."

"You're not miserable, are you, dear?" Vianney said.

"How's she supposed to know if she's miserable?" Jacob said. "Been here a week."

"It could have been a good week or a bad week," Vianney said.

"First week is always a bad week," Jacob said. "Cried my whole first week. Missed my dog."

"My first week, I thought I'd had a vision of the Virgin Mary," Vianney said. "I was scared silly. Turned out to be salmonella. I was in bed for a week."

"We aren't giving the poor child a chance to get a word in edgewise," Perpetua said. She patted Annie's knee. "Do forgive us the fault against charity, Sister. We're all over eighty and we get garrulous."

"You're over ninety," Jacob said.

"Over ninety and never missed a meditation in my life," Vianney said.

"It's not like us," Bonaventure said. "They don't dump it on them all at once anymore. They go slowly, in stages."

"Good thing," Jacob said. She shook her finger in Annie's face. "Don't listen to the idiots who'll tell you re-

78

newal was a bad thing. Renewal was a wonderful thing. Got rid of a lot of foolishness."

"All that silence," Canisius said. "My first week . . ." She looked at the others and shrugged. "Oh, well. Everybody's first week is the same, I suppose."

"Miserable," Jacob said.

"If it's God's will and you make up your mind," Vianney started to say.

Above them, the chapel bells rang the rosary. Vianney cut the word "mind" in half, bent her head, and stood up. Annie watched, fascinated, as the rest of them followed. She had heard about absolute obedience to the bell, but never seen it. Annie wondered how many sentences someone like Vianney had strangled in her lifetime, listening to the bells.

Suddenly, she felt better than she had all week. It was late September, not that far from Christmas and Epiphany. She could make it through another three months. Once she had a new name (Sister Mary Stephen?) and a new rosary and newly shorn hair, she wouldn't be Annie Bliss anymore. She would be someone new and different, almost a nun, almost free of Ellery Street and her mother's relentless, dental-drill drone. Who do you think you are?

3

Angela Louise caught up to her as she was going back to the main building. Agnus Dei looked more than ever like an enchanted tower, a place of mystery and magic, where straw could be turned to gold.

Angela Louise pulled at her cape. "Just one quick thing," she said. "We take care of the old Sisters here. They're very important to us."

"Of course they are," Annie said. She couldn't imagine Vianney not being important to her. She saw all those years of being a nun, stretching back through changes and renewals without number. Vianney was a living, breathing history of the Order in this century.

Angela Louise smiled, nodded, hurried away. Annie started hurrying, too. They were due in chapel directly after rosary. She didn't know what the penalty was for being late, and didn't want to. She thought of Clare Marie's shoes and couldn't stifle a shudder.

When she got near the North Wing–North Lawn wall, she was thinking about Stephen's letter, about what she would write him when they were called down to the library at the end of the month. She was imagining herself in the library, bent over stiff white paper with the Agnus Dei seal embossed at the top, when she tripped over the corpse of the bird. She looked down without thinking, her mind full of a vision of herself, in full habit, moving between the silver candlesticks to put her envelope on Clare Marie's desk. The black rubber sole of her shoe was spattered with flakes of dried blood, the toe brushed by stiffening feathers.

The bird hadn't just been killed. It had been *shredded*.

SHARING IN
THE SPIRIT

The pressure of the silence was like a helium balloon expanding in her head, pushing against her skull, threatening to cut fissures under her scalp. Kat looked down the length of the long folding table at Annie Bliss, calmly heaping large pieces of chocolate cake and butterscotch brownie on a plate. It was a good day, cold but clear, and they were holding Spiritual Discussion in South Yard instead of in the reception room. Northton lay in the hollow at the bottom of the hill, looking inert. Agnus Dei was behind them, a hulking, Gothic monstrosity with a will of its own. No wonder the ghost stories worked so well. Put the Motherhouse in a thunderstorm, kill the electric lights, and it became the perfect haunted house.

It was getting to all of them, Kat thought. Miriam had taken the seat beside her, keeping her eyes down and her face turned away, the picture of Custody of the Eyes, Custody of the Senses. There was nothing in the rules to say they had to keep their eyes averted from the world, their bodies stiff and separate from physical things. All that was supposed to come later. Even so, they were cutting themselves off, shutting themselves up, looking (or trying to look) "wholly inward."

Kat wished Annie had been the one to sit beside her—Annie who couldn't keep her mouth shut in instruction, who babbled through recreation like a talking doll with a broken switch. She could not get up, cross the circle, go to sit beside Annie. If there was one thing you never did in a convent, it was to seek out one Sister over the others.

At the far side of the circle, Clare Marie stood and rapped her wooden gavel against her metal folding chair. Most of them had been standing at the table, eating on their feet. Now they began to drift toward the circle, moving like nuns.

Every one of them looked terrified.

"Sister Postulant Martha," Clare Marie said.

Martha stood up in a rustle of linen skirt, held her reading book open in two flat hands, squinted at the lines. "*Today* we hold a memorial at Mass for Saint Januarias, Bishop of Benevento during the reign of Diocletian, martyred for the faith, with several companions, by beheading."

Kat rubbed the pages of her reader, ordering herself to settle down. Her mind hadn't been quiet all day. Protracted silence just *got* to you. Geraldine fought. Jane hid in strictness. Annie jumped from despair to euphoria, uncontrollable.

Kat bent forward at the waist, trying to make concentration as much physical as mental. Martha was saying prayers, reading the gospel. Kat was looking down the lawn to the edge of the road, seeing something that could not possibly be there.

There weren't that many cars like that left in the world, almost none that looked so clean and new.

It was like being spun around and around in the tilt-a-whirl at a roadside carnival. David was not a memory. David was a lime green Volkswagen bug, parked in the road at the bottom of South Yard, waiting for her.

"It's always been a war, Lieutenant. A war between women and the Church."

"Right now it's a violent death, Sister. A very ugly—"

"You think it's new, all this agitation, all this bitterness. But it's always been a war. There have been cease-fires, but never a permanent peace. Can you imagine the Church without teaching nuns, Lieutenant? Do you realize what Rome thought of the idea when it was first proposed? A scandal, Lieutenant, a minefield of occasions for sin. Unacceptable. Undiscussable. Jane de Chantal, Angela Merici, even Saint Vincent de Paul—forced to compromise, forced to fight, sometimes even forced to lie, just to put nuns in the world as teachers and nurses. A war, Lieutenant. A war between women and the Church."

"I don't see—"

"You don't see what it has to do with this? I do, Lieutenant."

"You mean, this will make you lose the . . . war."

"I mean, without the war, it would never have happened."

CALLING THE ROLL

The letter from Rome was on the desk, spread out across the green felt blotter. Clare Marie didn't have to read it to know what was in it. Their Motherhouse General in Rome was undoubtedly "very disturbed."

Clare Marie knew what Reverend Mother was counting on. The notice had gone up on the bulletin board outside the reception room yesterday. As of September, the option to wear lay clothes for Sisters on apostolate was withdrawn, the option for full habit reinstated. They would send nuns onto the streets of New York and Chicago and Los Angeles, and those nuns would "look like nuns." That these would be mostly first-year tertiary professed, still romantic enough about the habit not to care that the starched linen of the wimple stripped the skin from the sides of their faces, wouldn't matter. The conservatives would have their public display of compliance. The American Province would keep the substance of renewal unmolested.

With any luck.

Maybe, for the first time since renewal, there was hope. A postulant class of over twenty, instead of the five or six they'd been getting since Vatican II. Katherine Mary O'Brien. Miriam Bender. Clare Marie wished there was some way over the cavern of silence. She didn't think she and Reverend Mother Christopher had addressed a word to each other except for courtesy, charity, or necessity in over forty years. It was one of the things they had both worked hard to change. Someday, twenty years in the future, two of the postulants now sitting on the lawn would sit in this office instead, calling the roll and actually able to talk to each other.

She sat down next to Reverend Mother's desk. "I don't think we have to worry about outbreaks," she said. "There haven't been any yet."

"Nobody's thought of breaking into the tower and clanging up and down witn a cowbell?" Reverend Mother said.

"It's not that kind of class. Two of them tried to climb a pine tree and had to be helped down, but that's the extent of it. Nothing serious."

"O'Brien?"

"And Bender."

"That's all right," Reverend Mother said. "The only thing that worries me about O'Brien and Bender is that they'll leave." She tapped the papers on her desk. "Short list?"

Clare Marie looked away. This was the part of her job she liked least. She didn't know who belonged on the short list, not yet. She didn't know who should go and who should stay. Except, of course, for Geraldine Harrigan. If they didn't get Geraldine out of here soon, they were all going to go crazy.

They had made a rule, during renewal, to make no negative decision on a postulant until the end of the first phase. In the old days, too many girls had been sent home after a few weeks, merely because they'd had a more difficult time adjusting—or hiding their maladjustment—than some of the others.

They stared at each other. Clare Marie kept her hands folded in her lap.

Reverend Mother said, "Margaret Mary Connoley."

"I was thinking the same thing myself," Clare Marie said.

Reverend Mother sighed. "I remember when that happened," she said. "I thought we'd never be finished with it, and we won't be. Is she suicidal, then, our Jane?"

"No," Clare Marie said. "I wasn't thinking of that part of it. I was thinking that she spouts religion because it's what she has instead of friendship, instead of self-esteem. Not that she's not religious. As far as I can tell, she's very devout. But the verbal expression of it is overblown."

Reverend Mother relaxed. "That's not so bad," she said. "If she doesn't believe the things she comes out with, if it's just an act . . ."

"It's a particularly dysfunctional act. They hate her."

"*Hate* her?"

"I'm not overstating the case. They don't want anything to do with her. She plays Sister Mary Perfect Postulant. She points out their faults. She won't bend the rules for anyone or any reason. She takes exception to their jokes. Even little things, like talking about their families at recreation. It's like having another superior around. They resent it."

"I remember when talking about our families at recreation was not a little thing," Reverend Mother said.

"I remember when they told us which drawer to put our underwear in. Things change."

"Yes, yes," Reverend Mother said. "And mostly for the better. But you said they hate her. We have Sister Mary Perfect Postulants all the time. It's one of the great annoyances of formation. But the rest of the postulants don't hate them. They ignore them."

"That's what made me think of Margaret Mary," Clare Marie said. "The scapegoating. I said there had been little rebellion—no after-hours parties in the bathrooms or the tower, no contraband cigarettes or magazines, no letters from old boyfriends smuggled in from the Lord only knows where. None of the things we're used to this early in postulant year. I don't think they need them. They have Jane."

"I've heard her tell ghost stories on occasion," Reverend Mother said. "She's very good. They crowd around her to listen. They don't hate her there, do they?"

"No."

"But you still think she's being scapegoated?"

"She's desperate to be included, not just in the ghost stories, but everywhere. I've told you about her first Guidance session. She said she had an antipathy to Annie Bliss and asked if I could help her. She just wanted to get closer to Annie Bliss, of course, to be given a chance with the group. I gave it to her."

"And it didn't work."

"It hasn't yet."

Reverend Mother sighed, heaving her round bulk away from the desk. "You're sure there's nothing wrong with her? Seriously wrong?"

"I'm not God, Reverend Mother. I don't think she's unstable. She feels left out. She gets, admittedly, obnoxious on the subject of other people's faults. And I have no intention of asking her to leave because a lot of girls who are old enough to know better want to play high-school in-crowd at her expense."

"Maybe we should just bull it out," Reverend Mother said. "Forcing her on them might be worse than letting the situation ride. They'll be moving to the next phase in November. They'll have more on their minds. Too much, perhaps."

"She could be gone by then."

"You have something you want to do," Reverend Mother said.

Clare Marie looked out the window. The bell ending recreation was ringing. The old nuns were on their feet and moving. The postulants were picking up yarn and thread from the grass, making an effort to keep silence and only half succeeding. Annie Bliss had thread caught around her shoes. She was tripping, laughing, fighting off Martha's attempts to help her up. Kat was standing to one side, clutching Martha's cat to her chest, biting her lip, holding her laughter in, letting the tears stream down her face without impediment.

Jane stood fifty feet away, arms behind her back, leaning against a tree. Her face was blank and smooth. Her body was still. She was watching them.

Clare Marie turned away.

"The first thing we have to do," she told Reverend Mother, "is protect Jane. The second thing is to breach the group."

"And you know how to do both those things?

"Oh, yes. We start with Annie Bliss."

"Look down there on the lawn, Lieutenant. I could order them away, of course. Maybe I should. Do you think voyeurism is a sin?"

"I don't expect it of nuns, Sister."

"Of course not. We're not real. The postulants think that way when they come here. They can't forgive themselves anything. They try to be perfect at once, in all things. And when it doesn't work, when coming to the convent isn't a magic spell that makes them automatically selfless and detached, when they find themselves wanting the same things, sinning the same ways they did at home, well then—"

"Then they take knives and start to carve up the scenery? And each other?"

"I wish I could take this whole thing and dump it in the lap of our good Cardinal Archbishop, who feels so free to tell us not to change the rule of silence at breakfast. As if he knew anything about the rule of silence at breakfast. He won't touch this, of course. This will be all my responsibility."

"Sister—"

"Of course. I was telling you about postulants who expect to be perfect, just because they've come."

"I want you to tell me about the rope, Sister. How they got the rope. Who got the rope."

"Some of them learn to accept the fact that they must bend, that they will break the Rule, that they will commit faults and have to confess them, that their lives will be a struggle against imperfection. Others bend because not to bend is to break down, but they never accept their imperfection. They hate themselves for their failure. They tear at themselves every time they accidentally speak during silence, every time the pressures get too overwhelming and they blow off steam."

"Sister, please."

"You can't necessarily tell who is doing what, you know. That's the problem."

MOUSE

1

On the day David's first letter came, Kat found a dead mouse on the mat outside the pantry door, headless, crushed. It must have been there most of the night. The blood on the mat was dried into flakes. The torn muscles coiling from the stump were gray and limp and crusted with powder. Kat prodded it with her toe, feeling sick. The fur at the edge of the stump looked as if it had been wound through a corkscrew. It was twisted into a frill. Minuscule feet curled tinier claws into the faded green "W" of "Welcome." The thing didn't look dead. It looked *savaged*.

Damned cat, Kat thought, and then, I'm going to kill that animal. She stepped away from the mat, squinted into the late-October early-morning sunshine, ran an index finger under the uncomfortably stiff veil fastener at the nape of her neck. It was one of the best days for Northton—the place looked like a *National Geographic* cover on the glories of autumn in New England—and here she was staring at the drying blood of a dead mouse and swearing at a half-witted cat.

"You want to tell me what's wrong," Angela Louise asked, "or should I pray on it and see what I come up with?"

Kat shrugged. Angela Louise was bent over a large industrial iron, feeding sheets of white linen into oiled metal rollers that gave off steam when breathed on. Sister William, seventy-five years old and sixty (come Epiphany) in the Order, sat on a high stool with a book open in her lap. The book was *True Following: Living with Christ Day by Day*. Sister William was supposed to read aloud from it, "edifying" them while they worked.

"Unfortunately," Sister William said, the first day they met for ironing, "this is really the most embarrassing claptrap ever given an imprimatur."

Kat got another stack of white veils from the sideboard and handed them to Angela Louise. Something like this would have to happen the morning after the first full night's sleep she'd had in five weeks. Last night she hadn't dreamed, and that was a kind of miracle. She'd offered thanksgiving for it this morning in chapel. The dreams about David were driving her crazy.

Kat let Angela Louise step aside and moved in with her stack of veils, trying not to notice the sweat pouring off Angela's face into the gathered white linen of her wimple. It was one of those things—like assigning Sister William, whose cataracts were so bad only decades of stubbornness, years of practice, and a nearly pathological fear of hospitals made it possible for her to get from her cell to chapel every morning, as "reader"—that were so senseless, so arbitrary, so patently illogical, Kat despaired of understanding what the administration of this convent thought it was doing. What would be so terrible about Angela Louise taking off her wimple to do the ironing? Especially since she wouldn't have to wear a wimple (unless she wanted to) once she left the novitiate.

Kat bent at the waist and concentrated on the iron's feed, a complicated system of rollers and slots that would have tested the ingenuity of a master mechanic. She did not dream of things David had done to her. She didn't even dream of the places where they had once made love. In her sleep, she was not in their flat in London, not in the hotel room in Hong Kong, not even in the field behind the mission church in Malapur where he had touched her for the first time. In her sleep, she was always on the *Queen Elizabeth*

II, stretched out on a deck chair, wrapped in an ancient, ragged mink against the ice-hard wind.

They had spent the entire trip arguing about Agnus Dei. They had not touched each other once.

In her sleep, he had her on the deck chair, on the deck, on a table in the dining room. No, she thought, that was a lie. *She* had *him*. He lay passive, motionless. She reached for him, covered him. First she made him hard and then she used his hardness, rolling it along the insides of her thighs, ramming it into her as if it were a stake and she was trying to impale herself. In her sleep, his hardness was eternal. He was like a metal rod, rigid and cutting, reaching deep, causing pain. Except, of course, that she was causing the pain.

She felt Angela Louise tug her cape. She turned, feeding the last of the stack into the iron, feeling the linen slip through her fingers.

"She was frightened by a werewolf," Angela Louise said. "She doesn't want to tell us because the werewolf had the face of the Cardinal Archbishop, and—"

Kat took the stack of veils Angela Louise was holding out to her. "It was a mouse," she said. "Martha's cat brought us a mouse. Dead. Bloody. Disgusting."

"That's all," Angela Louise said. "A mouse."

"That's all."

"What happens in flood and famine?" Angela Louise said. "You go catatonic?"

"I speak in tongues." Kat started to feed the new stack into the machine. Sister William sat on her stool, staring mistily, dreamily out the window at the multicolored blur.

There was a knock at the door, a soft "Beata Maria Semper Virginis" that was almost inaudible over the rattle of the machine and the sound of Miriam singing "Ave Maria" down the hall in the kitchen.

Angela Louise said, "Regina Coeli" at the top of her lungs. Kat winced into the steam and wondered why they couldn't just knock or say "Come in" like ordinary people.

Marie Bernadette edged through the door, her eyes black holes in their cavernous sockets. Sister William looked her up and down, studying her as if she'd never noticed her before. Kat and Angela Louise kept their eyes on their work.

Marie Bernadette curtsied to Sister William. "Reverend

Mother would like to see Katherine Mary in her office as soon as possible," she said. Her voice came out in a rasping, breathless buzz, like the voice of a ham actor dying badly in a third-rate gangster epic. She gave Sister William one of her death's-head-rictus smiles.

"Suicide is a sin," Sister William said, tugging at Marie Bernadette's oversleeve. "You remember that, Sister. You remember that at lunch."

2

Kat was halfway to Reverend Mother's office before she realized what had upset her so much about the mouse. The fur had been all twisted, as if something had wrung its neck. She tried to imagine the cat doing that, holding the body of the mouse (the wriggling body) in its paws and twisting the neck. It seemed patently impossible.

It was like the night Annie had heard "footsteps" on postulant corridor, heard them and not been able to let them go. She had come rattling at the curtain of Kat's cell, insisting (silently, with gestures) on an investigation. Kat had gone with her, though she knew they wouldn't find anything. God only knew there was nothing to find. Clare Marie and Reverend Mother had the only keys to North Wing. On another night it might have been Jane, but Jane was off the corridor, probably downstairs in the Mary Chapel. Kat had heard her leave.

They had been in the bathroom when she first had the feeling something was wrong. The bathroom was a long, white-tiled room stretching the width of North Wing, serving both postulants and senior novices. The lights were harsh and very bright. The lavatory stalls were painted a dull metallic green. The absence of mirrors made the room look blank. Kat stood in the center of all that cruel white light, turning around and around on her heel, trying to identify an anomaly she wasn't sure existed.

It had taken her half an hour to find it. When she did, she didn't know whether to be relieved or disgusted. One wall of the bathroom was divided into wooden cubicles where postulants and novices kept their "personal items." The rules for cubicles were as strict as the rules for responses in choir.

Toothbrushes and soap were kept in plastic boxes. Washcloths, when dry, were folded and left lying flat. Bath towels and face towels were folded in thirds and hung over swinging metal rods, curtaining off the cubicle's interior. That night the cubicle fourth from the left and third from the bottom—Annie's cubicle—had its towels folded in squares and piled over the toothbrush and washcloth, leaving the frame exposed.

Annie had turned green at the sight of those towels, insisting she'd folded them correctly only a few hours before, but Annie was forgetful and high-strung. Even so, Kat had to give her the footsteps. In the bottomless darkness of Grand Silence, all the odd night noises that were probably just the wind sounded like someone pacing above her head. Except there was nowhere up there for anyone to pace.

Tortured mice. Footsteps on the ceiling. If she didn't start getting some sleep, she'd probably be seeing Lady Macbeth in the underpantry before Christmas.

3

Reverend Mother Christopher had the large corner office on the first floor of East Wing. She had a cherrywood desk, an ink blotter with amber leather borders, and a set of plain wooden chairs Kat was sure were early Chippendale. A sixteenth-century Italian painting—plump madonna and plumper child, both in the robes of empire—hung on the wall behind her head. The good Catholic laity, unable or unwilling to quit the service of Mammon, rewarded the nuns for doing it for them.

Reverend Mother gestured to the chair beside her desk. Kat sat down in it, only then seeing Clare Marie in the rocking chair in the corner. Kat stared at the clutter on Reverend Mother's desk. There was a letter from Rome, official-looking, with the seal of the Motherhouse General in the upper left-hand corner.

Reverend Mother folded her hands on her desk. "I have something specific to ask you," she said, "but first—" She frowned at Clare Marie, then patted the mess on her desk. "But," she said again, "I would like to ask you a question. A rather unusual question."

"Of course," Kat said, wishing she could tell if old Christopher was really confused and hesitant, or just playacting a calm before the storm.

"We want to know," Reverend Mother said, "is, are you *happy* here?"

Kat blinked. "Happy?"

"I said it was a rather unusual question," Reverend Mother said.

It was irrelevant. You were not supposed to be happy in the novitiate. She smoothed her skirt, buying time. What was she being asked? What was she supposed to say? "I'm not going to say I haven't had any difficulty adjusting," she started. She winced. She hated the word "adjusting." It was a typical twentieth-century coward's word, al lie in its denial of emotion. But Reverend Mother Christopher was nodding, looking pleased.

"Yes, yes," she said. "You've been trying to quit smoking. We know about that. But are you happy?"

Kat had a moment of panic—completely irrational panic —that Reverend Mother had seen David's car that day, parked at the bottom of South Yard. It was ridiculous, of course. It was weeks ago. She didn't even know if the car had actually been David's. She had done nothing to find out. She had tried not to think about it.

"I know it's very hard to quit smoking by just stopping all of a sudden," Reverend Mother said. "I know it's likely to make you moody. We don't mind."

Kat rubbed her hands against the sides of her dress. There were always stories going around about "tests," seemingly innocent questions used to determine whether postulants were "really suited" to religious life.

She took a deep breath and tried to think of something neutral, something that would commit her to nothing. The two old ladies sat looking expectant, their faces determinedly bright.

"I don't think I have any complaints," Kat said cautiously.

"Of course, you're older than the others," Reverend Mother said.

"Actually," Clare Marie said, "Miriam is the oldest."

"But Katherine Mary has the most experience," Reverend Mother said. "Of the world."

"Of course," Clare Marie said.

Reverend Mother sat back in her chair and sighed. The chair, built for space and grace and comfort, barely contained her bulk.

"The thing is," she said, "you look happy."

"I look happy," Kat repeated.

"Of course," Reverend Mother said, suddenly impatient.

Kat straightened. "You want to ask me something else, Reverend Mother?"

"Oh," Reverend Mother said. She pawed through the papers on her desk, came up with a blue air-mail envelope, passed it to Kat. "It's this," she said. "Page four."

"Actually," Clare Marie said, "I was the one who brought that up."

Kat turned the letter over and over in her hands, thinking how odd it was to be holding something from David while she sat in a chair next to Reverend Mother's desk. The letter had been opened carefully at the top. Sand turned to glass in her stomach, scraping her raw. They would not have given her the letter if David had said anything outrageous.

"Page four," Reverend Mother Christopher said again.

"There's really nothing objectionable in the letter," Clare Marie said, "and I'm sure this isn't objectionable either, but we don't know, you see." She nodded gently. "He sounds like a most *upright* young man."

"Yes," Kat said. "He is that."

Page four was the last of the letter. At the bottom, under his signature, David had written two of the only nine Chinese characters she knew.

The first was the character for "town."

The second was the configuration for "Tuesday."

VIRGINITY

1

Geraldine started it, just before the noon Angelus bell.

"The question we have to answer," she said, "is, are you a virgin?"

93

"Why do you do these things?" Annie said. "Of *course* I'm a virgin. Of course I'm a virgin."

"It's not so cut-and-dried," Geraldine said. "Everyone who comes here isn't a virgin."

Annie snorted, a sound like a minor explosion going off midway up her back. Jane heard the sound of a book slapping open, pages rustling, binding creaking.

"I'll read from the Thomas Merton," Annie said. "We can prepare for instruction. Is that all right with you? Jane? Would you rather read and let me work?"

"No," Jane said. She gave them her very sweet smile, the one meant to let other people know she was being accommodating. "Does it have to be Thomas Merton? Can we do Saint Francis? The Saint Francis on prayer."

Annie went through the books on the readings shelf. "I've got it," she said. "Can I start at the beginning? I've never read it."

"I don't mind," Jane said. "I could read it over and over again. Saint Francis has such wonderful things to say about prayer."

Annie got down on her knees, made the sign of the cross, kissed the book, and said, "Dear Lord, may the teachings of Your priest and saint, Francis, lead us to righteousness and virtue. Through Christ Our Lord. Amen."

"That we may be worthy of the promises of Christ," Jane said. "Amen."

Geraldine said nothing. She stood in her corner, arms crossed over her chest, looking murderous. Jane knew why Annie had wanted to let her read. Geraldine almost never did any work. To punish them for thwarting her, she would do nothing for the rest of the hour. Whoever was stacking trays would have to stack all of them.

The proof that Annie was part of "us" and Jane was not was that Annie felt guilty for Geraldine's behavior, but saw no reason for Jane to be. Jane felt the frustration rise and pushed it away. It was taking so long. She had been working on Annie for weeks now, and she didn't seem any closer than she had been at the start. How long was it going to take?

Jane counted Class D trays on the serving cart's fourth tier, stood up, then drifted across the room to the drug cabi-

94

net on the west wall. The cabinet was unlocked, its metal door swinging open in the Lysol-acrid infirmary air. Sister Elizabeth, who ran the infirmary, was over seventy, almost senile, and always forgot to lock the cabinets, just as she always forgot to package used hypodermics before throwing them away.

The west-wall cabinet was the "dispensary," the repository of sleeping pills and Darvon, quick remedies for minor ailments (mostly psychosomatic, Jane thought), to be passed out to Sisters "for emergencies." A clipboard hung on the wall next to the cabinet, where Sister Elizabeth was supposed to write dispensary information. The paper on the clipboard had columns headed "Sister," "Drug," "Quantity," "Purpose." They were blank. Antoinette had been up for a pain-killer for her arthritis, four novices had been in for Darvon for cramps, Jeannette (whose mother was dying of cancer) had carried away a ten-milligram Valium, but the columns were blank.

If Elizabeth wanted accurate information about who had received what drug, she had only to ask Reverend Mother for the log, or the hebdomadaria for the announcement list. Every time a Sister reported to the infirmary, she was required to report to her superior as well, explaining her complaint and the treatment administered. Her name would be read at the beginning of the next office, and her Sisters asked to pray for her. The practice was supposed to reduce hypochondria. It was embarrassing to hear your name read at office. If you were really sick, you'd be too sick to *attend* office. But Elizabeth was old, and frightened of being "retired." To be retired was to be sent off to wait for death. No Sister was retired until she literally could not work anymore. Besides, the clipboard was not really important. No Sister would so much as ask for treatment without Reverend Mother's permission, although that permission was automatic, never denied. Elizabeth had a tendency to sit down with the clipboard at the end of the day, "remembering."

If her drug counts came out wrong (and they always did), she "remembered" again.

Annie stopped reading. "There's a passage about prayer in work," she said. "Prayer of the hands. Do you want a meditation?"

"I want you to start acting normal," Geraldine said.

Annie ignored her. "I wish they'd give us a regular reader," she said. "This stuff makes me feel so inadequate."

"Being young in the religious life is like being a little child," Jane said. "We have to learn to walk all over again. I'm sure Our Lord will forgive us for not being as adept as the older Sisters."

"Give me a break," Geraldine said.

Annie looked at Jane uncertainly, half admiring, half exasperated. Jane turned away, thinking she must have sounded like a recording of Clare Marie again. She had promised herself to stop doing that, but it wasn't easy. She had to say something sometimes. She couldn't always say what she thought.

The tranquilizers were out of sequence. They were supposed to be arranged in alphabetical order on the second shelf, but were instead jumbled up, spread through the cabinet. An untouched bottle of Thorazine was on the balms shelf, wedged between a Bactine dispenser and a tube of Nupercainal ointment.

Jane put the Thorazine in its place on the tranquilizer shelf, conscious she was moving silently, almost furtively. Geraldine had started a monologue. Jane squinted at a Darvon bottle, lying on its side next to a jar of Vaseline. For once, she was not the one left out. Annie had roped her in as an ally against Geraldine. Did this mean Annie had begun to accept her? Or only that Annie had begun to reject Geraldine?

She did not want this to be just Annie's rejection of Geraldine. She did not want to leave this room and find Annie allied against her again, with Kat, with Martha, with Miriam.

She put her head against the cool metal of the cabinet, wishing Elizabeth weren't so insane about keeping the heat up in the infirmary. The heat made her logy, drowsy. Too often she found herself floating into memories of the worst kind, memories of her mother and her father, of before the divorce, of being seven and being chosen to lead the class for First Holy Communion. There were good things about that memory, and bad. The good thing was being out front, walking down the center aisle at church in her white lace dress and white lace veil, with everybody looking at her. The bad thing was her mother's voice ("fifty dollars for a dress for a child Michael for God's sake she's a seven-year-old child I've never spent") coming sharp and shrill through the four-inch plaster walls and the fitted oak doorway until it was *in* her room, filling it with thick poisonous smog. Her father always took her side. His eyes were like spotlights, always turned on her. Her mother saw right through her, but her father illuminated her.

She was becoming nauseated. She could feel it climbing her throat, spreading sharp and hot through the lining of her stomach. She was trying to decide what to do. All she could come up with was the need to dart, to keep the doors open, to make no decision, *not to fuck it up*.

"They always tell you girls who enter the convent are nice, normal American girls," Geraldine was saying. "You call this normal? You call kneeling on the floor when you read some saint dead God only knows how many years normal?"

"I'm going to read a passage on Holy Poverty," Annie said stubbornly.

Jane looked over her shoulder. Geraldine was sitting on a gurney, swinging her thick legs in the air. She had an odd look on her face, half smirk, half curiosity. Annie had her hands folded under her cape, her eyes on the floor. It came over Jane in a wash; the fear, the hope, the hatred—the hope. Sometimes she thought her whole life had been a desperate lunge at hope.

Geraldine was looking at her, then at Annie, then at her again, eyes as bright and dark and hard as black diamonds.

"I'm not going to let you get away with this," Geraldine said.

Jane turned away. She would not tell Annie she was not a virgin. She would not tell anyone.

The beach was not a travel-poster beach, not a long clean curve of white sand with the ocean rocking gently against it. What sand there was looked like bald patches on the head of a woman with eczema of the scalp. Scrub and rocks wound their way to the waterline, to be replaced by waterlogged dirt. The sea was insidious and full of slime. It slithered onto the shore like an amoeba working its way across a microscope slide.

They came there every morning, all that long hot August she turned thirteen. At least, she and her father came. Her stepmother (Muriel) sometimes left them to go into town to shop. Jane's mother was sure Muriel did a lot of shopping, just as she was sure Muriel wore a lot of makeup. Jane had come to Florida expecting to find a Lana Turner kind of woman, all puff and pout and cheap perfume. Muriel and her father were not, after all (by the laws of the Church), really married.

Muriel was a small, square woman with freckles and an overcompetent brusqueness of manner. She wore no makeup, no jewelry but her wedding ring, no scent of any kind. Her bedroom smelled of witch hazel. She was (score one for Jane's mother) twenty years younger than Jane's father. She was not, however, a Playboy bunny. Her chest was so flat, her calves so undeveloped, she looked younger than Jane. Aesthetically, she was prepubescent.

"What this is," Jane's father said, on one of those mornings Muriel had gone to shop, "is a cliché. You know what a cliché is?"

Jane knew what a cliché was.

"Older man runs from nagging wife to marry younger woman," her father said. "Christ, I know what a cliché is."

Jane kicked her feet against the scrub and looked out at the ugly, disturbing ocean, wondering what was going on this time. She was wearing a one-piece bathing suit with a pleated skirt like a cheerleader's frill that covered her hips and the top of her thighs. She had picked it out herself at Malley's in New Haven, while her mother sat on a chair in the fitting room and provided a running commentary on her choices. Every time Jane looked at that suit, she was furious.

Her father found sand, dug his toe into it, flipped it into the air. "The thing is," he said, "I worry about you. I worry about you living with *her*."

Jane looked out at the ocean—it was better than looking at her bathing suit—and tried to make the puzzle unravel. She hadn't seen her father in five years. Instead of the shining knight she remembered, she was sitting next to a haggard man in his forties, eyelids creased, jaw slack, Camel unfiltered stuck in the corner of his mouth. He was still a good-looking man, but it was a David Carradine kind of good-looking—dissipated, corrupt, almost threatening—not the well-scrubbed Paul McCartney of her imagination.

"She always says we don't have enough money," Jane said, "if that's what you're worried about."

"I'm not worried about the money," her father said. "Your mother gets more of my money than she did when I was married to her."

Jane wanted to say he was *still* married to her mother— the Church said so—but he was looking at her so oddly, making her so uncomfortable, that she kept her mouth shut. She had had too many cross-conversations lately. She'd come barging into a group of girls she'd known all her life, saying the things she'd said a hundred times before, and suddenly they'd be the wrong things. There was some secret she'd missed. They were laughing at her. One day she was sitting at lunch with Patty, her best friend since fifth grade, and Patty stopped her in the middle of a sentence and said, "Oh, for God's sake, Jane, stop talking to me. You *bore* me." The words, Jane knew, were copied from a parent or older sister. The sentiment, however, was sincere. What was she supposed to do about it? She wasn't even sure what it meant to be bored.

She did not want to bore her father, or make him disgusted with her (lately, a lot of girls at school claimed she "disgusted" them). She said, "Money's the only thing she complains about. Other than that, I think we're okay."

Her mother made dire predictions about what would happen to the bodies and souls of Muriel and her father (if they did not repent), but that was not what her father was asking about. At least she did not think it was.

Her father looked at his hands, rubbed them together, stared at the sky. "I worry about you," he said. "I worry about your being there with her, without me to set you straight."

"You could write," she said. "You could phone." Marilyn Donner's parents were divorced and her father called her every week, all the way from Alaska.

"I keep getting the feeling this is the only chance I'm going to have," her father said. "The only chance to set you straight. Before she ruins you."

The next time they came to the beach without Muriel, her father took her climbing on the rocks. It was a badly over-cast day, the sky full of heavy, dirt-gray clouds, a pair of waterspouts like pillars on the horizon. Jane felt hot and cold at once—the air was broiling but somehow clammy—and as they slid down to the water she wished they hadn't come at all. They could have gone shopping with Muriel, or stayed home, playing cribbage or keeping out of each other's way. She had started keeping a journal. She was listing all her confusions, all her mistakes, all her sins. With any luck, she would have it worked out before summer ended, before she had to go back to school and try again.

"There's a cave," her father said. "At least, there used to be a cave." He pointed out over the rocks. "We could go there."

She nodded, not thinking about him, thinking instead that she wished she had a Protestant bathing suit, a two-piece Bobbie Brooks bathing suit that showed her middle. Patty would have such a bathing suit, no matter what the nuns said. Rebecca would have something shocking, like a bikini. If one of the old nuns saw her in it and complained, Rebecca's mother would tell the nun to mind her own busi-ness. Jane didn't want a bikini—she didn't have much of a chest and didn't think she was very pretty—but she would have liked one of those Bobbie Brooks two-pieces, with a matching tote bag.

They were all the way to the edge of the promontory before she realized they were going there. Her father called it a "ness." He took a stubby aluminum flask from the canvas bag he carried his rubber swim fins in, tipped it to his mouth, and sucked on it for a long time.

When he put it down, Jane could see he was sweating. He was sweating the way people sweat with a bad fever, slick oily drops coming off his upper lip and down the side of his face. He was shaking like a drunk with the DTs.

He got out his cigarettes, stuck one in his mouth, lit it. He looked at her over the flame.

Jane wet her lips. Careful, she thought. "I've tried it," she said. "Once or twice."

He rubbed his mouth with his hand. "Is this the kind of thing I'm supposed to do?" he asked her. "To make you feel adult? The 'divorced fathers' make a kid a pal' code?"

She took the pack of cigarettes from where he had put it down on a rock, extracted one, put it experimentally into her mouth. She took his matches and held them in the palm of her hand. She was doing this all wrong, but she knew doing it wrong was better than not doing it at all. She would not tell him she had never tried to smoke before, any more than she'd tell Patty or Rebecca if (by some miracle) they dragged her behind the rock wall for a little experimentation. Letting her father know she had never tried to smoke before would ruin everything.

He sucked at the flask again, capped it, put it in his pocket. Then he sat on the rock beside her, looking out to sea.

"There's nothing wrong with it," he said. "That's what I've got to tell you. There's nothing wrong with what you're feeling these days. It's perfectly normal."

She stayed silent, not because she was afraid, but because she hadn't the faintest idea what he was talking about. He looked into her eyes, the sweat beginning to gleam over his back and arms, every muscle fluttering in spasms so that his body looked like one of those animated cartoons of molecules in random motion. She thought he was going to cry.

"Your mother," he started. He tried to look away and couldn't. His eyes looked like black holes. "Your mother has—she's—God, she's all screwed up inside." He gave a hiccuping, whooping crane laugh. "All screwed up inside," he said. "Oh, Jesus Christ."

It hit her like a spotlight. She thought (*porked, fucked,*

101

screwed, planked, stabbed, rode, hid the salami) of all the words for it, girls'-room words and playground words and hide-in-the-balcony-at-the-movies words. For a moment there was even emotion, a hot revengeful spear like the one she felt when her mother called her ugly or her (almost former) girlfriends told her not to be such a baby or Sister Agnese stopped one word short of calling her stupid. Maybe she also felt fear, but if she did, it was so well buried under fury, it was negligible.

A moment later, she felt nothing at all. She was sitting on a rock promontory in the middle of a bay on the Gulf of Mexico, watching her father stare at the tiny nubs of breasts that had so recently become visible under the thick cloth of the bathing suit her mother had goaded her into buying because it was ugly and cheap.

Her father licked the sweat from his lips. "Your mother," he said.

She shook her head. He reached for her, fumbling at the top of her bathing suit, rubbing much too gently against the nipples that hardened more in protest than from desire. Even at thirteen, Jane knew he was clumsy and inept. She could see the bulge in his bathing trunks. It would, she decided, be a larger version of the protrusion she had seen on Marilyn Donner's infant brother. If it hurt, it hurt. If it tore at her (the books said it tore at you, the first time), then she would hide her bleeding with a Kotex pad. She pushed her father's hands away from her breasts, annoyed.

"That's not what you want to do," she said.

She could see it working in him—the evasions, the explanations—and felt a weary contempt. He would find a way to blame it on her, she knew it. If anybody found out, it would be her problem and her responsibility. It would not be true, but nobody would believe her.

He was scrabbling at his trunks, tearing into the flesh of his stomach with his fingernails in his haste. She stood up and stepped out of the ugly bathing suit, out of the thick cotton panties she wore under it in an effort (encouraged by her mother) to maintain her "modesty." She had put so much effort into maintaining her "modesty," into developing the kind of chastity the nuns said was a direct ticket to Heaven. There was only one real sin in the Catholic Church,

102

and here she was, naked and somehow softened by the light breeze, getting ready to commit it.

She put her feet on either side of her father's waist.

"Oh, God," her father said. "What are you *doing* to me?"

But she wasn't doing anything to him, and they both knew it.

As she lowered herself onto him, it occurred to her to wonder why she was doing this, why she wasn't running away or screaming or forcing him into the rape he wanted to commit. Then she was on him and he was clutching her. In his clutching, she could find no answer.

In the years that followed, she never did.

3

In the East Wing tower, the bells rang the Angelus. At the end of the corridor, Elizabeth crossed herself in a voice calculated to wake every Sister in the infirmary and started in.

"The angel of the Lord appeared unto Mary."

Jane closed the dispensary cabinet and said, "And she conceived of the Holy Spirit." Annie had her eyes closed, "doing" the Angelus, trying very hard to be devout. Geraldine was glaring, her hands in the mess of hair that spilled from the front of her veil. Jane began her Hail, Mary. Geraldine hit the flat of her hand against the metal filing cabinet, making it ring.

"I can't believe you, Bliss. The religious maniac over here is one thing, but *you*."

"Behold the handmaid of the Lord," Elizabeth shouted.

Annie bit her lip and tucked her chin against her chest. Jane thought she was near tears. She knew Annie was near words. Annie wanted to tell Geraldine to shut her mouth. She was mouthing Hail, Marys by sheer force of will.

"How can you be so damned dishonest," Geraldine shouted. "You *know* what a crock this all is."

There was a rustle of skirts. Jane looked up and saw Clare Marie standing in the door, staring at Geraldine, looking infinitely sad. Her anger boiled up, hot and unquenchable. Clare Marie would have to tell Geraldine to go now, and it made her sad. Jane didn't think Clare Marie would be

103

so sad to see *her* go. She didn't think Clare Marie would be sad at all.

It was always like that. It was always going to be like that.

Jane bent her head and finished the Angelus, drily mouthing prayers that seemed to be coming out of Annie's throat like lava out of an erupting volcano. Annie sounded devout. All *she* sounded was distant.

When the Angelus was over, Annie got up from where she'd been kneeling, crossed the room, and kissed first Jane's shoes and then Clare Marie's. Jane could see she still hated it. Her face was red. Her eyes were wet.

Annie said, "I beg the forgiveness of this community and of my Postulant Sister Jane and my Sister Superior Clare Marie for allowing a disturbance to occur during Angelus without trying to stop it."

Jane hesitated only for a moment. It was ludicrous, to hold herself responsible for what Geraldine had done. It was, however, the form. She went to Clare Marie's shoes first, saving Annie for last, like a special dessert.

When she was done, Clare Marie said, "I think we've covered everything. Geraldine?"

Geraldine shook her head. She had her arms wrapped around her body, holding herself in. There were tears in her eyes, but angry ones. She had none of Annie's sweet vulnerability.

"I'm not having any part of this," she said. "I'm not kissing anyone's shoes, and I'm not apologizing for not taking their hypocrisy seriously."

Clare Marie nodded, first to Geraldine, then to Annie and Jane.

"Why don't you go on to rosary," she said. "You're going to assist Perpetua, aren't you, Annie?"

"Yes, Sister."

"Well, go along. If you don't hurry, you'll be late."

Jane held her breath. Hadn't she and Annie just made an alliance? What could be more natural than Annie asking if she wanted to come along to the old ladies' rosary? And once that happened—It made Jane giddy just thinking about it. She had been alone for so long. Once Annie took her up, the walls would come down, the house would no longer be empty. And Annie would have to take her up, sooner or

104

later. They were so much alike. They had so much in common.

Annie whirled away and plunged into the hall, nearly running. Jane nearly jumped. It was like a slap, that exit. It was as if Annie wanted to get away from her as much as from Geraldine or Clare Marie. The old anger began to bubble, the frustration to seethe and steep and send out promises of violence. There was a red mist between herself and the world.

She got herself under control. Rome was not, after all, built in a day. Geraldine had stopped crying. She had her chin in the air, her feet planted apart. She obviously had no intention of giving Clare Marie any reason to keep her.

With Geraldine gone, everything might change. There would be a vacancy in the core. And she was getting closer to Annie. She could feel it.

With Geraldine gone, she just might find a way in.

Just in case she didn't, she had put half a dozen fifty-milligram Thorazine capsules in her pocket.

For the second time this week.

T R E A S U R E

1

There was one thing Kat knew she couldn't do: she couldn't meet David in town, this or any other Tuesday, for at least three months. She wondered why he thought she could. Was she supposed to wear a disguise, hide herself in the convent van, and smuggle herself into Parkman's Dry Cleaning with the Belgian-lace tablecloths? Convent schedules were ritualized, formulaic. Some postulants and senior novices went into Northton—Martha to the vegetable market, Annie to the post office—but her work details were determinedly housebound. There wouldn't be a new work schedule until after Christmas. She couldn't just saunter out the front gate for an assignation with her lover.

Former lover.

Kat reached to the night table for her devotion beads,

picked them up, dropped them, picked them up again. The corridor was quiet. She was probably the only one here, unless Martha was resting, lying on her gray-and-white quilt, fat stupid cat wrapped in her arms. Most of the others used Private Hour to walk on the grounds or hole up in the library or (in the case of saints-in-training, like Jane) spend some time in the crypt chapel, praying over the bones of Mother Provincial Foundress Mary Imelda for demonstrable miracles. Kat rubbed the wooden devotion beads against the pad of her thumb. The problem with not smoking was that it made her so irritable, so nervous. After five weeks, it was getting worse, not better. She spent too much time snapping at people and biting her fingernails. What did David want of her? What did she want of David?

She wanted to see David, meet him in town and sit somewhere for lunch. She wanted him to drive her to Essex, to walk with her on the beach, to tell her about his novel. She didn't believe in his novel any more than he did, but she wanted to hear him talk. Never mind the dreams. If she could have him with her every day, the dreams would stop. She'd be no more interested in sex than she'd ever been.

She also wanted to be free of David and everything he represented.

She headed into the corridor, thinking she might as well check on Martha. If Martha was off somewhere, she could go to the North Wing Mary Chapel and practice her meditation.

If Martha wasn't asleep, she was probably playing with the cat. Martha was always playing with the cat.

Martha wasn't playing with the cat. Martha was standing in the middle of her cell, looking down into cupped hands filled with dozens of bright red capsules, any one of them big enough to put a horse out for a week.

7

Kat stared into Martha's eyes, trying to determine what was really happening. Martha looked like victim of shock. Martha was going to cry.

"For God's sake," Kat said. "What *are* those things?" Then, as if she were on automatic pilot, without even think-

106

ing what effect it would have, she got to her knees, kissed Martha's shoes, and said, "I beg the forgiveness of this community and my Postulant Sister Martha for taking the Lord's name in vain and subjecting her to a near occasion of sin."

Martha jumped half a foot in the air. The pills scattered, hitting the floor with muffled pings, skittering across the overpolished wood. Martha dropped to her knees and went after them, grabbing at them ineffectually, frantic. The cat, hidden until now behind Martha on the bed, jumped to the floor and began playing mouse games with a pile of them. Every pill Martha caught slipped through her fingers and hit the floor again.

Kat got to her feet and grabbed Martha's shoulders, pushing her toward the bed. "Sit," she said. "I'll get them."

Martha bounced against the bed, clawed the edge of the mattress, jumped. "Oh, Lord," she said. "We aren't supposed to sit on the edge of the bed. We aren't supposed to go into anyone else's cell and they're everywhere, they're under Jane's bed and Geraldine's and—and—"

"Stop," Kat said. "Stop." She took the cat's small pile from under its protesting nose, reached under the bed, and picked up five more. "Sit down."

"You've got to promise me not to do that again," Martha said. "Not to get down on your knees and apologize and kiss my shoes. Not now. Can I ask you to do that? Should I kiss your shoes for asking you to do that? I don't—"

"You can ask me to do anything in charity," Kat said. "Sit down."

"I did what you did," Martha said. "I took the Lord's name in vain. I should—"

"*Sit down.*"

Martha sat down.

"I'm in your cell," Kat said patiently, trying to sound calm. "If we have to, we'll sneak into everybody else's and get the rest of these. Martha, what—"

"Everything's all mixed up," Martha said. "It's all so against the rules. Everything and everything. And I don't know what to do and—"

"Clare Marie always says the Rule isn't the ten commandments," Kat said. "Martha, what are those things?"

"They're some kind of speed," Martha said. She looked

107

ready to cry again. "Or some kind of tranquilizers. I'm not sure. Elizabeth keeps them in the dispensary cabinet and it's practically illegal to *look* at them. Kat, they were just *here*. I came in at the beginning of the hour and I was going to lie down and just think, I had the cat, I wasn't going to sleep because I know we aren't supposed to sleep in Private Hour, but I get so tired what with going into town and all the bending at Children's House and then all that chapel and I was going to lie down and think and—oh, God, they were under my *pillow*. Fifty of them. Just lying in a pile under my *pillow*."

"All right," Kat said. "All right."

"It's not all right," Martha said. "Kat, what if Clare Marie had done an inspection? How long have they been here? What if Clare Marie had done an inspection and pulled off the quilt and run her hand over the sheets and they'd come falling out? I'd have been thrown out of here at least. I could get arrested. I could have, I could have—"

"All right," Kat said. "All right. We've got it under control."

Martha took the regulation broad white linen handkerchief from her pocket and sniffled into it. "I'm sorry," she said. "I didn't mean to go to pieces."

"It's all right," Kat said again, and thought: three times makes it true.

The cat climbed onto Martha's lap and stretched out on its back, feet in the air, wanting its stomach rubbed. Martha patted it absently. "I came up today thinking how perfect it all was," she said. "I went to chapel to do my novena to Saint Jude because I'm doing a novena to Saint Jude that William agrees to have the cataract operation, she's going to kill herself if she doesn't and it can't be fun not to see, and I came upstairs and I was thinking how I love it here, I really love it, and then—Kat, what are we going to do?"

Kat sat down on the insubstantial chair next to the bureau and looked at the pills in her hand. How did someone swallow something this size?

"We can do one of two things," she said. "We can pick all these up and take them to Clare Marie and explain the situa-

108

tion. Or we can pick all these up and flush them down the toilet."

Martha licked her lips, rubbed her hands, hunched her shoulders. "We can't take them to Clare Marie," she said. "That's the one thing we really can't do."

"Why not? Clare Marie is a sweetheart, Martha, you know that. Somebody put these in your bed. If we don't tell her, somebody may put more of them in your bed. Somebody—"

"Geraldine," Martha said.

"What?"

"Geraldine," Martha said again. "That's how I know what they are. Geraldine works in the infirmary. She told me about the cabinet and how it was unlocked and how Elizabeth never keeps accurate records. And she said it would be easy. To steal some. To . . . get high."

"Geraldine always talks like that," Kat said. "It's just bravado."

"She does things," Martha said. "Practical jokes."

"This is hardly a practical joke."

"Geraldine doesn't think."

"Martha—"

"And even if she didn't do it," Martha said, "if she said those things to me, she said them to other people. You know she did. And people will remember and think she did it even if she didn't. Even Clare Marie. She could get thrown out of here."

"From what I've heard, she's already been thrown out of here."

"Geraldine?"

Kat sighed. "Annie was telling us about it at lunch. And Geraldine wasn't *at* lunch. She apparently pulled some nonsense during work detail and then wouldn't kiss Clare Marie's shoes and then—I don't know. It was one of Annie's patented confusing explanations. I think what it amounted to was Geraldine crossing her arms, sticking out her chin, and giving Clare Marie a royal to-hell-with-you."

Martha looked shocked. "I don't *understand* some people," she said. "I go from day to day and it's perfect, it's not even subduing the will, or whatever they call it. Their will

109

and my will don't seem all that different. I like working in Children's House and I like chapel and I don't mind most of the rules. And then people like Geraldine—she used to get so upset and I wouldn't know how to help. I wouldn't know what to do."

"Maybe there was nothing you could do. Maybe she just didn't belong here."

"She came here. If she came, there was a chance she had a vocation. Not everybody has an easy vocation. Maybe we failed her."

Kat gave it one more try. "I think we should tell Clare Marie," she said. "Maybe Geraldine did it before she left, as a kind of revenge. Maybe somebody else did it. It's a dangerous situation."

"Who else would do it?"

Kat had a sudden vision of hard black eyes passing from one to the other of them along the length of the dinner table, fathomless, triumphant. She laughed shakily. "You know what I want to say? I want to say: Jane."

Martha grimaced. "The day Jane Galloway breaks a rule, the walls of this convent will shudder and fall."

"I know," Kat said. "It's just . . ." She shrugged. "I still think we should go to Clare Marie. If it's Geraldine, she can't get into any more trouble. They wouldn't bother."

"If it's anyone else, we'd be responsible for getting them sent home," Martha said. "I don't want to do that. I won't do that."

"All right," Kat said. "How many of these are there?"

"Fifty exactly."

"You could kill someone with fifty of these," Kat said. Martha said nothing. "You take the cells from here to the window," Kat said. "I'll take them from here to the door. When we've found them all, we'll flush them down the toilet."

"You won't tell anybody?"

"I won't tell anybody in authority. I might do some private complaining to Miriam."

Martha nodded. "All right," she said. "Miriam won't tell anybody."

"No," Kat said. "Miriam won't tell anybody."

They found only forty-nine, but that was not the strangest thing. Martha was happy with forty-nine. She stood in the toilet stall, watching the water suck them into the pipes. The fiftieth one was either lost down a floorboard or somewhere in Jane's cell. There was something about Jane's cell that made them both nervous. God help them if Jane found them there.

"She's infected the place with disapproval vibes," Martha said.

"I thought you said she was lonely."

"She is lonely," Martha said. "But it's a weird kind of lonely. If you try to help, she gets lonelier and lonelier. It eats you up."

Kat let Martha go back to her cell. Twenty minutes were left of Private Hour. They both needed rest, silence, the mundane comfort of mundane devotion. Kat lay on her bed, weaving her devotion beads through her fingers. The pills were gone. Martha was happy. Everything should be all right.

The bell for chapel woke her. She jerked bolt upright, swung her legs over the side of the bed, hopped to the floor —and there they were. Five of them. Five huge horse pills. Their gelatin casings were puckered and dented from the weight of her body.

They had not been there when she got up to look for Martha. They had to have been put there while she and Martha were taking care of Martha's pills.

She and Martha had been alone on the corridor. They had been in the lavatory, but not for long. Not long enough for someone to come onto the corridor, put the pills in her bed, and get off again. Not long enough for that.

The pills could not have been put in her bed.

The pills had been put in her bed.

She opened her window and threw the pills down four stories to North Lawn. She had an instant stab of remorse.

Birds would eat them. Birds would eat them and die.

SLEEPWALKER

1

After Compline, Clare Marie kept them in chapel until all the others had filed out, then made them form two perfectly straight lines for the walk back to postulant corridor. It was the forming into lines that made Annie begin to feel uneasy.

She put her head down until her chin touched her breastbone and wished she could take her hands from under her cape and rub them against her face. Sometimes, at the beginning of a headache, rubbing her hands against her face made her feel better. It didn't take the headache away, or stop it from getting worse, but for the few moments of rubbing everything seemed easier. Hands, however, belonged folded under her cape. Eyes belonged trained on the heels of the postulant in front of her. Kat and Miriam and Martha and Jane floated along in front of her, effortless, uncomplaining. Geraldine was gone.

She couldn't escape the fact that she felt a sneaking admiration for Geraldine. Geraldine had been angry and said so. I am a person, someone in particular, and I am not to be changed.

Geraldine had been asked to leave. Annie didn't want to be asked to leave. She only wanted it not to be so hard. She wanted to do it right. She wanted to be right. She wanted Stephen to be proud of her.

Had Geraldine's conscience books looked as awful as her own? Had Geraldine bothered to tell the truth? Annie blushed in the darkness. She hadn't been telling the truth herself. She had dutifully written "obedience" at the top of the page this morning, and duly written every fault against obedience she could remember on the lines under it at Greater Meditation. She had been specific and exhaustive, finally listing over a hundred faults. Clare Marie would call it "overscrupulous" and scold her. But she shouldn't have chosen obedience in the first place. Obedience, no matter how

112

bad she was at it, was not her major problem. Poverty was her major problem.

They turned into South Yard just as it started to rain. In the beginning, she had liked having chapel in a separate building, liked the five-times-daily walk across the yard, but lately the dry, turning leaves had begun to feel threatening, especially at night. When she dreamed about Agnus Dei, it was a dark house, a house without lights or windows.

She was afraid that if she told Clare Marie about her problem with Holy Poverty, they wouldn't let her have Stephen's letters anymore. Of course, the fact that she couldn't bear the thought of giving up Stephen's letters was part of her problem with Holy Poverty. She didn't care. Stephen's letters were a contrast to examen of conscience and preparation for confession and evening recreation. They made her happy.

The great double doors were open in the wind. They passed through them into the foyer, into the reception room, into the anteroom to North Wing. Clare Marie opened another set of double doors and they went into the stairwell. She would never stand up like Geraldine and tell them to leave her alone, just as she would never stand up in evening recration and tell them what she thought of them for telling all those ghost stories. Dear God, she hated those ghost stories. She had talked to Clare Marie about it, but Clare Marie, for once, had not been sympathetic. They were required to talk with everyone. They should think of the pleasure of others, not their own. Annie hated evening recreation, knowing she would have to sit placidly on the couch while Marie Bernadette or Jane or even Kat started another tale of blood and howling set in some undusted corner of the convent. Tonight had been one of the worst. Jane had been launched on another tower story, complete with clanking shades and ghostly admonitions. It had gone right into her, down to the deepest part of her memory, touching things she thought had been exorcised years ago. When it was over, she'd been in shock. She hadn't been able to rid herself of the feeling that Jane had done it on purpose, had *meant* to upset her. Then she had looked around at the others and gone into deeper shock still. They had been

113

laughing and appreciative, applauding Jane and the story and themselves.

"Oh, dear," someone said. "All that blood."

"No, no," someone else said. "Death. You know, the worms crawl in, the worms—"

"Oh, stop."

"—crawl out—"

"*Stop.*"

"They wrap you up in a dirty sheet and put you down about thirty feet—"

"Stop, stop, stop."

There they had all been, laughing, hysterical, unable to contain themselves. They thought it was funny.

They turned onto postulant corridor. Clare Marie stood beside the door, holding it open. Since it was her turn to intone the Divine Praises, Annie waited beside Clare Marie, giving the others time to get to their cells. They were supposed to undress to the Divine Praises and evening prayers, then take their things to the laundry chute, then shower, then (if they could) go to sleep.

Annie took her place at the lectern, signed herself, and said, "The Divine Praises." On the corridor, the tempo quickened. They would have to hurry to be done in time. Their voices rose in answer to her own, the echo-chant of an unseen choir.

She didn't think she would ever be able to joke about the things they joked about in recreation.

2

Later, lying in bed, she thought about her mother. It was less disturbing than thinking about Stephen. She was trying to modify her responses to his letters, to bring herself in line with the ideal of Holy Poverty. Stephen had written about a house he had visited, a big stone house on Edge Hill Road in New Haven. Annie could see the curtains and the windows and the translucent china the woman had brought out to serve Stephen tea, feel the heaviness of heirloom silver, smell the soft underscent of sachet.

She could not think of Stephen's houses without thinking:

114

if it can be done, I can do it. Not: if it can be done, maybe I can do it. There was no maybe about it.

Her mother came every Sunday, driving up in the inevitable rented Lincoln Continental Mark IV. They ate in the reception room, side by side on the worn brown couch. Mother wore Aunt Belle's fox fur stole, Grandmama's pearls, an ancient black silk dress that must have been expensive at the start of the Second World War. She kept trying to readjust her clothes, as if they made her itch.

"You stay in the convent," her mother said. "You don't know what a relief it is to me, with what's happening to everyone else's children. They think they know everything, but you know how it is, trouble's waiting, it always is, and the first sign of trouble is *pride*, and they surely have *that*. Mary Beth Martin sticking her nose up at me because her husband's a contractor. Everybody knows what he is, anyway, those Italians he knows. Everybody knows it was blood money bought that house."

"Yes," Annie said. "Yes, of course."

"And that Linda," her mother said. "Fancy rich girls' college. Nearly died from a lot of pills, that's what happened to her, became some kind of drug addict and had to go away someplace in New York State."

"Yes," Annie said.

"It's not like here," her mother said. "No one cares who they hurt in the world. Or what they do. It's not peaceful and holy out there."

Annie turned over in bed. She wished the weather hadn't turned so cold. Vianney and Perpetua and the others couldn't say rosary in the arbor anymore. The wind and damp got to them. She said the rosary with them in chapel, but it wasn't the same. From the arbor, Agnus Dei looked like a fairy castle. In the chapel, she was always noticing the worn places in the kneelers, the scratches in the wood at the back of the pews.

The muscles in her back began to unkink, the muscles in her legs to liquefy. Her body always felt heavier just before sleep, as if "sinking into sleep" weren't a metaphor but a stage direction. She sank into the mattress, out of sight of the conscious, watching world.

If she had any sense, she would thank God hourly for

bringing her to Agnus Dei. Outside, there would be nothing to stop her pride, nothing capable of stopping her pride. She would go rushing headlong at her mirage of an Edge Hill Road mansion, and she knew what would happen then. They could take death and purgatory and hellfire, souls and devils. What you got for thinking you could have those things wasn't damnation, it was

he committed suicide

failure.

CONFITEOR

1

Kat started to say her Confiteor in bed, but as soon as she was on her back she found herself drifting through a heat-mirage jungle, dressed in leopard skins, followed by David.

She got her rosary from the night table and slipped out of bed. The rosary should have been on her bureau, between her devotions book and her pincushion, but she had had it in her hands when she lay down and forgotten to get up and put it back. She got her examen book from the bureau and wrote the lapse on the first line of a new page, squinting and straining in the dim light of a hidden moon.

She got her robe from its hook, shrugged it over her shoulders, and tied the cloth belt around her waist. At her last Guidance session, she'd had a talk with Clare Marie about her difficulties with prayer. It had been a very odd discussion. She'd begun hesitantly, honestly. It had become almost impossible for her to concentrate on the words of the prayers, or even the essence of the lesson for rosary and the Stations.

Clare Marie had looked at her over the glare the sun made on the polished desktop and said, "There's something called the Dark Night of the Soul, of course. Or this could be a crisis of faith. Is that what you're trying to tell me? Are you losing your faith?"

"No, Sister."

"Are you sure?"

"Yes, Sister." It was her vocation she was afraid she was losing, or had never had in the first place.

Clare Marie tapped her fingers on the windowsill. "Under other circumstances, I would suspect this was a bid for attention. At this stage of the postulancy, we often find girls with sudden cravings for attention, shy girls who tend to fade into the group. But I can't see that would be a problem for you. You get quite a bit of attention."

"Yes, Sister."

"Possibly not as much as you're used to?"

"Well, um, actually, Sister, maybe more than I'm used to. Maybe too much." In fact, she got so much more attention than she wanted, she wouldn't have been able to begin to explain the scope of the problem, even if Clare Marie had been willing to listen. The weaker members of the class— poor, miserable Constance, the homesick Italian girls, clumsy little Maria Luisa, even Martha—had spontaneously appointed her Postulant Mother. They trusted the strength they thought they saw in her. They loaded her up with their pain and fear until she felt the weight of all that sadness would crack her bones. It would have been easier if they'd told her what was wrong. Instead, they kept the Rule that legislated against personal disclosure. They came to her mute, demanding to be comforted.

Clare Marie didn't want to hear about any of it. Clare Marie had something on her mind. But what? What was this all about?

Clare Marie came back to sit behind the desk. Her eyes were hard and bright, probing. "Well, then," she said. "If it's not the Dark Night of the Soul, and it's not a loss of faith, what do you think it is?"

Kat felt as if she'd been invited to confess to murder. She said, "Sister, I just can't seem to concentrate. I go to chapel and rosary and I just sort of drift. Instead of thinking about the prayer, I think about something else."

"Very good," Clare Marie said. "And why do you think this should be?"

Kat had to sit on her hands to keep from plucking her skirt or readjusting her veil from sheer nervousness. Clare Marie was not trying to find out what Kat thought the prob-

117

lem might be, but to elicit an answer she had decided on in advance. But what answer? What was she supposed to know that she didn't know?

"Sister, I don't know. That's what I wanted to talk about. First the why and then the how to make it stop."

Clare Marie looked mortally offended. She stood up, ending the interview, dismissing the irritant. "Sometimes, if we do not do what we are supposed to do, if we act unworthy of the promises of Christ, God cuts us off from the Divine Presence until we have made amendment and are pleasing to Him again."

Kat let herself onto the landing and started down the stairs. If Jane was in the Mary Chapel, she would try the rosary long enough to know if she could pray at all with Jane kneeling beside her. If she couldn't, she'd try thinking through her sessions with Clare Marie. What sin did the old woman think she'd committed? It couldn't be David. That Guidance session had come a week before David's letter.

The Mary Chapel was empty. She squeezed into the small, low-ceilinged niche and lit a candle from the "eternal flame" oil lamp at the Virgin's feet. The face of the statue glowed smooth and talc-powder white in the yellow light. She crossed herself and went to her knees, listening to North Wing, wishing she could walk outside in the darkness. For all the talk about Grand and Minor Silence, there was never any real silence within the walls of Agnus Dei. Sisters snored. Sisters opened and closed doors. Sisters sneezed. At meals, the tin tableware made atonal jug-band music through the readings.

She placed her devotions book on the slanted holder, open to the first of the Five Sorrowful Mysteries. There was a miniature reproduction of an Italian Renaissance painting of the Agony in the Garden. Christ was on his knees, his face tortured, his pores beginning to open in anticipation of the scourging.

She was drifting again—walking along the beach in Rhodes, holding David's hand, on her way to the concrete, earthly, tangible kind of love, the kind she understood best, the kind that would live in her body no matter how long she dedicated herself to love in Christ—when the screaming started. It came up from under her, like a helium balloon that had somehow penetrated brick and plaster on its journey to the stratosphere—a high, sharp, single-note wail that, once started, went on and on and on without a break.

2

When the screaming started, she was crouched against the wall under the rope hook, listening to the bats in the rafters over her head. She had intended to catch one, or, failing that (they were hard to catch), take a walk on the roof. Then she had heard Kat get up and move through the corridor to the Mary Chapel, and she had been afraid. She was safe in the tower, out of sight, but on the roof she might be seen. She hated Kat for her restlessness, for her inauthentic midnight piety. Kat was cutting her off, shutting her down, forcing her to hide.

Ever since the conversation with Geraldine in the infirmary, Jane had been thinking things over. Some of it still looked possible. Annie was still cold, but there might be a way to break that down. In fact, she was sure there was. What was impossible was the idea of explaining, to Annie or anyone else, what had happened between her father and herself. That first story was just the beginning. Maybe she would make it a novel, the first novel about the positive side of incestuous love. Dear God, wouldn't *that* get her on the best-seller lists. Maybe she ought to drop the novel and make it a how-to book instead. *150 Ways to Seduce Your Father. Theory and Practice of Paternal Love.* Her mother would probably set off for Florida with a shotgun.

Her mother would never understand that the sex had not been the point.

They wouldn't even understand the sex. They would sympathize with her or shun her or tell each other that explained why she was such a dork, but they would never understand.

She got up and went to stand at the narrow window overlooking North Lawn. From just the right angle, she could see the light of Kat's candle in the Mary Chapel. No sane person had ever believed what Kat was trying to make herself believe. No sane person could.

119

She didn't want to kill bats tonight, she wanted to kill *them*. Them, the giant ants.

A shift of mood, like a change in the direction of the wind, presented her with another possibility. She could sit down with the rest of them at the next recreation and—instead of giving a lecture on the Rule—giggle and confess to a weakness for whispering during Silence or a nostalgia for romantic movies. She could try. With Geraldine gone, no one would come right out and laugh at her. There might be a chance, as she was sure there was a chance with Annie. She saw herself trying and succeeding. She saw herself with her feet drawn under her, listening to their talk. Then she looked past it, to all the days that would follow that success, and it was a pit, a black hole, an abyss.

(It could obliterate you, as if you'd never been.)

She wished she could calm down long enough to catch a bat. She was making mistakes, losing things, forgetting things, getting sloppy. She had been trying too hard not to be herself. Martha had talked to her and she had listened. Clare Marie had talked to her. She had talked to herself. The effort was too much for her, and besides, she didn't believe in it. She made them uncomfortable, but she wanted to make them uncomfortable. They deserved to be uncomfortable. It was an accident, what they had and what she didn't have. They ought to apologize for it, make it up to her—here in the convent especially, where humility meant the recognition that none of them deserved anything.

She moved away from the window and got her robe from the floor. She was going to have to do something about the robe. It was covered with dust. Somebody in the laundry would notice. They might start thinking, and that was all she needed. Christ. If they even found out what she did up here, they'd have her head.

She belted the robe around her waist—she was losing too much weight—and went to sit under the rope hook again. She would stay and watch Kat's candle in the Mary Chapel. When it went out, she would go out on the roof, sit in the air, think things through. Then she would come back into the tower and catch her bat. Protect the nest, she thought.

She had just begun to drift into a daydream, her favorite

120

daydream, about the awards ceremony and the girls she'd known at school, when the screaming started.

3

"It's coming out of the walls," Constance said. Her eyes were red and full of precariously balanced tears. "It's coming out of the *walls*."

Kat came up the steps onto the landing, brushing by her, brushing by Miriam. It was coming out of the walls. A wall. She looked over her shoulder and found a small knot of senior novices standing on the stairs in their robes.

"What is it," Angela Louise said. "What in the name of God—"

"I don't know," Kat said.

"I don't know either," Miriam said.

"It's coming out of the walls," Constance said.

4

Annie was dreaming. She knew she was dreaming, because she was talking to her mother, and mother was back home on Ellery Street. Safely out of the way. That was the important part. *Safely out of the way.*

She looked down at the thing in her hands, the liver, the squirming liver spewing bile and blood all over her arms. She could hear her mother giggling in the background. It was the giggle that set off the scream. The scream went on and on, even after the earthquake started and she was being shaken so hard her head was snapping back and forth on her neck, snapping in sharp, clear cracks until it would have to snap off. Her head would snap off and start rolling over the rutted ground like a wild marble, right into Kat and Miriam and Angela Louise, who had appeared, suddenly, from nowhere. Then Kat was talking to her, saying something over and over and

("It's just a bat Annie it's all right it's just a dead bat") all of a sudden she was someplace else, out of the wind, someplace that smelled like clotheslines in summer. Kat was standing in front of her, holding her shoulders, saying that same thing.

121

"It's just a bat, Annie. Can you hear me? It's just a dead bat."

It *was* just a dead bat. The last Annie remembered, she had been lying in bed, drifting off to sleep. Now she was standing in the linen closet on the fourth-floor landing of North Wing, holding a dead bat.

A dead, bloody, mutilated bat.

"There's a man looking for you, Lieutenant. He has—"

"Ah, yes, Sister. The pieces. Would you like to sit down? You look—"

"Old, Lieutenant. What I am is old."

"I know how you feel."

"Does he have to carry those things around like that? The clothes and other things? Does he have to pull at them like that?"

"He doesn't mean to be callous, Sister. It's just—"

"Yes?"

"Usually there wouldn't be anybody else here. Any outsiders. We would have cleared the area."

"Why didn't you? Because we were nuns?"

"Because I fucked up. Excuse me, Sister."

STEPHEN

In the end, Stephen didn't ram it up her ass, or make her suck on it, or make her get on her hands and knees and pretend to be a dog he'd had when he was six. He tried for something simpler, something (he had to laugh at himself) the Church wouldn't mind so much. He tried because he felt more for Candy than he should. What he felt was silly, possibly stupid, certain to cause him pain, but there it was. He didn't want to get rid of it. He didn't even want to get rid of Candy, which was what he should have wanted. Every once in a while he just wanted to do things a little . . . less vigorously.

Candy could not do things less vigorously. Sex for Candy was not a form of communication, but a professional responsibility. If you wanted to communicate with Candy, you talked.

She painted a watercolor tattoo on his prick, a coiling snake, with an apple impaled on its fangs. When he didn't like it, she licked it off and replaced it with a butterfly.

"Only food coloring," she said. "It won't hurt you."

"My sister joined a convent," he said. "My sister's becoming a nun."

She looked at him, frowning. "What's that supposed to mean? I'm supposed to feel like shit?"

"Why should you feel like shit?"

"Your sister's becoming a nun," she said. "Shit."

He considered arguing with her, and gave it up. He was, after all, living on her for the moment. Not that it was going to last—he'd get his shit together any day now—but right this second, if she threw him out he'd have nowhere to go but the street. Besides, she'd only start harping on him to "get realistic," and he didn't want to hear it. He didn't want one damn thing half the dorks he'd known in high school didn't have already.

What he liked best was writing letters to Annie. In his letters, he could be the person he should have been, the person he would have been if the bastards hadn't screwed him six ways to Sunday every time he tried to get a break. Thank God she was safely locked away in that place and didn't need to lean on him.

Someday, though, he was going to be the person he was in Annie's letters. If the bastards ever gave him half a chance.

Candy stopped painting and looked up at him. "You're lying to her," she said. "I've seen those letters. What are you going to do if she gets in trouble? What are you going to do if she needs you?"

"She can't get in trouble, for God's sake. She's in a convent."

"There's all kinds of trouble."

"She likes to read about society houses. And country clubs. It's what she has instead of television."

"She likes to read about you."

She flexed her fake fingernails against his balls. The pressure was pleasurably painful, like the pinches she sometimes gave him at the top of his penis. He could sit here and let her do this to him forever. He could—

"You should take it more seriously," she said, stopping everything. "Anything could happen. Even to someone in a convent."

"Nothing's going to happen," he said.

"Yeah," Candy said. "Well, I've spent my *life* in situations where nothing was going to happen. And I've spent my *life* getting dumped by the people who said they'd be there to catch me."

"Stop worrying about it," he said. "Nothing is going to happen to Annie."

She took him in her mouth, biting him half seriously at the place where his penis met his balls. He closed his eyes and let it take him over.

He knew it was true. He might end up on the street, sleeping under newspapers. He might get in trouble and finally land in jail. Anything could happen to him.

But nothing was going to happen to Annie.

Annie was a unicorn.

"*I was here when this happened before, Lieutenant. I should have known. I should have been watching.*"

"*Sister?*"

"*Oh, nothing so bizarre. No knives. No superfluous people in the tower. But it was the tower. They're children, Lieu-*"

tenant. They believe in fairy castles and dragons and ghosts. And..."

"And?"

"And none of them ever comes alone. Remember that if you're ever in my position. They bring the soap operas with them. The brothers and sisters and mothers and fathers and aunts. Families are lethal, Lieutenant."

"Families are lethal."

"They'll tear you apart. They'll pull you in their direction and God will pull you in His, and one day you'll find yourself ripping in two, and it won't be along a seam."

FIELD TRIP

1

The book was in a small wire revolving rack next to the canned clams in the grocery store part of the post office— or, as the clerk had explained it, in the grocery store *rather* than in the post office. The grocery store and the post office were separated by a pasteboard wakk that came up only to Annie's shoulder. She could check the price of Swiss Miss or the cover of this month's *Beaver* while standing in line for stamps. It didn't make much sense to Annie, but Kat said it was done often in England. Annie went to the post office and pretended she was in a very small English village, the kind where an aristocratic murder happened every fifteen minutes.

Annie looked over her shoulder at Sister Scholastica, resplendent and unencumbered in black and gray, and Sister Daniella. Daniella's white novice's veil was tangled in a pile of packages. She was putting them down on the counter next to the clerk's cage. Scholstica was looking through her black change purse, like a dead woman looking for the coins to pay her passage to Hades. Annie looked back at the book. Kat had told her about Hades, and Scylla and Charybdis, and putting coins on the eyes of the dead. Kat had told her about burying corpses barefoot, too, and that was right here in the twentieth century. Kat was on an edu-

125

cation campaign, the way Clare Marie and Reverend Mother were on a reassurance campaign. Annie had been given permission to absent herself from ghost stories at recreation, even if it meant sitting alone on the other side of the reception room. Usually it wasn't necessary. Kat or Miriam or Martha came if no one else would. She felt guilty about taking them away from something they enjoyed, but not about staying away from the group. No one wanted a repetition of the night she had been (sleepwalking) frightened by the bat.

Annie liked Kat's methods better than those of Reverend Mother and Clare Marie. Kat told gruesome stories—as far as Annie was concerned, all stories about death and dying and burial were gruesome—but she told them matter-of-factly. Kat leached the mystery from the ghost stories, hoping she was draining them of power. Maybe she was, or maybe the dream had spewed up some buried psychic poison. Annie had been feeling better since the night she found the bat than in all the time before. Her unhappiness was muted, if not gone. She was bored more often than depressed. She had settled into the routine, ceased to fight it, become inured even to kissing shoes. The only thing that continued to worry her was her examen book. Somehow the list of faults got longer and longer every day, and more and more complicated. She hated Greater Meditation with a passion. By the end of it, she always felt as if she were drowning in imperfections, being buried alive by faults.

Clare Marie and Reverend Mother weren't worried about her examen book. They weren't worried about her sleepwalking, or finding bats, or screaming until all North Wing was awake in the night. Annie couldn't figure out what they were worried about. The day after she found the bat, she was summoned to Reverend Mother's office. She went, feeling on the edge of an ulcer, convinced she was about to be expelled from the community. At best, she expected a religious third degree: Why were you there? Where were you going? Can you promise never to do it again?

Clare Marie and Reverend Mother wanted to talk about faith.

"Faith is supposed to help us through times like this," Reverend Mother said. "But sometimes, for very young religious, adversity has the effect . . ."

"Yes, yes," Clare Marie said. "Sometimes very young religious, when they have trials, think God had deserted them, or maybe that He never existed at all."

They looked at her expectantly. Annie sat in the God-awful straight-backed chair, wondering how long she was going to be able to sit absolutely erect without her spine touching the back. She was having a hard time keeping her mouth from dropping open. She had heard about atheists in religion class, had even suffered through her friend Susan's crisis of faith in eleventh grade, but she didn't really believe there were people who didn't believe in God. "Atheists" were lying. Crises of faith were bids for attention.

"We're here to let you know God loves you," Clare Marie said. "God looks after you. God understands doubt and forgives it, if you search for Him."

"But I don't have any doubt," Annie wanted to say. She didn't say it. Clare Marie and Reverend Mother were floating in their idiosyncratic ether, inhabiting a world where the things she had to say would make no sense.

She touched the book on the rack with the tip of one finger, feeling the raised lettering, the raised edge on the gold frame that enclosed the pictures of four half-sexy, half-insipid actresses. *Lace*, by Shirley Conran. It must just have come out in paperback. She usually read all the books like this as soon as they hit the stores. She watched the miniseries, too. This one would probably be full of beautiful, ostentatious clothes and restaurants with gold leaf on the menus. She wished restaurants like that had secret rooms with one-way mirrors where people afraid to eat in them could watch people unafraid to eat in them eat in them. If there were a room like that, she would find the money to sit in it, no matter what it cost.

"Air mail to Zambia," Sister Scholastica was saying. "That's what I said."

Annie took the book off the rack. In her pocket she had the six hundred stamps it was her responsibility to buy every Tuesday afternoon, and the money for the paper and envelopes in special colors and sizes and weights she would have to buy at Holland's Office Supplies. She also had Kat's note to David Marsh. Kat said (from something in the letter everyone thought so innocuous) he would be under the clock at the bank. Annie hoped he was. She had to pass that note while she was still in the Paper-Supply side of Holland's, while Scholastica and Daniella were out of sight in Equipment. If David was under the clock at the bank, Annie could motion to him, meet him, turn over the envelope while no one was looking. Then she would be out of it.

She wanted to be out of everything. She wanted to watch beautiful women in expensive jewelry eat escargots and octopus from china plates with heavy silver seafood forks. It was like Stephen's letters. He wrote a lot about her vocation, but she skipped those parts. She wanted to read about the fifty-room house set among topiaries in Greenwich, the country club in Darien with real Oriental rugs on the floor of the members' library. If she weren't committed to the convent, she could drive through those streets. She could see the houses and the topiaries and the women driving to their country clubs in long dresses and family pearls.

She opened the book as close to the center as she could. There was a girl named Pagan. Pagan was being presented to the queen. Her curtsy was wobbly, uncertain, off-balance.

"Dear Heaven," Daniella said. *"Trash."*

Annie nearly jumped out of her skin. Daniella was right behind her, looking over her shoulder. Annie hadn't heard her come up. She put the book back in the rack and rubbed her palms against the side of her dress, trying to dry them.

"I don't understand how anybody reads that stuff," Daniella said.

Annie looked at the book on the rack. Even the pale imitation sunlight coming through the grimed windows made the cover glisten, like the dense satin of prom dresses in candlelight. Somewhere between those covers, Pagan was being presented to the queen and eating at restaurants with gold leaf on the menus.

"I was just looking," Annie said.

Daniella shrugged. "It's not 1965," she said. "Get your mother to bring it for you next time she comes. Nobody's going to tell you not to read it if you want to read it."

"No," Annie said. "Of course not."

"Scholastica's making out the forms for Express Mail," Daniella said. "What's-her-name out in San Diego has to have more Baltimore Catechisms. What does she do with

Baltimore Catechisms, eat them? Oh, never mind. I'm going over to see how it's coming. When she's done, we're going across the street. Be ready, will you? Scholastica isn't in what I'd call a good mood."

Annie nodded. Daniella hesitated, then drifted off. Annie reached for the book again. Scholastica was never in a good mood. Annie didn't want to think about it. She was tired of nuns. She wanted to think about money, about girls her age who were debutantes and got presented to the queen in long ball gowns imported from Paris and went to Europe the summer after high school. That world was real for somebody. It had been real, for instance, for Kat. The cover of *Lace* looked even shinier when she held it than it did on the rack. She could never ask her mother to buy it for her. Her mother would be scandalized. Stephen would be disappointed in her. They each in their own way expected her to be perfect, as perfect was defined in 1951.

At the package window, Sister Scholastica said, "That's it," in a loud, almost angry voice.

Outside, clouds shifted, uncovering the sun. In her hands, *Lace* gleamed and shimmered, like the hood of a highly polished Rolls-Royce left under Japanese lanterns at the foot of a curving drive.

2

He saw them as soon as they got out of the gray-and-black van to go into the post office—saw them and knew none of them was Kat. He stood, flexing his knees, wishing the cold weren't just damp enough to make his joints ache. He had a hard-on larger and more painful than any he'd experienced since seventh grade. It was the kind of hard-on you got when, still virginal, you allowed yourself an uninterrupted half hour with the magazines on the top shelf of the back rack in Bronxville News and Tobacco. It made him ashamed of himself. Everything he did lately made him ashamed of himself, except the things that terrified him. Sitting on the freezing marble steps under the clock in front of Northton Savings and Loan terrified him.

The town cop had come by every half hour, checking on him.

He put his copy of *I, The Jury* in the back pocket of his jeans and squinted across the town common at the entrance to the post office. He was prepared for the possibility that Kat wouldn't be able to get into town. He had picked the date at random and protected himself by writing her a long letter. He was beginning to think he hadn't protected himself enough. He couldn't possibly put that letter in the mail. If it was picked up by the censors, they would never let her hear from him again. Somebody would have to deliver it. It was beginning to look as if no one would come.

Should he cross the common and go into the post office? He couldn't face those nuns without a newspaper to cover the bulge in his pants. Even then, he was sure his voice would betray him.

Things weren't going well out in Eagleville. In fact, things weren't going at all. After Mary's visit, he thought he was on the track. He was going to devise a way to get Kat back. Instead of futile fantasies of fornication, he would concentrate on ways and means, plans and preparations. He would take control of the situation.

It hadn't worked out that way. His fantasies might be futile, but they were invincible. There was the one about the day of Kat's profession, the day she became a Bride of Christ. He saw her dressed in a bridal gown, although he knew the Society of Mary had never used that custom. Kat walked up the center aisle of the church, holding a bouquet of orange blossoms and sweet william. Other novices held the train of her gown, the sweeping net of her veil. Nuns sat in orderly rows, kneeling on hard wooden slats against the backs of pews.

He did nothing but stand at the altar, hands behind his back, waiting. Kat handed her bouquet to the novice on her left, unpinned her veil, and handed it to the novice on her right. Her head was shaven. He could see patches of her skull in the light from the altar candles. She climbed the two steps to the altar, unhooked her dress from behind, and let it fall off her shoulders. It caught momentarily on the jutting bone of her naked hip, presenting him with full, rounded breasts rising out of a sea of chiffon foam. She brushed her hand against the dress, dislodging it. It fell to her feet. She stepped out of it, walked to the altar, hoisted herself up like

130

a gymnast mounting a horse. When he looked down, she was stretched out among the Mass articles. Her hands caressed the chalice and the paten. Her legs brushed against the burse and the candlesticks. She was bucking and weaving, thrusting herself at him. He could see the pink tip of her clitoris in the candlelight. It looked swollen five times normal size.

Every part of him exploded. Kat reached for him and he let himself be drawn, let himself lie passive and triumphant as he sank into her, never to come out again.

Sometimes he told himself that that fantasy would be all right if *he* seduced *her*. It wasn't true. Nothing would ever make that fantasy "all right." Nothing would ever make it *acceptable*. Nothing would ever cure him of the self-disgust he felt every time he realized he'd enjoyed it.

Across the common, the two nuns and the postulant came out of the post office. The postulant lagged behind, her arms wrapped around her upper body, her head moving from side to side, looking for something. David walked forward across the sidewalk. She could be looking for him.

A moment later, he recognized her. Annie Bliss. He felt the sweat machine wind down. He wouldn't mind talking to Annie Bliss. These days, he minded the sight of any and all Catholic churches, any and all priests and nuns, any and all Latin Christmas music. He would not have so much as a picture of a crucifix in his house. He would not watch *Going My Way* on television. But he would not mind talking to Annie Bliss.

3

The man behind the stationery counter at Holland's wore a green plastic visor. Annie took the list out of her pocket and went up to him, glad not to have to wait in line. It wasn't the wait she minded as much as the people who caused it. They couldn't help staring. She could almost hear them thinking. Was she ugly? Crazy? Neurotic? Orphaned? Had she been jilted? Raped? Forced into the cloister by a fanatic parent? The people in Northton were not, in general, Catholic. It would not occur to them that there might be positive reasons for entering the convent.

She almost gave the man in the visor Kat's letter to

131

David. She switched envelopes and stood away from the counter to wait. It would take about fifteen minutes for him to find everything she needed. If David had seen her wave, if he had understood she wanted him to follow her, there would be time.

Across the common, he had looked taller than she remembered him.

"This bond," the clerk said, "We got sixteen-weight, we got twenty-weight, we got no eighteen-weight. What do you want?"

Annie choked. What did she want? The bond was for Sister Mary Thomas. Annie had no idea what Sister wanted it for. And—convent rules being what they were—she couldn't call to ask.

Someone came up to the counter beside her and said, "She'll take the twenty-weight." Annie jumped. People had been sneaking up on her all day. It was beginning to spook her.

"Twenty-weight is what you use for business letters," David Marsh said. "If it's not what whoever wanted, somebody will be able to use it."

"Oh," Annie said. The approach was so logical, so direct, it made her feel instantly better. She tried smiling at David Marsh. He was not only taller than she remembered him, he was better-looking. How could Kat have been in love with a man like that, seen him every day, even lived with him? He was so easy, so competent, so obviously rich. He terrified her.

David Marsh took an envelope out of his back pocket and handed it to her. "I thought she might not be able to make it," he said. "I came prepared."

She grabbed the envelope and stuffed it into her back pocket. Then she took the envelope Kat had given her and thrust it at him. "She sent you something, too," she said. "She— it's because of work detail. She can't get into town."

That was not strictly true. There were probably ways Kat could get into town, but it would be complicated, and much too risky. Annie didn't want to explain this to David Marsh. She didn't want to offend him. She didn't want to know what it would be like to have him angry at her. She wanted to get away from him before they got caught.

132

"Kat was always such an urban person," he said. "That's one of the things I find so hard to believe. How does she stand it in this town?"

"Oh," Annie said. "Well." She blushed. To think of all the times she had dreamed of sweeping into a ballroom, the cynosure (as her favorite writers always said) of all eyes. She couldn't even have a trivial conversation with a friend of a friend. She couldn't take her eyes off his shoes and train them on his face. She couldn't remember how to talk in sentences.

"Do you mind it?" David Marsh said. "Northton, I mean."

He was much too polite to ask her if she minded Agnus Dei. If he was in love with Kat, he probably hoped she did. He probably hoped they all did. Especially Kat.

"It's not bad," Annie said, hoping to sound ambivalent. She sounded inarticulate instead. "We don't get to see much of it. Northton, I mean."

"I don't suppose you do," David Marsh said.

"That's everything," the clerk said.

Annie rushed at the counter, suddenly wanting to put as much distance between herself and David Marsh as politeness would allow. He created a force field that made her feel as if she were choking. He made her muscles twitch.

The clerk put her order in two large shopping bags with twin handles. He put the bill on the counter. Annie fumbled for the money with one hand and grabbed ineffectually at the bags with the other. She was doing this all wrong. She was forgetting repose, and serenity. A nun was supposed to show the world only the face of certainty.

The clerk took her money. David took her bags.

"I'll take these out to the van for you," he said. "I'd better. You'd never lift them."

"Oh," Annie said again. She took her change from the clerk, not bothering to count it. She wouldn't have been able to make sense of counting, anyway. "You don't have to do that," she said. "Sister Scholastica and Sister Daniella are here. They'll—"

"Don't tell me," David said. "The convent's gone women's lib."

He was smiling at her again. He had a broad smile, showing strong teeth.

"Scholastica and Daniella," she said again, "will help."

He gave her a half-wise, half-disgusted look, as if he'd just caught on to the code. "All right," he said. "I don't suppose you want me to bring these where Scholastica and Daniella *can* help."

"No," Annie said.

"Figures."

Annie rubbed her palms against the side of her dress.

"Can you at least give me a hint?" David said. "Can you at least tell me if she's all right?"

Annie blinked at him. Why wouldn't Kat be all right?"

It suddenly occurred to her that David might be a Protestant, maybe even the kind they wrote about in *Time* magazine, that never went to church. Thinking of David as a Protestant made her feel funny.

"Of course Kat's all right," she said. "She hasn't even had a cold."

"Is she happy?"

"She looks happy," Annie said. "As happy as any of us, I guess."

"Meaning you don't know."

"I don't know that she's *unhappy*," Annie said.

David sighed. He looked suddenly older, tired, defeated. "I don't even know what I'm trying to ask you," he said. "I don't know what I want to know. Isn't that crazy?"

"You want to see her," Annie said. This she was sure of. "You should come Visiting Sunday. Any Sunday."

"Somehow, I don't think your Reverend Mother would welcome me with open arms."

She probably wouldn't, but Annie said, "Reverend Mother has nothing to do with it," as if she meant it. She was supposed to mean it. One of the changes since Vatican II had been their right to see anyone they wanted on official visiting days.

David Marsh leaned forward as if to pat her head, then backed away. "You're a nice infant, Annie Bliss," he said. "Tell Kat I said hello."

"I will."

"I'd give you a kiss on the cheek for her in proxy, but you'd probably faint."

"I probably would." She smiled. It was the first smile she'd managed for him, and he rewarded her with a half-sexy, half-humorous lift of his eyebrows. Annie felt the wind knocked out of her again. He was like someone on television.

"Maybe I'll see you later," he said.

She watched him leave Holland's Office Supplies, hands in his pockets, shoulders hunching against the cold that sucked inward when he opened the door. Stephen would be like that. Stephen would be like that and he would be hers.

4

"Who were you talking to in Holland's?" Scholastica said when they got back to the van. "Don't they tell you not to talk to strange men? You don't know what men are like. You don't know the kind of perverted obscenities they think about nuns."

"But," Annie said.

"*I* used to work in our mission in New York City," Scholastica said. "I've seen the kinds of things they show in Times Square. I haven't seen the movies, of course, but I've seen the posters. Pornographic movies about nuns. Pornographic books about nuns. It gives them a thrill, thinking about nuns."

Annie sat in the back seat, looking at the back of Daniella's head. Daniella was looking stiffly forward, pretending not to notice either of them.

"He wasn't a strange man," Annie said. "He was Kat's—Katherine Mary's—something. Half brother, I think." She made a short, silent act of contrition for the lie. It was, she assured herself, a white lie. "I met him the day we all came," she said.

Daniella turned sideways to look at Annie. "That's David Marsh?"

"I guess," Annie said. "David something."

"What was he doing there?" Scholastica said. "She can't come into town. If he thought he was going to effect an assignation, it was a pretty lame attempt."

135

Annie took a deep breath. If Kat and David were committing promiscuous fornication every midnight on North Lawn, she would not turn them in to Sister Mary Scholastica.

"I think he lives around here," she said. "I think Katherine Mary said he had a house in the country around here somewhere pretty close."

"I don't like it," Scholastica said. "It smells funny."

Annie looked out the windows at her side. Scholastica reminded her of her mother, and she knew the only positive defense in the face of an attack by someone like her mother. She kept her mouth shut and her eyes on the scenery. She kept her hands in her pockets, clenched.

In her pocket she had—what? Her mistake? It didn't feel like a mistake. She ran her fingers over the cover, feeling the ridges of the letters and the frame. She hadn't felt right since she realized she had it, but she didn't realize she had it until she was halfway across the common. Scholastica had been so sharp. Daniella had been so anxious. Annie had been hurrying, not thinking. She must have forgotten she had it in her hands. Called on to *get moving* (the first great rule of postulant life), she must have shoved it through her pocket slit the way she would her rosary beads at the sound of the chapel bell. On the way to Holland's, she had felt its heaviness against her leg. It seemed better to keep it than go back to the post office and try to return it. What would she say? What would she do if they didn't believe it had been an accident, if they accused her of shoplifting? It was better to keep it. And besides—

Besides, she didn't want to give it up.

She pressed her forehead against the cold glass of the window and closed her eyes. It would have been better to return it, she knew that. It would just have been so complicated. Scholastica would have taken her apart, probably right in the middle of the town common, in front of everyone. Then she would have had to go back to the post office and let herself be embarrassed in public *again*. Could you explain to a non-Catholic, who knew nothing of nuns but what he remembered of *The Bells of Saint Mary's*, that Vatican II had changed everything, that nuns could read anything they wanted now, even books like *Lace*?

"They're getting much too lax up there," Scholastica said, looking up the hill at Agnus Dei. "They don't tell you the truth about men anymore."

5

The van nearly scraped the Volkswagen when it passed on Main Street. David, looking up from Kat's letter, decided it was negligence rather than hostility. The nun who was driving was fluttering her hands, pounding the steering wheel with her fists, pumping her arms in the air. She had probably seen Annie talking to him, and was now making a point. David tried to catch sight of Annie, but the van was going too fast. It turned the corner of Main and Ridge Road and disappeared into shedding trees and neat brick buildings and hand-lettered signs for insurance agents and realtors and funeral homes.

He spread the pages of Kat's letter across his lap, hoping both that Annie was not in too much trouble and that she had the sense to keep her mouth shut. He put the map on his right knee and turned it until he thought he had it facing the right direction. There was a page of instructions, but like all Kat's attempts at giving directions, it was incomprehensible. There was a drawing of a small stone building in the middle of a pine clearing. That was what he would have to find.

His own letter was riding up the hill to Agnus Dei in Annie's pocket. He had written pages and pages of Byzantine sophistry, Jesuitical arguments, and rococo plots. He must have been crazy. Kat's letter wasn't even a letter, just two or three lines telling him everything he needed to know. It made him feel awful.

I've given you directions. Make it about 10:25. Try not to get caught.

He gathered the papers into an untidy mass and threw them on the passenger seat. He reached into his pocket for his keys. He was going to have to get out of here before he did something strange, made himself more of a curiosity

137

than he already was. He was going to have to check into a hotel somewhere and wait.

He was pulling into traffic when he started to laugh. The laughter bubbled up like danger, out of control. *Make it about 10:25. Try not to get caught.* Dear Jesus. Mary Mother of God. He wanted to stop the car in the middle of Main Street and laugh until he choked.

He would come walking to her out of the pines, and it would be as it had always been. It would be perfect.

PRECIOUS BLOOD

1

Kat kept a pair of pearl earrings with white gold rims in a satin-lined jeweler's box in the fourth drawer of her dresser, under her underwear. Martha kept a third of an ounce of Chanel No. 5, unopened, under the stiff, folded whiteness of her veils. Constance kept pictures of five small children in the back of her devotions book. In the envelopes from her brother Phillip's letter, Miriam kept a pile of ancient, yellowing notes from someone named Barret. Annie kept her high-school yearbook under her mattress.

Jane sat on the edge of Annie's bed and looked at the dead bird in her hand. Blood was crusting on the feathers at the bird's neck. Any minute now she was going to have to get up, cross the corridor, and throw the bird out her window. When they came upstairs form exercise, she had to be lying on her bed, looking (as Sister Agnes would put it) peakèd. That was how she had managed to get out of exercise and onto the corridor for an hour alone. Old Agnes thought doing calisthenics when you had "female trouble" would kill you,

Annie Bliss had no books except a convent-library copy of *The Dark Night of the Soul* and the *Anthology of Spiritual Reading* they had been given when they came. Even Constance had *All Creatures Great and Small* and a little gilt mirror with her initials etched into the glass. Miriam had the complete Rachmaninoff piano concertos on cassette tapes and a Sony Walkman. Searching through Annie Bliss's drawers, you would almost have believed she'd spontaneously generated in the reception oom the day they'd come to Agnus Dei.

Jane weighed the bird in one hand and riffled Annie's yearbook with the other. She didn't want to throw the carcass out the window. She wanted to leave it on Annie's pillow, or, better, under Annie's pillow. She wanted Annie to find it and scream and cry and make an idiot of herself. God, how she wanted Annie to make an idiot of herself. Preferably in public, and preferably irredeemably.

She had spent most of her time in Annie's cell trying to come to terms with the yearbook. It was as if Annie had been deliberately lying to her, passing herself off as something she wasn't so Jane would make her move and Annie could laugh at her. Did Annie laugh at her? Did Annie steal away in secret with Kat and Martha and Miriam and entertain them with just how idiotically stupid Jane was, thinking she could ever make it into the core?

She threw the bird on Annie's quilt and opened the yearbook to the pages that fascinated her: on one side, Annie in uniform, close to the center of a group of girls standing against a blackboard in a classroom, playing Secretary of the Student Council; on the other, Annie and her date with a lot of other girls and their dates in the Senior Prom Committee picture. It made Jane's head ache. Martha was probably a saint. Miriam and Kat—well, Miriam and Kat were special. They were brilliant, not just bright, and beautiful. Annie wasn't even high-school-cheerleader pretty. Annie wasn't one damn thing Jane herself wasn't. How was it possible that Annie had been what this yearbook said she had been?

Brianna Foley. Maggie Stander. Romana Cairn. Cecelia Mallory. Bridget Gallagher. Jane tapped the edge of Annie's Prom Committee picture. The names under that picture would be different, of course, but the names didn't matter. There were probably two thousand Catholic girls' high schools in the United States, and all of them had the same Prom Committee. And the same Student Council. And the same school newspaper, monitored by a young nun considered "good with students." Perfect Catholic girls from perfect Catholic families.

She put Annie's yearbook under her arm and headed for the lavatory.

2

She had not, in the beginning, intended to take any of the pills she stole from Elizabeth's cabinet. She had intended to use them, the way she had when she put them first in Martha's bed and then in Kat's, but that was different. She felt justified in that. She had taken all the red Dexedrine capsules and emptied them into a Ziploc bag she had stolen from the kitchen and refilled them with Bromo Seltzer, but that was just in case. Elizabeth might get organized any minute now. It was unlikely, but not impossible. Once Elizabeth got organized, she would be cut off. Besides, it seemed wasteful to use real Dexedrine to cause a fuss in Martha's cell. The capsules would be enough. No one would take the time to test them.

She closed herself in the fourth stall from the door and got to her knees to reach the loose tile behind the toilet bowl. She had discovered the tile the first week. It had taken days to pry it free and hollow out enough space beneath it to make it useful. She had taken a spoon from the sideboard and gone at the plaster that way, night after night, after lights out. She hadn't even known what she was doing it for. Making that hole was an example of unadulterated foresight, what her father would have called the "will to preparedness." You never asked her father, "prepared for what?" The answer was obvious: prepared for anything.

So far as Jane knew, the only thing her father had not been prepared for was Jane herself.

The Ziploc bag was on top, looking like a cache of heroin from a television movie. Jane took it out and laid it on the toilet-bowl cover. Under it she had fifty Thorazine capsules, twenty caps of Darvon Complex, a hundred sixteen Valium, thirty doses of Methadrine, and sixty Mequin. She'd taken the Methedrine from the cell of an illicitly dieting novice the day she searched the senior novices' corridor. The rest came from the dispensary cabinet. Valium and Darvon were for Sisters with cramps or temporary personal problems. The rest was for treating Sisters on the infirmary's locked ward.

"The most important thing you'll ever learn in life," her father said, "is how to put up a front."

Jane could see him standing on their beach, hands in his pockets, looking out to sea. According to her mother, Muriel had left him because she caught him sleeping with a thirteen-year-old boy. Jane wondered what she would think when he touched her this time—and he would touch her, it was the only reason she visited, they both knew that by now —knowing he had put it into a colored boy. The nuns at school said it was a sin to dislike people for their color, but she didn't even like thinking about colored people. She was sure if she touched a colored person's skin, it would be cold and clammy and feel like slime.

Her father took her hand and began leading her down the beach. "You have to make people think you are what you want them to think you are," he said.

Jane shook her head. She fuzzed out like this more and more often lately. The pills were spread out on the toilet-seat cover. She passed up the Thorazine for the Darvon, hesitated between loose Dexedrine and the Methedrine caps. She'd done this only twice before, once the day she left the pills for Martha and Kat and once a night about a week later, before she went to the tower. The second time, she miscalculated the Dexedrine. The first time, she had only meant to take a Valium to calm herself down. She'd been so furious that they'd got rid of the pills before she had a chance to report them, more furious that they hadn't seriously considered her as a source of the problem. It was as if they thought only the five of them existed. She'd needed something to straighten her out. The Valium had been stronger than she expected. The bell had rung for chapel and she'd been ready to pass out. She'd hardly been able to stand up. She'd gone through the cache in a half-immobile panic. The fear was as fast as fear always was, but the speed of it didn't reach her muscles. She'd licked her palm and stuck it in the Dexedrine and licked it off again.

And it had been a revelation.

Would her life have been different if she'd found this before, in high school, in grammar school, while her father was recording the growth of her breasts with the circular movements of a jagged thumbnail? She'd had the best chapel, the best dinner, the best recreation in all her time at Agnus Dei. She'd been infinitely poised, infinitely accepting, infinitely superior. When Martha told her to use the nail-studded spools to make leg warmers, it would take too long to teach her to do it "right," Jane's smile had not covered an inner explosion. When she caught Miriam and Kat passing notes, her reproof had been spoken in perfect charity. When she knelt in chapel for Vespers, her prayer had been a *prayer*, a celebration of herself. Then the stuff wore off and it came out of her, a Krakatoa eruption of paranoia and fury. *They* felt like that every minute of their lives. *They* didn't need pills to make them float free.

She had done it the second time as an experiment. She knew it was dangerous. Jane didn't think you could get addicted to drugs doctors were allowed to prescribe—didn't the Food and Drug Administration take care of that?—but she wasn't sure. Not being sure, she wanted to be careful.

She had not been careful enough with the loose Dexedrine. She'd swallowed half a handful of it with four Valium. From what happened, she didn't think the Valium had any effect at all. By the time she got to the bell tower, she might as well have been a booster rocket at Cape Kennedy. Her heartbeat was fast and faint at the same time. She couldn't stop walking. She walked until she was ready to throw herself off the roof. Then she went downstairs to the lavatory and swallowed four more Valium. Half an hour later, she dragged herself to bed, somehow convinced they would be waiting for her when she got there, grinning and ringing the bell for Sisters.

She put a single Methedrine beside the Darvon. She wanted just enough to give her that feeling of infinite superiority she'd had the first time. She wanted to float through dinner and chapel and recreation on a tide of perfection. She took out a second Methedrine. She dry-swallowed the Darvon first, then choked down the Methedrine. She put the pills back under the tile. The way things were going, she

142

would have to dig a deeper hole. She was running out of room.

She sat on the floor with her back against the stall partition and waited. After the first summer, she decided her father had divorced her mother because he didn't want to sleep with her. He wanted to sleep with children, touch them and squeeze them and stuff himself inside them. When he came into her, she felt stuffed full. Sometimes she felt stuffed so full, she thought parts of her father were going to come out her ears. She wondered what they looked like, sitting side by side on a banquette in the Oceanview Surf and Turf, her father's hand in her hair. He could barely stop touching her, even in public. He put his hands under the table and under her dress and finally under the thin nylon crotch of her panties. He worked his finger up inside her, grinning at the waiter and keeping a death grip on a Scotch with the other hand.

The Darvon was working faster than the Methedrine. She opened Annie's yearbook to the senior pictures. There was a solid square of activities under Annie's name, and not just things like "Sodality 2, 3, 4." Anyone could have that just by showing up at a meeting once a week. After "Math Club 1, 2, 3, 4" came "(Treas. 2, Sec. 3, V.P. 4)." After "Yearbook 1, 2, 3, 4" came "(Underclassmen editor 3; candids editor 4)." Annie Bliss had been elected to things. The lapel of her uniform blazer had probably been covered with pins.

When the Methedrine started to work, it made her mouth dry. She closed her eyes and let herself feel the jumpiness under the skin of her arms. The trick was to know how much was too much, how much was enough. Well, yes. Of course that was the trick. Wasn't it with everything?

The dryness persisted, but the jumpiness began to fade. She was losing track of time.

She lodged Annie's yearbook under her belt and stopped at the sinks to wash her face. No matter how the pills made her head feel, they always made her skin feel clammy and hot. She half drowned herself in cold water and dried herself on Miriam's towel. That was something else that hadn't worked, moving the things in Annie's cubicle. She had expected Annie to say something, to confide in her, but Annie had said nothing at all.

143

The clock on the landing gave her half an hour. She let herself onto postulant corridor, stopping to listen for someone who might have come up while she was in the lavatory. There was no one. She walked down to Annie's cell, let herself in, and closed the muslin curtains around her. Being here was like adding a third drug to the two she had already taken. She could feel the counterbeat in her temples. Everything she had ever wanted was in this room.

And the things she hadn't wanted didn't exist here.

She sat on the edge of the bed and stroked the dead bird's feathers, letting herself drift. She felt soft and gentle and slow and complete.

Annie Bliss was gone and she was Annie Bliss.

3

There was a noise below, scraping, as if someone had opened a door. She sat very still and listened very carefully, but it was nothing. Someone had come onto the senior novices' corridor. She could hear bedsprings creak. She turned Annie's yearbook over and over in her hands. All Annie had besides the yearbook was her spiritual diary, and Jane didn't want any part of that. She could just imagine what was in it.

She picked up the bird and stuffed it into her pocket. There was no window in Annie's cell. She would have to cross the corridor to get rid of the carcass. She would have to get up and get out and get ready to go back to this game they were playing. God only knew what they'd do if they found her looking through their things.

Throw her out. They were looking for an excuse to throw her out, and this would be it.

There were times she hated Clare Marie more than she hated *them*. Clare Marie's entire reason for existence was to find excuses to throw postulants out of the Order. Clare Marie would be overjoyed if none of them passed on to the novitiate.

She had taken too much Methedrine. Her heart was working like a jackhammer.

She got off the bed and put Annie's yearbook under the mattress. She wasn't doing anything wrong. They were threatening her and she was protecting herself. She was

144

crawling into the mind of the enemy and rendering it harmless. She had more right to be here than any of them. She would get more from being a nun than they ever could.

She took Annie's spiritual diary from the shelf above the robe hook. She flipped it open to the first page. What would she get? Flowers? Babies? Kittens playing in fields of clover?

This is what I'm absolutely sure of. Annie had overlarge, rounded handwriting, child's handwriting. Handwriting was supposed to mean something. You were supposed to be able to expose people with it.

When she was seventeen, after it was over, her father exposed himself to a five-year-old boy in a public park in Orlando.

Jane looked down at the next line in Annie's notebook and read:

He committed suicide.

SHIFT FOCUS

1

"This was the way it happened," Marie Bernadette said. "She was a junior novice, which in those days meant she lived on the second floor, because before Vatican II the real cloistered nuns were absolutely shut up in West Wing and couldn't talk to anyone but each other. The rule was to lock the second floor at night. The second floor particularly, not just the anteroom door to North Wing, so the cloistered novices couldn't get out and read newspapers or talk to outsiders. I know it sounds terrible, but . . ."

"It sounds ridiculous," Miriam said. "From what I hear, no one was allowed to read newspapers in those days anyway."

"Nobody was supposed to, but they did it," Marie Bernadette said. "Nuns are supposed to be perfect, but they usually aren't."

"Don't I know it," someone else said. And giggled.

"It was much better in those days," Marie Bernadette

said. "People took this life seriously. It wasn't like now. People respected the convent."

"I don't call wrapping a rope around your neck and hanging yourself from a rafter in the bell tower respecting the convent," Miriam said.

"Of course not," Marie Bernadette said. "But she was in despair. She still respected the life, you see. That's why she had to kill herself. Once she knew she could never be a good nun, there was nothing to do but kill herself."

Annie folded her hands over the papers she had spread out on the table and put her head down on top of them. Miriam and Marie Bernadette and the others were on the far side of the reception room, going over and over the same old ground. It made Annie uneasy to think that, in everything else, it was Jane who was left out and she who had a place inside. She did not want to be outside in any way. It made her feel detached, not in the conventual sense, but in the sense of "a detached limb." That was what Jane was, most of the time—a detached limb, or a detached *organ*. They carried her with them the way some people carry their appendix with them after an operation, pickled in a jar.

She picked up Merton's *Contemplation in a World of Action* and tried to make herself feel the visceral panic that had fueled her studying in high school. It wouldn't come. She was tired and floaty. The emotional rip of the trip into town had been compounded by the physical tear of exercise to drain her. Marie Bernadette sounded like a narrator on an old *Inner Sanctum* radio tape, but it washed right over her. Marie Bernadette could have sacrificed a goat on Annie's theology notebook without getting her the least bit upset. Or even getting her attention.

"The thing is," Marie Bernadette drawled.

Annie took Stephen's letter and the new Temporary Schedule from the back of her notebook and laid the pages out next to *Lace*. She'd read nearly twenty pages of *Lace* already. It was a wonderful book, exactly what she needed. It relaxed her just to look at it. She imagined herself at Pagan's Swiss boarding school, priming and polishing herself for a life of expensive cars and formal balls. Sometimes she remembered how she'd managed to acquire the book, and that made her feel guilty and uncomfortable, but she squelched it. She'd had enough lectures about "overscrupulousness." An action was a sin only if it was committed with full knowledge and intent. She had had neither. She hadn't even been aware of taking the book. She was sure of it.

If she hadn't committed a sin by taking the book, she didn't have to confess it to Father Duffy. If she didn't have to confess it, he wouldn't be able to tell her to take the book back, she could keep it.

There was something messed-up about that reasoning, but she was too tired to think what it was.

"She didn't die right away," Marie Bernadette said. "Hanging is supposed to break your neck, but it didn't break hers. She *strangled* to death. And while she was strangling to death, she *screamed*."

Annie folded Stephen's letter and the schedule, stuck them into *Lace*, and shoved the whole mess into her pocket. She couldn't stay here listening to Marie Bernadette. Marie Bernadette would give her another nightmare. Or Jane would start up, and *that* would give her a nightmare. As for the book . . .

She was not being overscrupulous. She was not castigating herself for an accident. It was just that Daniella was sitting by the fireplace, reading Saint Francis, and if Daniella saw the book she would ask questions. Once the questions started, the book would become an institutional matter. They would make her explain things four or five times and agonize over the ethical ramifications. Clare Marie had told her to begin making her own "informed moral decisions." She couldn't make her own moral decisions in the middle of a committee meeting, especially a committee meeting of nuns. Clare Marie scolded her for being conscientious to a fault, but as far as Annie could tell, all nuns picked over the moral and religious implications of every problem until the problem itself disappeared in the discussion of it.

"What happened," Marie Bernadette said, "is she had the rope around her throat, so her screaming didn't sound like someone screaming. It sounded like someone drowning."

Annie got out of her chair. She would put the book out of her mind, and go to talk to Kat.

Kat was lying on the grass in the middle of North Lawn, talking to the air. Her copy of *Contemplation in a World of Action* was under her left forearm, open at the center. Annie let herself out the side door and hesitated against the building, listening to Kat lecture the birds on discipline and obedience.

Kat looked better than she had in days. Annie had given her David's letter right after exercise, and whatever was in it must have been good. Kat was relaxed, undistracted, as if she had nothing on her mind but Thomas Merton's ideal monastic community. Was Kat still in love with David? Annie couldn't imagine falling out of love with someone like David Marsh, but she couldn't imagine someone like Kat wanting to be a nun, either. If Annie had had what Kat had—especially money of her own—she'd be in Paris at the Ritz or in London at Annabel's, not in Northton worrying about contemplation and obedience and getting enough sleep before the morning bell rang. Of course, the call of God was supposed to strike rich and poor alike, but—this was where she got tangled—she had an underlying conviction that it shouldn't strike the rich. The rich had other means of escape.

Kat started lecturing the birds on repose of the soul.

Annie stumbled forward over the grass, being careful to kick stones and knock loudly against benches, in case Kat was going to be angry about being disturbed.

Kat looked up when Annie was halfway across the lawn. "Oh, dear," she said. "Do I have something to apologize for?"

"Apologize?" Annie stopped. "Why would you apologize? I'm interrupting you."

"There's always David," Kat said. "He could have barked at you."

Annie thought of David Marsh, tall and smooth and confident in Holland's Office Supplies. How did anyone fall in love with someone like David Marsh? How did you get past the fear? What made you feel worth it? She took a seat on the bench closest to Kat's head. "He didn't bark at me," she said.

"Thank Heaven for small favors."

Annie brushed at her skirt. "I don't want to bother you if you're working," she said. "I mean, it's not anything important. I just wanted to talk . . ."

Kat was already sitting up, closing her book, stretching her arms. "Talk away," she said. "That book didn't make any sense the first time I read it, and it doesn't make any sense now."

"I haven't read it at all," Annie said. She looked across the lawn at the wall of evergreens that separated them from Retreat House. What would it be like to be someone like Kat?

"Were you in love with David Marsh?" she asked.

Kat burst out laughing. Annie felt herself go hot—not at Kat's reaction, that was better than she had any right to expect—but at what she'd said and the fact that she hadn't realized she was going to say it. She had been thinking of Thomas Merton and going to instruction unprepared, and it had just come out.

Kat leaned back on her elbows, grinning. "Is that what you wanted to talk about? If I was in love with David Marsh?"

"No," Annie said. "No. I mean—I didn't mean to pry."

"You wouldn't know how to pry." Kat leaned forward and tugged the hem of Annie's skirt. "And it was a good question. I wish I had an answer to it."

Annie went blank. "You mean you don't know? How can you not know?"

"Annie, I'm twenty-four, not seventeen. The situation gets more complicated as you get older."

"I thought you must have been in love with him and then fallen out of love with him," Annie said, "but that didn't make any sense. So I thought maybe you were still in love with him but you loved God more. But that didn't make any sense, either."

"You mean it didn't make any sense for me not to be in love with David Marsh?"

"Am I making a fool of myself? Do I sound like a complete idiot?"

149

"No," Kat said. "You just sound like you're getting a crush on David Marsh."

"I'm not getting a crush on David Marsh. I couldn't. He makes me nervous."

"You mean he scares you to death."

"Maybe."

"He's a nice man, Annie. He might even be a good one, and that's much rarer."

"I don't know," Annie said. "I don't know a lot about this stuff. As far back as I can remember, all I've ever wanted was to be a nun." She grinned. "Or to wake up one morning impossibly rich."

"Impossibly?" Kat laughed.

Annie looked back at the tree wall and shook her head. "It gets so confusing," she said. "Sometimes I feel like I'm in one of those snowballs. You know, where you shake it and it snows on a little plastic village. I'm in there looking out, and I can only see parts of things. You and David Marsh. Being a nun when being a nun doesn't seem to mean anything anymore. Even Catholics think you're crazy for doing it, and they don't support the Orders or the missions. And then being here. Everybody here is so different. Different from me. Different from what I expected."

Annie felt a tug again, Kat's hand back on the hem of her dress.

"Hey," Kat said, "are you all right? Annie?"

"I'm all right," Annie said. "I don't know why I brought all this up. I mean, it wasn't what I was thinking of. I wasn't even feeling particularly..."

"Disoriented?"

"That's it. Disoriented. Only sometimes it's like that about *everything*. And then I start to wonder if I know anything at all. If anything anybody ever taught me was true."

"Annie," Kat said gently, "it's all right. It happens to people all the time, when they start something new, something they're not familiar with."

Annie stared out at the wall of trees. Her headache was a mad doctor's hypodermic, coming in at the base of her skull. This was all she needed. Now she'd have to sit through instruction with a headache. Things were jumbled up enough, what with David and the book and Stephen and not having

150

understood the assignment. Now she'd be a complete basket case. When the headaches got really bad, she could hardly talk.

She felt another tug at her hem and looked down. The headaches always did something to her eyesight. Kat looked ripply.

"Are you sure you're all right?" Kat said.

"Fine," Annie said. "Just getting a headache."

"That's the bell for instruction. I'll walk you upstairs. We'll stop and get you an aspirin on the way."

Annie almost told Kat that aspirin had as much effect on her headaches as sugar pills had on malignant melanomas, but it was too many words. She said, "I left my things in the reception room."

"Go get them," Kat said. "I'll meet you in the ante-room."

It seemed wrong, somehow, to let Kat help her when she couldn't be helped. That was too many words, too. Kat was striding across North Lawn, leading the way inside. Annie followed her slowly, wishing she knew what caused the head-aches, what she could do to stop them. They came at her out of nowhere, ruining everything.

3

Standing alone near the door to North Wing, watching the others make their way upstairs, Annie could feel her headache receding. Jane Galloway disappeared into the staircase in a clutch of the more pious postulants and nov-ices. Annie's pain dissolved into fragments, diffuse. Instead of a needle, it became the low, dull throb most people meant when they said "headache." When Kat dropped the aspirin into her hand, she took them.

"I got you a present," Kat said, pushing something into her hand and pulling her into the stairwell at the same time. They were late. They would have to run to make it to the instruction before the second bell.

Annie looked at what Kat had given her. It was a photo-graph of a boy nine or ten years old, dressed in gray slacks and white shirt and navy blue blazer, looking uncomfortable in front of a latticework gazebo in a rose garden.

151

"It's David," Kat said. "Wasn't he an obnoxious little boy?"

"Obnoxious?" Annie frowned at the picture. "He looks perfect."

"That's what I mean," Kat said. "Obnoxious."

Annie put the picture in her pocket, working it under the cover of *Lace* so it wouldn't get bent. She wondered where it had been taken. Had there been a gazebo and rose garden at David's parents' house? How much would it cost to buy enough property—to own enough property—to have a gazebo and rose garden?

"Every time he starts getting to you," Kat said, "you look at that picture and remind yourself he's human. He was a child. He'll be an old man someday."

"But he won't get to me," Annie said. "I'll probably never see him again."

Kat gave her a funny look. "Of course you'll see him again. He'll visit you when he visits me, if we can talk him into coming to Visiting Sunday. He told me he liked you."

They had reached the third-floor landing. The stairs had begun to narrow and wind. Annie let Kat go ahead. What had David meant when he told Kat he "liked" her? Not what it sounded like he meant, surely.

Kat had given her the photograph to be kind, because she thought David had upset Annie, nothing more. Annie didn't care about David Marsh. She had never cared about boys, and she didn't expect to care about men. It was one of the ways she'd known she ought to be a nun.

The rose garden and gazebo were something else, like the book, or one of Stephen's better letters. She could imagine herself at the gazebo's edge, looking out over the people at a garden party where all the women wore broad hats and silver tea services were rolled across the lawn on silver serving carts.

She had not taken the book on purpose. She had *not*.

152

WAITING

It started to get dark a little after five. At five-thirty, someone in the manager's office at the Northton Superior Wayside Inn and Home Food Diner flipped the switch that turned on the neon sign planted halfway into Route 8, setting off a hurricane of technicolor Day Glo. David Marsh stood at the window of Cabin No. 4 and wondered what the sign was about. It was the great granddaddy of neon signs, the neon sign to end neon signs. The main body blinked off and on forty-six times a minute. The arch (rainbow?) laddered and darkened, laddered and darkened, laddered and darkened, in a machine-gun staccato of aggressive gold arrows. There were two cars in the Home Food parking lot (one for the cook, one for the waitress, he supposed) and three at the Wayside Inn. The manager's was a rattletrap '64 Buick that looked like a reproach. His own green bug sat next to a shiny sky-blue Toyota that had to belong to the people he thought of as "the strange man and his wife." There was no traffic on Route 8.

He put his half-finished bottle of Heineken Dark on the windowsill and wandered back to the disintegrating Danish-modern armchair. When he first decided to get a motel room, he thought he'd look for a Holiday Inn, or, better yet, something local and quaint. Surely Northton, with that great Motherhouse on the hill and all those visiting parents, would have something local and quaint. Not so. Northton had the Superior Wayside Inn and Home Food Diner. He wondered how it managed to stay in business. He wondered about the strange man and his wife—the man in two hundred dollars' worth of Brooks Brothers tweed blazer and ten ninety-five Alexander's polyester slacks, the wife looking like a bedraggled porno queen with all her Frederick's of Hollywood underwear deflated. He had rather liked the wife.

There were three unopened bottles of Heineken on the

153

night table. He pushed them away. He now had less than five hours before he could start for Agnus Dei, less than five hours to keep his act together. Keeping his act together had taken on mystical significance. His sex fantasies had begun to get competition from fantasies of another kind. He was being haunted by Kat-as-he-had-known-her, Kat in Malapur, Kat sitting on the step outside the unheated villa they had rented for fifty dollars a month in Rhodes. If he could banish the Kat of the sexual nightmares to the limbo where she belonged, everything would be all right.

He took his mail from the night table. He had put Mary's letter at the bottom of the stack. If it was anything like the last two, he didn't want to read it.

He couldn't sit alone long, in silence, without thinking of what he didn't want to think about. Kat in the Aegean Sea, coming out of the waves with the water falling in sheets across her naked shoulders, her naked breasts, into the discreet hollow and swell of her waist and hips. God, that had been a night. She had come out of the water, walked across the sand, sat down beside him, lit a cigarette. She had put her free hand under his trunks and stroked him, laughing.

"I thought I'd appraise you of my progress," Mary wrote. "Maybe this will shame you into some action. Maybe it will make you *realize*."

If he started thinking of Kat on Rhodes, the memory would become the dream, and the dream would be as full of anger and violence as all his dreams were lately. David-and-Kat would disintegrate into David Triumphant, and David Triumphant would be on a rampage. David Triumphant would bring down the Catholic Church and all its fanaticism, destroy it before it could eat another young woman alive.

"I talked to another lawyer," Mary wrote. "I went up to see her and they wouldn't let me. They kept telling me Sunday was the only day. I thought I could get them on *habeas corpus*. The lawyer looked into it, I'll give him that much. He really looked into it. All I got was advice from a judge (it didn't go to court, the lawyer knew a judge) to go up Sunday like everyone else. Tell me how that's going to help. Tell me how it's going to help to follow the rules and look like I'm accepting this thing. Tell me how it's going to help to cooperate with those dyke bitches."

He put her letter back on the night table, face down. In another page, she'd start railing about involuntary servitude, white slavery, things that had nothing to do with anything. Maybe she'd start talking about the hit man again. For Kat or the Reverend Mother, he wasn't sure which. Maybe she wasn't, either.

Her letters always smelled of rye whiskey.

He got out of the chair, found his fisherman's sweater, pulled it on.

He locked his door in the intermittent glare from the neon sign and started across the parking lot. What would Mary say if she could see him here, holed up in a motel filthier than anything he had to put up with in Asia, on his way to see Kat? She'd probably ask if he'd remembered to bring a rubber.

He had remembered to bring a rubber.

He was standing in the Home Food Diner vestibule, looking down at the empty newspaper rack, when the strange man came in from the parking lot. He was trying to pick apart the morality and the practicality the way a hair-dresser works through a tangle—if she asked, he'd tell her he had it; if she insisted, he'd use it; if she said nothing, he wouldn't use it and hope to God she got pregnant.

Getting Kat pregnant was a plan Mary would appreciate. Worse, Mary would applaud.

Behind him, the strange man said, "Sometime, someday, we're going to see Annie."

The strange man's wife said, "Fuck that."

David felt himself drowning in fear: fear that Kat wouldn't come; fear that she would come but not let him touch her.

He turned to the strange man and his wife and said, "I know someone named Annie. Annie Bliss."

155

FORGIVENESS

1

Annie stopped just inside the reception-room door and raised her eyes slowly, a practice of humility. Her happiness was a bubble threatening to make its way to air and burst. Even Jane's pious statue kissing (Jane always kissed the feet of the statue of the Queen of Heaven when she came through the reception-room door) couldn't depress her. The evening had been a dream. It was as if God had given her a sneak preview of what she would be like when she was trained, when she was perfect. Ever since she had stepped into chapel at six o'clock, she had done everything right.

She had bobbed and weaved through Vespers without a hitch. She had remembered the distinction between proper and improper religious authority in instruction. She had read the passage from Luke in spiritual discussion in a high, clear, unhurried voice that had made Clare Marie smile and nod in congratulation. She had come to her feet as soon as the bell rang, moving with automatic and accepting obedience. Annie loved doing things right. She loved doing things right and being recognized for it even more. It even made up for the fact that she had been taken out of her place in line and chapel (for no reason that had ever been explained to her) and paired with Jane.

Annie made her way across the room, thinking it was unlikely that Jane would be telling ghost stories with Reverend Mother in attendance.

"Ah," Reverend Mother said, when Annie stopped to pay her respects. "Annie Bliss. What about you? Who do you want to be after Christmas?"

"Excuse me?" Annie said.

"Names," Martha said, frowning at her knitting. "That's what we've been talking about. Day after Epiphany, we take names." She gave Jane a swift, sour look and began to unravel a row.

Annie got wool and knitting needles from the box (why

156

was it every time you got into a good mood around this place, something happened to ruin it?) and said, "Sister Mary Stephen. I have a brother named Stephen. And my father was named Stephen and he died."

"I don't see why not," Reverend Mother said. "We try to give you what you ask for. We don't want you laboring in the vineyards for forty years with a name you hate."

"You mean Polycarp *asked* for that?" Miriam said.

Jane Galloway sniffed. I don't think you're getting the point," she said. She looked significantly at Reverend Mother. "We're supposed to dedicate ourselves to a saint, not commemorate our families. Or Heaven knows who else. Polycarp was a wonderful saint."

"All right," Miriam said. "Take Aloysius." Her voice was dry and hard, but not as dry and hard as it would have been if Reverend Mother had not been there to hear. "Assuming he's still a saint."

"I want to take Euphemia," Jane said. She grinned at Miriam with pitying condescension. "She was a virgin martyr, you know. She was thrown to wild beasts because she wouldn't renounce her virginity. Not like a lot of nuns you hear about today. Getting married. Having affairs with the parish priest."

Annie looked up at Reverend Mother. The huge woman was staring at Jane, her eyes deep and suddenly fathomless. She turned, found Clare Marie, hesitated. Annie could almost see the internal debate, like a Ping-Pong match, going on behind Reverend Mother's eyes. Reverend Mother came to some kind of decision and turned back to Jane.

"You know," she said, "we do promise to forsake family for Christ, and it's a very important part—"

"Oh, no," Martha said, rising from the floor in a single, swift motion. "Oh, dear merciful God."

"What is it?" Annie jumped up. She wasn't fast enough. Others had jumped up around her. She was blocked by a wall of bodies, all staring in the same direction. Annie felt her stomach cramp. The look on Martha's face had been the announcement of disaster.

"What is it?" she said again. She could hear the beginning of panic in her voice. Everyone around her was suddenly tight, watchful, edgy. She wished she could see through the

157

crowd. She felt like a prehistoric bug in amber, trapped in this thick air of emergency.

That was the trouble with Agnus Dei, she thought. You could be going along fine, you could get everything under control, and then it would hit you. She felt the headache coming up. She put her face in her hands, willing it to stop. She had been fine. She had been *fine*. Now what?

Kat came up behind her, stroking her shoulder, soothing. "It's just Marie Bernadette," she said.

Martha shifted. Constance turned away. Annie could see through to the far side of the room. To Marie Bernadette, collapsed on the floor.

To Angela Louise, arms rising, hands fluttering, blunt, squarecut fingernails scratching at the air in the direction of Daniella. Angela Louise was protecting Marie Bernadette from them. She was keeping Marie Bernadette safe, insulated, unchanged. Annie didn't know which was the worse shock: Marie Bernadette on the floor, a blue tinge in her cheeks; or Angela Louise, the perfect novice, transformed into something—not someone—else.

Her headache was like heavy surf, pounding and inescapable. There was nothing she could trust in the place. Nothing she could hold on to.

Angela Louise was close to tears. Her voice wavered. "I can take care of her," she said. "I've done it before. I can take care of her."

"She needs a hospital to take care of her," Daniella said. "Angela, in the name of—"

"She's just fainted," Angela Louise said. "Sometimes she faints."

"Angela."

Annie felt herself moved aside. Kat was breaking free, making a way for herself in the crowd. Annie watched Angela Louise, the angry, trapped face, the tense arms and shoulders, the hands twitching, ready to strike. Marie Bernadette was a doorstop, curled forgotten on the floor. Angela Louise circled her, marking territory.

"We promised each other," Angela Louise said to Daniella. "You and Lucy and I. We *promised* each other."

Kat stepped out of the crowd, slipping into Angela

158

Louise's magic circle. Angela Louise looked at Kat and then at her hands.

"I can't let it go," Angela Louise said.

"You have to let it go," Kat said.

They looked at Marie Bernadette. Annie looked too, trying to make it real.

Marie Bernadette was like a bad statue, too thin and limp and formless to be convincing. She didn't seem to be breathing. She didn't seem to be made of anything that could ever have breathed.

Angela Louise stepped away from her. "We promised each other," she said again.

"She didn't promise us," Daniella said.

Kat moved closer. Marie Bernadette was laid out in tribute like one of the mice Martha's cat brought home. Annie wished her headache would go away, wished Marie Bernadette would sit up and laugh and put a stop to this craziness.

Kat held out her hands. Angela Louise turned away from her, from Marie Bernadette, from the rest of them. When Clare Marie started to come forward, Angela swung around and glared.

They left Marie Bernadette on the floor until Angela Louise was gone.

2

"It's not just our problem, you know," Reverend Mother said. "It's a problem with the whole Church. And it was a problem before renewal, though nobody likes to think about that."

Kat kept herself still on her chair. She did not want to be in Reverend Mother's office, but she was, and she was just going to have to survive it. Reverend Mother looked edgy and depressed. Kat didn't blame her. Marie Bernadette was stretched out in the anteroom, still unconscious.

David was probably pacing Main Street in Northton, anxious to get started.

Kat put her right hand in her pocket and ran her finger along the gutted paper tube of her prize. She'd found it behind the cushions of the couch, when she first sat down at recreation. She'd put her hands behind her, stretching, and there it had been. She wondered what anxious father or brother or mother or aunt had dropped it there. She wondered what she was going to do with it. It was a Benson and Hedges regular, longer and stronger than the Merits she used to smoke. If she sneaked into the bathroom after lights out and smoked it, she would be in an agony of nicotine fits for days after. If she had any sense, she'd get rid of it first chance she got. She didn't think she had any sense. What she needed, with Angela Louise in tears and Marie Bernadette passed out in the anteroom, was half a pack and a few good belts. She couldn't even feel guilty about it. One look at Christopher and she knew the old woman could have stood a few good belts herself.

Angela Louise came in, looking pale and drawn and shaken. "I gave Annie Bliss a shot of brandy," she said. "She looked ready for hysterics."

"Annie Bliss." Reverend Mother sighed. "She's high-strung, our Annie."

"Reverend Mother," Kat and Angela Louise started together. They looked at each other and shrugged.

"Reverend Mother," Angela Louise said again. "Sister Mary Peter called the paramedics. She says Marie Bernadette has a . . . I don't know. Something wrong with her kidneys."

"Acute kidney malfunction," Reverend Mother said. "You think we haven't been here before? We've been here before. Has she been vomiting?"

"Vomiting?" Angela Louise said.

"After meals," Reverend Mother said. "That's the usual. We can make them eat, but then they vomit."

Kat felt herself swimming through Jell-O, battling fog. "Reverend Mother," she said. "I think they're worried Marie Bernadette is going to die."

"She won't die," Reverend Mother said.

"But kidney failure," Kat insisted.

"Kidney malfunction," Reverend Mother corrected.

Kat subsided into her seat, wishing she'd asked for a glass of brandy for herself. Angela Louise stood near the door, on the edge of some further explosion.

"You young people don't realize it," Reverend Mother said. "This Order has survived for over a thousand years. It

160

seems eternal to you. Sometimes I sit in this chair and wonder if we'll survive the decade, never mind the century."

"All I want," Angela Louise said, "is for you to do what's right for Marie Bernadette."

"At the moment," Reverend Mother said, "what's right for the Order is right for Marie Bernadette."

Angela Louise closed her eyes. "You're going to send her home," she said.

"I'm going to send you downstairs to see her," Reverend Mother said.

"Giving us a proper good-bye?" Angela Louise said.

Reverend Mother turned to look at Kat. Kat sat up sharply. She was, she knew, being cast as the rational one. She had talked Angela Louise into letting the rest of them help with Marie Bernadette.

Reverend Mother ran her hand over the beads hanging from her belt. "You should go down and stay with her," she said to Angela Louise. "And Katherine Mary should go see to Annie Bliss. I'm not sure that was the right thing to do, leaving Annie with Mary Peter and Marie Bernadette."

"Better than leaving Annie with the rest of the postulant class," Kat said. "Who knows what they're talking about down there."

"Perhaps." Reverend Mother turned to Angela Louise. "Don't confuse yourself, Sister. Don't think the good of the Sisters is unconnected to the good of the Order. The good of the Order *is* the good of the Sisters."

Angela Louise turned her back and walked stiffly to the door.

3

They had to go down the stairs and back across the reception room to get to the anteroom. The stairs were shallow and winding, difficult to descend in the dim light. Kat followed Angela Louise at four paces, regulation when they processed into chapel, prudent now because she didn't want to disturb Angela Louise's anger or the healing of that anger.

There was a painting of Saint Agnes holding a lamb at the bottom of the South Wing steps. Someone had lit a votive candle at its feet. Angela Louise stopped to dip her fingers in the holy water and sign herself, eyes closed, lips moving. Then she swayed, grabbed the edge of the table, and bent over at the waist.

"I'll be all right," she said. "Just give me a minute and I'll be all right."

Kat sat on the last step, drawing her knees to her chest, wrapping her arms around them. "Angela," she said.

Angela Louise looked up. Her eyes were very red. the tears were coming down her face, a slick, soft screen obliterating the acne scars on her cheeks. "It's not as straightforward as it seems to you."

"Angela, if she wants to leave—"

"Marie Bernadette does not want to leave." Angela Louise rubbed the tears from her eyes, her cheeks, her lips. She looked up into the dark of the stairwell and shivered. "The good of the Order," she said. "The good of the *Order*."

Kat reached into her pocket for the cigarette. Then she remembered the promise she had made to herself, and the crazy agony of going cold turkey. She started to put it back.

"Can I have that?" Angela Louise took the cigarette from her. She lit it with the matches kept on the shelf under Saint Agnes's votive candle. "It's been nearly three years," she said. "They make you dizzy."

"I kept telling myself I was going to throw it out," Kat said.

"You don't want to do anything wrong," Angela Louise laughed faintly. "I didn't either. I haven't, most of the time I've been here. I kept telling myself I was going to be a good nun. I was going to keep all the rules. And I did."

"Except for shielding Marie Bernadette."

"There's nothing against the rules in that." Angela Louise held the cigarette like a joint. "Do you know what's going to happen after they send her home? She might not survive, mentally or physically."

"At the moment," Kat said, "she's barely surviving physically."

"At the moment, she's going through a very bad time. The adjustment isn't easy, you know. It hasn't been easy for me and it won't be easy for you. Or for Martha or Miriam or your precious Annie Bliss."

"Those are sirens," Kat said. They both stopped to listen.

162

"People should never be asked to leave before they're ready to go," Angela Louise said.

Kat started to move toward the door of the reception room. "Come on. First see Marie Bernadette. Then Compline."

"It will kill her to be outside," Angela Louise said. She looked at the picture of Saint Agnes with the lamb, sobs catching in her throat, chest heaving. Kat wanted to get her moving.

Angela Louise straightened by herself, looked at the still-glowing tip of her cigarette, and plunged it into the holy water.

"To hell with them," she said.

4

"I think she committed a sin," Jane said. "A really awful sin. An unforgivable sin. She didn't confess it because she was afraid to face the priest. And she stayed here anyway, trying to be a nun. And God got her, finally."

"Maybe she was trying to commit suicide," Miriam said, sounding tired. "That's what you said before. She knew she couldn't be a perfect nun, so she tried to kill herself by starving herself to death."

Jane sniffed. "That's what *she* said. Marie Bernardette. I never said that. I think the girl in the tower was just like Marie Bernadette. She committed a terrible sin and was too ashamed to confess it and so she killed herself. And that was a sin, too, so God made her death really horrible. God made her death a judgment."

Annie leaned backward until her neck was touching the wall and closed her eyes. Jane and Miriam were right outside the door. Sister Mary Peter had heard sirens and gone to the foyer to wait for the paramedics. Annie had been left alone with Marie Bernadette, to watch. She wished she had more of that brandy Angela Louise had given her. Another half glass and she would fall asleep.

She opened her eyes and made herself stand away from the wall. She didn't want to think about her father. Clare Marie was always telling her to work at being happy. If that meant she should try not to think about what happened to her father, she would be glad to oblige. She only wished she could make such a ferociously determined effort to be happy that she would blot out the sight of Marie Bernadette's body on the couch.

Breaths that were so difficult to draw ought to make some sound.

"You can smell it on them when they die," Jane said. "The sin smells like bad food left in the heat. It comes off them in waves."

Marie Bernadette was turning a soft blue, like the aura of a blue fox coat.

Annie snatched the chair from the side of the couch and dragged it into the corner farthest from the North Wing door. She took out her copy of *Lace*. She was near the door Mary Peter would use to bring the paramedics. She would be able to hear them coming. She put the book on her knees and opened it carefully to page fifty-one. Judy was hanging from the side of a cliff, screaming for rescue. Pagan and Kate and the French girl were trying to save her. Everything in *Lace* was exciting, without being important. People worried about their careers, but not their souls. People worried about their boyfriends, but not if they could pay the rent. Rich people's problems were not only more interesting than poor people's problems, they were less urgent.

"You've got to be careful," Jane said, in a mock-sepulchral voice. "Sin haunts the living and the dead."

JOURNEY'S END

1

Halfway between the main building and Retreat House, it hit her—here she was, skulking through the trees like Dracula's henchman making safe the way to Lucy Westenra's bedroom, keeping an assignation with a man who had been her lover for over two years, thinking of Sister Mary Ligouri. She almost came to a halt for a little self-analysis. David was waiting, Marie Bernadette was in the hospital, Angela

164

Louise was going crazy, Annie looked like she'd been run over by a truck, but she was zigzagging through the pines thinking about an old woman she'd spoken to exactly once.

North Tower rose out of the trees, looking separate. Kat walked backward, staring at it, wondering why it always made her so uneasy. The lights in the windows were an illusion, moonlight streaming from one wall of open archways to the other. She turned away and headed toward Retreat House, where the path was hidden behind decorative shrubbery beside the rectory door.

They had gone to Kathmandu because she wanted to say she'd been in Kathmandu. There were other places in the same category—Baghdad, Kabul, Khartoum—but most of them had been taken over by communist insurgents or Moslem fanatics. She'd had to satisfy herself with Kathmandu, and she'd put David to a lot of trouble getting her there. Then she'd looked out the window of their stifling British, frighteningly expensive hotel room and nearly cried.

"I said I'd get you to Kathmandu," David said. "I didn't say I'd make Kathmandu look like you wanted it to look."

What Kathmandu looked like was a primitive joke of a suburban subdivision. Houses and barns spread out from the city in every direction, neat little rectangles of private space.

She left David on the terrace of their hotel, surrounded by waiters and busboys and the ritual implements of tea, and went for walks. She walked from one end of the city to the other, buying cheap felt backpack patches and rope cigarette lighters from every boy who approached her. The boys laughed when she gave them money. She was making a fool of herself.

The day she found Saint Dominic's, she was looking for a bakery shop that sold samosas. She went down a twisted street, through a courtyard, around a corner, and suddenly she was in open country, looking across a long, dry field at a collection of huts with a wooden cross over each one. She thought she'd stumbled into an eccentric graveyard.

The two nuns came out of one of the huts while she was still standing at the edge of their land. At the time, she

165

thought only one of them was a nun. The other was in lay clothes. The one she knew to be a nun was in full Dominican habit, complete with flat headdress and ground-draping white robes. They saw her standing there and waved, nodding to each other.

She made her way across the stony field, wondering where they had come from, what language they spoke, what they were doing here. When she was less than a yard away, the one in habit said,

"If you come any closer, Sister's going to eat you for breakfast."

"She might be a Lutheran," the one in lay clothes said. "I wouldn't bother her if she were a Lutheran."

"Sister has her prejudices," the one in habit said. She bobbed her head, remembering a courtesy. "I'm Sister Mary Ligouri. The radical nun here is Sister Joanna Reilly. *Are* you a Lutheran?"

"I'm a Catholic," Kat said. "But—"

"Just give Sister five dollars," Sister Mary Ligouri said. "You're doomed anyway, might as well get it over with."

"Five dollars."

"We run a clinic here," Sister Mary Ligouri said. "And a school, for that matter. That's what makes it so difficult, you see. You can't skimp on a clinic. We can only skimp on ourselves. We've got a student who wants to go to America and join our Order, but we have to find a way to get her there."

"And you need five dollars." Kat felt like someone who'd come in late to a movie.

"No, no," Sister Mary Ligouri said. "We need fifty dollars. More than we have. We promised the Motherhouse we'd come up with the fare. We can get twenty by minor fasts in the next two weeks, but we have to have her on a plane by the nineteenth. Otherwise she won't be in time."

"If she doesn't persevere, the Motherhouse will come up with the fare back," Sister Joanna Reilly said. "The way things are, that's very fair."

"I'm sure it is," Kat said faintly.

"It would be easier if there were a lot of Catholics here," Sister Ligouri said. "English Catholics. But the English community is mostly Anglican anti-Papist. So."

Kat had a sudden vision of the Port Authority. You could collect fifty dollars in three hours panhandling in the Port Authority, no worthy cause necessary. You could probably collect a hundred wearing a nun's habit.

"It's all right if you don't have any money," Sister Joanna Reilly said. "Most of the hikers who come by don't. They use all their money getting to Nepal."

"I'm not a hiker," Kat said. She was painfully ashamed of herself. She must have spent a hundred dollars on rope cigarette lighters alone. Never mind what the hotel room cost, or the room service, or the English liquor she and David drank when they spent an evening in the bar. She stuffed her hands into her pockets and came up with cash—Nepalese cash, Hong Kong dollars, French francs left over from her trip out. At the deepest reach she found three American twenties, matted and sweaty and pressed into a cube.

"Here," she said. "I don't know how much that is, but don't skip lunch. In this cold."

Sister Joanna Reilly looked delighted. Sister Mary Ligouri looked concerned.

"You can't be left in this country without money," she said. "You have to keep some back for yourself."

"I've got enough traveler's checks to choke a horse," Kat said. "I've got three credit cards. I don't think I'll starve."

The old nun hesitated so long, Kat thought she was going to insist on seeing proof of solvency. Then she nodded slowly and turned toward the hut she'd come out of.

"Come this way. If you've got all that, you ought to have a receipt for your taxes."

Inside, the hut was cool and dark. The floor was dirt, but well packed, without ruts or weeds. It looked freshly brushed. Sister Mary Ligouri went to the small table near the only window in the main room and sat behind it, thumbing through papers in a square metal box.

"Can you help me? I don't know where Sister's gone. I can't read the receipt, you see."

"Do you need more light?"

"I need a new pair of eyes. I wouldn't be able to get around this room if I didn't know it so well. Didn't you realize I was blind?"

"No," Kat said. "You don't look blind. Your eyes—"

"I am going blind very late in life. In the last two or three years, I suppose, though it must have started sooner. It's not that much of a problem, you know."

There was a seat on the far side of the table. Kat took it, moving carefully, feeling horrified and not wanting it to show. She took the receipt book and the pile of bills and started counting.

"I thought you said you run a clinic here. And a school," Kat said.

"*We* run a clinic here," Mary Ligouri said. "*I* don't run anything."

"But how can you teach, or nurse, or whatever? And isn't it bad for you, going without food and the climate and God-knows-what-else out here?" The horrified feeling was coming through. She couldn't stop it. "Isn't it—"

"My blindness is hereditary. It wouldn't have mattered where I was. As for the rest—" Ligouri shrugged, taking the receipt from Kat's hand. "In another few months, I won't be able to do the work here, even the teaching. So I'll go to Calcutta and learn to teach Braille. Being blind will be a great advantage in teaching Braille." She smiled.

Kat smiled back, wondering if Mary Ligouri could see the smile, wondering what planet this frail old woman had been born on.

Two years later, David waited in the trees, not on a hotel terrace. She still wouldn't be able to explain it to him.

She turned into the path beside Retreat House and hurried into the pine woods beyond, thinking there was no need for caution anymore. She couldn't be seen this far from the main building. She just wished she'd remembered to take off her white veil.

Ten feet into the woods, the path disappeared, becoming an obstacle course of ruts and tree roots and sharp fallen branches. She should have remembered to bring a flashlight. She should have remembered to bring stones to mark her way.

She felt like Gretel, lost in the woods on the way to the gingerbread house.

He had brought, not a flashlight, but candles. Kat saw their wavering flames while she was still caught in the flora fifteen feet away. The candles were white and tall and dripless, stuck into brass-colored tin holders and set at the corners of the rug he'd stretched across the ground. Kat ached for him. He hated dripless candles, hated makeshift replicas of what he called "real things." Silver candlesticks were "real things." She stood silently in the darkness, watching him put out plastic wineglasses and mass-produced French bread and fake-crockery tubs of cheese spread and pâté. All those years on lacrosse fields and handball courts showed. His body was hard and well formed and promising. He looked good in clothes. He would look better out of them.

She took a stone from the ground and pitched it, without much force, in his direction. He jerked up, his eyes straining at the trees. Kat was surprised. She hadn't expected him to be so wired, so nervous. The David she remembered was never wired, or nervous, or out of control.

"It's me," she said. "I didn't want to just burst in on you."

"Where are you?"

"Right in front of you." She moved slowly toward him, her feet catching on the carpet of damp, moldering pine needles. Her foot brushed against a pinecone. She kicked it away. "I never came this way in the dark," she said. "The path didn't do what it was supposed to do."

"I thought I'd be caught," David said. "Jesus Christ."

He stood up. Kat hesitated. For some reason, she didn't want to get too close to him while standing. Her skin felt like energized sandpaper.

"Kat?" he said. "Kat?"

He sounded frightened. Kat laughed, shaky. "Sit down," she said. "David, please sit down." She fought her way through the last of the debris until she was standing at the edge of the rug. David sat in the center, surrounded by his low-rent picnic. She sat down next to one of the candles in the corner.

"I'm sorry," she said. "I know I'm being bizarre. I don't seem to be able to help it."

"That's all right." He reached into the Styrofoam ice chest and pulled out a bottle. "Beaujolais," he said. "I got you three bottles of Beaujolais."

"Good. I think I need to be drunk."

"I've been sitting here going nuts, thinking you'd been caught. Thinking I was going to get caught. Every tree in this place is the ghost of a nun." He poured Beaujolais into a stemmed plastic glass. He handed it to her and poured another for himself. "Do they lock you up? Is that what took you so long?"

"No." She was beginning to feel easier. This was David. He would never jump her, or force her, or rush her. "There was some trouble. One of the novices got sick and had to be taken to the hospital."

"To the *hospital*?"

Kat smiled faintly. From the sound of David's voice, you'd have thought she'd said "to the rack." "Why are we talking about Marie Bernadette?"

"I don't know," David said.

There was a pack of cigarettes lying on the rug at David's feet. They beckoned to her, the way he beckoned to her. She could feel the smoke inside her and his hands on her breasts. The tension was a wall. The wall had spikes, shards of broken glass, that were the traces of what they had always felt for each other. She took a long swallow of wine and put the glass down in front of her. It tipped precariously, subverted by the unevenness of the ground beneath the rug.

"I can hardly think," David said. "I haven't been able to think in weeks. Or sleep." He made a fumbling production of lighting a Camel and looked into her face, his eyes hot and dark and miserable. "I've always tried to be a good person, Kat. I really have. I've always tried to treat women the way I'd want to be treated myself. I've always tried to respect your decisions. But, Kat, I just can't right now."

"I miss you too," Kat said.

"It's not a question of missing you."

"What is it?"

He dropped his eyes. "Your mother came to see me," he said. "And she writes. She wanted me to kidnap you."

170

"Are you going to?"

"Do you want me to?"

"No," Kat said. "Not yet. If I did, I'd be smoking."

"There it is," David said. "Not *yet*." He refilled his wine-glass. "I sit around the house and think about us. Before. In Hong Kong that time. In Rhodes. The time we bought the sweater. And that all seems so real to me, Kat. That's the problem. That all seems so real to me, and this doesn't."

"David, women become nuns. Men become priests and monks. Sometimes relationships don't work out and people don't marry. Or don't make it together. There's nothing unreal about this."

"Yes there is," David said. "Yes there is, Kat. Because things didn't go wrong. We didn't fall out of love with each other. I keep coming back to the day you went in, and that's what I can't get rid of. You didn't stop wanting me."

Kat looked into her wine. A few flakes of ash had collected on the surface and were beginning to drown. "Yes, I did, David. I did stop wanting you."

"Bullshit," David said.

Somewhere in the dark, the chapel bells rang eleven. Kat ran her tongue over her lips. They were dry, hot, chapped. The rest of her was cold. They'd be changing to winter habits soon, and after that would be the naming. All their steps were measured, timed, ritualized. With David, things were not so orderly. With David, hesitation was sin.

The first time they'd made love, he'd been careful with her. Every time after that had been an explosion. He waited, knowing she did not need it as much as he did, until the waiting became painful. When he came for her, he was magnified. The skin on the inside of his thighs and on his testicles was dry and scratchy. When they were finished, she dried the sweat and rubbed powder there. Had he brought powder with him, brought protection, come equipped the way some toys came with batteries? She wanted to run the flat of her hand down the side of his face and under his shirt. She wanted to feel the skin of his thighs and his testicles and wipe away the dryness.

She crossed her arms over her knees and put her head down. She felt as if someone had wrapped a tourniquet

171

around her throat. Her head was throbbing the way her arm throbbed when she had her blood pressure taken.

"I can't do this now," she said. "I can't even think about this now."

"I can't think about anything else."

"What do you want from me?"

His silence went on so long, she looked up. She looked up even though she was thinking of William and Angela Louise and Marie Bernadette, of generation after generation of nuns in community. The long gray-and-white-and-black line went on forever. At the end of it was the thing that had started long before she went to Asia, long before she met David or Sister Mary Ligouri. The thing (God is a place) that made what happened to her at San Sulpice possible, that had brought her finally to Agnus Dei.

He was taking her glass and pouring wine into it, measuring it so that it came exactly one half inch from the rim.

"You always had such a thing about the right way to fill glasses," she said.

"I want you to come back," he said, giving her the glass. "Here. I want you to come back and talk to me here."

"I haven't left yet."

"You will. We'll have some more wine and you'll tell me funny stories about the convent and then you'll leave. And I'll let you go. But I want you to come back."

She thought: I shouldn't do this. I shouldn't promise this. If I promise this, I'll do it.

If she wanted him now, she'd only want him more the next time. And more the time after that.

She would only want Agnus Dei more, day after day. She knew she should tell him to come Visiting Sunday. She knew he wouldn't do it.

"All right," she said. "I'll finish this wine and I'll tell you about buffing wood floors. And then I'll come back."

"Next week," he said, "Same time, same place."

"Yes."

He took one of her hands and laced her fingers through his, playing with the skin of her palm and the pad of her thumb. It was nothing he hadn't done a hundred times. She had never attached any significance to it. I ought to take my hand away, she thought, the way he took his away that time

172

in the reception room. She held on to him instead, not wanting to let him go. She had always loved the feel of men's hands. She had loved David's hands most of all.

There was a sound in the woods. He pulled away from her, tensing. They sat listening to a silence broken only by leaves.

"Sorry," he said. "I'm a little edgy."

Kat laughed. It sounded false. "Guilt," she said. "Guilt always makes you edgy."

David lit another cigarette. "We don't have anything to be guilty for. Yet."

TRANQUILIZER

When the lights went out, Annie was in the last stall near the window in the lavatory, reading about Maxine falling in love with the heir to a vineyard and finally marrying the château. She'd begun to be upset about what had happened to Marie Bernadette. She'd thought about it all through Compline, all through Particular Examen of Conscience. She had begun to think Jane's voice was in her head instead of in her memory, that nattering voice going on and on about unconfessed sin and God "getting" you and the will to hell. She was grateful for Grand Silence. Postulants moved through the lavatory noiselessly, giving her the peace she needed to lose herself in Maxine's château and Judy's poor days in Paris. Clare Marie would undoubtedly have preferred her to read the Bible for comfort, but she had tried the Bible. It didn't help. *Lace* helped. When the lights went out, she was able to glide back to her cell, her mind empty of everything but speculations on the cost of having something made by Christian Dior.

She put the book under her pillow and got into bed. She said her *Confiteor* lying down, asking God's mercy for needing something like this to soothe her. She played Part II of her own private mini-series, *Lace Goes to Greenwich*.

In the beginning, the symphony played. She leaned across

173

a Belgian-lace tablecloth, lighting candles. Candle heat made the skin above her breasts warm. Candlelight made the diamond choker at her throat sparkle and glitter.

In the end, she was standing on top of a high mountain, talking to her father.

"You could have stopped it," he said.

The air was so thick, it was like breathing tomato paste. She thought: it's not true it gets clearer. It gets muddier and muddier the higher you go. Her father was inching his way around the nipple of the mountain, moving like a yodeler on a Swiss clock. She inched after him, stumbling, afraid to fall.

"I was only seven," she said.

He turned to face her. "You could have stopped it and you didn't."

She ran after him, not caring that her hands were bleeding from steadying herself against the rocks, not caring that the air had gotten thinner—there was no oxygen left in it—and her lungs had become a set of inflexible steel bands bent on choking her to death.

"You could have stopped it," he shouted.

She opened her eyes. She was lying in bed, head aching, muscles tensed.

She heard someone walking, creeping up the staircase. The footsteps were slow, measured, somehow covert. They made her skin crawl. Who would be creeping like that, when there was nothing against their moving around after Grand Silence in the first place? Maybe whoever it was was just being careful, trying not to disturb the rest of them. She didn't believe it. What she heard was nasty. It was deliberately secretive.

She got out of bed and struggled into her robe. She was wide awake. She wouldn't be able to get back to sleep for hours. If she let herself lie in bed, she would only start imagining things. Left to herself in the infinite darkness of Grand Silence, she could do more to scare herself silly than a hundred of Jane's stories.

The main lights to the corridor were on a key only Clare Marie had. They were forbidden to turn on a light in the lavatory to read by. There was, however, a night light on the half-landing outside the Mary Chapel. She had seen Kat there once, hunched over a copy of *The Way of Perfection*.

174

She slipped out of her cell, along the corridor, to the fourth-floor landing. She was already on her way downstairs when she heard the footsteps again.

Footsteps above her. Footsteps in the tower.

She felt the book in her pocket, the edge of the picture of David in the rose garden protruding from the back cover. She was being ridiculous. No one ever went into the tower, except on cleaning detail. They were forbidden to go there. And it was locked.

Agnus Dei was old. The floors creaked in the wind. She had been upset by the dream she couldn't remember and everything that had happened to Marie Bernadette.

She turned away from the sound. There was a pen and a pad of paper next to the door of the Mary Chapel, so they could write notes to the Virgin and put them under her statue. She'd use the pen to write "Anne Fairchild Bliss" on the inside front cover of the book. Then she would read until she was tired, or until she heard Kat coming back from wherever she had gone to meet David.

An hour of Pagan and Judy and Maxine and she would stop imagining she heard someone walking in the tower.

"I haven't heard anything I need to hear, Sister. I haven't heard anything about knives or ropes or chairs dragged up five flights of stairs."

"What is it, Lieutenant? We can't just have a tragedy, we have to have a mess?"

"Sister—"

"One of my postulants killed herself, Lieutenant. That should be enough."

175

CHRISTOPHER

When she first came to Agnus Dei, a clothed Sister had been required to keep her head covered at all times. There were the wimple and veil for outside. There was a soft, frilled, elastic-rimmed cap, like the mobcaps worn by spinsters in Dickens novels, to sleep in. There was a hard shell of linen to wear on East Wing when the headdress got wearisome. "A covered head," her Novice Mistress said, "is a sign of your consecration to God." Christopher didn't know about that—they'd abandoned the covered-head rule in 1952, well before renewal—but she was sure it was a reflex. She still wore her mobcap to bed. She still wore her shell of linen on the corridor. She felt like a complete idiot. There she was, wandering into the East Wing recreation room to make herself a midnight cup of tea, that white unyielding halo slanting welts in her ears. There was Vianney, more than twenty years her senior in religion, trying to read the instructions for Mocha Cocoa through a tangle of thick white curls.

If it hadn't been for the lights in North Wing, she could have stayed in bed.

She stood very still, listening to nuns. Nuns slept deeply, snoring. Nuns slept badly, tossing and turning and moaning with dreams. Nuns slept not at all, getting out of bed to pray in chapel or keep each other company over tea and hot chocolate. Christopher always felt more comfortable here than in North Wing. Postulants and novices were unknown quantities. They were so restless, so doubtful and questioning. In her day, postulants knew what they wanted. They didn't expect paradise when they walked in the door.

Except, perhaps, for Margaret Mary Connolcy.

She heard the sound of the chocolate maker going on in the East Wing recreation room and went toward it, wondering if she were trying to postpone her trip to the other side of the building. Somebody had to go over there and find out

176

what was going on—lights moving back and forth across windows, and sometimes...sometimes other places. Clare Marie thought Jane was another Margaret Mary Connoley, but that was silly. Clare Marie hadn't known Margaret Mary Connoley. Clare Marie had been in Alaska, teaching religion to the Aleuts, when the poor girl hanged herself. Christopher thought she was the only person alive who knew what had happened and why. There had to be more than "scapegoating." The girl had to be unstable. Jane, so far as Christopher could tell, was one of the more flagrant examples of overcomplacent piety, but nothing worse. More important, the family had to be unstable. Margaret Mary's parents had been a pair of vicious, bigoted psychotics bent on seeing their daughter in hell. They had sold the girl on her own damnation. Christopher remembered following old Reverend Mother Peter Claver out of the reception room after they'd spent an appalling half hour with the grinning, satisfied father and his maliciously triumphant wife. She remembered thinking that their daughter's death vindicated them. Then Peter Claver, the gentlest, most generous woman she had ever known, had kicked over the brass urn in the back hall and said, "I don't want to die with a mortal sin on my soul, so I suppose I'll have to confess what I want to do to those people. But a request from Christ Himself couldn't make me sorry for it."

Twice in the last two weeks, the lights had come from North Wing tower. The second time, she had hauled herself out of bed and nearly pitched herself out her window, leaning into the night to see who was there. She couldn't. The angle was wrong. She had ended up pacing back and forth in her cell, feeling frustrated.

She supposed it could have been fireflies in North Tower. Or she could have imagined it. On the other hand, she didn't imagine much. The ghost stories she had been listening to for over forty years left her cold. She found the very premise ridiculous. She believed in miracles—Lazarus rose from the dead, and Bernadette saw the Virgin in a grotto—but God was not an omnipotent two-year-old. He wasn't going to throw a lot of petty, irrational nonsense into the world for no good reason.

She let herself into North Wing, closed the door behind

her, locked it, listened. She could hear someone praying in the Mary Chapel. The words were unintelligible. The rhythm was clear. Someone was saying a rosary.

She climbed the North Wing stairs and stopped on the third-floor landing to look into the senior novices' corridor, two blank walls of muslin closing off the cells. The curtains of the third cell on the right were open, to show that Marie Bernadette was gone. Now, there was a mess: Marie Bernadette in the hospital, and Angela Louise doing a month's penance for that ridiculously childish act of sacrilege. Christopher wished these girls would have more perspective. Everything was life-and-death to them. It had to have something to do with all that television they watched at home.

She started up the stairs again. She stopped on the half-landing, just outside the Mary Chapel. Someone had lit a devotional candle under the statue of the Virgin and left it burning. She listened to the muffled Hail, Mary coming from the chapel itself. Katherine Mary? Perhaps Katherine Mary had lit the candle, meaning to put it out when she went upstairs.

Was that what she had seen from her window, a devotional candle? The lights she had seen had been moving. They had moved for a long time, much longer than the few seconds it would take for Katherine Mary to light a candle and go into the chapel.

She was on the fourth-floor landing when she realized the North Tower door was open. She felt the rain-wind in her face, heard the sound of trees straining in the start of a storm. For a moment, all she could think of was how bad the storm would be. The first November storm forecast the winter.

She climbed the stairs to the tower and looked inside. It was vacant and clean. She could have sworn no one had entered it since the last cleaning day. She walked to the middle of it and stood, listening for she didn't know what. She heard sounds above her head and looked up to see bats in the rafters.

Bats.

She stifled a laugh. Bats. She had been standing at her window for nights on end, worrying herself into insomnia over a lot of bats. Dear Lord. What had she expected to find, the ghost of Margaret Mary Connoley trailing from archway to archway, rattling chains and crying "Damned! Damned to all eternity!"?

She locked the door behind her and went down to the Mary Chapel. Katherine Mary was at the front, near the statue of the Virgin, on her knees but no longer saying the rosary. She went up and tapped the girl on the shoulder.

"You'll know how important this is, Sister, because I'm breaking Grand Silence to say it."

Katherine Mary nodded, solemn, anxious.

Christopher said, "Put some sleep into your life, Sister. It's what God made nighttime for."

Katherine Mary stifled a burst of laughter, nodded, got to her feet. She shrugged.

"I know," Christopher said. "I can't sleep on command either. But we can both try, once in a while."

Katherine Mary shrugged again. Christopher watched her go, the best candidate they'd had in twenty years, the kind of candidate who'd been rare even in the old days. When she heard the door to postulant corridor open and close, she knelt at the Virgin's feet, to say a prayer for the postulant class.

To say a prayer for Katherine Mary, who left the Motherhouse some nights, and had yet to tell anyone why, or where.

The face of the Virgin looked waxen and stiff in the candlelight. Christopher said a final Hail, Mary. Postulants. *Nuns*. If nuns ever started making ordinary common sense

She stepped onto the half-landing. She could hear sounds coming from the tower. Bats. She had never realized how heavy bats sounded—heavy and human, like children clomping across wooden floors.

She would have to get the exterminator in, in the morning.

"*Ah, here we are. Here's the difficult part. Here's the part where everybody lies to us and thinks they're not.*"

"*Sister?*"

"*I'm sorry. I'm getting very tired.*"

"*I'm already tired. I've been tired.*"

"*Yes, of course.*"

"*Was that supposed to mean something in particular, Sister?*"

"*I was thinking of Ignatius Loyola. Do you know Ignatius Loyola?*"

"*I knew a Sister Ignatius Loyola. She taught geometry at Saint Bridget's.*"

"*Ignatius Loyola founded the Jesuits. They made him a saint. I suppose they were sorry for it later. He was a famous ascetic.*"

"*Sister?*"

"*Yes, yes, Lieutenant. I know. But it's relevant. Loyola wrote a book of spiritual exercises, you see. To help youths determine God's plan for them. Except, of course, we know what Loyola's plan for everyone was. He wanted as many people as possible in the religious life. He wanted an army of God.*"

"*Sister—*"

"*Sister, Sister, Sister. You keep saying 'Sister.'*"

"*I'm dead tired. It's almost five o'clock in the morning. I still don't know what's going on.*"

"*Neither do I. Neither do they. You think they know, they ought to know, but they don't. That's where Loyola comes in.*"

"*Because he wrote a book of spiritual exercises?*"

"*Because we took the first week of those exercises—we all did, every active order in the Western world—and turned it into a life. A life, Lieutenant. A life where the most important*" word is 'sin.' And the most important sins are mental, emotional, ephemeral."

"I don't see—"

"Do you know what happens to people who spend their time chastening themselves over the smallest faults, conscious and unconscious?"

"No."

"They learn to lie, Lieutenant. Mostly they learn to lie to themselves."

BARRIER

1

On the morning they were introduced to Chapter of Faults, Kat woke up thinking she was pregnant.

She heard the electric bell go off above her head and tried to sit up. She had a vague sense that this was a very important day. The night before, there had been a call, their first. Reverend Mother had come to evening recreation and read a list of names. Constance, Maria Luisa, and two of the Italian girls had disappeared, never to return. Kat felt as if she'd been walking through a gentle countryside sheltered by trees, only to look back and discover she'd been walking through a minefield.

According to Angela Louise, calls always came before progressions. Progressions were "changes in their relationship to the Rule"—admittance to choir, introduction to Particular Examen, stricter observance of silence. Progressions meant, Kat assumed, more rules. Angela Louise had refused to be specific. Progressions meant more *Pressure*, she said, over and over again. Progressions meant moving into waters some people wouldn't be able to navigate. Hence, the calls.

Kat imagined Constance and Maria Luisa and the two Italian girls, waiting in the dark for their parents to drive up to the door.

She tried to turn over. She vaguely remembered intending to sit up, but she was still lying down. She tried to roll over on her side. The movement made her stomach rock against her rib cage. The first wave of nausea drowned her. The second forced a spasm of bile into her throat, hot ragged bile like incompletely melted rock. She lay still for a moment and then turned, slowly and carefully, onto her back. She opened her eyes and watched the room rock and sway. She felt the nausea shrink to a threatening lump in the pit of her stomach, replaced by an awareness of dizziness and pain. She ached. Her breasts felt as if someone had battered them with a tire iron.

In another country, Clare Marie slid from the Morning Ejaculation to the Our Father. Kat could hear Annie's voice, coming one beat ahead of the rest. Annie's voice called up Annie, sitting round-eyed at Angela Louise's feet while Angela Louise explained calls and progressions. Annie had looked more frightened of calls and progressions than she ever had of ghost stories.

She was making her third attempt to sit up when it hit her, cracking through the nausea like a knife through an eggshell: a perfectly formed vision of the last time she'd made love to David. She saw the apartment in Boston. She saw the oversized bed with its self-contained, winged table-ledges. She saw the date like the page of a tear-off calendar in an old movie: March 19, 1983.

Eight months ago.

2

David rented the apartment because he wanted to be near Kat, but far enough from Mary so he wouldn't have to deal with her. It was Mary he worried about in the beginning. Kat had written to the Society of Mary from London, but he had not been able to take that seriously. Mary frightened him. He thought Mary was trying to eat Kat alive.

"I don't understand how you can live with that bitch," he said. "I don't understand how you can let her do what she's doing to you."

Kat wanted to tell him Mary was doing nothing to her. That battle had been fought and won years ago. It was their friends who frightened her, all the bright, pretty, ambitious people who cluttered their lives—her friends from Farmington and Vassar, his friends from Groton and Amherst, New

182

England preppies with an eye to the fast track and a passionate commitment to self-actualization, self-realization, self-promotion. They lived in a magazine.

"They just want to lead nice lives," David said. "It's finally occurred to them they're not Rockefellers. They're going to have to work for what they want."

She was thinking about the work these people did and what it meant to them when she got to his apartment the night that became the last real night they spent together. She had spent the night before listening to Mary harangue the Catholic Church. She had spent the afternoon with her old friend Cass, in Boston on "a flying business trip" for the brokerage firm she worked for in New York. Kat felt stuffed full of other people's inconsistencies, other people's inconstancies. Mary smoked endless cigarettes in the dark, discoursing on the evils of bishops. Cass wore her hair above her earlobes and her silk blouse tied at the neck in a floppy bow. They both talked endlessly about being the best you could be. They both urged her to feel good about herself. Neither made any sense whatsoever.

"All connections are temporary," Cass said. "No one can say 'forever' and mean it."

Cass had been married nine months.

Kat let herself into David's apartment, got a sixteen-ounce beer mug from the kitchen cabinet, and made herself the largest Rusty Nail in recorded history.

3

When David got back, she was lying in the dark with the Rusty Nail half drunk, staring into dead black air at a ceiling that seemed too far away to be part of this room. She was what she thought of as a little drunk. She had lost the need to care, but not the caring. She was thinking about nuns going down on their knees to the Archbishop, promising forever. There seemed to be long lines of them in the room with her.

She saw his body as a dark shape in the light. She said,
"Americans are always reinventing the wheel."
"Right." He laughed. "What's in that thing?"
"I was trying to be serious."

"You were trying so hard to be serious, you probably didn't bother to put ice in it."

He came to sit at the edge of the bed. It was a platform bed, low to the ground. When he sat down, he took up his separate piece of it without disturbing hers. He put the grocery bag on the floor and said,

"Bad day?"

"Cass grew up to be a psychopath."

"Cass grew up to be a stockbroker."

"Nobody grows up to be a stockbroker. You have to be a two-year-old to take it seriously."

He took a swig of the Rusty Nail. "Dear Lord Jesus," he said. "Straight alcohol."

She made herself sit up. She could smell him under the plaid wool of his jacket, woodsmoke and pine. She took his cigarettes out of his pocket and lit one, watching his eyes in the light of the match. He looked much more serious than he sounded. His eyes were old and dark and sad, waiting. Waiting for her? How long had he been waiting for her? She started to drink more of the Rusty Nail and stopped herself. Any more and she'd go numb, deaden the nerve endings once and for all, and she didn't want that. It was what she had wanted when she first let herself into the apartment, but now something in her was changed. He had changed her, just by being there.

She thought: he's the only chance I've got.

She put a hand on his arm and said, "Make love to me."

He jerked away as if she'd dropped a match on him. "Jesus Christ," he said. "Why do you do this? Why do you keep on doing this?"

"I'm not doing anything."

"It's been four months."

"I know how long it's been."

He took a deep, steadying breath in the darkness. Then he stood up and looked down at her. She wondered what he could see. There was light coming from the doorway. Was she like a girl on a bed in a spotlight? Was she there at all? He said, "Give me a minute," and walked out of the room.

When he came back, she was lying on her back again. She had taken one more chug of the Rusty Nail. It hadn't made

184

her numb, but it *had* broken her train of thought. She wasn't thinking about anything.

David sat down, putting his own drink—something small, in a whiskey glass—beside hers on the shelf. Kat could feel her skin shrinking, getting itchy and thin. She ran her hand against the soft flannel of his shirt. He had discarded his jacket in the other room. He had left the grocery bag beside the bed. She could see a carton of milk in it.

He took the cigarette out of her hand and put it in the ashtray. She could feel the fear coming out of him, the fear of touching her, the fear of failing again. She was afraid of being swallowed alive.

"I'm a damned idiot," he said. "You have the right to tell me I'm a damned idiot in the morning."

Her bra had a front clasp. She undid it and let her breasts hang in the still, damp air, feeling their weight and the pull of gravity. She took David's hands and put them against her. Her nipples were hard and extended, pricking against his fingers like the raised dots on a page of Braille.

"Make love to me," she said again. She did not say, "make it something else than what those people have, if they have anything, with the husbands and lovers and one-night-stands who make them feel good about themselves."

He pulled the tie on her wrap skirt. She touched the severe planes of his face, the disciplined muscles of his neck and shoulders. He felt solid and sure and eternal. His fingers moved into her, their probing tentative and gentle, waiting for instructions. The hard edge of a single fingernail moved along the muscles inside her, scratching in a pleasant, promising way.

She lay back and closed her eyes and let the barrier break, the barrier that seemed to have been in place for a thousand years. He pushed into her, first with little stabs and half-panicky retreats, then with longer, surer strokes. She opened herself wide, giving him the room he needed. She pushed against him until she could feel the tip of him at the mouth of her womb. He was the only man who had ever been able to get that far into her. She loved the hiccupy rhythm of that contact. She was always surprised by the strength of it.

He drew his hands to her sides, holding her in place. She

185

took him by the shoulders and pulled him down. She wanted to wipe herself out, to lose herself in him. She wanted to know what people found in orgasm that made them willing to devote their lives to searching for it.

When it came, he had his face buried against her neck, the dry tip of his tongue against her skin. She felt him first in parts: his penis stretched into her vagina; his leg against her leg; his hands knotted into fists against the small of her back. Then he became whole and she became whole and she let herself go into it. She became spasmodic, a series of muscular contractions she had not caused and could not control.

Even before she began to surface, she knew it wasn't working. Whatever they had started with was slipping away. She lay very still beneath him, trying not to give herself away. They had started with something, some feeling, they would never have again. It would never be entirely gone, but it would never be entirely with them, either.

And it had never, really, been enough.

She looked down at his head and watched his hair shudder like aspen leaves as his release followed her own, as his release blotted out the shift in her own.

When he was still, she got the cigarettes from the shelf and lit one.

She had not wanted him to see her face.

4

She did not want to get out of bed. She did not want to stand, when she knew she wasn't going to be on her feet for long. She steadied herself against the bureau, wondering what was wrong with her, why the waves of nausea kept coming, one after another, with no end in sight. Eight months. If she were eight months pregnant, she'd be as big as a house.

She could have been pregnant, that time. It was the one time in her life she hadn't been meticulous about birth control.

She swung her feet over the side of the bed, fighting the dizziness like a drowning swimmer fighting an enemy ocean current. She closed her mind against the prayers and tried to

186

think it through one step at a time. She looked up and saw Annie standing at the open curtain of her cell.

The floor was very cold. It sent a needle of pain into her leg, as if she'd stepped on a tack. She put her head between her knees and breathed deeply, pressing her heels into the bare wood. She felt Annie tap her on the shoulder and sat back. She couldn't make herself straighten up.

Annie was making the sign for "help." She looked like an image on a badly functioning television screen, wavery and intermittent.

Kat was fumbling over her stockings, shaking off Annie's efforts to help and offers to fetch Clare Marie, when it hit her. Tuesday. It was Tuesday. She couldn't let herself be confined to the infirmary on Tuesday.

She couldn't possibly be sick on Tuesday.

David came on Tuesday.

PICTURE

The snapshot was at the very back of Stephen's letter, folded into a sheet of onionskin, a small, square, harshly colored studio shot reduced to wallet size and cracked along the diagonal. Annie pulled it out and laid it on top of the dispensary cabinet. She had been thinking about Kat—why would someone so obviously sick refuse to come to the infirmary?—and then about what Stephen had said at the beginning of his letter. She'd only had time to read the first paragraph, but that had been enough. The part of her that was upset about Kat sick was submerged under the part of her that wanted to kill Reverend Mother. The anger had come at her like one of her headaches, a molten eruption. She heard Stephen's voice in her head, saying, "I came Tuesday and they wouldn't let me in." How could they have sent him away without telling her he was there? How could they have sent him away at all?

She had taken the Class E trays out of the serving cart, tried to count them, and given up.

On the sheet of onionskin, Stephen had written, "Here's a picture of Stephen, Sr. I found it in my papers. I thought you'd like to have it. God only knows *she* doesn't keep pictures of him around."

Stephen senior was a pale blond man with delicate bones, water-blue eyes, and the hint of something angry and bitter at the corners of his mouth. Annie tilted the picture back and forth, catching the light. It drew her in, whether she wanted to go or not, and she certainly didn't want to go. The picture made her feel clammy.

Somewhere in the middle of Stephen's letter would be the description of another house, another Fairfield County adventure. When she had a chance, she'd go down to the lavatory and read it. She wished her copy of *Lace* were still intact. All that was left of it was a handful of loose papers she kept in an envelope under her mattress. She'd read the book to shreds in less than three weeks.

She tried counting trays again. She came up one short, then two over, then two short.

Behind her, Jane opened and shut the office door, then leaned against it.

Annie shoved Class E trays back onto the cart. She had no idea how many there were. "I can't seem to count today," she said, making it sound as if it were entirely Jane's fault. "I've done it four times and all I get is a mess."

Jane sat down in the chair next to Elizabeth's desk. "I'll count them in a minute," she said (patiently, Annie thought, letting her irritation escalate into anger, and feeling immediately guilty for it). "I've got to tell you something."

"If you're going to tell me you think Constance is off cutting her throat right this minute," Annie said, "I don't want to hear it."

"I was going to tell you about Scholastica," Jane said mildly. "I saw her in Reverend Mother's office when I went up to—" Jane hesitated. "Get a permission," she said finally. "For some medication."

Annie supposed this was Jane's way of saying she had menstrual cramps. The unnecessary euphemism made her even more irritated. The irritation made her ashamed. The shame made her head ache. It was always like this with Jane. The more time Annie spent with her—and Annie was spending more and more time with her; the Order seemed to be shoving them together at every opportunity—the more she realized Jane's perfection was not the simple mastery of rote some of the others (Kat) could claim. Jane thought like a nun. She offered up the abuse Annie was heaping on her. She made her suffering an act of charity. Was this why Clare Marie had assigned her so much time with Jane, because Jane was perfect, because Jane's perfection might cure her own imperfection? She bit her lip and turned away.

She had spent the night wondering why Constance and Maria Luisa and the two Italian girls had been sent home, when she had been allowed to stay. Constance had fit more easily. Maria Luisa had been more tractable. Annie had no way of determining how the decision had been made, on what basis, by what standard.

She gave up on the trays and started to uncrate a box of bandages. The invoice said, "200 sterilized gauze wraps." The box contained what looked like five hundred eye patches. Annie sat down on top of it, defeated.

"I'm sorry," she said. "I didn't get a lot of sleep last night. I'm not coping very well."

"Coping." Jane made a face.

Annie shrugged. "We're going to have to look this up," she said. "It doesn't have in it what it says it has in it."

Jane smiled charitably. "I was going to tell you about Scholastica," she said. "It's a scandal. She's running off with a seminary student."

"A seminary student?"

Jane's eyes were very bright, the pupils wide and fathomless. "He's going to leave his Order and leave the Church and join the Episcopalians," she said. "I heard Reverend Mother talking about it."

Annie picked at a lock of hair that had come loose from her veil, not knowing what to say. She thought of Scholastica's habitual bitchiness and wondered how the seminary student expected to live with it. And why was the story so important to Jane? Jane had hardly known Scholastica.

"You know what I think?" Jane said. "I think suicide is the way God punishes people who betray their vocations. That's what happened to the girl in the tower. She wanted to leave, but God wouldn't let her leave."

189

"For God's sake," Annie said.

"Some people don't come at all," Jane said. "They hear the call but they don't listen to it. They try to live as if they'd never heard it."

Annie felt the crest of the headache wash over her in a rush, propelled by the knowledge that if she told anyone what Jane had just said, and how she'd said it, they'd laugh in her face. She made one more stab at ramming the stray lock under her veil, grabbed a stack of magazines, and headed for the door. She looked back at Jane, and found a bland smiling face with expressionless eyes.

"You shouldn't take the name of the Lord in Vain," Jane said placidly.

Annie had a wild urge to grab Jane by the shoulders, shake her hard, and make her admit she'd done what she'd just done. Instead, she took Stephen's letter out of her pocket and shoved it among the papers on top of the dispensary cabinet.

She did not want the picture of her father, or anything it had touched, touching her.

CONNECTIONS

1

By the time the bell rang for Extraordinary Instruction, Kat's head had cleared enough so she was at least making sense to herself. She went out the pantry door and down the steps, because she had a feeling something was wrong out there she had to take care of. She was trying to wipe the slush snow out of her eyes when she stumbled over the bird, a tiny, cold-weather bird with brown feathers and wings that had been (severed?) broken and torn. Martha's cat was perched on a branch above her head, watching the kill. What was happening between herself and David was like a chess game played by mail. It was ritual contact. It was too much and not enough at the same time.

Martha's cat came down from the branch and took up a station a foot from the bird, shoulders hunched, teeth bared, stomach heaving out spit-hisses. Kat looked first at the cat and then at the bird, trying to clear her mind for something else, something wrong.

Her mind did a loop, her stomach gave a final, nostalgic heave, and she *saw* it. She looked from the bird to Martha's cat to the bird again. She kicked at the bird and watched the wings fall away, wings that had been separated as cleanly as a surgically amputated limb.

She had a sudden need to vomit, a swooning rush with an almost indiscernible backbeat that had something to do with the cat hissing at the kill and the bird having been gone after with what must have been a razor and the ceiling over her head on postulant corridor being heavy with something that sounded like footsteps and then—

Kat stood up and brushed the freezing rain out of her hair, leaving Martha's cat and the bird to hold their adversarial pose in the thickening storm.

She folded her arms across her chest and waited for the woman walking across the lawn to reach her.

Mary.

2

Maybe it was the dim light, or the way her head still felt full of cotton candy. Kat didn't know. Mary looked older. The lines at the sides of her mouth were deep black slashes. The lines at the sides of her eyes were fly-strangling spider-webs. There were three broken capillaries on one side of Mary's nose, the punishment God visited on the Irish for one bender too many.

Mary took out a cigarette and tried three times to light it in the rain and wind. She dropped the match on the grass. If it had been dry, she would have started a brushfire.

Clare Marie, on her way to chapel, stopped in the middle of North Lawn and stared at them.

"You should have come to the front door," Kat said. "That's the usual procedure. You come to the front door and ask Sister Portress if you can see me. Sister Portress sends you to Reverend Mother. Reverend Mother sends you to me."

"Reverend Mother sends you to hell," Mary said. "Don't think I haven't tried."

Above them, two low notes of warning rang in the chapel and towers. Kat had a crazy urge to cut her sentence in half, turn her back, and walk off as if Mary didn't exist, a model of nunly perfection, circa 1958. She would have done it if she hadn't been sure Mary would follow her right into chapel.

"I have something to do, Mother. I've got five minutes before I have to get there. That's it."

"This is it," Mary said. "I'm giving you one last chance."

"For what? What are you doing here? If you just wanted to visit, you could come on Sunday. I'd even like that."

"A nice Sunday visit with my daughter the nun."

"Why not?"

Mary reached into her trench coat and came up with a fistful of newspaper clippings. The clippings were matted and smeared, as if they'd been handled day after day for months.

"I brought you a few things, Katherine. I brought you some news of what your precious God-damned Catholic Church is doing out there. Trying to get books taken out of libraries and magazines taken off newsstands. Aren't you the one who walked out on me for three months because I said Hugh Hefner should be castrated? Or are principles something they make you give up?"

"Mother, I've known you all my life. You wouldn't know a principle from a hole in the wall."

"Ah," Mary said. "We've returned to the mama-baiting of your college days."

Clare Marie was no longer standing alone in the middle of North Lawn. She had pulled Reverend Mother out of thin air, Kat could see the two nuns huddled together, discussing them. Dear sweet Jesus Christ, she thought. I wonder what the penance for this is going to be.

Mary looked at the wad of papers in her hand, shrugged, and let them fall to the ground. They turned to something that looked like plaster of Paris in the slush.

"There was quite a lot of information in those," Mary said regretfully. "Not that I expected you to read them."

"Not that you expected they'd do any good if I did read them. Mother, what are you doing here?"

Mary got out another cigarette. "I'm giving you a fair demonstration of how I'm going to behave if you don't go upstairs this minute, pack your things, and leave with me."

3

By the time Reverend Mother and Clare Marie reached them, Kat knew Mary was drunk. She wasn't high, or slurry, or comic-falling-down. She was fueled. She was like a finely tuned engine running on the highest-octane gasoline.

"Ah, here now," Mary said. "We have visitors."

Clare Marie and Reverend Mother were expressionless. They were always expressionless. It was only in crisis, when anyone else would have been hysterical or angry or at least surprised, that you realized it.

"Watch me," Mary said. "Watch me make it through fifteen common terms for abnormal sexual intercourse in under thirty seconds."

"For God's sake," Kat said.

"I don't believe in God, Katherine, and neither do you. I thought I'd made that clear."

The lift of Clare Marie's eyebrows was almost infinitesimal, but Kat caught it. Mary must have caught it, too. She blew cigarette smoke at them.

Finally, Reverend Mother held out her hand. "I'm Mother Mary Christopher." She bowed. "You must be . . ."

"Kat's mother." Mary didn't take Christopher's hand.

Christopher put her hand back under her cape. "Welcome to Agnus Dei," she said. "We're always glad to see the parents of our girls take an interest in their progress."

"Are you," Mary said.

Clare Marie coughed. The cough bounced into a silence broken only by rain. Kat wanted very badly to cry.

She said, "For God's sake, Mother, you sound like something out of a bad movie."

"My daughter," Mary said, "is going to pack her things and come with me."

193

"Your daughter," Kat said, "is going to instruction where she belongs."

"I was going to take a picture of David's prick and bring it with me," Mary said, "but I thought you'd remember it well enough not to need a reminder."

Kat was moving, swinging, before she realized she was angry. "What are you trying to do," she shouted. "What are you here for? What are you—"

She felt a hand on her arm and stopped—in the middle of a sentence, she thought wildly, just like the old nuns stopped for the bell. She reeled herself in and said, "Excuse me, Sister."

"It's quite all right," Clare Marie said.

"Sister, can I go to instruction? I mean, I know—"

"It's quite all right," Clare Marie said again. She was looking calmly at Mary. Mary, not calm, was looking back. A little more agitation, Kat thought, and Mary's eyes would actually begin to roll.

"I don't give a flying shit what any of you think is going on here," Mary said. "I'm not going to have her in a convent, and that's final. She can come with me or you can *live* with me. It's the only choice you've got."

"For God's sake," Kat said again.

"Don't *give* me that," Mary said. "You like to suck cock just like the rest of us, sweetheart. You're not Saint Joan and you're never going to be."

"What do you think this is going to accomplish?" Kat thought she must be shouting again. Only shouting could make her throat hurt so much.

Mary snatched her arm, pulling her forward, almost pitching her into the mud. Kat stumbled against Reverend Mother, slid on the slickness of the grass, and tumbled into Mary's side.

"You just get your things," Mary said. "I'll buy you and that friend of yours some French ticklers as a coming-out present."

"All right," Reverend Mother said. "That's enough."

Kat shook herself free of Mary's hand and backed away. She was shaking, but she was finally out of it. Reverend Mother and Clare Marie and Mary stood in a badly proportioned triangle, getting wet.

Mary was very calm. Whatever had set her off was gone. She was looking at them as if they were some particularly unintelligent form of rodent. Kat recognized the expression. It was the one Mary used at cocktail parties, with men who should be, but were not, trying to make her.

Kat felt the nausea of the morning coming back, making her stomach feel full of petroleum jelly. She wiped the rain off her face with the palms of her hands.

"Sister," she said.

"It's quite all right," Clare Marie said. Kat thought of herself saying that to Martha, the day they found the pills, thought of herself thinking: three times makes it true.

"You don't want to go home?" Clare Marie asked her.

"No, Sister."

"All right. Go up and change into dry things. Then come down to instruction."

"I'm not that wet, Sister. And I'm already late."

"You can't be late," Clare Marie said. "I'm here."

Kat blinked. A giggle came up like a sneeze. Clare Marie bowed slightly, pleased. "Dry things," she said again.

Kat nodded, turned, started to back away. Mary said, "Go ahead and do whatever the hell you want. I'm not leaving. And I'm not shutting up until I've told you how she's spent the last five years of her life."

Kat pulled the veil off her head. It was saturated, like a rag left overnight in a pail of water.

4

Kat was halfway back to the main building before she remembered the bird. There was something about the bird, but it was gone, buried under Mary.

Somewhere at the back of her brain the jungle drums said: Jane, Jane, Jane.

195

CHAPTER OF FAULTS

1

"You are now sitting," Clare Marie said, "as you will sit when you make your first Chapter of Faults, exactly one week from today."

Jane slid into the only empty seat in the double row of cane seats lining the chapel's center aisle. She'd almost been sorry to be late. It was difficult to get anything past this mood she was in. She looked covertly at Annie Bliss across the aisle, listening wide-eyed and ramrod-straight to Clare Marie's extended discourse. It had been a bad day for Annie, that was the truth. Jane thought it was probably going to get worse.

She leaned left until she felt safely hidden by Martha's bulk. It was more than the Biphetamine she'd taken in Elizabeth's office, more than the extra half dozen she'd taken away in her pocket. Annie had felt so guilty about leaving her alone to count trays, but Jane had never been so glad to get rid of anyone in her life. Ever since Geraldine's departure, she'd had the hardest time getting pills. Annie was always there, always watching. It wasn't safe to haul away an entire bottle. Elizabeth might be senile, but she wasn't dead. Lately, with the stuff she'd been taking herself and the stuff she'd been putting in Kat's coffee at evening recreation, her supply had been getting low.

She had given Kat too many of the damned things the night before. She'd known it at the time. She'd had to add two Dexedrine caps she'd brought for herself, to counteract the barbiturates, and then she'd nearly started kicking furniture. If O'Brien slept like a normal person, she wouldn't have to do these things. She could just wait until the corridor was quiet and go up and feed the birds.

Except that feeding the birds didn't have the effect it used to. The birds felt like cheap tin mechanical dolls. Kat had almost caught her at it twice, and on one memorable night —the night, of course, when she'd taken one Amphaplex

196

too many, so she was bouncing off the walls like a psychotic Ping-Pong ball—Reverend Mother had locked her in. She'd been intending to go downstairs for some phenobarbital to take the edge off when she heard heavy footsteps on the stairs. When she heard the door lock (she was on the roof, lying flat, so she couldn't be seen), she'd almost risen up and strangled the old woman. Reverend Mother wasn't likely to be back, but she had to do something about Kat. Kat with her Godforsaken insomnia was ruining everything.

Maybe, just maybe, she had just done something about Kat.

Jane sorted through the pills in her pocket, looking for a couple of Librium to cool herself off. It had been such a good day, she almost thought she'd come favorably to the attention of some saint. First Annie and that Kodak, that awful letter from her brother, full of suicide and death and melodrama. She'd started out telling Annie about Scholastica, meaning to build another bridge between them, and it had fallen apart. There *was* a bridge between them, but she was beginning to realize it wasn't the kind she'd thought at first. She had been so convinced that Annie had been given to her as a key—a key to unlock the empty house, a key to open the door of the fold. Annie would take her up and she would become part of the core.

It hadn't worked that way. Jane wasn't sure what had gone wrong, but something had. Annie was as wrapped up in Secretary-of-the-Student-Council as Bridget Gallagher had ever been. However it was going to work—and it was going to work *somehow*—it wouldn't be by Annie taking her in.

She'd said that about Scholastica to see what kind of rise she could get. You could always get a rise out of Annie, talking about suicide. Annie thought she didn't think about it, but she was wrong. Jane had watched her and read her notebooks and read the pile of her brother's letters she kept with her spiritual diary. Jane had said that about Scholastica, and been rewarded with a full-scale eruption. Even the whites of Annie's eyes had paled into transparency.

Jane slipped a Librium under her tongue and held it there, waiting for enough saliva to build up so she could swallow it. Thinking about Annie made her very restless these days. Annie confused her, and Jane was never confused about anything. Mary Connor O'Brien was a different story. There was nothing confusing about that.

Mary Connor O'Brien was the best thing that had happened all day.

2

She had been thinking about her own mother when she heard them, her mother and her father, the summer they knew she was pregnant. She remembered that summer as hot and still and silent, but she knew it hadn't been. For once her mother had resorted to screaming, and her father ... That was what she had been considering, when she reached North Lawn. She was beginning to realize she could obliterate it, wipe it out as if it had never happened, because it *would* never have happened. She could do it with the pills, and with Annie Bliss.

Mary Connor O'Brien was standing under the maple tree near the S-shaped stone bench that marked the division between North Lawn and the chapel yard. Jane was reaching into her pocket for another Biphetamine—as if that would jolt her out of memory, back to the business at hand—when she'd heard voices on the lawn.

"How the *fuck* am I supposed to know what you've been doing?" her father said. "I know what you *are*, maybe I can guess what you *do*."

Jane stopped just inside the first line of trees—pine trees, easy to hide in, like the trees she hid in when she followed Kat out of the Motherhouse at night. She swallowed two of the pills in her left pocket—red ones, from her lavatory supply; she wasn't sure what they were—and tried to get close enough to hear the conversation. Close enough and high enough. Or normal enough. She always thought of the pills as making her normal, as giving her back what *they* had taken from her.

Mary Connor O'Brien was interested in getting back what Agnus Dei had taken from her. Jane struggled onto a low branch and watched the tableau. Reverend Mother and Clare Marie were very relaxed. Mary Connor O'Brien was tense. The theme was simple. Kat wanted to be a nun. Mary didn't want her to be a nun. Mary was going to get her back.

The motivations weren't so simple. They should have been, but Jane could feel the warp, the way she could feel the warp whenever she said "suicide" to Annie Bliss.

"I'll go for the moment," Mary Connor O'Brien said, "but I'll be back."

Mary had said it to dead air. Reverend Mother and Clare Marie were walking across the grass in the direction of the chapel, their heads bent to the wind, their veils whipping out behind them. Mary was wearing a trench coat and smoking a cigarette. Her eyes were red.

Jane slid off her branch. The red pills were beginning to work. God only knew what they were—God only knew what any of that stuff was—but it worked. Jane was beginning to think all the scare stories about overdoses and withdrawal symptoms and ending up with your brain cells looking like mush were just so much horseshit handed out by the people in control.

She thought of Kat in the Mary Chapel, on the corridor, in bed with the window open and her eyes closed, awake, awake, awake. Kat was always awake.

She thought of all the pills in all the cups of coffee, every night she wanted to feed the birds.

"Tell her anything you want," her father said. "She won't believe you."

She got to Mary just as the older woman started toward South Yard.

"I know how you can get her out of here," she said. "I know something guaranteed to work."

3

Clare Marie had Martha at the front of the room, lying flat on her face with her arms stretched out at her sides to make a cross.

"When you have prostrated yourselves in front of Reverend Mother," she said, "you will tell your faults against the Rule. This is called a proclamation. You will proclaim yourself to the community. When you are done, the community will have an opportunity to proclaim you."

Clare Marie tapped her foot. Martha said, "I proclaim myself for a fault against charity in ignoring my Sister Mary

199

Lucy's needs at dinner. I proclaim myself for a fault against obedience for speaking after the Grand Silence. I proclaim myself for a fault against poverty for discarding a tube of toothpaste before it was completely empty."

Jane sat back. Annie was petrified. One of the remaining Italian girls was near tears. They were going to be stupid about it. They always were.

Had Jane been much later than she thought? Or had she blanked out and missed the whole lecture? Over the last two weeks, she had begun losing pieces of days, whole hours that just seemed to have dropped out of existence. That was the kind of thing being tired got you, and not having enough pills. She was going to have to do something about Annie in the infirmary.

She looked at Kat sitting thoughtful and still in her straight-backed chair. Kat, who was probably wondering what she would and wouldn't say in Chapter of Faults, what she could and couldn't get away with.

Jane didn't think Kat had to worry about Chapter of Faults.

DECISION

1

She must have been looking for him. Subconsciously (did they believe in the subconscious?), she must have been hoping to see him standing under the clock at the bank, his hands in his pockets and his chin jutting out, defying nuns.

Annie followed the top of Sister Annunciata's veil into the post office-grocery store. Sister Annunciata should have been a pleasure—after Scholastica's dissatisfied acerbity, anyone should have been a pleasure—but Annie couldn't see her without remembering Scholastica, couldn't remember Scholastica without remembering Jane, couldn't remember Jane without remembering that damnable picture. Her head hurt. Instead of the darning needle she was used to, she had a bed of nails. The bed of nails pulsed.

The book, the new book she wanted above all others, pulsed too.

She had put her father's picture next to the one of David in the rose garden. They seemed to go together. She wasn't sure how.

She felt a tug and looked down to see Annunciata peering through the post office window at the common. Annunciata was hardly five feet tall. She dithered.

"Oh, dear," Annunciata said. "He's still looking at us."

"Sister?"

"That man. He's been staring at us since we got out of the car."

"It's all right," Daniella said. "He's something to Katherine Mary. He lives around here."

"He wants to know if one of us is Katherine Mary?"

"He wants to know if any of us is anyone he's met," Daniella said. "If he recognizes us, he stops and says hello."

"Ah," Annunciata said. Annie squirmed. Did Daniella suspect her of carrying messages for Kat? Did Daniella suspect her of being involved with David herself? She'd been like this all morning, ever since she'd picked up Stephen's letter. It seemed to be getting worse. Her mind was like a photograph album being riffled in the wind. Stephen. David. Her father. Jane. Chapter of Faults.

It was too much. The bed of nails said it, every time it pulsed. Too much. Too much. Too much. Particular Examen of Conscience had been bad enough. Examen books had been nearly impossible. The tin utensils in rectory and the worn carpet on the fourth-floor landing were killing her. Chapter of Faults was acting on her like a sharp jolt on a vial of nitroglycerin.

The cover of this book had a warm, glowing brown background, and a picture of a woman in a tiara, with pale blond hair the color of some exotic metal.

"If we know him," Annunciata said, "we ought to go get him. He'll get deathly ill standing there in the rain."

"Hail," Daniella said.

"Is it hailing already?" Annunciata said.

The hailstones were the size of golf balls. Daniella smiled.

201

"He knows Anne better than he knows me, Sister. Maybe we should send her out to get him."

"I don't care who goes," Annunciata said, "just as long as somebody does. I won't be able to concentrate thinking of him outside in that weather."

Annunciata turned on her heel and marched up to the clerk's window, a tiny figure in medieval clothes embarked on an impossible mission. As far as Annie could tell, the woman couldn't read numbers on a speedometer, never mind add up a postage receipt.

Daniella tugged on Annie's sleeve. "You look like death," she said. "Go talk to David Marsh."

"You did that on purpose?"

"I had to do something. You look ready to burst into tears." Daniella looked out the window at David. "Not that I wouldn't like to go myself," she said. "He really is a remarkably good-looking man, isn't he?"

"Yes," Annie said, feeling numb.

Daniella gave her an impatient look. "We're supposed to be chaste, Bliss, not discorporeal." She nodded in David's direction. "I wonder what it takes to get a man like that interested in you."

"Black hair and violet eyes," Annie said. "If you *want* a man interested in you."

"The more I know you, the more I wonder how anybody survives postulant year." Daniella sighed. "It's Kat I'm wondering about, Annie. Don't you, sometimes?"

"No," Annie said. She wondered about Kat constantly.

"Go," Daniella said. "Annunciata is beginning to look alarmed."

Annie looked back at the book on the rack. It wouldn't be hard. She'd just have to wait until Annunciata (inevitably) did something unbelievably illogical. Then, when everybody had crowded around to get it straightened out, Annie could just pick up the book and—

And she had to be out of her mind.

She opened the door and eased herself into the storm. At the last minute, she remembered why she had been looking for David. David had met Stephen. Stephen had said so, in his letter.

2

"She wants to meet me? How can she want to meet me?"

Annie wrapped her arms around her body. Hail whistled when it fell. Now that she was standing next to him, she couldn't look at David Marsh at all. He made her stomach queasy and her head light.

"Annunciata's just that way," she said. "She doesn't want you standing here in the cold."

"I don't want me standing here in the cold. That's not the point."

"I know you came to talk about Kat. We can talk about Kat on the way back."

A sound like a sigh escaped from David's stomach. Annie looked up at the flat, sharp lines of his face. He was staring into the distance, toward Agnus Dei. He seemed impatient.

"Actually," he said, "I didn't come to talk about Kat."

"You didn't come to talk about Kat?"

"I've been seeing Kat. Did you know that?"

"Yes." Everyone on postulant corridor knew it. They wouldn't turn Kat in, but they knew it.

"I'm sorry," David said. "We should get out of this storm."

"You came to talk about me?" Her mind was too full of debris to consider the implications.

David said nothing.

"Sister Annunciata is going to be having kittens," Annie said.

"She doesn't want to ream me out for pestering consecrated women?"

"No. She may want to get you into dry clothes and feed you honey tea."

"All right." David smiled. "That doesn't sound impossible."

Annie led the way back to the post office-grocery store. The hailstones were getting bigger. Daniella stood at the window, watching them.

"Tell me about Stephen," she said, trying to talk to David without facing him. His body was too hard, too supple, too

203

graceful. When he stood still, she didn't notice it. When he moved, he made her shiver. "He wrote and said he'd met you."

Somewhere behind her, close but not too close, David coughed. "That's right," he said. "He said you hadn't seen each other in ten years."

3

"So you're a writer," Annunciata said. "Do you write books I can read, or books with a lot of sex in them?"

Annie bit her cheeks, wondering if she wanted to laugh or cry. David hadn't refused to talk about Stephen, but he had come close. Why didn't David want to talk about Stephen?

Stephen had written a great deal about David. David had impressed him. No, David had floored him. "If I had to describe the man I'm trying to become," he wrote, "this guy would be it." It had been one of the few things in Stephen's letter that had made her happy. There had been no descriptions of houses or stories of country clubs. Everything had been about her father, or her vocation.

She looked at the book rack for what felt like the millionth time. It wasn't a woman on the cover, but a girl not much older than herself. Princess Daisy.

"I haven't written any books," David was saying. "I wrote magazine articles. I was a stringer for UPI in Southeast Asia for a while."

"Oh," Annunciata said. "You wrote about the war."

"Well, the war was over by the time I got there. I wrote about local conditions."

"There's nothing to say I can't read books with sex in them," Annunciata said. "I just can't get used to it."

"That's all right, Sister. Sometimes neither can I."

Annunciata beamed at them. They each tried to beam back. David looked mildly puzzled. Daniella looked infinitely amused.

Annie rubbed her forehead again. She was suddenly tired of it all, tired of David, tired of Jane, and tired, most of all, of trying to be the perfect postulant. Her headache was back, worse, all-encompassing. She had run into the wall again. She had crashed headfirst into the fact that she had made the only possible decision. She was in a box. She was (as Kat put it) being buried alive.

"Annie?" David said.

"Oh, dear," Annunciata said. "I think she's feeling faint."

"I'm all right," she heard herself say. "I'm just—I have a headache."

"Chapter," Daniella said, meaning David not to understand.

"Oh," Annunciata said. "Oh, dear."

"Why don't we get her someplace she can sit down?" David said.

Annie felt a hand on her arm, another on her back. The hands pushed her across the small, crowded space to the bookrack. Panic flooded in on her again. They knew she wanted the book. They were going to stand her in front of the rack and confront her with it. Then she realized where they were going. The bookrack was next to a window whose sill was a wide, empty shelf. David sat her down there, her back to the dirty glass.

"What she needs," David said, "is some bourbon."

"Coffee with three sugars," Daniella said. "That'll get her to the van."

"Coffee with three sugars," Annunciata repeated. She hurried to the four-stool soda counter, a horror of cracked linoleum and unpolished chrome.

David knelt beside her. "Annie? Can you hear what I'm saying?"

"I'm all right," she said again. Tears were pushing into the corners of her eyes. She held them back. Her panic was absolute. "They send you home," she told David. "If they think you can't handle it, they send you home."

"Oh, my God," Daniella said.

"What's she talking about?" David said.

Daniella knelt down and took Annie's hands. "Bliss, listen to me. Nobody expects you to be a saint. Nobody expects you never to get upset, or sick, or make mistakes. Nobody's going to send you home."

"They sent Constance home. They sent Maria Luisa home."

Daniella sighed. "She should probably burst into tears and get it over with," she said, standing up, "but she won't."

205

"What's all this about?" David said again.

"Nothing." Daniella looked across to Annunciata at the counter. "I'd better find out what's going on over there."

Daniella moved away from them. Annie watched her go, wondering if she had left them alone on purpose. Everything was crazy today. She thought of the picture of her father and felt her stomach give a heave.

"It's all right," she said. "I get migraines. Everything gets awful."

David sat beside her on the shelf. "Is it me?"

"You?"

"Before, I upset you."

"No, you didn't." (Yes, he had.) "It's what I said. It's a migraine."

"I was worried about you. You didn't seem happy, last time."

"I'm very happy," Annie said. "I've always wanted to be a nun."

On the rack, the book gleamed dully, a warm, inviting-in color. Annie was close enough to touch it. She put her hands in her pockets, carefully avoiding the picture of her father. The thing was like a snake.

Daniella and Annunciata came back, bearing coffee in a Styrofoam cup. Annie hated Styrofoam cups. They reminded her of greasy spoons on Chapel Street.

She took the cup in both hands and drank the coffee, so thick with sugar it was almost a syrup, in a single, endless swallow.

4

After a while, they left her to sit by herself. Daniella and Annunciata went back to the postal window. David went out to the common, in the direction of his car. Daniella took Annie's stamp money. Annunciata brought her two aspirin and stood over her while she ate them.

She waited until they had their backs to her, until David was out of sight around a corner.

Then she took the book out of the rack and put it under her cape.

LINE OF DEMARCATION

1

The hail had turned first to rain and then to ice, leaving the soft ground near the Retreat House path pockmarked with hard, slick ruts full of frozen water. Kat moved carefully between them in the dark, wishing the soles of her shoes were not so thick and pliable. You could break your ankle on the idiot things.

The chapel bell rang ten forty-five, a single note, ghostly and ominous in the unrelieved darkness.

She turned off the Retreat House path and down the shelved fieldstone steps, trying to correct for the curve in the hill she couldn't see. She had never felt much better than she had when Mary showed up. Her nausea had (finally) disappeared, but her head was full of cotton wool and strangeness and she wasn't thinking straight. She had snapped at Annie at dinner. She had come out the North Wing first-floor lavatory window, as if trying to avoid being seen going out the wing door. She had been convinced someone would be waiting for her at that door.

She stepped onto the Retreat House patio, a small square of irregularly shaped stone tiles with a statue of Saint Francis of Assisi in the center. The tiles were coated with ice. She slipped, recovered, slipped again. She caught herself on a low stone ledge and leaned against it. If postulants were allowed to proclaim each other at Chapter of Faults, she would be caught. Annie and Miriam wouldn't say anything, but Jane would, and Kat was sure Jane at least knew she was leaving the building at night. The way it worked, they wouldn't be allowed to proclaim anyone until they became novices. Kat was sure no one else knew, none of the novices, none of the professed Sisters. She could go on meeting David in perfect secrecy until they went into retreat before Epiphany and the naming.

Did she want that? Did she want to lie in Chapter of Faults, even if only by omission?

She heard sounds coming from Retreat House and stood up, catching a sudden gust of frigid wind under her cape. The last thing she needed now was pressure. She had tried to pressure herself at Compline—tried to *make God listen*— and all it had gotten her was exhausted. She needed time. Time to find out if what she had felt in San Sulpice had been an illusion, or a self-delusion. Time to find out what she really wanted of David.

She stuck her head in the door of the Retreat House garage and said, "Are you here?"

"Jesus Christ," David said. "It's cold as hell in this place."

2

From the sound of his voice, Kat expected to find David edgy, nervous, distracted. She had closed the door behind her before she realized what was really going on. The air was thick with it. She thought of the lecture her biology professor had given on the odors animals emitted in heat, and found herself backing against the door she had just closed, wrapping her arms around her stomach as if to protect herself from assault. She felt him crouched out there, hidden by the shadows cast by a cheap bayberry candle, ready to attack.

He poured wine into a paper cup and put it down beside the candle nearest her. "Kat? Aren't you going to sit down?"

"I don't know." Her laugh was shaky and weak in the half darkness. "You seem . . . strange."

She saw the flare of his Zippo lighter, the glow at the tip of his cigarette. He said, "I'm all right. Come and sit down, Kat."

"Right," she said.

"I won't do it," he said. "I was going to, but I won't."

"Do what?"

"Make you make up your fucking mind."

Kat stared at the candle long enough to make her think her eyes had adjusted to the light. Then she began to move forward, haltingly, searching for the edge of the blanket with her feet.

"Sit down and drink your wine."

She found the edge of the blanket at last, tripped on it,

came down hard on her left leg. The pain shot into her hip and died. "I did something bloody to myself," she said.

"Pick a topic of conversation," he said. "Any topic of conversation but the one we should be having a conversation about."

"David—"

"What, Katherine?"

She sat far enough away so she had to lean and reach to get to the paper cup. She set it in front of her, afraid to drink it. She had promised herself, after the first night, that she would talk to him but not get drunk. Breaking one rule at a time was enough. Right now, dead drunk looked too good to flirt with.

"Maybe we should have that conversation," she said.

"If we start talking about that now, all I'll do is give you ultimatums. And I promised myself I wouldn't give you an ultimatum until I was ready to hear you say no."

"You think I'm going to say no."

"I think you could."

Kat sucked at her wine. If she drank it out of the far side of the glass, the way you drank water to cure hiccups, she couldn't drink it too fast.

"Mary came today," she said. "Unannounced and unadmitted. She just showed up on North Lawn around eleven o'clock and caused a scene."

"That must have been a zoo."

"Yes. Yes, it was."

David didn't say anything. Kat could hear him dragging on his cigarette, see his eyes slanting over the candle flame. "For God's sake," she said. "You don't want to talk about what you want to talk about. Do you want to talk at all?"

"Sleep with me," David said.

3

What she did instead was take one of his cigarettes, the first she'd had in over two months. It felt like a defeat. She put it down in the tin holder he'd brought to keep the candle upright and leaned back on her hands. She wasn't aware of being hot, but she could feel sweat on her neck. She wasn't

209

aware of being crazy, but she could feel herself a breath away from saying yes.

She tried another drag on the cigarette. She hated the way it tasted. She was going to have gut-wrenching nicotine fits for a week.

"It wouldn't be fair," she said finally. "I made a promise. I can go back on the promise, God knows, that's why they have postulant year, but I'd have to, I'd have to—"

"Tell them first?"

"Yes."

"Tell them. Go back, go to sleep, wake up tomorrow, and tell them. I'll be waiting for you at the front door at nine."

She took one more drag on the cigarette—the last, she promised herself—and said, "No." She had to force the sound out of her throat. There was something stuck in there, trying to block it.

She heard movement on the other side of the candle and realized David was standing up, stretching, moving back and forth just out of sight. She stiffened. God only knew what she would do if he came near her. She could practically feel his skin from where he was now. More of her ached than her head. Dear God, more of her ached.

She heard Mary saying, "You think it's going to be easy."

She heard herself telling Angela Louise, "I don't want that from him anymore."

She put her face in her hands. "David."

He stopped pacing and knocked something metallic and hollow against the concrete floor. "David what? It's all you say anymore, Kat. David, David, David. You want to make love to me. You know you want to make love to me. I know you want to make love to me. I don't understand."

"I know you don't understand."

"Oh, for God's sake."

"Don't keep saying that." She took another hit of the cigarette. It was a hit, not a drag. After two months, it was as good as marijuana for getting high. It made her feel light-headed and detached, almost calm.

"All right," she said. "Now, listen. I'm a little upset."

"So am I, Kat."

She rubbed her face. Her cheeks felt numb. "You. Mary. Something, it's going to sound crazy, but something about a bird. And something that happened today. We had an extraordinary instruction."

"Sleep with me."

"Listen to me."

"You're changing the subject."

"No I'm not." The cigarette was half burned down. Seeing so much of it gone made her panicky. She sucked on it again. Her heart started to trip-hammer, from nicotine or stress, she didn't know. She could feel the shift in David's mood. The urgency had lifted. She no longer needed to give him an answer in the next thirty seconds. She felt the knots begin to pop in her back and legs. "Mary came," she said, "and I was thinking about you. I've been dreaming about you. And I was walking across North Lawn and I saw this bird, this cut-up bird, and there was Mary. Do you see?"

"No."

"Neither do I, exactly. But David, a cat couldn't do that to a bird, could it? The wings looked *severed*, as if something had gone after them very carefully with a razor. The cuts were clean. And the eyes were out. A cat couldn't—"

"What is this conversation about?"

"Nicotine," Kat said. "I've got a nicotine high."

He disappeared from her awareness and popped up again, very large and real, kneeling beside her on the blanket. She could feel his breath in her hair. She should have been afraid of him, but she wasn't. She thought she could settle against his shoulder and be comforted as innocently as a child by its mother.

"I'm sorry," she said.

"*I'm* sorry." He let his fingers trace the high, wide contours of her cheekbones, the slightly boxed curve of her jaw. She felt the need to lean against him rise in her again, and almost gave into it. The skin of his fingers gave off electric sparks. They connected to something not so comforting inside her. He sat back. She started to breathe again.

"Let's have a toast to David Waltham Marsh," he said. "He has a positive genius for blowing it."

"David."

He waved her away, but he didn't move back to his side of the candle. His long legs stretched out beside her knees, touching her lightly, without insistence. Then he put his

211

hands in her hair. "You look like hell, Kat. I didn't realize until I got this close."

Kat shook free of him. "I look like hell because I got sick this morning," she said. "Some kind of food poisoning."

"It's me."

"No."

Had she really intended to come here and tell him about the bird, and about Jane? She supposed she had. It all seemed very far away now. Her suspicions of Jane were chimeras.

She curled into the blanket, keeping her distance even though she didn't want to. When she was close to him, she could feel the effort it cost him. He was a good man. She had no right to put him through this pain.

She rubbed her hands together, wondering how they got clammy so fast. "David? If you gave me an ultimatum right now, if you said if I didn't sleep with you, leave with you, if you said it was that or never see you again, I couldn't say no."

This time, when the Zippo went off, she was close enough to smell lighter fluid.

"For that, I should give you six kinds of ultimatums and drag you out of here by your hair."

"Oh." Kat laughed. "Maybe that's the answer."

"I don't think so." He moved away. "We never pulled a lot of bullshit on each other. I could give you an either-or, but I don't think I could mean it. But right now, the way I feel, if you decided to spend the rest of your life in this place, I'd still be here for you. I could lie about that, but I won't. Maybe that makes me a first-class asshole."

"What it probably makes you is a saint."

"God forbid."

"The thing is," Kat said, "with things the way they are, I could go on for years, never making up my mind. Nine years before final profession, David. I could just drift, the whole time."

"You'll make up your mind. And it won't take nine years."

"No, just until I've turned myself into a psychotic."

He took her face into his hands and kissed her nose, as if

212

he were playing. If it hadn't been for the stiff violence in his hands, she would have been convinced he was playing.

"Go," he said. "Say hello to Annie for me."

Kat smiled. "You came into town to see her today."

"I saw her practically faint. Tell her I hope she's all right. And go, Kat. Go *now*."

"Yes."

She turned to look at him when she got to the door. The candlelight made his face seem full of hollows.

He looked haunted.

4

She was halfway back to the main building before she realized there were lights on the first floor of North Wing, unusual lights, emergency lights. She was thinking about choice, and lines of demarcation, and what she would do if she was pushed, now, into making a decision. She was intensely relieved David hadn't pushed her. She would opt for a middle space—complete irresponsibility, catatonia, self-denial. It was already coming at her from too many sides. There were already too many decisions to be made on too little data. She didn't think she could stand one more thing, one more person, pounding at her.

Which, of course, was why she was thinking so obsessively about the bird. There was nothing really wrong about the bird. It was just that thinking about the bird was easier than thinking about David.

She was already on North Lawn before she realized why there were lights on the first floor of the wing. They were waiting for her. Reverend Mother. Clare Marie.

And Mary.

"Sometimes I think the Buddhists have more sense than we do. More psychological sense."

"Sister?"

"The Buddhists. Thomas Merton was very big on the Buddhists."

"I don't see what the Buddhists have to do with it. I don't see what the Buddhists have to do with anything."

"They don't believe in sin, Lieutenant. They have an ancient monastic tradition, as old as ours or older, but they don't believe in sin."

"This is sin, Sister. I thought we had that much straightened out."

"This is crime, Lieutenant. And the other part, the part that had me so worked up I was blind to everything else, that wasn't even crime."

SUNDAY

Mrs. Bliss came in another rented Lincoln Continental, a blue one this time. David saw her pull up half a minute before he realized he was being watched. He saw her get out of the car, holding a pocketbook of some unyielding, man-made material over her stomach. She looked like she was protecting herself from a bayonet charge. He thought of Annie breaking down in the post office. Would she be required to see her mother? If they were so big on charity in there, they could at least protect Annie Bliss from her mother.

There was no one to protect him from Mary Connor O'Brien, but he had seen her before she'd wanted him to.

He was almost prepared for her. He watched her pick her way through the ruts and ice of the entryway road. Mary still looked too much like Kat not to make him ache. She had also developed (for him) a personality of her own. She made him need cigarettes.

What did Kat do up there, when everybody else had visitors? Did Annie's brother come, to make an Electra triangle with Annie and her mother? He got his cigarettes out and lit one. There was no point thinking about Annie's brother. It made no sense to want to strangle the man.

Mary tapped on the passenger-side window, a dull tap make by knuckles in thin stretched kid. David leaned sideways and jacked the door open for her. She folded herself in, looking amused.

"I should have brought my detective," she said. "He doesn't believe in you."

"You hired a detective."

"Of course I hired a detective. You weren't doing shit."

She took out her cigarettes—tapered Dunhill customs in a silver case—and lit one with the dashboard lighter. David wanted to laugh. They were less than seventy feet from the Agnus Dei gate. He had been sitting in the car for half an hour, trying to muster the courage to pull into the drive. Kat wanted to see his name in the visitors' book, to greet him and pour him tea. She'd been asking him for weeks. He'd been sitting outside this gate every Sunday for a month. He couldn't make himself risk it. Mary, who, so far as he knew, had nothing to risk, was sitting out here with him.

"If you're going to give me another lecture about getting her out," he said, "don't bother."

"I told you. You weren't doing shit. I took care of it my own way."

"You hired a detective."

"Not right away. What I did right away was follow you."

She couldn't possibly have said what he just heard.

"I followed you," she said. "Actually, I followed Kat, it was easier. I lost her, but I followed her, and after I lost her I made enough fuss so somebody took notice for once. Then I went out and hired a detective, a lawyer, and a press agent. All in less than a week."

"What the hell are you trying to do?"

"Exactly what you're trying to do. Get her out of there."

"I'm not trying to get her out of there."

"Like hell you're not." She swung him around to face her. She was much stronger than he'd thought. She was right, too. He'd never taken her seriously. What would have happened if he'd driven up to the front door and signed the visitors' book and asked for Kat? What would have happened? He thought he was going to vomit.

"Listen to me," she said. "I had him go through your house. I had him go through your 'papers.' Your 'novel.' All that wretched pornography about nuns and altars and High Mass sanctified by menstrual blood. Very melodramatic, David. I'd hardly have thought it your kind of thing."

"My sexual problems have nothing to do with Kat."

"That's what he said. And *they* won't read them. But I can use them anyway, David. I don't give a damn what you do or don't have the balls for. I'm going to get her out of there."

His eyes were dry and hot. "She would have left, for God's sake. She would have left if you'd just given me time."

"Left for what? For you?"

"I thought that was what you wanted."

"I want to make sure she doesn't get away with it." She grabbed his head and wrenched it toward her. "You're all shit, David, every last one of you. You're all shit and you turn us all to shit. We let ourselves be turned to shit because it's the only choice we have. The only choice. Listen to me, David. This is what mothers pass on to their daughters. This is the *truth*."

"If you don't open the door and get back on the road, I'll open it for you and dump you."

He heard the door latch click, felt the sudden sucking shock of cold wind. "Behold the new man," Mary said. "No balls. No prick. No God Almighty self-respect."

"You're drunk."

"I'm winning."

The door slammed, closing him in alone. The air went hot and stale and rank with cigarette smoke. God takes care of drunks and little children. When he looked up, Mary was chugging across the ice in her Brooks Brothers stack heels, not even swaying.

From the back, she looked like Kat-turned-suburban-matron, the Kat he supposed he had wanted Kat to become. It would have been impossible for them both. He wouldn't have wanted her that way.

What was he going to do now?

"Why don't they come down from there?"

"They're taking statements, Sister."

"Statements?"

"They're trying to find out what happened."

"I've been telling you what happened."

"You've been giving me a history of monasticism in the Church. Or here."

"What do you want from me? Just to know the knife came from the kitchen? The knife came from the kitchen."

"The knife came from the kitchen and the stool came from one of the other towers and the rope came from the basement. She must have been planning this for weeks."

"Maybe she was."

"What were you doing all those weeks?"

ULTIMATUM

1

Kat had expected recriminations, or restrictions, or penance. She had not expected silence, which was what she got. By the time she was called to Reverend Mother's office, a week to the day after she was caught, Kat had almost begun to believe it had never happened. She had stepped into the light, seen Mary, and expended a frantic

217

burst of energy convincing herself not to cut and run. She had been sure they had followed her, even eavesdropped on her conversation with David. She thought they were going to expel her on the spot. Then she had calmed enough to notice the expression on Reverend Mother's face. Whatever else was going on, they weren't going to expel her.

She stopped outside Reverend Mother's office and gave two loud taps. A voice inside said, "Come in." Kat pushed open the door.

Reverend Mother was sitting behind the desk, looking squat and uncomfortable. "Come in," she said again. "Sit down."

Kat closed the door behind her. "Yes," she said. "I—ah. Could I not sit just yet? I—"

"I didn't mean to imply sitting was a matter of religious obedience," Reverend Mother said. "At the moment."

"No," Kat said. She walked to the window and looked out. Behind her, Reverend Mother creaked uneasily on her chair. Kat gripped the windowsill and rocked. "Is there something I can do for you?" Kat bit her lip. Of course there was something she could do. She wouldn't have been called unless there was.

"Your mother," Reverend Mother said, shuffling papers on her desk, "is a very determined woman. Very imaginative."

"Is she?" Kat said.

"Quite," Reverend Mother said.

Kat sat down in the chair next to Reverend Mother's desk. "I'm sorry," she said. "She gets drunk and when she gets drunk she gets—"

"I know what she gets."

"I guess you do." Kat rubbed her arms. "She, um, that's what happened with my father, you see. She—I mean, it's not that he wasn't a bastard. Excuse my language, but there isn't any other word for it. God only knows he was a bastard. Is. We haven't seen him for six or seven years. He used to *hack* at her. He'd pick at her hair and her body and her clothes and her conversation. Sometimes he'd do it in front of company, in front of her friends. In front of his friends he was always all right. Anyway, she'd go to the priest and he'd

218

give her a lot of nonsense about it was her Christian duty. She was supposed to put up with it. And then she'd come home and finish the Scotch."

"A priest is not God."

"Yes, Reverend Mother, I know." Kat smiled faintly. "I went to the same priest when I was applying here. For my papers. He said you'd never let me in."

"Did you believe him?"

"I don't know. It didn't seem important at the time."

"Katherine—"

"No," Kat said. "Let me finish. I mean, excuse me, Reverend Mother..."

"It's all right."

"It's just that he was a bastard, but she was crazy. When she drank. I was away at boarding school, so I only caught it at vacations, but it was awful. She would never look drunk. She'd just start doing things. She took a razor and shredded all his shirts once. Another time she put his shoes out in the rain. She smashed his shaving mirror."

"She never did those things when she was sober?"

"When she was sober she was just bitter."

Reverend Mother picked up a pencil and stared at the eraser tip. "This has been going on for how long? Six or seven years?"

"No, Reverend Mother. When I was about halfway through my junior year at Farmington, she went stone cold sober, left the Church, and got a divorce. As far as I know, she never touched another drink until after I came here. She drove me up here. She wasn't happy, but she wasn't drunk."

"I thought that man drove you up here. The one she's accusing you of meeting."

"David Marsh, Reverend Mother. He came by himself. To . . . see me off."

Reverend Mother gave Kat a look that said she knew exactly what *that* meant. "I told you I wasn't going to treat you like a child, Katherine, and I won't. But we seem to have run across a complication in the last few days."

"Don't tell me. She tried to set fire to the refectory."

"I only wish she had." Reverend Mother found what she was looking for, a pale green folder. "I said your mother was

219

a very imaginative woman. Maybe I should have said resourceful. Do you know a publication called the *Confidential Observer*?"

"It would be hard not to. They sell them at the check-outs in supermarkets."

"I haven't been in a supermarket in thirty-six years. I sent Sister Annunciata into town for a copy. If I'd known what we were getting into, I'd have sent a lay person. However, the publication was described to me only as a magazine. It was very interesting reading."

"I think it used to be on the Index. When there was an Index."

"There was an article purporting to tell readers how to protect their families from being kidnapped by unidentified flying objects. I was unaware that people in the world were now worried about being kidnapped by unidentified flying objects."

"Reverend Mother—"

"No, no. I'm being facetious. I understand. They're lonely and lost and old. None of this would be a problem, you see, if it weren't for the Cardinal Archbishop. Your mother has contacted a reporter for this magazine. She has made it perfectly clear—your mother, that is; the reporter is a man—that if you do not leave this house by the end of the week, she will give this publication material for an article. Very ambiguous material. Very volatile material."

"About me?"

"In part. In part, the material is about community practices."

"She's going to say we beat ourselves with whips and sleep in our coffins."

Reverend Mother drew a small black bag from her pocket. She opened it and took out a long knotted-cord rope. "Do you know what this is, Katherine?"

Kat's throat was very dry. "No, Reverend Mother."

"It's called a discipline. When you have been a canonical novice for six months, you will be given one of these to use, every Saturday, when you make the Stations of the Cross. You will use it in secret. You will swing it first over one shoulder, then over the other, very lightly and always over your clothes. In that way, you will participate symbolically in the scourging of Christ."

Kat held her hands tightly in her lap. "That's hardly beating ourselves with whips, Reverend Mother."

"No, it's not. However, the use of the discipline as symbol is very new with us, instituted in the past twenty years. A great many of the older Sisters still use it as it was traditionally used in this Order. On bare skin. And meant to hurt. Not to wound, not to maim, but to hurt."

"The Order doesn't forbid it?"

"The Order forbids fanaticism, and morbidness. It does not forbid corporal penance when properly used. Needless to say, 'properly used' is defined here according to Church tradition, not modern psychology."

Reverend Mother returned the discipline to its bag. Kat turned away. "I suppose there are other things like that. Things I don't know about yet. But she does. Somehow."

"The 'somehow' isn't difficult to work out. We lost almost two thirds of our Sisters between 1964 and 1975. They wouldn't be that hard to find."

"So the *Confidential Observer* runs a story on how she's trying to get me out of here, and they bring up all this, and they make us look . . . crazy."

"Katherine, as I said, none of this would be a problem for me if it weren't for the Cardinal Archbishop. I don't think this publication is much respected. Or much believed. If we all kept our silence, nothing would come of it. But the Cardinal Archbishop is a passionately loyal man with an unfortunate tendency to speak his mind. He will denounce the article. His denunciation will bring it to the attention of more reputable newspeople. And, as I said, former members of this Order are not hard to find."

Kat stared past Reverend Mother to the trees on North Lawn. She was numb. "You're right," she said. "My mother is a very imaginative woman."

"Katherine Mary—"

"Do you want me to leave, Reverend Mother? Is that what all this is about?"

"No," Reverend Mother said. "I want you to make up your mind."

Kat stared at her hands.

"I have problems," Reverend Mother said, "both with the hierarchy and with this Order's Motherhouse General in Rome. This . . . situation . . . will only make them worse. If I must deal with it and its effects on our continuing difficulties, then I want to do it to good purpose. Normally, we give postulants a year to sort themselves out. I can't give you that time, Katherine. If I'm going to ride this out, if I'm going to protect you when the consequences to this Order are possibly destructive, then I have to know you intend to stay with us. I have to have a commitment, at least for the novitiate. You have to make up your mind."

"Yes," Kat said. She thought of David, waiting in the Retreat House garage. Usually when she thought of him he seemed to call her, to draw her. This time, he was only a statue in a room of statues, a companion piece to the Reverend Mother statue and the Mary Connor O'Brien statue and the Agnus Dei tableaux. The stress had finally got to her. She was wrung out. "I don't know what you want me to do," she said. "Sign something? Make a declaration in chapel?"

"I don't know what I want you to do, either. I just want you to do something. By Friday, I must have some sign that you are committed, or that you are going out."

"What kind of sign?"

"I don't know."

"Reverend Mother, I don't even know how to start thinking about this."

Reverend Mother tapped her desk. "Are you in love with this man?"

"I don't know, Reverend Mother. No, that isn't true. I love him. I don't know *how* I love him. If that makes any sense."

"I think it makes sense. I'm not going to ask you if you've been meeting him. You're not a child, and this is not a game. But sometimes the most impossible things are less impossible when you have help. When you have someone to listen."

Kat stood up. She wasn't supposed to dismiss herself, but she couldn't sit any longer in this room. A week ago she'd been telling herself the last thing she needed was pressure. Now the walls were compressing, the sides of her head were

222

compressing, the air was thickening in her lungs. She made an awkward, halfhearted curtsy. "Reverend Mother."

"I wasn't suggesting that as a sign, Katherine. I was only offering to help."

"Yes, Reverend Mother."

"All right," Reverend Mother said. She stood up. "I'm not going to keep you. But, Katherine . . ."

"I know," Kat said. "By Friday."

2

In the East Wing second-floor hall, two windows, open as if it were midsummer, sucked cold and snow onto the floor. Kat stopped at one of them. The deciduous trees had gone bare. She could see the roof of Retreat House and the Mary shrine planted in the high rocky hill that made up most of the back acre.

It was late morning. She should go back to the laundry room. Angela Louise would be struggling against the load of wimples and veils, against William's eclectic conversations, against herself, probably, to keep Minor Silence and her equilibrium. It was remarkable how well Angela Louise kept her equilibrium.

She went down a flight of stairs into what was called "old cloakroom," a long, wooden-floored room with hooks for choir cloaks on the walls. At the back of it, she let herself into the switchboard office.

The switchboard office was dark. In the old days, four Sisters manned the board continually from seven in the morning until nine at night. Now, no one manned the board until Vespers. Any day calls were picked up in Reverend Mother's office.

Reverend Mother's office had a single line. The switchboard had two lines. Sisters with urgent family calls were sent to the switchboard and its second line.

Kat didn't know if this constituted an urgent family call. She didn't even know if she cared. She plugged in the auxiliary line and dialed David in Eagleville.

THE FORGIVENESS
OF SINS

After the bell rang for Particular Examen, Annie could hear pens scratching against paper, dozens of pens on dozens of notebook pages in dozens of choir stalls from one end of the chapel to the other. Her stomach rose and fell and settled into the sickened anticipation she remembered from rides on the roller coaster at Savin Rock. Things always fell farther than they rose. Anticipation was worse than actuality.

She bent over her examen book and wrote: *proclaim myself for behaving uncharitably toward my Sister Postulant Jane.*

It was very hot. On the other side of the stall, Jane finished writing, put her pen upright in the well, and began to read silently, lips moving. Annie folded her hands over her examen book and willed herself not to look sideways at Jane's neat, blocky confession. Her own was sprawling, a disordered mess, incomplete. It had been like that all week. Once or twice she'd written furiously for fifteen minutes, only to find she hadn't been listing faults at all. She'd been writing about the book, or Stephen, or (worse) her father. This time she'd remembered to list faults, but couldn't force herself to write all of them. She had "snapping at Sister Gervase in the library" and "being inattentive to Martha's needs in refectory," but not "indulging in distractions during Mass." She had nothing on *what* she had allowed to distract her during Mass, that lumbering daydream that had become as much a part of her as a Siamese twin, where she descended a staircase dressed in backless, strapless black satin with diamonds in her hair. She could not be corrected for posture in line without getting desperate for ten minutes in a lavatory stall with Stephen's latest.

224

At the far end of the chapel, a light went on over the third confessional, announcing Father Duffy's availability. Annie hesitated. It was the perfect opportunity. Most Sisters took confession in the morning. She could go in now and talk as long as she liked without worrying about holding someone up. On the other hand, what could she say? When I think of my mother, the world goes black? When I think of this house, I want to run? When I think of my father . . . She felt compulsively for her father's picture, found it, pulled away as if burned. She had been trying to get rid of the thing for a week. She hadn't been able to do it. It was alive in there.

"Idolatry," Jane told her once, "is the principal sin of modern man."

Annie didn't remember what had started Jane on idolatry that day—they'd been hosing out apple barrels in the kitchen yard—but Jane had scared her to death.

"People think it has to do with putting a metal animal on an altar and kneeling in front of it," Jane said, "but it doesn't. They think just because the only thing they kneel in front of is a Catholic altar, they're not idolaters, but they are. They worship money, and success, and beauty, and sex, and sometimes even their own bodies. They put their faith in everything and anything but God. They *believe* in progress and they *make* their Easter *duty*. And you know what happens to them? They end in the blood and death they've been worshipping all along."

"Why do you think of these things?" Annie said. "How can you?"

"I don't think of them," Jane said. "They just sort of come to me. When I'm praying. You talk to God and He talks back, and if you're listening you hear Him."

"I don't hear Him."

"You're letting yourself be distracted. You're letting yourself be an idolater."

"Don't be ridiculous."

"What do you think of when you ought to be listening to God?"

What she thought of was *Princess Daisy*. Or her father.

And Jane was a prophet.

The light over the confessional went off. A moment later,

the light over the Reconciliation Room went on. Father Duffy, having had no luck with traditional confessions, had resigned himself to face-to-face. Annie closed her examen book. Isolation was the worst part of being at Agnus Dei. Jane told her things and Annie had no one to ask about them. She could ask Kat—the group as it had existed the first few weeks had been carefully broken up, but she still had chances to talk to Kat—but she knew what Kat would say. "Be sensible and it will be all right." Except the frightening thing about the things Jane said was that they made ultimate, apocalyptic sense. She felt battered against rocks by a windstorm.

Stephen. Her mother. Her father. Agnus Dei. David Marsh. Jane. Kat. *Princess Daisy*. The prison of Holy Poverty. The *prison*.

She got out of her prie-dieu and headed for the Reconciliation Room, wishing she'd been fast enough to catch Father Duffy in the old confessional. She could always ask him to move—he'd be delighted—but maybe the request would look suspicious. What sin could a nun have that was so terrible, she'd be afraid to tell the priest face-to-face?

She knocked on the Reconciliation Room door, heard Father's creaky "Come in," and pushed through. He was sitting on one of the two unvarnished chairs. The other was pulled close beside him.

Annie signed herself. Father Duffy said, "May the grace of the Holy Spirit fill your heart with light, that you may confess your sins with loving trust and come to know that God is merciful."

"Amen," Annie said.

Father Duffy patted the empty chair, beaming. "Sit down, Sister, sit down. There's no need to look so nervous."

Annie sat down. Father duffy patted her shoulder and beamed again. Even the deep rutted lines in his face looked forced.

"It's not exactly a confession," Annie said. "There was something I wanted to ask you. Something doctrinal."

Father Duffy nodded patiently. Annie hesitated. Father Duffy meant well, but he wasn't very bright. Annie didn't trust him. Then she remembered the picture of her father and felt her throat go tight.

She took a deep breath and said, "Father, why do people commit suicide?"

"Suicide?" Duffy's voice was a squeak. "Are you thinking of committing suicide?"

"No, no," Annie said, feeling a heavy wash of guilt. She had panicked the man out of his chair. "Father, no, it's not me. My father—"

He turned sharply to stare at her. "Your father," he said. "Your father committed suicide."

"Yes, Father."

"Ah." Father Duffy relaxed. He shuffled to his chair and sat down again. "Your father committed suicide," he said again, "and this disturbs you."

"Yes, Father." It did a good deal more than disturb her. "It happened when I was seven years old. He was buried in the Church. Our priest said he wasn't in his right mind, and I guess the bishop believed him. So they—"

"Yes, yes," Father Duffy said. "That happens some-times."

He had become preoccupied. His preoccupation made her jumpier than his meretricious beaming.

"Someone here said it was idolatry. That people commit suicide because they worship something, money or fame or social position, something not God, and then because it's false they fall into despair and kill themselves. And it doesn't matter if they're mentally ill, because idolatry can *make* you mentally ill. If you persist in sin it can make you mentally ill."

"Ah," Father Duffy said again. He was staring into the distance. He didn't seem to have heard a word she said. "I don't understand," he said finally, "what all this has to do with you."

"I don't either. But I persist in sin myself. I do the same things wrong over and over again, even when I know they're wrong. So you see . . ."

"No, no," Father Duffy said. "I don't see. Did you tell your Reverend Mother about this?"

"About my father?"

"That he committed suicide, yes. That he was thought to be mad."

Annie had never heard anyone use the word "mad" in

that sense except on Saturday-afternoon Creature Features. It was a nineteenth-century word. She couldn't make it apply to her father or herself.

"Nobody ever asked me about my father," she said. "They asked for my parish records. They got them."

"It might not have been in the parish records. At least not the ones they sent here. Was it the same priest, the priest who buried your father, who wrote your recommendation for the religious life?"

Annie coughed uneasily, involuntarily. "The priest who buried my father is dead. He died not long after my father did."

"Ah," Father Duffy said. "So the new one might not have known."

"That my father committed suicide?"

"That he was considered insane." Father Duffy beamed again. "That explains everything, you see."

"Explains what?" Annie asked desperately.

"What you're doing here. How you were accepted into this Order."

Annie rubbed her temples. "I don't understand how my father's suicide could have anything to do with my being accepted into this order."

"No, no," Father Duffy said. "It's not the suicide, it's the madness. Of course, things have changed. I may be completely behind the times. You'd have to ask Reverend Mother about that. They don't accept girls for the Society of Mary where there's been madness in the family."

Annie bolted out of her chair. "What?"

"They're afraid of the heredity, you see. It runs in families, madness does. There's always the worry madness will imitate true vocation, and we can't have that."

"No," Annie said. "We can't have that." The headache hit her without warning, a vicious jab at the soft core of her brain, releasing her mother's voice, her mother's face, her mother's smile. The panic that followed was uncomplicated and direct, a desperate fear that Father Duffy would go to Reverend Mother. Then she realized she was in the confessional. They had made the form when she walked in. There was nothing he could do.

"You must tell your Reverend Mother," Father Duffy

said again. "When you do, come back and I'll give you absolution. And then" —he shrugged— "you must ask God to reveal His plan for you. He has a plan for every one of us."

"Yes," Annie said.

Father Duffy had gone back to beaming at her. She let herself into the chapel, closing the door of the Reconciliation Room behind her. Kat was bent over her examen book, immobile, stolid, even more tense than she had been all week. Jane was leaning back on the kneeler.

The bell rang the end of Minor Meditation. Sisters began to move, clearing their stalls of examen books and writing implements.

Annie didn't know which was worse: that she couldn't rid herself of the memory of her mother's living room, or that she now knew the Society of Mary would not take girls with madness in their families.

TRANSFERENCE

The copy of *Princess Daisy* was under Annie's mattress, resting on the ledge created by the joining of the wooden slat and the metal frame. Jane found it when she went to postulant corridor to get their aprons. She held it in her hands, turned it over and over, and wondered what it was supposed to mean.

The copy of *Princess Daisy* had a sticker on the spine that said, "Northton General Store."

Jane picked at it. There was something here she could use, but she couldn't for the moment think what it was. She was not feeling well. She hadn't fed the birds for a week. Sometimes the rage was so red and hot it made her blind. There was Kat, and there was Annie. She couldn't tell if what she'd done to Kat was working. As for Annie —Annie was not what Jane had thought she was, at first.

She put *Princess Daisy* back on its makeshift ledge, thought about it, and moved it down one slat. She had been moving more and more things in Annie's cell. Annie either didn't notice, or did and thought she was going crazy. She probably thought she was going crazy. As, of course, she was.

She got Annie's apron and threw it over her arm. Kat was only a diversion. Kat was close to Annie. Kat could get in her way. It would be just as well to get rid of Kat. On the other hand, it wouldn't matter one way or the other, as long as she succeeded with Annie. Jane had been deluded, in the beginning. She had thought Annie was meant to be her friend. She had suffered Annie's impatience meekly, swallowed her rebuffs, tried harder and harder week after week in the face of that all-encompassing rejection. It had been worse than what had happened with Bridget Gallagher in eighth grade. This time, it had been humiliation by choice.

The pills had finally made her realize. Annie was not her friend. Annie was Jane *herself*. She had stolen Jane's life, sucked it out of her the way a cat sucks breath from a baby. It had come to her in a vision one night in the tower, the last time she fed the birds. Annie was her twin, a secret part of her that had split off and taken everything of value with it. Annie had left her with her mother's hatred and her father's hands, dressed in torn and borrowed clothes, shut out, shut in, caged forever. If she hadn't been afraid of running low on pills, she would have spiked Annie's coffee the very next night, just to see if Annie recognized it, too.

She crossed the corridor and went into her own cell. She took her apron off the hook and weighed it, feeling for bulk. She couldn't risk being cut off from the pills. The pills cleared her.

It was going to come out right. She wouldn't even have to do anything. She would just prepare the ground, and Annie would take care of the rest herself. She was not quite sure what "taking care of it" would entail, but that didn't matter. She would make Annie ready. Annie would know.

She put her apron over her arm. The pills gave her visions all the time now. She saw her mother's bloody hands in the light from the flashlight. She saw Annie swimming like a lemming out to sea. She saw Martha's cat, writhing and tear-

230

ing against the knife that came down over and over again on its belly, on its throat. She saw that even though it hadn't happened yet.

The anger came out of her hands like the light had come out of the Virgin's fingers when she revealed the Miraculous Medal.

There was something about *Princess Daisy* she could use. She just had to figure out what.

She went back into the corridor and headed for the door. She was always very calm these days. Especially when she was having her visions.

AN INWARD AND
SPIRITUAL GRACE

1

Kat was halfway to Retreat House before she realized how stupid she had been, all day, all week, maybe ever since she'd come to Agnus Dei. She ducked against the wind and snow that pelted her like a swarm of wet, vicious gnats. She was supposed to be at rosary or work or choir. Instead, she was making her way to Retreat House in broad daylight, asking to get caught. She could have waited for David to come tonight. She could have sent word through Annie. She could have behaved like a responsible adult.

There was crazy, urgent music under her skin, saying: hurry, hurry, this is going to be the last time. She couldn't get past it.

The wind whipping through her thin veil was making her ears raw with cold. The music under her skin changed to: *now or never.* Now or never what? Did she intend to wrestle David to the floor of the Retreat House garage and impale herself on him? Did she want to climb over the wall like the eloping Juliet and disappear into the night? What did she think she was doing?

She made it to the Retreat House courtyard and stopped to catch her breath. Reverend Mother's talk had not pushed her into this. She had been like this all week, ever since she had realized, while trying not to, that she was going to have to commit herself, blind. She had gone down on her knees in chapel at four o'clock in the morning and begged God to let it happen to her again, prove to her it had been real, tell her she had come to the place where she could find it again. She had lain cold in mind and body on the stone floor in front of the altar and felt nothing but the constant, ever louder beat of urgency. She had to make up her mind.

She took some snow off the ground, made it into a loose, wet ball, and lobbed it into the trees. It came apart in the air. It did nothing to relieve the crippling ache in her arms.

David opened the garage door and said, "Kat?"

"I'm here," Kat said.

He came into the courtyard and stopped in front of her. He was doing his best to keep his hands off her and his face free from worry. She wanted his arms around her shoulders and her panic mirrored in his face. She kept her arms wrapped around herself, as if cloth and skin could keep blind terror from breaking the surface. It didn't work. She had started to cry. She was seeing him through water, wavy, like a figure in a distorting glass. His eyes were wide and afraid, confused. He was frozen by indecision.

She dragged her voice out of some dungeon and said, "I need help."

Her face was against the sheepskin collar of his jacket and the dry hot skin of his neck. His chest rose and fell, rose and fell, against her breasts. His hands stroked her hair, feeling for the contours of her skull.

She cried until she was dry.

2

Later, when he had calmed her, she sat on the floor of the garage with a Thermos cap of coffee in her hands and tried to talk to him. He had retreated to a far wall, edgy and wounded, a little afraid for her. Now that she could think again, she couldn't look at him. His pain hurt her.

"It's been here all along. They think I'm level-headed. But it's been building up. When Mary showed up last week, when she came at night, not the first time, it was just too much. I could feel it . . . coming out. Feel myself being shredded. She had a piece and you had a piece and Agnus Dei had a piece and it was just . . ."

"Don't," David said. "You're just getting yourself upset."

"I know." She took a deep breath. "Maybe it's my fault. The rest of them have religious crises once a week. They cry in Guidance. They get angry and blow up, or they get upset and drop the dishes they're wiping. I just, I don't know. Keep calm. Try to look calm."

"Maybe you are calm."

"Right."

He pushed himself away from the wall and came toward her, but only halfway. He stopped before she was at arm's length. "She gave you an ultimatum and it upset you. Maybe you're turning this into more than it is."

"I wish it was more than it is. I wish it meant something."

David lowered himself to the floor. "How can it not mean anything? She's asked you to make a choice between Agnus Dei and me."

"No," Kat said. "That's exactly what she hasn't done." She tapped David's knee. The need to touch him hadn't disappeared with her panic. She wanted to learn the shape of his body all over again, with her hands. She contented herself with the pat on the knee. "What she didn't do," she repeated, "is tell me to choose between you and the Order. She asked me to promise I would remain through my novitiate, that's all. She never asked if I was meeting you and she said she wasn't going to. And she won't. I could stay for the next two and a half years and go on meeting you once a week. Nothing has to change."

"She didn't mean that," David said. "She meant to tie you down, make you choose. She just put it badly."

"No, she didn't."

"She couldn't possibly put up with this."

"There's a chance we could get caught. We have this thing, called Chapter of Faults, where you tell the Sisters what you've done wrong for the week and they fill in what they think you've missed. Someone could see us. Someone could report me in Chapter. She'd have to do something about it then."

"She could send someone to be sure you were seen."

"She wouldn't do it."

David got to his feet again. Kat thought he was avoiding her. He wanted to withhold himself until he was sure of her. She didn't blame him.

"You're making the woman out to be a saint. She isn't, Kat. And even if she is, she's got responsibilities. To the Order. To the Church. To the tradition you're always talking about. She couldn't let something like this go on. Unless she thinks we're not really meeting."

"She knows we're meeting."

Kat put the Thermos cap at her feet. Now that she was calm, she was cold. She wondered what time it was. She had no idea how long she'd cried, or if bells had rung while they were talking.

"Maybe what I'm trying to tell you," she said, "is it doesn't matter what you believe about Reverend Mother. This is what I believe. And that doesn't matter either, because—sit down, for God's sake."

He stopped pacing and got out his cigarettes. He lit a match and dropped it on the floor. It gave him an excuse not to sit down.

She thought of the first time he had made love to her, of his body coming into hers, of the hard swell of him stretching her, stretching her, until she felt huge. She slid against him without abrasion. The world was a dark tunnel. He put down roots in her.

She said, "I love you."

He said, "I've waited three years to hear you say that. Now it sounds so damn much like good-bye."

)

She stayed until she heard bells. Then she got to her feet and brushed off her skirt and cape. Their conversation had disintegrated into hollow politeness. She still wanted him to touch her. He wanted them out in the air, where he wouldn't feel caged in with her.

He held the door for her, a dancing-school gesture that

234

was, to him, probably as automatic as breathing. She went into the courtyard and stared at heavy clouds that promised snow.

"You don't wear a watch," she said. "I have no idea what time it is. I have no idea where I'm supposed to go."

"Does this get you in a lot of trouble?"

"It probably gets me a few meals on my knees."

He ran his hands through his hair. "I'll be here tonight," he said. "Usual time, usual place." He smiled. "If you don't come, I'll know you've given up on me."

"If I don't come, I might not have been able to get out."

"If you want to get out, you'll get out. You being you, it's a good thing for the Catholic Church you don't want to be Pope."

"Maybe I do."

She looked back, expecting to see him still holding the door, and found him instead right behind her. She turned into his arms without thinking, without caring, knowing only that he was reaching out to her and she didn't want to turn him away. When he bent over her, she parted her lips and drew his tongue into her mouth, imagining she could feel the naked shape of him pressing against her, even under all those layers of clothes.

When the second warning bell rang, she broke away from him.

And ran.

TOWER

"Marie Bernadette said you could see blood on the floor," Jane said, "but it isn't like that at all. You don't bleed from hanging."

Annie stepped away from the arch toward the middle of the tower room and got one of the floor brushes from the pile Jane had made in an empty bucket. Kat was coming back through the pine cover. *Running.* She had to be coming from Retreat House, which meant she had to have been meeting David. The sheer craziness of it made Annie's mind reel. God only knew what they would do to her if they found out.

They wouldn't do anything worse than they'd do to Annie if they found out about Annie's father. Annie dipped the brush into the water bucket and carried it, dripping, to the archway directly across from Jane. The archways left the room open to the wind. It was so cold it was hard to breathe, but Annie was sweaty and clammy under her cape, feverish. Her headache had been getting steadily worse since confession. Her heart rate had to be double whatever was normal. Her eyes had grown psychic cataracts, making everything misty. She did not want to spend the afternoon in North Tower with Jane. The place made her flesh creep.

Everybody had to spend an afternoon in North Tower. Kat had already been here. So had Constance before she was sent home. Martha had brought the cat. North Tower had to be kept clean. It was a shrine, like Lourdes, where the small square patch that held the miracle was kept always pristine, waiting for the return of the lady.

She took the can of abrasive and poured sand-gritty lines of it into the cracks between the stones at the base of the archway. She had been driving herself crazy all afternoon, waiting for herself to go off like an unstable chemical. Madness runs in families. What if it did? What if it didn't but they believed it did and sent her home? She saw her mother's face, pinched and satisfied. She saw her father turned to fragments of blood and skin and bone. She saw the girl who had hanged herself in this room, swinging on her rope, keeping time to the World Clock. She put all her arm strength behind the brush and ground abrasive into the mortar.

"What I can't understand," Jane said, "is how she fooled everyone for so long."

"Probably no one was awake," Annie said. "It was the middle of the night."

"I don't mean the night she came up here. I mean before." Jane made a trip to the water bucket and retreated to her archway. "There had to be signs. She had to have been unstable. If she was being in the least bit honest, her examen

236

book had to be a mess. Long *lists* of things. Pages crammed so tight you could hardly read them."

Her examen book had to be a mess.

Annie wiped crystals from the stone with the palm of her hand. She spent all her time with Jane now. Jane was a saint. She had a visionary quality, a bright glow in her eyes and the skin of her face, that left Annie feeling awed. And she was perfect. Annie was sure Clare Marie had put them together so she could learn from Jane's perfection. Just right now, though, she wished she'd been assigned with someone else. Someone who could have cared less about the girl in the tower, or the theology of suicide, or the real meaning of vocation.

"Would that have proved she was unstable, if she had a long list of things in her examen book?"

"Of course not," Jane said. "That would have proved she was evil."

"Maybe she was just conscientious."

"If she wasn't conscientious, she wouldn't have written it all down. If she wasn't evil, she wouldn't have had it to write down."

"How could she be conscientious and evil at the same time?"

Jane tapped the metal edge of the water bucket with her brush. "That was what I was trying to tell you the other day. You try to make it straightforward, but it isn't."

"I'm trying to make it make sense."

"It does make sense. She let her vocation be eaten away by her evil. She committed faults and didn't ask for correction. She committed sins and didn't ask for absolution. There was everything to cure her, but she loved her illness. More than she loved God."

"If she wrote it all down, then she offered it for correction."

"Maybe she didn't offer it in chapel. Or maybe she didn't write it *all* down."

"I think you make this stuff up," Annie said. "I think this is just another ghost story."

"I'll tell you what isn't a ghost story," Jane said. "You can feel it up here. You can feel her dying."

This time the abrasive crystals scattered into the air and onto the wooden floor.

Now that Jane had said it, Annie *could* feel it. The weight of the girl's body shifted and swung, making a heavy wind. The stench of that girl's dying was faint, like a strong scent caught from a long distance.

"You know why they send us up here to clean?" Jane edged across the room until she was standing next to Annie. "If you're like her, you can see her here. See her and hear her. That's how they know. They send us up here to find out who she comes to, and then they know."

Annie cut sideways and broke for the center of the room, for the air, for the cold, for the end to this headache that seemed to have escaped the confines of her skull and invaded the atmosphere. She tripped over the water bucket and knocked a set of scrub brushes to the floor. She sat down, hard, on the stool. The wind rushed at her ears like bees, stinging her.

Jane was standing where she had left her, relaxed, hardly curious. Annie felt the panic rise and fought it. She couldn't afford to panic, couldn't afford to lose control. She'd just done something outrageously stupid and she hadn't been in control of herself, she hadn't, she couldn't blame it on the headache, she'd had headaches before and never been like this, this was—

She took a deep breath and counted ten. Jane said, "Annie? Do you have one of your headaches? Are you all right?"

"Yes," Annie said. "Yes. I'm sorry. Headache."

"You ought to go to Elizabeth and get something for it," Jane said.

"Yes," Annie said again. How had she wrinkled her skirt? "I'm being stupid. I don't like to take pills."

Jane nodded wisely. "You feel it's a weakness," she said. "That's what I was trying to tell you. About the girl who died here."

"What?"

"Maybe in this case it was an end to her weakness. Not just despair, like they tell us. She was evil and she deserved to go to hell and in the end she loved God so much she offered herself for the worst punishment. Because she knew

238

she deserved nothing better. And God took her up on it. He accepted the gift. Do you see?"

"No," Annie said. The headache was coming back.

"She was ashamed," Jane said. "She deserved punishment and didn't want mercy."

"Excuse me," Annie said. "Excuse me. I—"

"You have to go down to Elizabeth. I'm sorry. I get so caught up in all the theory."

"That's all right," Annie said. She did not want Jane to kiss her shoes. She didn't want anything but to get out of the tower. She stumbled at the doorsill.

Out of the tower, things were better. Her head was clearer. Her muscles stopped twitching. There was nothing crazy or sinful about this. She just wanted to read. Father Duffy had upset her. Waiting for Chapter of Faults had upset her. Jane had upset her. There was nothing surprising or sinful or crazy about any of it.

Except that, the second time, she had stolen the book.

CULPA

1

The candles at the chapel door looked like the torches the townspeople of Rhodes carried to the harbor on bonfire night. Kat remembered the bonfires. She and David had spent a long night watching them.

She slipped into the cane seat third from the front on the right, the seat that would be hers for the rest of the year if she decided to stay. She had been trying all afternoon to force herself into one kind of total experience or the other. She had tried to feel David's body, David's hands, David's tongue. She had tried to feel that place. She felt nothing. She would have considered herself (as Daniella put it) "discorporeal," if she hadn't thought she was very close to being violently ill.

She had to make up her mind.

She listened to Reverend Mother and Clare Marie making their way up the center aisle and made one more stab at it. She closed her eyes. She held herself still. She tried to imagine the Blessed Virgin standing beside her, Christ Himself standing before her. It didn't work. God was an unleavened abstraction.

She closed her hand around her rosary crucifix and said: *Tell me what to do.*

Nobody answered.

Reverend Mother signed herself and said, "May the Holy Spirit fill our hearts and minds and souls. May we be granted the grace to speak with wisdom and charity."

"May we be granted the grace of perfect humility," Kat said, "and the strength to amend our lives, that we may be made worthy of the promises of Christ. Amen."

Reverend Mother sat down. Novices and professed Sisters bent over their hands. They would not look up during any Sister's proclamation, unless they were proclaiming her themselves. Even then, they would look only to the dais. This was supposed to be an act of charity, but Kat couldn't think of it that way. The averted heads threatened indifference.

Reverend Mother took a wooden chit out of the wooden box beside her chair. Kat had a sudden vision of Shirley Jackson's "The Lottery." They had pulled wooden chits out of a box there, too. Then they had stoned someone to death.

She told herself to calm down. They didn't stone people to death in this house. They made them beg soup on their knees. They made them kiss shoes. They made them keep silence for a week. But they didn't stone them to death.

No matter what she decided to say, this was going to be hard to take. For once, Kat could understand Annie without an active effort. This whole production made her jumpy and rebellious. It was like undergoing analysis in full view of three hundred people. Worse, there was no way to control it. Reverend Mother could ask questions. Clare Marie could ask questions. Any Sister above postulant status could make amendments. It could go on and on.

For her, it wouldn't go on and on. She wanted someone to force her to make one decision or the other, but Reverend Mother wouldn't do it. Even David wouldn't do it. Mary, who wanted to do it, didn't know how. What happened to

240

her would be only what she made happen. And she couldn't make up her mind.

She *wouldn't* make up her mind.

Reverend Mother said, "Sister Postulant Martha."

Kat relaxed. It was up to somebody else for a while.

Martha walked up the middle of the aisle to the open place before the dais. She got down on her hands and knees. Then she spread out her arms in the shape of a cross, with her forehead on the floor.

"Reverend Mother and Sisters, I proclaim myself for a fault against obedience in having spoken three times without necessity during Grand Silence. I proclaim myself for a fault against charity for having spoken sharply to my Sister Postulant Antonia four times during work charge."

Kat winced. Antonia was dense to the point of impenetrability. Saint Francis would have spoken sharply to Antonia.

"I proclaim myself for a fault against" —Martha hesitated— "against poverty," she said doubtfully, "for having allowed the cat to sleep in my cell six times." Her voice picked up. "I proclaim myself for all my faults, remembered and unremembered, and ask my Sisters in charity to speak to my correction."

There was a long silence while Reverend Mother waited to see if any Sister would speak to Martha's correction. Kat wondered what they could say. What fault could you find in a Sister whose failings all seemed to come from an excess of enthusiasm?

You could find great fault in a Sister who slipped out of the Motherhouse at night to walk in the woods. Even if all you knew was that she walked in the woods.

Reverend Mother said, "I would speak to my Sister Postulant Martha, in charity, of the will of her superiors, for the good of her soul."

Martha got to her knees, doubled forward, and touched her forehead to the floor.

Reverend Mother leaned forward as far as her ⸮ would allow. "The cat," she said. "Do you have the ⸮ your cell because you want company, or out of s⸮ for the cat?"

"Both, Reverend Mother."

241

"Both?"

"If I put her out, she comes to my window and cries. It makes me feel guilty. And I like having her there. It's ... comforting."

"The cat is pregnant?"

"Yes, Reverend Mother."

"She's close to delivery?"

"I think so, Reverend Mother. Maybe ten days or two weeks."

Reverend Mother tapped her ring against the arm of her chair. "For now," she said, "keep the cat in your cell when she wants to be there—this is every night?"

"Every night for the past month, Reverend Mother, yes. She's usually waiting for me when I get up from Compline."

Kat looked up sharply. There was something ... She caught Clare Marie staring at her and looked down again.

Something was caught in the tangle, but Kat couldn't extract it. Reverend Mother was giving Martha a penance for her rudeness to Antonia. Kat knew she should listen—they were supposed to listen to everything, it was all "edifying" —but it was all going around and around in her head, making her dizzy. David. Agnus Dei. That place. Martha's cat. What was it about Martha's cat?

"Go in peace," Reverend Mother said.

Martha said, "I thank you, Reverend Mother, and my Sisters in this community, for speaking in charity to my correction."

Martha kissed the floor, swung back, and got to her feet. Her face was glowing rosily. Her eyes were shining. Kat sighed. For Martha, Chapter of Faults was a healing ritual. Would it be like that for her? Would it be like ... going home?

squirmed in her soul. Going home to what? What had in San Sulpice had been like going home. So had know David. She was always "going home," and trying up to find herself lost, confused, out in the ht to be rational about it. She ought to ask anted to give up Agnus Dei. Every time she apart. When she tried to ask herself the same question about David, all she got was: it would never be enough.

It was entirely possible that nothing would ever be enough.

She made an Act of Hope that she would be able to use the time before she made her proclamation to make up her mind.

Reverend Mother pulled a wooden chit out of the box and said, "Sister Postulant Katherine Mary."

2

The aisle seemed very long, much longer than she remembered it. By the time she got to the mark in front of Reverend Mother's chair, she was exhausted. Her feet hurt. Her muscles ached. The cold detachment that had kept her flighty and distracted since she first came into chapel was gone.

No one would force her to make any one choice. No one would show her a sign. She would have to make her decision as an act of blind faith—to David or to God.

She had a sudden, violent desire, as strong as any urge she'd ever had for sex, to be walking down this aisle in full habit. They said the traditional veil cut off your peripheral vision, the wimple cut welts into your skin. She wouldn't care. She would rather have that than this feeling of being naked before three hundred women who had more courage and resolve than she could ever hope for. Three hundred women who had already made up their minds.

She stopped at the mark, got to her hands and knees, stretched out until her forehead touched the cold stone of the chapel floor. The slide felt endless, as endless as the tearing indecision of the past three months. She could not live any longer without knowing, without deciding. Equivocation always got to her in the end. She was not a good hypocrite.

She opened her eyes and looked at the folds and patterns in the stone beneath her face, chips of rock and dust scattered across the polished surface like sand blown up from a desert floor. The polish of the stone was wear. Thousands of hands and feet and foreheads had ground it smooth.

Faith was believing in a reward nothing in reason could guarantee.

She thought of David coming to her in Malapur. David who had made her whole. David who had seen inside her. David who had taught her to feel for him something she had thought impossible for her to feel at all: a will to have him exist in the world, whether he was with her or not, whether he cared for her or not, whether he gave her what she wanted or not. He was an absolute value to her, like trees or honesty. She would not have wanted any world she lived in to go on without him.

She closed her eyes and thought: I love you. I told you the truth about that. I love you.

Somewhere behind her, someone coughed. She wondered how long she had lain prostrate here, silent. It felt like hours, but it had probably not been long. Nothing ever lasted very long.

Except what she felt for David.

Except what she wanted from God.

Except this endless wait on the floor of a dark chamber.

Sadness was a citadel she would have to abandon. Now.

She took the longest breath of her life and said, "Reverend Mother and Sisters, I proclaim myself for a *maxima culpa* against obedience and against charity, in having five times left the Motherhouse to meet without supervision or permission the man who, in the world, was my lover."

She pulled David out of her memory and set him down in front of her. He stood in his thick down jacket, looking larger and heavier than he was.

I love you, she told him, thinking she was being very silent and very loud at the same time. I will always love you. If I had stayed with you, I would have hated you for never being enough.

He disappeared, like a dream image in a trite movie. She began to slide, unobstructed, toward what she had been looking for since she walked out of an ancient church in Paris into the rain.

God was a place. He would take you in, keep you safe, whenever you were ready to come.

She was very ready to come. She slid into that calm white light, like a diver so skilled she hardly disturbed the surface of the water.

In that place, the citadel of sadness was changed to wine, and memory was a friend.

STAIRCASE

Falling asleep, Annie couldn't decide if it was God or the Devil who had saved her. She had been shielded from scrutiny as effectively as a nun's face under an exclaustration veil. Kat had made her proclamation. No one had had ears to hear anything else. Oh, Annie had had to go up and speak for herself, but no one had been paying attention. They were all in shock.

So she was saved. For another week, another month, maybe long enough. She conjured up a daydream about Princess Daisy at the final, glittering party that marked her triumph. She saw the diamonds and the silk, the carriages and limousines. She saw Stephen standing on the grass in Central Park, holding out his arms to her, saying, "I'll keep you safe." She drifted into sleep smiling, protected from the day. Protected from Father Duffy. And Jane.

She was going to have to be careful about Jane. She was beginning to think Jane could see inside her, to the dreams of Belgian lace and diamond tiaras, to her fear of the dark. She was very, very afraid of the dark. She imagined things moving in the dark. She thought she had always heard them moving, but she couldn't be sure.

There was nothing so odd about having nightmares, after a day as bad as this. She saw herself climbing into a dream pulpit, setting herself up to lecture herself. Her fear that she might be losing her mind was all in her mind.

The dream Annie grinned down at her from the dream

pulpit. The real Annie looked down to find her feet—it suddenly seemed very important to know exactly where her feet were—and she was standing on top of the North Wing staircase, on the rail, so that if she slipped forward half an inch she would fall into the stairwell and down the eighty feet to the portress room at the bottom. She would break her neck or crack her head open or impale herself on the cast-iron spikes of the fence that surrounded the statue of Saint Benedict near the door. She slipped backward instead, rapping the base of her spine against the wood of the landing outside the tower. When she looked up, she knew she wasn't sleeping anymore. She was really here. She had come here in her sleep the way she had come to the linen closet in her sleep. She had nearly killed herself in her sleep.

Something in the bell tower laughed. She heard it. Somebody laughed. Was she hanging in there, that girl? Hanging night after night in spirit as she had once hung in body? Hanging and laughing?

It was not normal to walk in your sleep. It was not normal to climb onto a stair rail in your sleep. It was not normal to hear a ghost laughing in a bell tower.

It took everything she had not to scream, or call out for Kat, or run down the stairs in a clatter of wood and beads until she was safely in her cell and under the blankets.

She got to her feet and walked quietly, silently, back to postulant corridor. She walked between muslin-curtained cells to her own. She got *Princess Daisy* and Stephen's letter and the picture of David in the rose garden and the picture of her father. She got the robe from the hook behind her bed.

In the Mary Chapel, she put everything on the floor under the picture of Saint Agnes. She lit a votive candle. She watched the light. Then she took the picture of her father from the pile, tore it into pieces, and held them over the flame.

She was nothing like him. Nothing at all. She didn't look like him. She didn't think like him. She would certainly never do what he did.

She felt the tears start and bent over, grabbing the book and David's picture and Stephen's letter and holding them

246

against her chest as if they could protect her from whatever was happening to her, whatever was breaking her apart and reducing her to a fetal agony on a wooden floor in a dark hallway in the middle of the night.

Maybe she wasn't crazy. Maybe she just needed this release the way some people needed a drink after work. Just touching the book made her feel better. Just thinking of Stephen's letters calmed her.

She picked herself up. She was all right. She had had a bad day. She had had a nightmare. She had been (sleepwalking) under a little too much pressure.

She would go downstairs and lock herself in one of the stalls and read.

BLINDSIGHT

Kat kept herself on her knees in front of the main altar for thirty minutes before she knew she wouldn't be able to stop herself. Then she got to her feet and went to the window. She couldn't see the Retreat House garage. It was hidden in the trees. Even so, just to make sure, David had covered the small high windows with cardboard, to block the light.

She went back to the front pew and knelt down. She felt sure, and that was all she had ever asked for. Sure about Agnus Dei. Sure about what she had to do. When she looked at the altar, she knew she was not alone. Christ was more than "present in the Host." God was a friend who sat with her during a long and difficult convalescence, to divert her while she healed.

Sometimes, instead of saying the prayers she had been given to say—the penance had been a whopper—she talked to that Presence in a general way, about convent practice and her own stupidity. She was getting her sense of humor back. God didn't seem to mind. She bent over her prayers again, determined to do what she had to do and do it right.

She was in the middle of a Hail, Mary when it struck her, the thing that had hit her in Chapter but that she hadn't been able to interpret.

The cat slept with Martha every night.

If the cat slept with Martha every night, it wasn't out killing birds.

Which meant something else was.

"I think that's daylight, Lieutenant. Look at it."

"I'd rather not, Sister."

"Really? I keep thinking it won't last. There'll be another storm."

"Probably."

"You sound tired, Lieutenant."

"Aren't you?"

"You asked me where I was, all those weeks. Do you want to know?"

"Sister—"

"I'll tell you where I was, Lieutenant. I was hiding behind the dictates of common sense."

GROUNDWATCH

In the chapel, the bells made two o'clock, a hollow sound, what David had always imagined John Donne's tolling bell would be like. John Donne. Henry James. Wonder Woman. Stephen King. Bad fifties music about teenagers dying in car crashes. Kat.

He hoped she was happy in there.

He stepped back and looked one last time at the fourth

floor, where she said she lived. He was surprised to see lights there—not on the fourth floor, actually, but in a window that seemed halfway between it and the floor below, and in the oddly off-center tower at the end of the wing. The tower light flickered and died, as if made by out-of-season fireflies. The light in the half-story window flared, then dimmed. A figure moved against the glass. Annie Bliss, he realized. She was bent crooked at the waist, as if she had a pain in her stomach. He flapped his arms against his sides for warmth. If he'd known how well he'd be able to see, he'd have come sooner, looking for Kat. Maybe, when enough time had passed so his being discovered would get her in the minimum of trouble, he would come back.

A light went on in the chapel. He started back toward the trees, cover and safety. Then he turned for one last look at Annie Bliss. Maybe he would come to Northton one last time to talk to her. He didn't like the way she was walking. It could be the light, or turned food at dinner, or insomnia and exhaustion, but he didn't like it all the same. She had been very upset the last time he talked to her. Thinking of her gave him a black twinge. Something was going wrong for her in there.

Even so, maybe he'd go into Northton next week and waylay her at the post office. Just to ease his mind. He could ask her about Kat.

"Sister?"

"I'm quite all right, Lieutenant."

"Are you?"

"What was that man carrying? The—"

"It was a piece of that man's jacket. From the wall outside. He climbed the wall outside. Sister, what is he doing here?"

"I don't know."

"Who is he?"

"I don't know that either. I suspect, but I don't know."

"Sister—"

"Do you think he killed her, Lieutenant? He hardly looks the type."

"They never do."

"She killed herself, Lieutenant."

"She died in that room with her throat cut, Sister. That's all we can know for sure."

ECHO

1

Kat had been enclaustrated. That was what they called it, when they announced it in chapel. To Annie it sounded like a disease, or the kind of medieval punishment that had something to do with outsized hooks. Maybe it was both. Kat did not seem to be part of them anymore. She didn't even seem to be on earth. She spent all her time practicing for Christmas Choir, or making devotions to Our Lady.

Or walking North Lawn looking for dead birds.

Annie pulled her legs up under her and put *Princess Daisy* on the bed. It was a wreck, battered and torn. A few nights ago, she had fallen asleep on the half-landing. When she woke, she found wax dripped across the length of a page, melting paper and ink and gluing a whole section together. It stuck out of the book now like a board. It could not be fixed.

She had a headache all the time now, except when she was reading.

This morning, she had taken Communion, even though she'd been denied absolution at her last confession.

She got off the bed, got her apron, tied it around her. She had been waiting all morning for lightning to strike her dead, or for the Host to burn a hole in her stomach. She knew that was ridiculous. All that happened if you took Communion with a mortal sin on your soul was that you went to hell if you died before it was forgiven. Even so, as soon as she'd felt the Host on her tongue, all the grade-school stories had come flooding back.

She wasn't going crazy. She was going *senile*.

She heard Jane coming down the hall and tried to move, to look active and happy and one with the spirit of the house. It was impossible. These days she approached everything, even dinner and recreation, with the leaden torpor of a condemned man.

Taking Communion in mortal sin wasn't the worst thing she had done. She had "taken Communion in the hand" three times in the past week—and crushed the Host to crumbs in her pocket.

The Host was the body of Jesus Christ. It was the real body of Jesus Christ, even though it looked like a wafer. That was transubstantiation. Wafer and wine became Body and Blood. In reality.

She had taken the body of Jesus Christ and crushed it into crumbs and shoved it into her pocket with *Princess Daisy* and Stephen's letter and David's picture and three Bic medium-points, all leaking.

If she didn't take Communion, Clare Marie would want to know why. She would ask questions. She would get answers.

Annie wiped the sweat from her upper lip. Her heart was out of control. It sped up and slowed down, trip-hammered and thudded.

Jane rapped twice on the metal curtain rod. Annie grimaced. Jane always remembered to knock. Why did it make her so angry that Jane always remembered to knock?

She pulled the curtain open. "Almost ready," she said.

"That was the warning bell," Jane said. "You have to move faster. You're going to do the Lord's work. You should fly to Him."

"Yes," Annie said. "Of course."

"You have another headache," Jane said.

"No."

Jane shrugged and walked to the window. "Kat's in the rose garden," she said. "Pacing. Like the lady in white."

"Margaret Nunnally left this morning," Jane said. "*Before Mass.* Did you hear about it?"

Annie put her armload of flowers on the bare stone steps in front of the altar. The flowers were a gift from a benefactor. She and Jane had been pulled off infirmary duty to decorate the chapel with them. They were supposed to be under the direction of the Sister Sacristan, but she'd been called to Reverend Mother's office. Annie took three long-stemmed irises and put them aside. Jane knew she hadn't heard about Margaret Nunnally. She never heard these things.

"I'm too tired in the morning to notice things," Annie said.

"Martha was telling me about it. She was telling everybody about it. Margaret was confiding in her."

Annie nodded. Almost everybody confided in Martha. Even she had, before she'd had too much to confide.

"People leave," she said finally, wondering where they went and what they did after they were gone. She ran into a blank wall.

"Everybody who leaves can't be rejecting their vocation," she said. "Even Clare Marie says people come who think they have a vocation but don't really. When they find that out, they leave."

"But that's not the point," Jane said. "It wasn't any of that. She saw the ghost."

"Don't be ridiculous," Annie said, angry. "There is no ghost."

"Margaret Nunnally thinks there is. She says she heard footsteps in the tower. And *laughing*."

Annie licked her lips. She'd once thought she'd heard laughing in the tower. She'd been convinced she heard it. "It's all those ghost stories," she said. "I don't care what the tradition is. They drive everyone crazy."

"So Margaret elaborated a little," Jane said. Annie took the irises down the middle aisle to the card table where Sister Sacristan had put the vases. Her headache was a firestorm. It had been joined by the old familiar panic, as if she'd just desecrated another Host or looked through her examen book. She rubbed her temples frantically. When it got this bad, it affected everything. She reached for one of the tall vases and knocked one of the clear glass bud vases with the side of her hand. She caught it just in time. It was Steuben glass. It was worth hundreds and hundreds of dollars.

She had to get to the lavatory. To the book.

"It gets spooky on postulant corridor at night," she said shakily. "Especially if you're the only one who can't sleep. Margaret was imagining things."

"Maybe," Jane said. "But you can't have God without the Devil. The supernatural world exists or it doesn't."

"The supernatural world exists in Heaven and Hell and Purgatory. Not wandering around the North Wing bell tower cackling madly in the middle of the night."

"I didn't say Margaret said anyone was cackling madly."

If Margaret had heard the same thing Annie had heard, it hadn't been mad cackling. It had just been a laugh.

Annie shoved an iris into a vase so quickly, the stem broke. She took it out and laid it aside. She had to get to the lavatory and the book before she lost control completely. She looked quickly, reflexively, at her stomach. The Host was not burning through the wool. There was no radioactive glow under the cloth, announcing her sin to the world.

"I think it's all superstition," she said. "'Superstition and paganism. Peopling the world with departed spirits and Lord only knows what else."

"Maybe it's just echoes," Jane said. "Maybe the things people do live after them, and the things they feel very intensely live the longest."

"You've been reading too many horror novels."

"They're the best way to get ghost stories," Jane said. "But she'd have to be feeling something very intensely to commit suicide, wouldn't she? That has to be part of what suicide is all about. The emotions being out of control. Exaggerated."

Annie thought of her father, the week before he died. He had not been "exaggerated." He had not been "out of control." If anything, he had been too controlled. Too still. And yet . . . She shook her head. She didn't want to think about her father. It wasn't safe. It was never safe. It was especially unsafe when she was like this, when everything seemed to be getting to her.

As soon as she was finished with the irises, she would make some excuse and go off to read her book. Then it would be all right. It always was.

"I think it's important to consider these things," Jane said. "God has a plan. He doesn't reveal Himself in words. We have to—oh, good heavens."

"What?" Annie turned around. Jane was standing at the edge of the altar steps, near the stained-glass window overlooking North Lawn. She was bending over the sill.

"Look at this," Jane said. "Who in the name of Heaven would bring something like this into a convent?"

She turned very slowly, very gracefully. It took her forever. It didn't matter. Annie knew what she was going to see before she saw it. Then Jane was standing right in front of her, holding it in the air, exposing the cracked cover and mottled pages.

The book, the book, the book.

Princess Daisy smiled and smiled and smiled in the brown haze of soft focus.

Annie's mouth felt full of sawdust.

BODY AND BLOOD

The animal on the lawn was a large spraddled bat with what looked like penicillin mold around the rim of its mouth. Kat poked at it with a twig. It was difficult to look at. Bats were ugly animals. This one had lost its eyes. Its corneas—did bats have corneas?—were tattered clots of blood in deep sockets. Its claws were like tiny, deformed human hands.

Kat threw the twig away. Since the first Chapter of Faults, she had been calm, even happy, except for the animals. She did not make it into that place every day, but

254

she made it often enough. And she had not died to David. She loved him more easily for having given him up. She remembered him without becoming obsessed by him. She prayed without feeling she was mouthing alien words in a dead language. She worked and knew her work was being watched, directed, by the Christ she had once thought it impossible to meet face to face. Score one for Saint Teresa: it was possible to live always in the presence of God.

Everything was perfect, except for the animals.

A wind rippled the grass. The bat shook and rocked and fell over on one side. The animals were driving her crazy.

Because something was very, very wrong.

And she didn't know what.

She was heading for the twig she'd thrown away when she heard someone behind her. Angela Louise was standing by an ice-slicked stone bench. Kat rescued the twig, wondering which of them would break silence.

Angela Louise made an ineffectual swipe at the bench and sat down. "I can talk to you, can't I? If it's a matter of conscience?"

"I think you can talk to me if you want to," Kat said. She made her way to the bench, slowing to look at the bat as she passed it. God help her, the thing was ugly. "I think I'm just supposed to keep silence until somebody talks to me."

"It wasn't much of a penance, was it? Under the circumstances."

"Maybe they thought it was," Kat said. "Maybe it means a lot to them, being able to leave the grounds and go to town, being able to have visitors. Of course, I never had a legitimate visitor. And the only one I could have now is my mother, and you know how I feel about that."

The starch in Angela Louise's veil was melting in the rain and fog. "I had a whole conversation worked out," she said. "I made it up for an excuse. I wasn't sure what the rules were. But—I was worried about you."

"I'm not Marie Bernadette," Kat said gently. "I'm all right, Angela. In fact, I feel better than I have since I got here."

"I don't think you're Marie Bernadette. I'm just glad you did what you did."

255

"Even if half the postulant class thinks I'm a heroine out of a romantic novel?" Kat laughed. "It's driving Clare Marie bonkers, truly. Martha and Annie mooning around after me like I've just gone gloriously to martyrdom and the little Italian girls clucking and saying rosaries for my sanctification. I've given up my earthly love for God. I'm a movie star."

"They're very young. At least you gave up your earthly love for God, instead of the other way around. Which is what everybody else seems to be doing these days."

"I couldn't have. It would have been too much of a sixties cliché."

Angela Louise tapped her knee impatiently. "It means something to me," she said finally. "The Order. Vocation. Maybe just religious life, giving up this world as witness to your faith in God's promises for the next. I *believe* in separation. There aren't a lot of Orders like this anymore, at least in the United States. And it's very hard when no one seems to understand."

"I understand, Angela Louise. If I didn't, I wouldn't be eating my meals from a plate on the floor."

"Does it make you terribly self-conscious?"

"Not in the least. The lower back pain, however, is going to kill me." She saw Angela Louise suppress a smile. "Listen," she said. "The next thing..."

Out on the lawn, another wind redirected her attention to the bat. It was tilted on its side. She could see its underbelly. She got up and walked to it, crouched down, prodded it with a twig. The skin on its belly had been cut to ribbons and stripped from the organs and muscles beneath, as if it had been peeled.

The smell was overpowering. Kat could feel the odor seeping into her skin.

"Kat?" Angela Louise said.

"Come here."

Angela Louise came up beside her. "Dear God," she said. "Throw that thing away."

Kat prodded it again instead. It was inert. It did not bleed. It took a long time for blood to clot in the rain.

"Do you remember Martha in Chapter? She said she kept the cat with her at night. If the cat's with Martha at night,

256

she's not running around North Lawn killing bats. And most bats are rabid. If the cat had been killing bats, the *cat* would be rabid."

"You mean the bats do that to themselves? To each other?"

"No," Kat said. "Look at that thing. It's been ripped apart."

"Kat—"

"It's not just the animals," Kat said. "There are things going on on postulant corridor. Margaret Nunnally went running out of here this morning saying she heard ghosts walking in North Tower. Everybody thinks she's crazy except me. *I've* heard something walking in North Tower."

"That happens. Half the postulants my year thought they heard something up there."

"I'm not prone to an overactive imagination. Something's wrong."

"What?"

Kat kicked the bat with her toe. "Jane," she said finally.

"Galloway?"

"Angela, listen, please. I know this sounds crazy. I don't have one reason to think Jane Galloway's killing small animals in the night. Not one. But she's gotten weird. Really strange. There's something wrong with the expression on her face. Something off. And she's never in her cell at night. I don't think she sleeps."

"There's something wrong with the expression on her face," Angela Louise repeated.

"And something's wrong with Annie Bliss," Kat said. "Jane's with Annie all the time. Clare Marie has them doing everything together. Annie looks worse every day. She's jumpy and scared. She won't talk to me. And me— every once in a while I wake up feeling like I've been on a first-class binge. Head stuffed up, stomach a mess, nauseated, dizzy. Every time I wake up like that, I find more birds. Or bats. Or mice. Or something. All torn up."

"You've been under a lot of strain."

"Maybe. But it's another one of those days. I feel like hell. I don't know why. And here's a bat. I'm not crazy, Angela. Something's wrong."

"It's the silence," Angela Louise said. "And the isolation. It does this sometimes."

Kat poked at the bat. She wanted to do something now, immediately, without losing another second. She could not figure out what, or why.

A month ago she would have believed everything Angela Louise said. She would have been sure she was getting the night terrors. She would have put it all out of her mind. Now she couldn't do any such thing.

There was something about Jane's eyes, something she should recognize.

"It's not the isolation," she told Angela Louise. "And I'm not crazy."

CORRECTION IN CHARITY

It had taken her a long time to get it down. The principle was simple. All she had to do was bump Annie broadside and take the book while Annie was worried about the bump. The execution had not been so simple. She hadn't had a chance to bump Annie. She hadn't even had a chance to get close to her more than twice, and each time she'd been very wound up, nearly flying, and scared to death she wouldn't get another shot. It was a miracle she'd managed to get the book at all. It was a miracle, and it had happened to her. That proved—something.

Jane slipped into the cloakroom and headed for the switchboard. She'd taken too much of that stuff this morning. Nothing she'd fed herself since had been able to cool her down. She'd been in outer space, and that made it difficult to get everything straight. So many things needed attention at once. Kat had wriggled out of it and was using up more and more of Jane's pill supply. Annie was coming apart like a rag doll with her stitches pulled. Her father...

The thick root of her father's penis stuck in the air like

a sentient tree. Her father and her mother. Blood and screaming. Her father calling her *whore*, shoving it into her one last time, shoving it into her as if he were trying to tear her insides out, calling her *whore* and demanding to know who else, what else, where else. She saw his hand in the air, felt the flat pain of it hitting her jaw in a hard *whack* that nearly broke the bone. He wanted details. There had never been anyone else. His hand was a fist coming down at her. The blood filled her mouth and her windpipe. It came up under her skin and was pounded back, smashed in on itself. The fist went up and down and the bones in her nose cracked lengthwise along the rim, and the bones in her jaw shattered and her teeth went loose in her gums and her father said *whore you're a whore you're a fucking piece of cunt.*

Blood and screaming.

The hospital hadn't asked any questions. They had known, but they hadn't asked. Her mother hadn't asked any questions, either.

She sat at the switchboard and made herself go blank. She could control it if she worked hard enough. She counted to ten twice and then stretched, pushing her arms out as far as they would go. Now her reflection in the switchboard's polished black face looked like a wild white bird. She was purging herself dry. She would be clean.

But not now. Now she had something to do.

She took the slip of paper with the number out of her pocket. It glowed, only for her.

She thought of her father's fist in the air and the sand under her bare buttocks and the stiff part of him grinding into her and the blood on the table.

Now she knew how to fix it. Now she knew what it was about Annie's book.

She had been right from the beginning. Annie was meant to lead her to salvation.

Annie would never be able to live without that book.

She dialed carefully, pausing between numbers and rechecking. She held the receiver to her ear and waited until someone (an old man?) said, "Northton General Store and Post Office."

"You ought to keep people from stealing things," she

259

said. "Even if they're going to be nuns. Especially if they're going to be nuns."

"Whore," her father said.

"Rip it out," her mother said. "Rip it up. Rip it to pieces."

OVERBOARD

1

Annie sat in the back of the van, listening to the engine coughing and the wheels hitting rocks in the road. She saw trees and houses and stores and one glimpse of the Sound. Passing through it was like looking at a side show. Still-frames came and went. But nothing moved.

The slide show stopped in front of the post office–grocery store, the frame frozen on the screen.

She had a letter from Stephen she had picked up in the hall as they were leaving the Motherhouse. She hadn't had time to read it. If they would give her time, she would be all right.

Maybe.

Daniella was leaning between the driver's and passenger's buckets, frowning. Annie willed her eyes to focus.

"What's the matter?" Daniella said. "Are you asleep?"

Annie jerked away. "I'm all right," she said.

"Oh, dear," Annunciata said. "What is it? Another headache?"

"No, Sister. I didn't get much sleep last night. I'm sorry. I dozed off."

"It's those chapel bells," Annunciata said. "How anybody gets to sleep up there is beyond me. Sound like bombs going off in your head. What Reverend Mother was thinking of—"

Daniella shot the woman a look of pure exasperation and leaned between the buckets again, pushing her face as close to Annie's as she could get it.

"Are you sure you're all right? No headache?"

260

"No, Sister." Annie tried a smile. "I fell asleep in chapel and Jane had to kick me awake. I'm just tired."

"You look dead."

"I'm fine," Annie said again.

"We'll get some aspirin when we go in to get the mail," Annunciata said.

Annie got out of the van and held out her arm to help Annunciata down. The slides were going by just fast enough to imitate movement. It looked phony. Annie kept one hand behind her back and one stiff in the air, serving as a rail for Annunciata. She did have a headache. She just couldn't afford to miss the post office.

How could she have dropped the book? How could she have dropped the book and not known?

Annie edged Annunciata over the ice toward the sidewalk, feeling the old woman's weight against her arm like the Ancient Mariner's albatross. Sometimes, when she looked sideways, she thought she saw her mother there.

2

As soon as David saw them get out of the van, he knew something was wrong. Daniella was agitated and edgy. Annie moved like a wooden doll, joints stiff, hinges creaking. David shivered. He wanted to get *over* there. He'd intended to wait until they went into Holland's, to make it look casual. He had no way of knowing what trouble he'd get them into by being here.

He kept himself still just long enough to wonder why he was so worried about Annie. He hardly knew Annie. He knew Kat cared for her. He knew she was a "good infant." He knew he hated her mother and her brother. None of it was enough.

He thought of her walking on the landing in the dark. He thought of her walking into the post office, wooden and terrified. That was the word. The child was terrified. But why? Convents weren't torture chambers where girls were buried alive and forced to wear hair shirts and scourge themselves.

261

Then he thought of the story Mary had fed that newspaper. It was all nonsense, of course, all lies.

But.

He started across the street toward the common.

3

When she had bought the stamps, she went to the bookrack and stood, very quietly, in front of the last copy of *Princess Daisy*. They had other books of the right sort, but she didn't know what they were like. If they were awful, she could be stuck for a week or more with nothing to cure the headaches and take away the nightmares. She could be taken off post office duty. She could find herself going into retreat before Naming with nothing. She couldn't spend a week in strict silence, concentrating on her sins, without *something*. She would go crazy.

Besides, *Princess Daisy* was perfect. It wasn't like some of them, full of blood and awfulness and divine retribution for success. Princess Daisy got everything in the end. Annie touched the cover with the tip of her finger. When she'd first seen the book, there had been five or six copies on the rack. Now there was just this one. Everybody in Northton wanted to read about Princess Daisy.

Something had happened to her headache. It had grown, not in intensity, but in area. It surrounded her like a wall.

She looked into the security mirror over her head and saw Daniella and Annunciata at the parcels window. The parcels clerk was bent over them. His eyeshade hid his face.

Stephen's letter was burning through the nylon lining of her pocket. According to the last one, he looked on her as his "personal prayer battery." Was she hurting him by not being perfect in prayer? By being so full of sin and craziness and so incapable of stopping herself?

It didn't matter. Nothing mattered except that she couldn't leave and she couldn't let herself go crazy.

She took the book off the rack and rubbed the cover between her palms. The cover was very smooth. It shrank the atmosphere. It ate away the fear.

She looked into the security mirror again. Daniella and

Annunciata and the clerk were still in their places. She swayed from side to side, checking the corners of the room. There was no one there.

She put the book in her pocket and prayed for invisibility.

4

When he came in, she was sitting where he had left her the last time, on the window shelf near the bookrack. She had her hands folded in her lap and her back very straight. She had her eyes trained on the ground, as if she were praying. David stood awkwardly in the doorway. She did not look terrified now. He had overreacted.

On the other hand, she did not look good.

He caught Daniella's eye just as she caught his. Her eyebrows went up. Her cheeks sucked in. David flushed. Something *had* happened up there. Something with Kat. He shouldn't be here.

He looked at Annie Bliss and realized he had no intention of leaving until he was sure she was all right, or found out what was wrong and how he could help. She looked so miserable sitting there by herself. Tight and miserable and scared.

He unzipped his jacket against the humid warmth of the room and started over to her. Daniella stopped him halfway there.

"If you're trying to get a message to Kat," she said, "don't."

David rocked uneasily from foot to foot. This woman would be a good nun. She was half a foot shorter than he was, but she had all the physical authority of Kareem Abdul Jabbar.

"She got caught," he said.

"She turned herself in," Daniella said.

"I thought something like that might have happened."

"Then what in the name of all that's holy are you doing here?"

David looked involuntarily at Annie Bliss. Daniella looked, too. The frown that spread over her face was tinged with impatience, and uncertainty.

"I don't think she feels well," Daniella said finally. "I think she has a headache and doesn't want to tell anyone."

"She's scared to death," David said flatly. "Look at her. She's scared to death."

Daniella licked her lips. "I know," she said. "I know."

"Of what?"

Daniella shook her head and shrugged.

David opened his jacket wider. Annunciata was still at the parcels window, stacking brown-wrapped packages on a counter. He jerked his head in her direction. "Am I the most-wanted man? Does every nun at Agnus Dei have my picture engraved on her eyelids and orders to shoot on sight?"

"Half the time, Annunciata wouldn't know her own mother from a hole in the wall."

David nodded. He started moving toward Annie Bliss. Daniella stopped him.

"We're really not crazy," she said. "We're really not. There's nothing so very odd about our life up there. There's nothing perverted about it."

"I never thought there was."

"Right," Daniella said. "So what's wrong with Annie Bliss?"

David made his way to the window shelf. "Hey," he said. "You look depressed."

Annie jumped half a foot in the air.

5

It took forever to work it out. That David was with Daniella. That there was nothing wrong in talking to him. The sweat came down Annie's forehead and ran into her eyes, making her wince. The wince made Daniella frown. Daniella's frown made Annie's heart speed up, then slow down and get heavier, a great thumping boom in her chest. Annie tried to control it with breathing, but couldn't. She could control it by putting her hand on the book, but didn't dare. Being in the store and having the book scared her. Even though she knew nothing could happen.

David sat beside her, his shoulders brushing hers. She moved away from him. She couldn't handle touching him.

He made her queasy and excited in a way she wasn't sure was entirely healthy. She wanted him to put his arm around her.

The book weighed a ton and a half in her pocket. It made it hard for her to move.

<h1 style="text-align:center">6</h1>

"Maybe you need to get some air," David said. "Take a walk outside."

"I'm fine," Annie said. "I bought the stamps and sat down to wait and it's what I do every week, and I'm *fine*." Annie glared. Daniella shrugged, turned, and walked toward Annunciata without another word. David took out his pack of Camels.

"I didn't mean to make you angry," he said.

"You didn't get me angry," Annie said. "I'm just very tired. I didn't get much sleep. Everybody keeps acting like I'm dying or something."

Her voice was a half step from panic, high and shrill.

"It's because of last time," she said. "I know I was an idiot the last time. I had a headache. But I don't make a habit of that kind of thing."

"It isn't because of the last time," David said, wondering how much truth he could tell before she turned on him. "You seem . . . unhappy."

"I'm not unhappy."

"All right."

"Besides, you're not supposed to be happy in the novitiate. It's a test. Like basic training."

"Kat's happy," David said. "All things considered."

"Kat's a very unusual person."

"So are you."

"Am I?" She looked at him full face. The skin around her mouth was lined. There were bags under her eyes. She was like the woman in *Lost Horizon*, aging centuries by the second.

"Annie," he said. "What's wrong?"

She jerked to her feet. "Nothing's *wrong*," she said savagely. "Nothing's wrong."

It wasn't until they were on the sidewalk that Annie began to relax. The door squeezed shut behind them and her lungs suddenly seemed to have so much extra space—as if she were recovering from pneumonia, very quickly.

When the door opened again, she was looking at her hands. Annunciata was making small talk. It was holding them up.

She looked up when the man coughed. It was one of the clerks from the grocery store, not the small man with the eyeshade but the taller one with the apron who stood behind the check-out counter near the display of International Coffee. Annie felt the bottom drop out of her stomach, leaving a hole.

"Excuse me," the man said. "Excuse me. But she really took it."

"What?" Daniella said.

"She realy took it." The man was shocked and agitated. His eyes were bulging. His lips were wet. Annie looked at him in horror and fasination, a monster from the deep come to snatch her from her bed. He couldn't have seen her take it. He *couldn't* have.

"She took a book," the man said. "She took it off the rack in my store and walked out with it. She really did."

"Don't be ridiculous," Daniella said.

"I'm not being ridiculous. She took a book."

David was looking at her, at the clerk, back to her. His face was closed. His eyes were stone. He had worked everything out. She kept her hands clasped very tightly under her cape. She could not take the book out now. She couldn't give it up under any circumstances.

She was drowning.

The man spread his feet. "I'm not being ridiculous, and I'm not leaving till I get it back. She *took* a *book* out of my store." He pointed at Annie's right side. "She put it in that pocket."

"Don't be ridiculous," Daniella said again. She snatched at Annie's pocket, plunging her hand into the slit. Annie felt the weight lighten. Daniella had her hands on the book. She was pulling it into the air.

If anyone had asked, Annie would have said she felt nothing. That had to be wrong. Tears were coming down her face, washing the sweat and snow out of her eyes.

IMPOSSIBILITY

When the van came back, Kat was standing on the parapet overlooking the drive, holding a set of rosary beads that felt like so much useless plastic in her hands. Something had happened to Annie. The word had gone through the class, devoid of detail, rich in emotion. Something had happened to Annie. Something *final*.

Kat leaned against the stone pinnacle and watched them get out of the van. Annie was white and wooden. Daniella was furious. Annunciata was... Annunciata. Kat plucked at the rosary beads. She couldn't take comfort in Annunciata's normality. Annunciata would maintain normality in the aftermath of nuclear war.

A police car pulled up behind the van.

Kat tugged at her cape. She didn't like this. She didn't like it at all. She couldn't think of anything Annie could have done that would bring in the police. Had Annunciata let Annie drive? Had Annie hit someone?

There was an odd scraping sound on the other side of the parapet. Kat looked up and saw Jane standing against a stone pillar. Jane was holding a bird—a dead bird, its neck twisted and torn. Kat felt the bile rise in her throat, insistent, undeniable.

She knew what was wrong with the expression on Jane's face.

"Barbiturates," Kat said. "You put barbiturates in something I ate."

"I'm going to throw this bird over the wall." Jane smiled. "I'm going to throw it over and everyone will think it's the cat. They always do."

"I'm allergic to barbiturates," Kat said. "They make me nauseated."

Jane walked to her, holding out the bird on the palms of her hands. "You can tell anyone you want to. No one will believe you."

"You're out of your mind."

"Am I? You all thought you'd get rid of me, but you won't. I'll get rid of you. No one will believe you. No one wants to believe you."

"Whether or not anyone believes me is entirely beside the point."

Jane smiled again. Her eyes were dreamy and vague, like a sleepwalker's. Barbiturates, Kat thought, and then: no, no, something stronger. Jane was all doped up. That was what Kat should have recognized before. That was what had been bothering her about Jane. That and the night walking. That and the birds and bats and mice with their heads torn off at odd angles and their limbs severed with something that cut in straight, clean lines. Congratulations, O'Brien. One and one and one make three.

Jane turned the bird so Kat could see the eyes pushed out of its sockets, the bloody hole that had been its mouth. The retch came up Kat's throat and stalled, making her lungs full of something thick and unbreathable.

Jane tossed the bird over the side of the parapet.

"I've taken care of Annie Bliss," she said, "and I'm going to take care of you."

She turned on her heel and walked away, toward the door to South Wing.

In the drive, the cars stood abandoned and still in the gathering night.

Kat started to run.

CONTRACT

Annie sat by the side of Reverend Mother's desk, her hands folded on the polished surface. They had taken the book. They had taken her picture of David. Stephen's letter was all she had left. She wanted to take it out and read it, but she didn't dare.

They were going to send her home.

She'd been thinking about going home ever since the police came. Maybe that proved she was crazy. She should have been thinking about what the clerk was saying, about being prosecuted for shoplifting. Instead, she thought of the stale smell of overcooked cabbage and hot dogs, the malicious, whining monologue that was really a paean to death. "Who do you think you are?" was just another way of saying "This is your tomb."

She could not go home. She would die if she went home. Her mother would sing the funeral dirge and she would put the barrel of the gun in her mouth and pull the trigger in blessed relief.

Or worse. She would *not* put the barrel of the gun in her mouth, not pull the trigger, not do anything at all. She would live year after year, aeon after aeon, in the unrelieved darkenss of that house.

It would be better to pull the trigger here at Agnus Dei and never have to see that house again.

Unless Stephen would come to get her.

Behind her, the door opened and closed, hardwood on hardwood, scrape and clatter. Reverend Mother and Clare Marie crossed the office to her. Their faces were hidden in the jutting shields of their veils. Their hands were hidden in their oversleeves. They weren't people. They were nuns.

There were spirit voices in the room. They said: get out of here get out of here get out of here.

Reverend Mother said, "They're not going to prosecute. That much we've taken care of."

Annie stared at her hands, mute.

"What were you thinking of?" Reverend Mother said. "What could you have been thinking of?"

"Reverend Mother," Clare Marie said.

Reverend Mother brushed her away. "Not once," she said. "Not just this once. Three times. Is that right? Three times?"

"Yes, Reverend Mother."

"Whatever for?" Reverend Mother slammed her hand

against the desk. "Whatever for? If you want a book all you have to do is ask for it. All you—"

"I don't know," Annie said, desperate and panicked. "I don't *know.*"

Reverend Mother sighed. She tipped her chair back until the swivel joint creaked. Annie thought of her mother's house and forced the tears down, down, where no one would ever find them.

"You're unhappy here," Reverend Mother said.

"I'm happier here than I've ever been anywhere else."

"This is inexcusable."

"Yes," Annie said. "Yes, I know."

Reverend Mother hauled herself to her feet, as if pacing would solve something. She was too heavy to pace. She leaned against the desk instead.

"Try to make this easier for both of us," she said. "Tell me what you want, Annie. Do you want to go home?"

"No," Annie said. And then the tears were there, hot and unstoppable, wringing her dry and making her gasp for breath. "No," she said again. "I can't go home, I don't want to go home, I don't want to leave here, I *don't.*"

"Do you know any reason why we shouldn't send you home?"

It was the wrong question, but the right tone of voice. Annie could hear the escape clause in that voice. She sat up straighter and looked from Reverend Mother to Clare Marie.

"It was an accident," Annie said. "The first time it was just an accident. I was looking at the book in the store and when I came out I had it and I didn't mean to. I didn't mean to take it. Then I had it and I read it and it made me calmer. I'm always messing up, always, I never do it right, I'm always failing, and it made me calmer and I read it to death and it fell to pieces and then my brother came—"

"Stop," Reverend Mother said. "Stop."

Annie stopped. It felt like erecting a brick wall in the path of a tornado.

"Annie, why do you want to be a nun?"

Annie looked out the window at North Lawn. Kat and Martha were walking to chapel. Particular devotions.

"There isn't anything else," she said, as quietly, as calmly, as she could. "There isn't anything else."

"Do you want to stay with us? Do you think you ought to stay with us?"

Annie knew what Reverend Mother wanted to hear. She wanted a clear "no." She wanted a decision. But it wasn't that simple. There was no "ought to." Nobody "ought to" be a nun. People just were.

"My father committed suicide," Annie said. "The Church said he was crazy and buried him anyway. I talked to Father Duffy about it and he said I should tell you, I wasn't allowed to be here if my father was crazy, but I didn't want to be sent home and he wouldn't give me absolution and I took Communion anyway and I'm in mortal sin and I—"

Reverend Mother grabbed Annie's wrist and pulled it, hard. "Calm down," she said. "Calm *down*." She let go and began to pound the table. "I've told them and told them," she said. "I've said it a thousand times. The man is senile and he's going to cause us trouble. Well, he's caused us trouble. God in Heaven."

"Reverend Mother," Clare Marie said.

Reverend Mother patted Annie's hand. "It's all right, Annie. Father is a . . . Father is a little out of date. No one would send you home because your father was a suicide."

"The Church said he was crazy."

"Maybe he was." Reverend Mother dropped back into her seat. "I knew it was going to be something like this. I knew it wasn't going to be simple."

"We're going to have to do something about Father Duffy," Clare Marie said.

"Do what? Threaten to send the Cardinal Archbishop a letter bomb if he doesn't remove the old fool? Oh, never mind. What are we going to do about this?"

Annie put a hand in her pocket and felt the edge of Stephen's letter. If Stephen would take her in, she wouldn't have to stay at Agnus Dei. She would be free.

Free for what?

She didn't know if she needed an answer to that. She would cook and clean for Stephen, like a rectory housekeeper. Stephen would be very successful, very rich. They would share a shiny new house with walls of glass, and no

271

heavy curtains. Her mother would never enter Stephen's house. Annie would be safe in Stephen's house.

Reverend Mother was staring at her. She waited.

"Do you want to go home?" Reverend Mother asked again.

"No." Stephen might not want to take her in. He might not be able to.

Reverend Mother sighed. "Would you be willing to start retreat immediately? Take a penitential retreat for a month?"

"Go to live in Retreat House?" Annie asked, confused.

Reverend Mother shook her head. "We use Retreat House when seculars make retreats here. Our own Sisters use an enclosure floor in East Wing. It's like being in contemplative enclosure, Annie. Strict silence. No magazines or newspapers or television. No visits or phone calls or letters. It's a way of directing our attention to God and God's will for us. That's why you make a retreat before Naming. To decide if you're doing what you really should be doing."

"For one month," Annie said carefully.

"Unless you decide to leave us. You could decide to leave us at any time."

And go where? Annie wondered.

She pulled nervously at the hem of her skirt. If she agreed to this, she would be volunteering for prison. She would be shut up in the dark and silence with nothing to help her. She would go insane in an hour. ut she would go insane in a second in her mother's house.

What if Stephen wouldn't have her?

What if he would?

The other side of panic was a cold room with steel walls, locking out every extraneous thing.

There had to be a way to talk to Stephen. There had to

She said, "I want to talk to my brother."

"You want to go home with your brother?" Reverend Mother was surprised.

"No," Annie said. It was hard to get this out. "I want to stay here, I want to make the retreat"—she could hardly say the words without gagging—"but I need to talk to him.

272

About my father. I was only seven, but he was seventeen. He . . . knows things . . . about our father."

Reverend Mother rapped her glass thoughtfully against the desk. "All right," she said. "We will call your brother. You will enter retreat tonight. When he comes, we'll make an exception and let you see him."

"Thank you." The words came out in a rush. Annie had to hold her breath to keep from smiling.

Stephen would take her home.

VISITATION

In the end, Jane took pansies and baby's breath and tied them with a ribbon she'd found in a wastebasket. If Elizabeth asked, she could say they were yesterday's flowers she was bringing to brighten up the ward. Or she could say she felt so sorry for old Vianney, stuck in bed all week with a cold, she didn't think the chapel would miss a handful. With any luck, Elizabeth wouldn't ask.

It was the stairs that were making her heart pound. She'd come tearing up here, furious at herself. She'd done the one thing she shouldn't have. It had looked so close, so *final*. How could they let Annie stay after that? When she saw the policemen getting out of their car, she thought it was all wrapped up. She'd run up to South Wing roof and waited for Kat to turn around and *told* her.

And then it had all fallen apart. She wasn't sure how yet, but she knew it had. The word was all through the class. Annie was going into retreat until Naming and then continuing with the class. It made Jane's head ache. It was just like what had happened with Kat. Jane could barely breathe out of rhythm without getting squashed, but Annie and Kat got deals.

She started up the stairs again, reached the infirmary door, hesitated. What she was doing was very dangerous. If she got caught, Reverend Mother would not make arrangements for her to stay. She was not among the elect. They

273

were looking for a reason to send her home. They were looking for a chink. And she would give it to them. If she didn't have the pills, she would give it to them.

If she'd had enough pills, she'd never have said what she said to Kat.

She let herself onto the ward and knocked on Elizabeth's office door. Elizabeth should have already gone downstairs. The only ambulatory people on the ward should be two novices patrolling for emergencies. She knocked on the door again and waited.

From somewhere down a side hall, she heard Lucy say, "Sister Agnes Bernadette needs to be changed again."

"Oh, dear," someone else said. "Do you think it was the bells?"

Jane listened to their footsteps retreat, probably to the linen closet at the far end of the side hall. She knocked on Elizabeth's office door again. No answer.

She let herself in and closed the door behind her, slipping the latch up so no one could come in without making a racket. Then she went to the dispensary cabinet and pulled the shutters back.

She swept plastic vials of Thorazine and Benzedrine and phenobarbital from the second shelf. She went through the third shelf and found a bottle each of Dexedrine and methamphetamine. She had to be careful with the uppers because there were never very many of them. There wasn't as much call for pepping nuns up as calming them down. Uppers were used mostly at Children's House, for therapy for hyperactive children, although that never made much sense to Jane. Nuns were supposed to pep themselves up. They were supposed to have inner strength.

The irony of it was, she had more inner strength than any of them. She was a rock.

She closed the shutters and started to arrange her flowers in the vase on the desk. Elizabeth would discover the missing bottles and there would be a fuss, but it would be all right. She would use what she had to and put the empty vials in Kat's underwear—or Annie's, if it came to that. She didn't think it would. Annie was close to a nervous breakdown. She knew she'd been discovered, knew Kat was on to her, knew the game was nearly over. Jane would find some way to get rid of Annie long before they started looking for the pills. She'd find some way to get rid of Annie once and for all.

She thought of the bird lying in her hand, the limp malleability of its neck, the blood where its eyes had been. She thought of the blood on the table and in her throat. It was an absolute equation. Annie had stolen her history. Annie would have to give it back.

She went to the infirmary door and slipped off the latch.

When she had taken care of Annie, she wouldn't need the pills. She would have it all inside her. Forever.

CONSIDERATIONS

When the bell rang for evening recreation, Kat was down on her hands and knees under Jane's bed, pawing through the dust for something she already knew wasn't there. Jane had to be keeping the drugs somewhere. She had to have a stash of pills and powder. Wherever it was, it wasn't in her cell. Jane had the ultimate nun's cell, bare of everything but regulation clothing and a few holy pictures. Her clothes were clean and pressed and folded. There wasn't a stain or trace on any of them.

Kat got up, brushed off her skirt, and went into the corridor. If she hadn't been such an idiot over the last three months, she could call David. David would know about drugs, what kinds produced which effects, where people who used them might hide them.

She went into her own cell and got her lint brush. Every time she tried to think it out, all she got was: call David. She couldn't call David. She shouldn't even think about it. In six months or a year, they might let him visit on Sundays, but it was part of her agreement with Reverend Mother that she wouldn't be the one to initiate contact. Besides, what would she tell him?

He would believe her about the conversation on the parapet, even if no one else would. That was one thing.

She put the lint brush back in her dresser. *Our* lint brush, her mind droned irrelevantly, *our* dresser. She was all keyed up, ready for an emergency, but the emergency was here and she couldn't think of a thing to do about it.

Her mind enforced the beat like a metronome: call David.

The second bell rang for recreation.

She put her rosary beads in her pocket and headed downstairs.

SOUND AND LIGHT

The anteroom to retreat corridor was large and empty and completely lined with wood. Even the ceiling was paneled. Annie sat on the single bench in front of the single table and stared at the lacquered pine boards, wondering why anyone would bother to panel a ceiling.

She was being locked away in a tomb for the living dead. Stephen was the only person who could rescue her. If she hadn't been convinced Stephen would rescue her, she would never have been able to walk into this room.

She could get through it just one night, as long as she knew Stephen was coming.

Stephen was coming tomorrow. Reverend Mother had called him, and he had promised.

Retreat corridor was on the fourth floor of East Wing, just across North Lawn from North Tower. If she looked out a window here, would she see lights moving there in the dark? Jane said the girl who had died called to postulants and novices and Sisters who ought to come to her. Jane had stopped Annie in the hall outside Reverend Mother's office and told her about it.

"They see lights," Jane had said. "They see lights no one else can. That's how they know they're supposed to follow

276

her. Of course most of them don't. Most of them hide under their beds and go running out of the convent in the morning. But it catches up with them. It always catches up with them."

Annie took out her handkerchief and mopped sweat from her face, carefully drying every square inch of skin. Jane had been using her ghost-story voice, but she hadn't been telling a ghost story. She believed every word she said. Annie could see it in Jane's anger, in the tight, belligerent way Jane held her body to block the path. Jane was furious, and Annie didn't blame her. Annie had screwed up everything, destroyed everything, made a mockery of everything. She had committed four or five mortal sins— more than she'd admitted to—and gone on committing them as if her only mission in life was to bring down everything the Order stood for.

She thought of the Hosts she had crumbled in her pocket. She hadn't told anyone about those. She hadn't dared. When Stephen came to get her, she'd confess that, but until she was one hundred percent sure she had somewhere to go if she left, she couldn't risk anything so irrevocable.

Her face was wet with sweat again. She dried it. Again.

There was a light above the inner door. It went on with a stuttering buzz. She put the handkerchief on the table and her hands in her pockets. Stephen's letter was in there. It could keep away the dark and the silence and the nightmares and the night voices. If she could keep it with her, she could come through the night whole.

If Reverend Mother knew she'd kept it with her, she'd be out of Agnus Dei and on the road before morning. On the road to her mother's house. In a Lincoln Continental her mother would rent for the occasion, just to make sure the Bliss women would not be snubbed, even in defeat.

If Stephen didn't take her, would anything really matter?

She took the letter and laid it on the table next to the handkerchief. The light over the inner door buzzed again, impatient, questioning. She didn't believe they wouldn't be watching her. Of course they would be. If she tried to get away with something, she would be stupid. And clumsy. She would be found out.

She pushed the letter away from her until she could no longer see Stephen's handwriting. The lights here were very bright, but uneven. They cast shadows in unexpected places.

The lights on retreat corridor would be turned off. She would be alone in the dark.

The inner door clicked, and Annie turned just in time to see it snap open. She thought of Gabrielle van der Mal leaving the convent at the end of *The Nun's Story*. When the door clicked then, there was a sunny street on the other side, and a city full of possibility and hope. On the other side of this door there was only a long, dark corridor.

She went through the door and shut it behind her. She heard the click and pulled against the knob. She had locked herself in.

She had locked herself in in more ways than one.

She went to the end of the hall, to the corner cell on the window side. Her clothes were hung on hooks and folded into the dresser. Her two pairs of shoes stood side by side under the bed. It was a cell like every other cell at Agnus Dei. There was nothing sinister about it.

Every Sister in the Order made a retreat every year. Every Sister spent at least eight days of every three-hundred-sixty-five in complete silence, complete solitude, complete communion with God. That was all they were asking her to do. That was all they wanted in exchange for saving her life.

She took off her postulant dress and folded it into the laundry basket in the corner, then put on her nightgown and robe. She went to the window and leaned against the sill. The lights snapped off, leaving her in darkness.

She would have to be very careful not to go to sleep. She would have to stay awake this one night. Tomorrow she would go home with Stephen and sleep in an ordinary bed in an ordinary room, or on the couch in his living room, or in a motel room he had rented for her.

Stephen would have to save her. She could see lights moving in North Tower.

"The gash goes up, Sister. That's what he said. The gash goes up."

"I don't understand."

"The cut in her throat. It starts at the base and goes up. The knife entered the base of her throat and was drawn up toward her chin. 'Jerked up,' I think the man said."

"But, Lieutenant—"

"Of course, it's not official. Nothing is official until the autopsy."

"But, Lieutenant, that doesn't make any sense."

CHARADE

Stephen had been at Candy's when the call came, sprawled across the end of her bed like a beached whale and puffing against the wind like the Little Engine That Could. Not that he would have been at Candy's for long. She was finished with him. She'd been finished with him since she found he was taking folding money out of her cigar box while she was in the shower.

There was nothing else he could have done. He couldn't get welfare. He couldn't get unemployment. He couldn't get a job. He'd heard winos could always find money for liquor, but he'd be damned if he could figure out how. At the moment, he couldn't find the money to buy gum from a gumball machine.

He stretched out on the bench he had had to dispossess a wino to get. It had been a stroke of luck that the convent had called while he and Candy were still fighting, instead of after she threw him out. It had been a stroke of the wrong kind of luck that Candy had thrown him out without throwing his shaving kit after him. He was going to look like a wreck in the morning. He was going to have to hitchhike to Northton, too, and that wasn't going to be easy.

What did Annie want him for? Maybe he could find something to do in Northton, or at the convent, that would at least put a roof over his head. Nothing permanent. He would never get where he was going if he buried himself in a burg like Northton.

Annie, he thought, would understand. Annie would understand everything. Maybe the God he was never sure he didn't believe in was sending him to Annie to get himself straightened out. Maybe he would lay the whole thing at her feet and ask her what he should do.

There were boys in the park. He could hear their laughter and their whispers. He could feel their dangerousness. No, he didn't want to sleep in the park.

He got up and let the newspapers he had been using to cover himself fall to the grass. Maybe he'd start hitching to Northton tonight. Just being in the same town with Annie would make him feel better. And he wouldn't have to worry about juvenile delinquents.

The wino he had dispossessed was lying in a mess of withered shrubs and dirt just off the path. He straddled the body, hesitated, then went methodically through the pockets. It made him a little sick. It was the worst thing a person could do. The wino was dying of booze and malnutrition and not hurting anyone but himself. He was stripping the man of half a day's relief.

He found twenty dollars in the right pants pocket and put it in his jacket. There was change in there, too, but he couldn't bear to touch it. He couldn't even bear to think about what he was doing. He was one step away from being that wino and he couldn't think of a single thing that would save him.

Except Annie.

Maybe Annie could tell him what to do.

"Sister?"

"I want it to make sense."

"So do I, Sister. And in a way, it does. If it happened the way they're telling us it happened, then this is the only way it could be done."

"The only way she could cut her own throat."

"Yes."

"They say they were struggling with her, trying to get the knife out of her hand."

"Yes, Sister. That's what they say."

CAT

Jane came up to the tower directly after prayers, not caring if anyone heard her. Annie was on retreat corridor. Annie was exhausted, and Jane wanted her to see the lights before she went to sleep. They were important, those lights. The ghost of the girl who had died in that room was calling out. Someone had to listen.

Did she believe in ghosts? No, no, it wasn't that simple. Ghost stories were fairy tales that hinted at a larger truth. They terrified Annie. That was the value of ghost stories.

Jane looked out the archway to North Lawn and watched Martha's cat pacing back and forth in the branch cage she had made for it. If Annie could hear the noise it was making, she'd *believe* in ghosts. The damned animal sounded like a child being drowned.

Jane slipped out the tower door and down the stairs. She had to be careful passing the Mary Chapel. Anyone could be in there. They all had crises of faith and confidence in the

281

night. She started to light a candle in front of the painting of Saint Agnes and stopped herself. Why leave a candle burning for someone to wonder about? The knife wouldn't be there anymore. She would throw it away after tonight. She took it out of the hollow gap between the canvas and the frame. It was small, meant for chopping celery or peeling apples, made to fit a tiny hand. She wrapped it in her handkerchief and put it in her pocket. She wouldn't cut herself a second time.

The first time, she had cut her thigh in a long, thin line, letting free a river of surface blood that had soaked her nightgown. She had had to tell Elizabeth she'd cut herself on a jagged tile in the shower. She'd had to *make* a jagged tile. She'd had to have tetanus shots. It had been a mess.

It had been a mess, too, that time on the table in the kitchen. She'd been thinking about it all day, ever since she realized they weren't going to send Annie home. The blood and the table and the shoes on the floor and the tinted wax paper her mother had put on all the windows.

"I'll help you murder it," her mother said. "Or I'll make you murder it. Take your pick."

Jane stepped onto North Lawn, letting the door swing shut behind her. The cold and wet came up under her robe and crawled along her belly. She could almost feel it there, the bright beating lump of it. At the time, she had thought she could talk to it. She even thought it could answer. She talked to it for seven weeks before her mother set up the arc lights in the kitchen.

She thought of all the methods she had ever heard of: knitting needles, coat hangers, lye, saline, buttonhooks, metal meat fasteners, knives. The old woman her mother had brought in—the bag lady with her dirt-streaked face and clean, clean hands—stood over her with the wood-handled butcher's steel in one hand, the dull metal catching light patterns from the arc lamps. Jane knew she was going to die. The old woman was going to stick the butcher's steel up there, where her father had been. Her mother was going to stand against the wall and watch. Her father was a black knight, but her mother was a witch. Jane turned her face away from the light and listened to the beat in her head and the beat in her belly and the jungle drums of fear and pain going up to Heaven from her nerves and skin and muscles.

She did not want this to happen.

The light from the arc lamps hurt her eyes. The bruises on her arms and legs and face throbbed. The thing she was breeding inside her pulsed and twisted, pulsed and twisted, reacting to her fear. She felt the metal of the butcher's steel between her legs, scraping against her thighs, and writhed away from it. It was coming for her. It had always come for her. Her mother was bent over her head, her mouth close to Jane's ear. "We're going to help you murder it," she said. "We're going to stab it through the heart and leave its blood on you."

Jane twitched against the metal, bending sideways, frantic to get away. It was inside her and growing. It would kill her and she would be dead in the little fenced-off area outside consecrated ground in the Catholic cemetery in Woodbury. They let the weeds grow there. They let the dirt show through the lawn. There were never any flowers. She would be dead and lying under barren ground, and if whatever it was lived, it would never visit her. It wouldn't even know her name.

The old woman pushed against her, slamming her backward until she hit her head on the flat of the table. She lost her eyesight in a shatter of sparks and colors. The butcher's steel came up into her, filling her vagina, filling her womb, tearing against the inner skin like splinters tearing against the soft arch of a foot. Jane felt the tear and the start of the bleeding, the incredible, endless pain of a cramp. The old woman was eviscerating her. Her insides were turning against her, sucking away from their moorings and struggling to get out. Jane could feel it moving away from the hollow shell of her skin, down the passage, into the light. She tried to hold it in and felt herself nailed to the table, the cramps coming at her like her father's fist, coming stronger and harder and from the inside out. She heard her father saying, "whore cunt gash." She heard her mother's voice from the far side of the room, screaming "get it out of her get it out of her get it out." The butcher's steel stabbed into her again and again and again, like a rapist's prick, like the devil's prick consummating a witch's union. The lump was traveling down the passage, it was halfway out, but the butcher's steel kept coming into her, meeting the cramps, meeting the pain, coming and coming and coming until she thought she was going to wake up and find herself stuck on it like a letter on a spindle.

The old woman dropped the butcher's steel on the floor. She was covered with blood. They were both covered with blood. Jane's mother was back against the wall, her eyes hot and feverish and furious, her dress white and unstained. Jane wanted to take the butcher's steel and kill the woman. She wanted to stab her through the stomach, tear her up, throw away the pieces. She sat up on the table in a sharp, swift motion that brought so much pain she nearly blacked out. There was blood on the table and the floor and the three pairs of newly shined shoes Jane had put down after dinner. There was blood on the walls. Only her mother was immune.

What was left of it was on the table between her legs, a mass of gore and blood and pulp.

"Drink some brandy," the old woman said. "We can't have you passing out now."

"Bury it somewhere," her mother said. "We can't have it here. We can't have it lying around in the trash for someone to find."

She took the brandy the old woman offered her and drank it down, knowing she would not be conscious long, knowing her mother would be true to her word. Her mother would make her bury it. By herself.

She looked down at Martha's cat in her hands. She had slit the belly carefully. The cat was still alive. The fetal kittens were still alive. It was like one of those plastic windows-on-the-body anatomy models. The kittens squirmed in their nest of blood. The cat screeched and clawed against her robe. She felt dizzy and faint and charged up all at once.

Two or three more days and they would have been born.

She picked the knife from the ground where she'd dropped it and cut into the cat and the fetal kittens, turning them to strips of fur and muscle. If they wouldn't send Annie home, she would have to take care of it. She would

284

have to do the only possible thing, what she should have done in the beginning. She would have to take care of it before she was lost in her own history, the history that should have been Annie's history, because Annie had stolen hers and—

It was too hard to think out. It was too hard to think. She had taken pills at random, hundreds of pills, familiar and strange. She had made herself a cocktail and swallowed it without having the faintest idea what it would do to her.

It had made her dizzy.

And it had made her sure.

Annie Bliss.

"It never occurred to you, Sister? Not once?"

"No."

"It was the first thing I thought of."

"Is it true?"

"You tell me, Sister."

ACCIDENT

In the end, the drinks were not one too many or two too many or three too many, but infinite. The bartender was getting ready to cut her off. Even the asshole who called himself a reporter could see it. Mary lit another cigarette and squinted into the smoke. She'd tried to tell the fool there was no such thing as a "classy" bar, but he wanted to show off the money they gave him to spend. She leaned across the table and tapped his wrist with the

285

hot tip of her cigarette. He jumped back, spooked and angry.

"Jesus Christ," he said. "I don't know what you think you're doing sometimes."

"I'm getting your attention," she said. "I want an answer from you."

He drank off his mint-new Glenlivet as if it were beer and made a face at the taste. "It's the lawyers," he said. "I told you. There's no answer until there's an answer from the lawyers."

"Screw the lawyers. I don't give a rat's ass if I'm arrested."

"So get yourself arrested. Just don't get us arrested."

"I'm not going to get you arrested."

"You want us sitting on the doorstep while you wave a gun around, you're going to get us arrested."

Mary sighed. He thought she was crazy. They all thought she was crazy over there. They were so used to crazy people, they didn't know sanity from a hole in the wall. Of course, maybe they were right. Maybe it was crazy to want to take a Saturday-night special into a convent Visiting Sunday and blow a few holes in the wall. On the other hand, it might work. There had to be some point at which Kat became just too much trouble for Agnus Dei to keep.

The Saturday-night special was in her handbag, wrapped in one of the lavender handkerchiefs she'd received from her mother as a "little wedding present." Little wedding presents. First Communion dresses ordered from the custom department of Saks. Public piety and private family planning. The great parade of upper-middle-class American Catholicism.

Any fool knew you weren't supposed to take it seriously.

She stood up, being careful not to sway. "I'm going down the hall," she said. "I'll be right back."

"Go ahead," he said. "Have a piss for me."

She made her way through an overgrowth of potted ferns to the back hall, followed signs to a flight of stairs, and started to inch her way down. Usually, movement helped. She used to say she was never so drunk she couldn't get rid of it by getting to her feet. Things were getting less and less like usual all the time.

She wondered what Kat was doing up there, sleeping or lying awake, thinking of her precious David Marsh or dreaming of becoming a saint. Maybe that was what Kat really wanted, to become a saint. Just to show it could be done.

Mary fumbled with the light switch and got a weak, hazy stream from a half-dead bulb. Right on target. If she knew her bars, the ladies' room would be "nice," clean and decked out in pink or ecru waterproof wall facing. There would be plenty of toilet paper and an old black woman on a stool next to a saucer with six quarters in it.

She felt the edge of her heel catch the weathered wood of the step after she started to fall—*after*, as if life had started running backward and any minute now she'd find herself falling up, stepping higher, returning to a point one step ahead of her mistake. It didn't work that way. She felt the edge of her heel catch the step and then she felt herself floating, hovering in the shadows too close to the bulb.

Then she realized she wasn't just falling. She was passing out.

"*This is what we have. Four of them in there. One of them is dead. One of them is in shock. Two of them saw it happen. The one in shock and one of the two still talking are covered with blood. They look like they took a bath in it. The guy—*"

"*Lieutenant—*"

"*Do you know what 'findings consistent' means, Sister?*"

"*No.*"

"*It means you're stuck with a verdict you don't believe. The guy says she turned the knife on herself. You know what's wrong with that?*"

"There are a great many things wrong with it. The Church—"

"To hell with the Church, Sister. The movies. That's what's wrong with it. It's from a Second World War movie about fighting in Japan. John Wayne, I think."

"Lieutenant—"

ENGAGEMENT

Jane was waiting for her when she got to chapel, kneeling in the prie-dieu, bending her head over her hands so she wouldn't have to look up and do something about the situation. Annie crossed herself and genuflected and got in beside her, staying in her corner, trying not to touch. She didn't want to touch anything. The place was alive with grace, God's grace, Christ's grace, the graces of the martyrs and the saints. The chapel was as blessed as Mother Seton before her canonization. She was going to go up to the rail and swallow the body and blood of Christ in mortal sin. Again.

She had not been able to stay awake. She had done everything she could think of. In the end, she had dropped off sitting at her window. She had wakened standing over one of the sinks in the lavatory, imagining she was looking at herself in a mirror. There had been ghost lights in North Tower, clear and alive across the dark of North Lawn. Her face in the mirror had been drawn and old and wreathed in a wimple, the face of an ancient, bitter nun who pours the black poison of her resentment over the children she is given to teach.

She should be prostrate at the foot of the altar. Kat was there. Angela Louise was there, too. It was the kind of optional penance Clare Marie was always urging them to make. It showed firm resolve, purpose of amendment. It was a public declaration of incapacity.

The chapel had stone walls and a stone floor and enough

288

drafts to power a windmill, but Annie was beginning to sweat. Where was Stephen? What was he doing? Was he on his way, or already in Northton, waiting for a "decent hour"? She hated "decent hours," convent rhythm, worldly etiquette, workday routine. She hated habits and chalices and religious observance. She had spent what wakefulness she had managed to maintain working it out. She could not stay at Agnus Dei. Agnus Dei would kill her as surely as her mother would.

Kat got to her knees, kissed the floor, stood up. The chapel didn't exist for her. Nothing existed for her. Annie turned away. It was frightening to look into Kat's face. It was terrifying to realize all those stories about feeling in the presence of God were not just stories. Someone she knew prayed, and the praying was a conversation.

When Annie prayed, the words went into the void, swallowed in blackness and smoke. Just like she was being swallowed in blackness and smoke by her sin and her pride and a God who was not a Supreme Court judge, but an executioner.

Annie bit her lip. Jane was glaring at her, Jane with the murderous eyes and the virgin righteousness, Jane whom she had never been able to stop hating for her perfection. She knew what that meant, now. She knew what it made her, that she hated someone for being perfect.

If she didn't escape from this place, God would get her.

"How could you come here?" Jane hissed at her. "How could you come into the sight of God after what you did?"

EXPLANATION

1

The remains of the cat were strewn across the rocks at the top of the garden, tucked into cracks and gulleys between the stones. The kittens were cut but intact. The mother cat was in pieces. Martha was leaning into the wind, doubled over, clutching her stomach, dry-heaving into the endless storm that was Northton's November.

Kat walked back and forth in front of the red-stained snow. Martha was crying. The crying and heaving were mixed together, grief and disgust and hysteria edging too slowly toward anger. Kat put her foot in the nest of fetal kittens. All she had was anger. And frustration. It was still Grand Silence. She was still doing penance for meeting David. She was not supposed to speak unless spoken to.

Jane had done it. She was worse than crazy, worse than dangerous. She was lethal.

Annie and Jane came out of chapel, walking in lockstep, like a sideways tandem bicycle. Annie was red and shell-shocked and exhausted. Jane was smiling.

It was more than that, Kat thought. Jane was smiling *at her*. Their communication held, shimmering, in the gray dawn. Kat's stomach shrank, forming a knot. She looked at the blood in the snow. She looked up again, but Jane was gone. Gone with Annie.

Martha stopped heaving and straightened up. Kat tugged her sleeve. They had been taught an elaborate sign language, a method of communication in silence that had been common in the Order before Vatican II. They had been taught but not drilled, because active Sisters almost never resorted to it anymore. Kat racked her brain to come up with the series of symbols for "talk to Reverend Mother," and got nothing but the hooked-finger symbol for "fork."

Angela Louise came up behind her, started to tug her sleeve, and stopped. Kat caught her face just as it began to drain of blood.

"My God," Angela Louise said. "What happened here?"

Clare Marie, standing at the chapel door, swung sideways, looking for the voice that had spoken in Grand Silence. She found the three of them. Kat nodded frantically, pointing to the ground.

"Jesus, Mary, and Joseph," Angela Louise said.

Kat threw her arms in the air. The frustration was unbearable. She was ready to break rocks.

Clare Marie stopped just behind Martha. "Dear Lord Jesus Christ," she said, signing herself.

290

Kat felt the hand signal for "Reverend Mother" come at her like one of James Thurber's phantoms. It brought a tremendous sense of relief.

She tapped her forehead twice and bowed in Clare Marie's direction.

2

"You must realize," Reverend Mother said, "what you're saying makes very little sense."

The light came at Reverend Mother from behind, leaving her face in the hood-frame of her veil looking dark and unreachable. Angela Louise and Martha sat to either side of her. They, too, were unreachable.

Kat's urgency was like a muscle spasm. She wanted to shake this old woman by the shoulders, smash a window, break furniture, do something that would get some attention. She wanted to calm down and speak rationally. She couldn't do any of those things.

At the very least, she wanted to make sure Annie wasn't left alone. Which was impossible, of course, because Annie was on retreat corridor. She was supposed to be alone.

"What you're trying to tell me," Reverend Mother said, "is that one of my postulants, a girl I see every day, a girl I have absolutely no trouble with, is running around this house murdering small animals and—and—I don't even know what to call that mess this morning."

"She admitted it to me," Kat said desperately.

"Yesterday," Reverend Mother said. "On the parapet."

"Yes."

"She came right out and told you she'd killed the bird."

"She implied it," Kat said. Reverend Mother's face was a mask of disbelief. Kat hurried on, as if getting the words in quickly would make a difference. "She had it in her hands and she was twisting its neck and she was drugged—"

"You don't know that either," Reverend Mother said. "You inferred that."

"Her eyes were black holes."

"Something that can happen from eyestrain or lack of sleep. Both common among postulants."

"She threatened Annie. She said she'd taken care of Annie. Maybe she got in touch with that man at the store and told him—"

"Told him what?" Reverend Mother exploded. "Why would she have to tell him? From the way it was described to me, our Annie was not exactly subtle. She just picked up the books and put them in her pocket. We don't need interference from Miss Galloway to explain how Annie got caught. Never mind the fact that it's just as well she did get caught. Katherine—"

"Never mind," Kat said. "I know, I know. That's why I didn't say anything to begin with."

"Reverend Mother?" Angela Louise was very pale. Kat wondered what was going on in her mind. Angela Louise, who wanted to protect the Order the way medieval knights had wanted to protect their queen. Kat looked at her hands. This had already gone too far. This conversation was not just futile, it was over.

"She's strange," Angela Louise said. "Reverend Mother, that girl is *strange*. I know she never breaks the rules, but she's—"

"She's vicious," Martha said suddenly. "She's a vicious little bitch and I'd be a hundred times happier if you'd send her away from here and never let her come back."

"Martha," Reverend Mother said.

"I'm sorry," Martha said. "I'm sorry for my language. But she holds her holiness over your head like a guillotine."

"That's hardly evidence that she murdered a cat."

"I don't think she did murder the cat," Martha said. "But she says things. And she sneaks. And—"

Reverend Mother tapped her desk impatiently. "She's strange," she said. "She's an outsider. I understand all that. But none of that means she killed a cat, or that she was threatening Annie Bliss, who's in quite enough trouble on her own." Reverend Mother looked from one to the other of them, magisterial, definitive. "We cannot send a perfectly adequate postulant home because she doesn't fit in, in a worldly way, with the rest of you. That is not what we are trying to do here."

Martha and Angela Louise bowed their heads, acquiescing to reason and authority. Kat wanted to be out of the room, free to act. Free to act at what? What could she do, lock Jane in a closet? For how long? To what purpose?

She knew Jane was dangerous to Annie Bliss. She didn't know how.

Reverend Mother said, "Katherine Mary."

"Yes," she said.

"The penance was never meant to break you," Reverend Mother said. "It's not a test of strength. If you're having trouble . . ."

"No." Kat stood up. "Thank you, Reverend Mother, but no. It's not breaking me."

Reverend Mother didn't look as if she believed it.

Kat turned aside and let Angela Louise lead the way to the door.

3

Kat was in the hall again when she thought of David, the white knight, the rescuer of damsels in distress. Could he see Annie Bliss as a damsel in distress?

The problem with David was that there was more involved here than asking help for Annie Bliss. Kat had not stopped loving him. She could not imagine hearing his voice again. She could still see the perfection of his body, barely hidden in a heavy jacket. It hurt her to remember him. It made her weak.

She wasn't making this up as an excuse to see him again. Jane had been on the parapet. Kat had not been "misinterpreting" or "exaggerating."

She thought of David in his heavy jacket. She heard him laugh, his deep voice bouncing off the walls of East Wing like a tennis ball off a backboard.

She stopped on the landing and looked down on North Lawn, at the mound of earth that covered the cats. Something was wrong. She could hold onto that. Something was wrong. And she had to do something about it.

She had to get to Annie Bliss.

VISIT

When they came to tell her Stephen had come, Annie was in the retreat corridor Mary Chapel, talking to the Blessed Virgin in a mumble. Retreat corridor was a hollow cave, a wind tunnel, a decompression chamber. She was not decompressing. Her father sat on the Mary Chapel altar and talked to her. His mouth was a hole. His lips were burned away. He smiled at her with his teeth. Annie resisted the urge to put her hands in his blood. He wasn't there, any more than her mother was, though she could hear the hiss of her mother's voice, the snake in the garden. "I told you so I told you so I told you so."

There had been lights in North Tower. Annie had seen them. She had watched them moving from one side of the tower room to the other, picking up speed, gathering brightness. She had seen the lights and Jane knew she had seen them and Jane had said, Jane had said—

"God can wait forever He can wait forever He doesn't have to let you go not a year not a hundred years He can wait forever and she can wait with him and—"

There was a sound behind her. Annie stood up, wondering how much of what was happening was real, how much fear, how much the madness that had been her father's and would be hers because the sins of the father are visited on the children and because she was so full of sin, she was an abomination in a religious house. She didn't need Jane to tell her that. She was an abomination in a religious house and here she was, pretending piety and devotion to Mary.

Out in the world, it wouldn't matter so much. Out in the real world—not her mother's house, but the *real* world—it wouldn't matter at all.

She counted time on her rosary beads. If I say three more decades, Stephen will come. If I say five more decades, Stephen will come. If I say a whole rosary, fifteen decades, fifteen minutes for each meditation, Stephen will come.

Kat was standing in the doorway, her veil crooked and a wild look in her eyes. Annie shook her head. She was imagining it. Kat never had a wild look in her eyes. She was the one who was wild. She was driving herself crazy, waiting for Stephen. She was already crazy, and Stephen was the only person who could make her sane.

Kat said, "Your brother's downstairs. They told me to tell you to come down."

Annie felt shot out of a cannon. The air cleared. Her head cleared. Her fear melted into the floor. She was standing in the retreat corridor Mary Chapel, an ordinary young woman in an ordinary universe where ghosts did not walk in towers and no one (careful, careful) had ever committed suicide. She felt like flying.

Stephen had come. Stephen would rescue her.

Kat stepped back, uncertain. "Annie? Are you all right?"

"I'm so glad he's here," Annie said. Her smile got wider and wider and wider, until she thought it would split her skin. "I'm just so glad he's here."

Kat hesitated. "Annie," she said, "why do you want to be a nun?"

Annie shook her head. In less than an hour, she would be free. She would tell Kat: I don't want to be a nun. I hate being a nun. I hate being a postulant. I'm full of sin and I don't care. I want to touch silk and silver and live in a world of stately processions. I want to be Princess Daisy and a girl named Pagan and a girl named Annie Bliss whose father did not commit suicide, who does not kiss shoes, who does not eat breakfast off cracked stoneware plates with tin utensils.

This was the mercy of God, that He had sent Stephen to rescue her.

She brushed by Kat to the door of the Mary Chapel, tripping over her own feet.

This was the mercy of God, that He would release her from her vocation, that He would not hold her to a promise that was killing her.

OMEN

Annie was running. Her footsteps sounded like lead on steel, rackety and harsh.

Kat stared down the empty stairwell. It was as if Annie had shoved a load of meth into an artery. She was higher than Jane had been on the parapet. She was flying, soaring, wheeling into space.

Jane was in the foyer, waiting. Kat had seen her.

What did Annie want of her brother? What did she expect?

Kat started down the stairs. She had seen the brother, up close. She hadn't liked what she saw. He was worse than a phony. He was a bum. And he was desperate.

She wanted to get David on the phone and make him talk to her, make him tell her what to do. She heard his voice in her head. She heard her own voice pleading with dead air.

Something was wrong.

Annie was flying.

Annie was going to crash.

Jane was going to be there when she fell.

SANCTUARY

The first thing Annie thought when she saw him was: he looks like our father. The next thing she thought was: he looks tired. She almost didn't go beyond that. Stephen was sitting in the great yellow wingback, his nose buried in a Royal Doulton cup, picking his fingernails with a toothpick. Annie watched the movement of his thumb. She should be running across the reception room the way she'd run down the East Wing stairs. Instead, she was standing in the doorway, frozen, wanting reassurance. She stepped onto the carpet, careful, trying to make no sound. It didn't surprise her that he looked so different from what she'd expected. It did surprise her he looked so much like the picture of their father, down to the way his collar seemed too large for his neck, his neck too scrawny for his head. She had expected a hero. What she had was a clerk.

Was it incest to want to put your arms around your brother's knees, to want him to put his arm on your shoulder and his thumb on your cheek?

She stopped in the middle of the room and coughed falsely into her hand. Stephen's head came out of his coffee, lifted above the shoulder line, fixed itself unsteadily in the air. Annie stepped back, shocked and a little queasy. Stephen looked—ruined. The tweed of his jacket was creased and stained with something green. His face was lined and not clean.

They had made a mistake. They had called the wrong Stephen.

Agnus Dei was an infinite weight, settling on her shoulders. Her headache was a knitting needle.

Stephen leaned forward and said, "Annie?"

"Yes." She came closer. He smelled of bitter tea and old bread. She took a seat in the middle of the couch, watching him. "Yes," she said again. "Stephen?"

"Shit," Stephen said. "You look like a nun already."

The chapel bells rang eleven o'clock. They both looked up at the same time, hearing movement on the floors above them. The professed Sisters were going to General Chapter. Annie waited for the headache to get worse, for the weight of Agnus Dei to grow heavier. Nothing happened.

Now that she was close, she could see that more than his jacket was wrinkled. His trousers were a mass of lines. His shirt was mottled and stained. He looked like one of those men who slept on the New Haven green. Something drastic must have happened to her on retreat corridor. She was hallucinating. She had to be hallucinating. Stephen could not be what he looked like to her now. He was her hero. He was her savior. He had come to rescue her.

She could feel the panic building inside her. Behind her

was a pit. Before her was Stephen, whom she had loved well, as well as Kat had ever loved David. She had to believe in him.

"They still wear habits in this place," Stephen said. "Gave me a jolt when I came in, this old lady all covered up. Then there was a young one dressed like you. Pretty. Better than pretty."

"Kat O'Brien," Annie said.

Stephen nodded. Annie looked at her hands. Stephen lit a cigarette. Annie got up and hurried to the hutch for one of the cut-crystal ashtrays. She put it on the coffee table in front of him and watched his nicotine-stained fingers shove the cigarette into it. The cigarette was hand-rolled.

He wasn't taking care of himself. She could do that for him. She would. She'd be very useful to him, he'd see, he wouldn't regret taking her in.

This scene was like an Escher print, disproportioned, oddly skewed.

Her headache was coming back.

"I didn't know what kind of habits they had," Stephen said. "I kept thinking of you in black and white. Like the Hayley Mills movie."

"You can wear them outside starting next year," Annie said. "But most people won't. They'll wear shorter things."

"Like you're wearing now."

"With a black veil." Annie tugged her veil.

Stephen smiled, a sick, pleading grin that scared Annie to death. "I always think of you in the whole rigamarole," he said. "I'm very old-fashioned."

Annie thought of herself in "the whole rigamarole." It made her dizzy.

It didn't matter how small Stephen's house was, how cramped. She could keep it clean for him. She could keep his clothes washed and pressed and decent food on the table. She could help him. He could keep her safe.

The reception room was getting smaller. The walls were drawing closer together. Her father waited just inside the anteroom door, her mother at the top of the stairs.

"Take me home with you," she said, closing her eyes and

298

forcing it out, pushing it through the force field of terror that was walling her in. "Let me live with you."

Stephen burst out laughing.

APPEAL TO CONSCIENCE

The light in Reverend Mother's office was brighter than it had been this morning. Kat thought the Holy Ghost must be illuminating the place. The sun was behind heavy storm clouds, a massing threat of snow.

Annie was downstairs, talking to her brother, asking his help. Somebody ought to be there when she crashed.

Reverend Mother patted her hands together. "The call came just after you left the office this morning," she said. "We spent a certain amount of time checking it out."

"It didn't come from the hospital?"

"It came from that—reporter—she's spending so much time with."

"It's a good thing you checked it out."

Reverend Mother nodded. "From what we can determine, your mother and this man were in a restaurant. She was on her way to the ladies' room. She fell on some stairs. That was how the accident happened."

"She fell down the stairs and shot herself?" Kat said. "Excuse me, Reverend Mother. That sounds a little farfetched even for Mary."

"The whole thing sounds farfetched to me." Reverend Mother smiled thinly. "She had a gun in her purse. A . . . what do you call them? An illegal gun."

"A Saturday-night special?"

"That's right. She fell on the stairs and it went off. According to her reporter friend, he'd spent the night trying to talk her out of coming up here and shooting a few rounds into the walls."

"At least he was trying to talk her out of it."

299

"The reporter says she's in critical condition," Reverend Mother said. "The hospital says she's resting comfortably and is in no danger, at least from the gunshot wound. She shot herself in the leg. Lost a lot of blood." Reverend Mother pursed her lips. "There is, I'm afraid, some evidence of cirrhosis."

"Cirrhosis," Kat said. She saw Mary at twenty-five, a vision in white tulle and beaded satin, bending over her bed to kiss her good night before going out to dinner. She must have been five. Or four. What happened to people? "Sometimes," she told Reverend Mother, "I get flashes of her. From when I was a child. She was a beautiful woman."

"She's in Mass. General," Reverend Mother said. "The hospital in Boston." She fidgeted. "The thing is," she said, "I want you to do us a favor. Something I'm not sure you'd do on your own."

Jane came onto North Lawn, carrying a basket of infirmary laundry. Kat tried to get a good look past Reverend Mother's broad shoulders. Jane dumped the contents of the basket through the East Wing pantry chute and started back across the lawn.

Why cross the lawn in this weather? Why not go around from inside?

Jane was walking oddly, stiffly. She made Kat's spine twitch.

"I want you to go to Boston," Reverend Mother said. "To visit your mother."

"Now?" Kat said.

"I know you don't get along well," Reverend Mother said. "And under the old rules, you wouldn't have been allowed a visit unless she was dying or dead. These days we're more flexible. If you don't want to go for yourself, go for the good of the Order."

"Visiting my mother for the good of the Order."

"Not visiting would be bad for the Order. It would make a remarkably effective, if completely inaccurate, magazine story." She picked a folder from the mess on her desk. "We're apparently making the *Time* religion section this week."

Out on North Lawn, Jane slipped under the arch between North and East Wings and disappeared. She must have let

300

herself into the central core of the building through the archway door. The reception room was in the central core. Annie was in the reception room.

"I have called the hospital," Reverend Mother said, "and made arrangements here. You can go up with Annunciata tomorrow morning after breakfast and stay at our Boston house. For three or four days, I think."

"Three or four days?"

"Under the circumstances, if you wanted to stay longer, you could."

"I don't want to see her," Kat said. "I—" She stifled it. It wasn't true she didn't want to see Mary. She didn't want her hurt, or lonely. She had never intended to abandon Mary, or anyone else, by coming to Agnus Dei.

North Lawn was empty. Jane was probably waiting in the East Wing anteroom, ready to pounce on Annie. To pounce and do what?

Would it matter if she spent three or four days in Boston? Or would Jane make her move, whatever that was going to be? Would something happen to Annie?

What in the name of God was Jane going to do to Annie?

"Katherine," Reverend Mother said.

"Yes," Kat said. "Yes, Reverend Mother. Boston. Tomorrow."

Reverend Mother relaxed. "You really don't mind?"

"No, Reverend Mother."

"I could have made it a matter of religious obedience," Reverend Mother said, "but I didn't want to."

"It isn't necessary. I understand the situation perfectly."

Reverend Mother stood up. "I just wish they were all like you," she said. "All this nonsense with your young man notwithstanding."

RESOLUTION

First there was laughter, sharp, hysterical. Then there was something that might have been a sob, but sounded more like a hiccup. Jane leaned against the anteroom door, trying to hear words. It was impossible. They had planted themselves in the middle of the reception room. Even with the door open, she got only the loudest noises. Laughter and hiccups and sobs. Nothing useful.

At first, when she heard Annie's brother was coming, she thought he was going to take her away. As soon as she saw him, she knew it wouldn't happen. He couldn't take anyone anywhere. Everyone who went where he was going went alone. God, his stink was awful. The state of his nerves was worse. She thought he was going to shake himself into molecules.

It had set her back a little. Stephen did not belong in Annie's life as Jane understood it. She had worked it out, and the dichotomy was absolute. Annie had taken the good and left her with the evil.

She had gone up to the infirmary and taken a handful of pills she hadn't bothered to identify. She'd spilled them haphazardly into her hand and swallowed them without water. She'd wheeled the laundry cart up and down the halls and let herself take off. And take off she had. Oh, yes. It was as if she'd been waiting for just this combination of pills. She saw it all very clearly. She saw Annie Bliss sucking the breath out of her, swallowing her soul. She saw her mother and her father. She saw the blood on the table and the blood coming out of the car. If Annie Bliss left Agnus Dei alive, she would take Jane's life with her.

Annie's voice rose to a dramatic squeak, desperate, lost, tearful. Jane put herself into the motion and color of it. Annie radiated panic.

Annie was her salvation. If she pushed it one more time, she could make it happen. She could free herself. Annie

302

would disintegrate. Jane would get her life back. The scales would fall from the others' eyes and they would see Jane for what she really was—not for what Annie had made her, but for what she really was.

She thought of the spirit lights in the tower, candle flames moving back and forth in an invisible wind. She could make Annie see what she wanted her to see.

COMMUNION

When it was over, Annie went to the main chapel and prostrated herself in front of the altar, to see what it felt like. It felt like nothing.

Stephen was nothing, no one, blank. He was what her mother had always said he was. Was that the secret? That her mother had been right all along?

She was afraid her mother was right about everything, and that all the things Jane said were true. She had been given a vocation. She had betrayed it. God was stalking her, cutting off her avenues of escape. If she made a good penitential retreat, He might let her live out her life.

She couldn't possibly make a good penitential retreat. She couldn't possibly be a nun.

She had taken the last two books deliberately, but she couldn't have stopped herself. The books were a part of her. She hated herself for being poor. She hated the poor for being poor. She wanted to take the bare boards and thin mattress of her bed and tear them to shreds. She couldn't summon anger at the thought of Catholics going to their deaths for the faith in Poland, but she could summon it for muslin curtains and canned baked beans.

She could summon it for Stephen.

She got to her knees, kissed the floor, got to her feet. There was one good thing about being on retreat. She was set apart, supposedly concentrating only on God, keeping strict and unrelieved silence. She would not have to talk to the Sisters through this fog of dread and prophecy. God was stalking her.

She let herself through the core archway door into the anteroom. Jane was standing just inside, her arms crossed over her chest. Annie stepped back, not surprised, but reluctant. She would never be surprised to see Jane. Jane was what God had given her instead of a conscience.

"It doesn't work that way," Jane said. "Didn't you know that?"

Annie put a finger to her lips, sealing her silence. Jane would remember she was supposed to keep silence and go away. Jane was always very careful about keeping the Rule.

Jane did not go away. Staring into her eyes was like staring over the roof of a tall building, hypnotizing, dangerous, irresistible.

"You were supposed to be a *nun*," Jane said, coming forward slowly, inching closer and closer. "You were supposed to be a *nun*. What do you think is going to happen to that?"

Jane was right up against her. "Even if you could go home, it woudn't help. God doesn't live in a convent chapel. God is everywhere. God is everywhere but inside you."

Jane pressed a finger in the air next to Annie's head, her fingernail making scratching motions at Annie's eyes. Annie flinched. Her mouth went dry.

"You're going to see lights in the tower," Jane said, "see them and know they're for you. You deserve to see her face-to-face. You deserve it. Don't you? You love to sin."

Annie closed her eyes. She wanted to scream at Jane. She wanted to scream. She could see it all, the girl in the tower swinging from the rafters and her father's head in pieces in her mother's bedroom and herself, swinging in the wind. Jane's shoulder was touching her shoulder. Jane's arms were touching her arms. They were breathing the same air.

"You love to sin," Jane said again. "You live for it. You couldn't give it up if you wanted to. And you don't want to. So there's nowhere to go." Jane stepped back, and smiled, and folded her hands under her cape. Chameleons were less changeable. The prophet had become the perfect postulant. "You shouldn't even want to live," Jane said, in the voice she'd use to ask for salt. "And you don't, do you?"

Annie's headache was a knitting needle someone had left too long in a fire. She tried to step away from Jane, and found she'd forgotten how to move.

"You shouldn't fight the will of God," Jane said. "That's the worst sin of all."

PHONE CALL

And that's the worst sin of all.

Kat sat down next to the switchboard. What was? If she'd been earlier, she might have found out. If the conversation had gone on longer—the monologue; Annie was keeping silence like a good little postulant—she might have done something to counteract it. Jane had thrown off that last line and disappeared. Kat had run down the stairs, thinking all the way of how she was going to record this in her examen book, and found Annie standing by herself in the middle of the anteroom, gazing fixedly at the ceiling, in some kind of trance. She grabbed Annie by the shoulders and shook her.

"You can't listen to her," she said. "She's crazy."

Annie smiled and shook her head, the picture of perfect charity.

Kat tried the only thing she could think of. "Somebody killed Martha's cat last night," she said. "Cut it into strips and killed the fetal kittens. It was Jane, Annie. It was Jane."

Annie's smile didn't falter. Her halo didn't dim. She raised her hands and began to make a series of bewildering signs. She made them over and over again until they got through: *It was me.*

"Don't be ridiculous," Kat said. "You were locked on retreat corridor last night. There's no way out once those doors are locked."

Annie signed again: *It was me.*

"What does she want you to do?" Kat said. "What was

305

she telling you to do?" Annie said nothing. She didn't even blink. Kat thought of herself shipped off to Boston, sitting at the side of her mother's bed, taking abuse and trying to forget all this. There was no time. She grabbed Annie's shoulders again. This time, she held them hard. "Annie, listen to me. David would take you in. You don't have to go to your mother. David will take you in. He won't even mind."

She caught the flicker of interest and jumped at it. "We can go right now and call him," she said. "I don't even care if I get caught. We can go *right now.*"

The interest jumped one last time and died. Kat gave Annie a final hard, snapping shake. It didn't help. Annie was beyond her. Annie was as stoned as if she'd swallowed half of Jane's secret stash.

"Annie," Kat said. *"Listen to me."*

Annie began to gesture again, a longer sentence, a more complex thought: *It has always been me.*

Kat picked up the receiver, started to dial, then broke the connection. Then she said aloud, "Dear Lord, please let me be doing this for the right reasons. And please let it *work.*"

She picked up the receiver again. She dialed the Eagleville number and waited. She heard the phone picked up on the other end.

"David, please," she said. "David, I need you."

"*That's the last of her, Sister. Going out the door.*"

"*You think one of them murdered her.*"

"*No, Sister.*"

"*You said—*"

"*I said we shouldn't believe everything we hear. And we shouldn't. I don't think it could have happened the way they said it happened. The girls say they followed her. The*

*man says he saw a light and became alarmed. It's all very
nice, Sister, but you could fit a submarine through the holes."*

*"I don't know how to tell if they're lying, Lieutenant. I
used to think I did, but I don't."*

*"They're not lying, Sister. I'd bet my life everything they've
said is the absolute truth, as far as it goes. She tried to hang
herself. She cut the rope with the knife and strung it up. When
they tried to stop her, she turned the knife on herself. The
absolute truth. But not the whole truth."*

"They're not telling us everything."

*"No. Sister. They're not telling us everything. And I don't
think they ever will."*

BLOOD OF THE LAMB

1

At the end of Compline, the members of the Christmas
Choir rose in place and gave the *Salve Regina* in Latin chant.
The last full tower-and-chapel-bell set rang the end of office.
The chapel lights snapped off. The choir rose in candlelight
and started through the measured, hypnotic cadence of the
Sweet Hymn, bouncing the solemn regularities of that incan-
tatory language off stone walls and stone floors and hard-
wood prie-dieux, making the place seem haunted.

Kat lost the beat, stumbled over the verse. She had to
hold her breath for half a minute while she figured out
where she was. She was still coming up for air after office.
Since she had given up David, God had given her complete
rest in office, complete rest in prayer. As long as she was
talking to Him, she was aware of nothing else. Usually she
emerged from this state tranquil, serene. Tonight she had
come up into the hard static of nervous anxiety. She felt
stung, as if she'd been slapped.

David had promised to take Annie. That much was done.
She had no idea why he was doing it. She didn't care. She
wasn't going to pick at his motives. She plunged into the
second verse and a prayer for him at the same time. He'd

probably save his soul all by himself, but it didn't hurt to make sure.

When she looked up again, everyone was standing, getting ready to process out. For over eight hundred years, Sisters of the Society of Mary had left chapel after Compline just this way, gone to their beds in just this order. Usually procession gave her a feeling of infinite peace, of belonging to something larger and more significant than herself. Tonight it scraped against the edge of her fear like sand across a blister.

Annie was behind her, walking through the night like a zombie.

And she didn't have any more time.

2

When they got to the reception room, Annie had to remind herself to go right, toward East Wing, instead of straight ahead with all the other postulants. Jane was gripping her elbow, holding it just under her cape, where no one could see. Jane's fingers bore into Annie's joints. Annie had to break away, bow to Sister Portress, go upstairs in silence.

She was very calm. She had been calm for hours. She hadn't needed Jane to tell her those things. She would have figured them out for herself.

God had demanded sacrifice of Abraham. God had demanded sacrifice from Christ, too. That was what God wanted from all of them. Sacrifice.

The East Wing stairwell was full of footsteps. The rafters were full of voices that weren't voices yet, but would get to be, if she let them go on long enough. The voices said:

No way out.

The voices said:

He committed suicide.

Kat had been careful not to take any coffee during recreation, not to give herself an excuse for insomnia. It hadn't helped. She went through night prayers in bug-eyed wakefulness. She lay in bed and counted every crack and stain in the ceiling. She sat up in bed and made a list of all the reasons for breaking the rules a second time in one day.

The need for a cigarette was climbing through her throat and lungs, making her crazy. It wasn't much of a list. She'd be embarrassed to present it to Reverend Mother. What had Jane been saying to Annie in the anteroom? What had Annie been listening to?

She got out of bed, went to the window, opened it against the night air. The cold usually sobered her. Now it just made her feel near pneumonia.

She leaned out the window and looked back and forth along the fourth floor of East Wing. It was dark. All of Agnus Dei was dark. Annie was up there somewhere in the dark.

4

In the next cell, Kat's window went up, jarring and creaking against the swollen wood of the frame. Jane sat very still, trying not to breathe. Things were a little hazy. She had eaten her way through nine small Dexedrine tablets and half a dozen phenobarbital at recreation. She had eaten more—she couldn't remember what, or how much of what—in the lavatory after prayers. The mix wasn't right. She was fuzzy and jumpy at the same time. She couldn't get her head clear. She had the rest of the pills laid out on her quilt, in descending size, so she could take what he needed to balance herself.

She had tried to feed Kat phenobarbital at recreation, but it hadn't worked. Kat wasn't drinking coffee. Kat wasn't eating chocolate cake. Kat wasn't doing much of anything but fidgeting. Annie was locked up in East Wing, beyond the sound of Kat's voice.

If things had worked out differently, she could have waited until tomorrow, when Kat would be safely in Boston, out of Annie's reach. Now the blood and the table and the cat and the pills were all descending on her, crushing her, suffocating time. Annie was ready in a way she would never be again. Tomorrow she might think of a way out, or just calm down. As soon as Annie calmed down she would remember what Kat had said about David. And then the chance would be gone.

She took out one of the green pills, swallowed it, reached for another.

Her mother floated through the dark air over North Lawn like a vampire, holding the butcher's steel like a magic wand.

5

On retreat corridor, Annie lit a votive candle in the Mary Chapel. Kat saw the flame go up, and leaned so far out her window, she nearly fell. Annie couldn't sleep either. Was that a good sign or a bad one? Was Annie afraid of the dark?

Kat sat on the floor, drawing her legs up under her. What was she afraid of? What did she think Annie was going to do, locked up on retreat corridor? There were two doors to retreat corridor. One led to the anteroom. The other led to a back staircase that went to the basement and the crypt. They locked simultaneously when the bolt switch was thrown. The bolt switch was in a small cubbyhole outside the anteroom door. Once it was locked, the only way someone could get off without being let out was to throw one of the two fire alarms. The fire alarms opened the bolts. They also set up an unbearable racket everywhere in the Motherhouse.

Annie couldn't possibly get off retreat corridor.

What was she afraid of?

In the next cell, Jane started singing to herself. Kat could see her through the curtain, sitting on her bed, rocking.

6

David came out onto North Lawn, telling himself for the hundredth time that he was being worse than an idiot. This was not what Kat had asked him to do. Kat wanted him to take Annie home and let her live with him. He'd known from the sound of her voice she'd promised Annie before asking him. He didn't mind. He'd promised to be there for her. He would be there. And he liked Annie Bliss. He'd show up at the door tomorrow and offer to take her home.

In the meantime, he couldn't sleep. He'd been out in Eagleville, pacing the cramped rectangle of his living room, and the next thing he knew he was in the bug on the way to Northton. God only knew what for. Now he was standing in the cold and damp, getting chilled to the bone, as if he thought that by sitting here, keeping watch, he could prevent anything bad happening between now and the time he came charging in like the cavalry.

The hall where Kat was supposed to be was dark. The hall where Annie was supposed to be had a single light, a candle shining at one end. It looked disembodied.

7

The tower was dark. Annie shielded the candle with her palm and looked again, to be sure. The tower was dark. The tower was empty. She was sure of that.

There were paper and pens under the statue of the Infant of Prague, to write letters to your Divine Spouse. You were supposed to write notes to Jesus and carry them on you, close to your heart. She had written a list instead. She had been very honest, very straightforward, very forthright.

She could not go home to her mother. Who do you think you are?

She could not go to Stephen. She had made him up.

She could not stay at Agnus Dei. She could not bear one more day of poverty and silence.

She started to write down what Kat had said about David, and stopped. She didn't think that was any more real than what she had dreamed about Stephen. It would be worse if it was. It would be like the things she had thought about herself when she read Stephen's letters, and the books. That she could do it, somehow. That she could make her way to mansions and limousines and restaurants with gold leaf on the menus. That those things were not just real, but real for her.

She was very calm. She was calmer now than she had ever been in her life.

The circumstances of her life were the walls of a box. The God who had made her was a vacuum pump.

If she stayed very calm and went very slowly, she would be all right.

But she wouldn't be like that girl in the tower. She wouldn't go out apologizing for what she was.

8

Jane could not let it go another night. The longer she sat in the dark, silent wakefulness, the worse it got. They filled her head with off-key music. They chanted in tongues. They smiled at her, like the guardian angels in My First Communion Catechism, making sure she safely crossed the street.

It had taken nearly all the rest of the pills, but it had worked. She was clear. She could see it all. She wanted to get started. She wanted to get started before it was too late.

There was a thin wash of moonlight over North Lawn. It came through Kat's window, turning her into a silhouette against the muslin curtain that divided her cell from Jane's. Kat was leaning out, watching Annie on retreat corridor.

Jane slipped off the bed one foot at a time. She moved as slowly and silently as the clouds that were closing in on the moon, and slipped into the corridor, into the nest of demons that had surrounded her always, walking toward the angels who had waited for her for so long. The demons fluttered and hissed, waving their malice like spears. She held her arms tightly against her sides and moved like a walking

312

board. She wanted to jump away from the butcher's steel and her mother's clawing fingers. She wanted to rake her nails against her father's cheeks and draw blood. She wanted to scream at all the dead bodies in their cells to come out and see what reality was, what God was, what heaven and hell were. She walked straight down the corridor instead, barefoot step after barefoot step, very slowly, very deliberately, very quietly.

9

Something that sounded like a snap jolted her. Kat hadn't been asleep, but she'd been lost in memory and worry, speculation and self-reproach. Dew had condensed on her hair, making her scalp cold and slick. She reached to the bed for the robe she'd left lying on the quilt. She stopped, her fingers closing on the thick terry-cloth nap. Through the muslin, she could see Jane's bed, unslept in, the quilt pulled tightly over the sheets and blanket and mattress. She could not see Jane.

She looked at Annie's candle. It had stopped moving. Annie had come to rest.

She got off the floor and went into the corridor and pushed through the curtains of Jane's cell. Jane's empty, silent cell.

Annie could not get off retreat corridor. But anyone who wanted to could get in.

10

Annie was thinking about Princess Daisy again, about the horse-drawn sleigh she rode through Central Park to her final triumph. The Tavern on the Green. What was it like? It was a real place. She'd seen ads for it in *The New Yorker*.

She started to rub her temples, then stopped. She didn't have a headache. She had what felt like a hangover, as she'd heard hangovers described—a hazy, muddy, lugubrious feeling—but no needle-sharp, white-hot, pulsing pain. Even thinking about her father didn't bring her pain.

Across North Lawn, something moved in the tower. Something rose and swayed. Annie sat up, alert. She had

313

waited and waited and here it was. Just like last night. Jane thought she was telling ghost stories, but she wasn't.

Annie took her rosary and examen book and devotion beads and Bible and crucifix and Little Office and put them in the pockets of her robe.

She went into the lavatory, past the stalls, past the sinks, to the wall of windows looking out on the place where the wings were joined.

The fire escape was rusty and unsteady, abandoned. It stopped at the second floor. The rest of it had come off, snapped by storm winds or ordinary rust. It didn't matter. She needed to go only one floor down. She could go through the window there, down the corridor, down the stairs, through the anteroom and the reception room. She could get to North Tower without sounding the alarm.

Her headache was coming back. She stood on the fire escape and felt the cold, hoping it would ease the pain. There was no wind. She could hear the coughing spit of the tide coming in on the Sound. There was even a moon, hemmed in by a few hazy clouds. North Lawn looked like the setting for a Nativity scene before the Magi arrived.

There were more lights in the tower now. Something was hanging from a rafter, swaying in the breeze in that open octagonal room. Something only she could see.

She pulled at the third-floor window, wedging it open, letting herself in.

She no longer knew what was true.

11

The bolt switch was a tall metal rod anchored in the floor. Kat had to tug at it twice to get it moving, and even then she got it only halfway. Her palm and fingers were slick. She planted her feet on either side of it and pulled, falling back ward, so that all her weight and strength worked on it at once. This was what she needed David for. How did Clare Marie get this thing shut?

She heard a grind and a pop, the inner door to the ante room coming open. She ran toward it, knowing she had no reason to be so terrified. The bolts had been thrown. They could be thrown only from outside. Jane could not be wandering around retreat corridor and outside it at the same time. But she could already have come and gone.

Kat stumbled through the anteroom, bumping against a table and a bench. There were no windows and no lights. She held herself against the wall and felt her way across the paneling, board by board, catching the skin of her fingers on bent nails.

She felt the wall move, sway, swing away from her. She stumbled into a dark, cramped space, reached out, felt the walls slope and widen into a broader corridor. She edged into the dark, wondering why all the cells were closed off when no one was using them.

She leaned against a wall to catch her breath. She said, "Annie?"

No answer.

Her heart began a slow, hysterical climb, louder and louder, faster and faster, harder and harder.

Annie could not have got off the corridor without sounding the alarm. Jane could not be on the corridor if the bolts were thrown. Therefore, Annie was on and Jane was off. Elementary.

Daniella had said something about Annie being in the corner-window cell. Daniella had put Annie's things there.

Kat made her way down the corridor, counting cells. She stopped dead in the center and almost kicked herself for being such a fool. She grabbed the curtains of the cells on either side of her and pulled them back. There was a window in the cell to her left. There was a shade drawn over it, tight. She went in and snapped the shade open. Then she went back to the corridor and made her way to the end. The last cell on the left was still and faintly illuminated. Kat put her hand on the curtain and tried again. "Annie?"

Nothing.

She drew the curtain back with a jerk. The cell was empty. The bed had not been slept in. Through the window, she could see North Tower, gleaming whitely against the clouds.

There were lights up there. *Lights*.

And something worse.

12

When David first saw the lights, he moved to the edge of the trees to get a better look. He moved because it was something to do. He had no idea what went on in Agnus Dei. Lights in a bell tower in the middle of the night might be perfectly normal.

He was still there when he saw something besides the lights. He didn't believe it. He looked at it twice and decided he must be getting drunk on rotgut whiskey. He advanced halfway across North Lawn and gave it another try.

He was not going crazy. He was not seeing things. It was actually there.

He took a good long swig of whiskey and didn't notice the burn.

There was a noose up there, hanging from the ceiling, swinging in the wind.

He thought of Kat's voice on the phone, saying: We've got to get her out of here *now*.

He took another swig and started across the lawn again, meaning to raise hell at one of the side doors until someone heard him who was authorized to go up there and stop whatever was going on. He stopped after a few steps. He couldn't do any such thing. If whoever was trying to do themselves in was neither Annie nor Kat—and it would never be Kat—he would ruin it all. He would get himself and Kat and everyone who talked to him in trouble. He would disqualify himself as Annie's refuge. He would screw it all up.

He turned back to the tower and the noose. He was going to have to climb.

13

Before she left retreat corridor, Kat went into the lavatory, the Mary Chapel, even the linen closet. The bolts were thrown, damn it. Annie had to be on the corridor. Annie wasn't on the corridor. Annie wasn't anywhere.

Kat took a votive candle from the Mary Chapel and lit it. It was inadequate, but better than nothing. Anything would be better than bumping through the anteroom again. A fumbling mania pounded hurryhurryhurry through her brain.

She stopped on the landing and listened. There wasn't so much as a snore coming from the professed Sisters' corridor.

She wanted to shake Reverend Mother out of bed and tell her there was a noose hanging from the rafter in North Tower, the place was lit up like a jack-o'-lantern, and now what? She wanted to scream "I told you so" over that undoubtedly bald head. There wasn't time.

She went past the empty portress station, through the reception room, into the main anteroom. The candle flame flickered and rose. She pushed her way through the chairs around the main anteroom table, catching her ankle every few inches, catching her robe and nightgown on splintering wood, not knowing what she was running to, what she was trying to prevent, what she thought was going on up there.

She grabbed the North Wing door. It was locked tight.

14

When Annie got to the top of the stairs, the tower door was open, letting cold air pour into the stairwell. The noose was swaying in the wind. Votive candles were scattered around the floor, every one of them lit. The stool was lying on its side, as if someone had kicked it over.

Now that she was here, she was no longer calm. Her headache was a geyser. The rope was frayed and rough. If she put her neck into that, it would sting her a hundred times and more. It would burn against her throat. All of a sudden, it felt like a terrible thing, a terrible, impious thing. She saw the Devil holding out the noose to her, drooling black goo that welled out of his gums and teeth. When she blinked again, she saw her father in Stephen's face, the defeat and the pain and the final, impotent protest.

Would it be like that? Would she kick the stool out from under her and in that last second twist away, plead and strain and fight, desperate to escape what she had started?

Agnus Dei was a wall at her back, an imperative. It would have what it wanted. The girl who had died here sat in

317

the shadows, watching. Annie could feel her here. She could hear the noise of some frantic animal in the ivy outside, looking for sanctuary in a wall.

The noose swung back and forth, like a hypnotist's watch.

If she did this, would there be an end to the pain?

It came at her then, a thought so clear and sharp with the cold air of sanity it nearly knocked her off her feet.

Where had the noose come from? Where had the candles come from? Who in the name of God was in here with her?

It was like rising from the dead, rising and learning to fear death all over again. It was like rising from the dead only to realize there was someone on the other side of the coffin lid with an ax, ready to murder you.

What in the name of Jesus, Mary, and Joseph had she thought she was doing?

She twisted around, needing to get out of here, needing to get as far away from this stage set for a séance as she could manage, unable to take her eyes off the noose or the candles or the tower door. The tower door, pulled all the way back when she first came in, was swinging forward, swinging forward, swinging toward her.

15

Locks could be opened by fiddling with hairpins. Locks could be opened by simple destruction. Kat gave half a second's thought to hairpins and none at all to relative strength. She threw her candle into the corner and grabbed the heaviest arch-backed chair. She had the chair off the floor and tilted arch forward before she remembered it was too heavy for her to pick up. She was ramming it into the door before she realized it might not do any good.

16

Someone was ramming the North Wing anteroom door. Everyone on postulant corridor was waking up. Jane could hear them coming out of their cells, gathering on the landing below her. Every part of her was pounding, head and skin and eyes and blood and teeth and heart and nerves and bone

318

and even her feet. Her mouth was a desert. The last Methedrine capsule had sent her up and beyond. She was looking
at Annie and she was looking at a mirror. The mirror had
leached the soul out of her and the life and the truth and the
faith and the Holy Catholic Church and now she had it cor-
nered. She had the knife in her hand and she had it cor-
nered, backed up against an archway with no way to get to
the door.

"Kat was right," Annie shouted at her. "Kat was *right*.
You're *crazy*. You're *crazy*."

Far below them, Kat was screaming, "Open the door,
God damn it, open the God-damned door."

Jane put out her hand until the tip of the knife was cutting
into Annie's cheek and said, "Bang, bang. You're dead."

17

David saw it as soon as he got his head over the archway sill, just as he heard the screaming start—Annie
backed into a far corner, doing a backbend into the wind,
and that crazy idiot standing over her with the knife,
laughing so hard she could barely stay upright. He could
see it all: the knife and the laughing and the hand on
Annie's shoulder, pushing her backward, backward into
dead air over a hundred-foot drop.

Then he caught a foot on a vine and slipped.

18

The last lunge took the skin off both her palms. Kat
dropped the chair and stared at the blood oozing out of her
from a hundred small pricks in her skin. She could see the
white stretch of muscle and the white stretch of bone. Above
her, Annie was screaming and screaming and screaming, her
soprano panic bouncing through the stairwell and piercing
wood.

The anteroom door shuddered and jerked. Kat dived for
it. Thank God, somebody had opened that God-damned
door.

Kat pushed past Angela Louise and headed for the stairs,

running, taking them two at a time, marveling at herself because part of her brain was thinking of the penance due speaking during Grand Silence and the penance due making unnecessary noise and the case she could make for this noise being necessary.

The rest of her was not thinking at all. It was just moving. It moved right past Angela Louise's question about what was going on around here and right past the novices clogging the landing on the third floor and right past the postulants huddled at the bottom of the tower stairs. Martha caught her at the last minute, held her, yelled, "What's *up* there?" into her face. Kat threw her off and kept running until she was at the top of the tower stairs and through the door and

19

they were all around Jane now, coming in from every side, trying to stop it at the last minute, but it wasn't going to work, it wasn't going to work, Kat coming across the floor, David Marsh slipping and sliding on the ivy and the maple leaves, Annie grabbing at her, grabbing at her, trying to get upright again, none of it was going to work. Jane was flying, literally flying, her feet weren't touching the ground, her body was smoke. There was nothing they could do about her now. There was nothing they could do to save themselves, they would all go up like smoke and

20

Kat was halfway across the room when she saw David coming through the archway, halfway across and in no mood to stop or wonder what he was doing there. Jane had a knife and the point of it was on Annie's throat. Kat could see the beginning of blood, drops of blood like the blood that fell from Jesus' hands. She got her hands on Jane's shoulders and pulled until

320

21

Jane was swinging around, swinging around, hands on her shoulders and her wrists, hands on her arms, the knife twisting out, twisting back, pointing backward over the bones of her hand and David Marsh stopped dead in the middle of the floor, staring from one to the other of them like he'd just walked into a lesbian orgy or a Black Mass or a George Romero movie come to life because

David wasn't going to be in time. He wasn't going to get there nearly in time. What in the name of Christ crucified did they think they were doing? They were

on her now, on her, like feeding vampires, like vultures, she would see them all in hell for it. They were standing above her, her mother and her father, they were holding the butcher's steel in the air and bringing it down, bringing it into her, into her throat this time, cutting up through the bone, forcing blood down her throat and into her lungs and there just wasn't ny *air*. The cramps hit her in waves, a mockery of labor. She was lying on the kitchen table and there was blood everywhere, on her hands and feet and arms, on the shoes she'd left on the floor, blood coming out of her everywhere in thick mottled masses, and the pain was unbearable. The pain had always been unbearable, the knife had always had a life of its own, it had gone on for years and years and years and now it was

gone.

24

"Jesus Christ," David said. "Dear Jesus Christ in Heaven, she's *dead*."

MORNING

"Sister? Are you all right? I can get some coffee if you're cold."

The light coming through the archway was faint but steady, gray and diffuse, filtered by fog. By clouds, too, probably, Annie thought. Another November storm.

There was blood everywhere, on the floor and the stool, on the noose that still hung from the center rafter and swung in the wind. Nothing but a lifeless piece of rope, now. Nothing to be afraid of.

And Jane was dead.

Jane was *dead*.

Annie picked up the pack of cigarettes David Marsh had left by her knees, extracted one, picked up the lighter, popped it into life in a great rush of fumes and flame. She must have smoked all of three cigarettes in her life. Every one had made her dizzy. At the moment, dizzy seemed as good as anything else.

Nuns did not smoke. But she was not a nun.

She looked across the tower room at Kat, standing with Reverend Mother and a man in an overcoat two sizes too large for him.

"Listen," Kat was saying. *"She committed suicide."*

EPILOGUE:
PART ONE

Testament

1

From a statement made by Anne Fairchild Bliss *to* Det. Lt.
R. F. Delaney, *November 7, 1983, Northton Municipal Hall,
Northton, Connecticut*:

She was trying to stick the knife in her throat. We kept
grabbing it, trying to get it away from her. It was very
confusing. When she couldn't get to the noose she had the
knife and she used that. I don't remember it that well.
There was a lot of shouting and confusion. What I remember mostly is a lot of noise and people running and
Kat, that's Katherine Mary O'Brien, I think Kat was crying. And the blood.

2

From a statement made by Sister Mary Anselm *(née Katherine Mary O'Brien) to the General Chapter of Inquiry, Agnus
Dei, Motherhouse, Society of Mary, Province of North
America, May 14, 1984,* Sister Marie Gabrielle *(for Reverend Mother General Marie Dolorosa) presiding*:

I don't think you could say anyone could have known. I
didn't know. She made me nervous and I thought she was
killing small animals. But I didn't have proof of that and
there was nothing in her day-to-day behavior to give it away.
Or to indicate she was taking drugs. Just the opposite. There
were little things and my mind made connections. Considering the kind of connections they were, what I had to go on,
I'd say I had a ninety-nine percent chance of being wrong.
On a day-to-day basis, she was mostly a perfect candidate. A
little stiff and unyielding, self-righteous, but that happens. I
didn't think she was going to commit suicide. It never even
occurred to me. It wouldn't have occurred to anyone under
the circumstances.

3

From a statement given by letter by Anne Fairchild Bliss *to the General Chapter of Inquiry, Agnus Dei, Motherhouse, Province of North America, May 15, 1984,* Sister Marie Gabrielle *(for Reverend Mother General Maria Dolorosa) presiding:*

You wrote asking if anyone could have known. Quite frankly, nothing was obvious to me at the time. I was under discipline and very upset because it was becoming clear I might not have a religious vocation. I was thinking about this all the time. Jane Galloway was my prie-dieu partner and I saw her every day during this period, in chapel and at recreation before I went on retreat, and also during work charge. She always seemed to me the model postulant. It never occurred to me she was anything else.

4

From a statement made by Sister Mary Beatrice *(née Martha Kowalski) to the General Chapter of Inquiry, Agnus Dei, Motherhouse, Society of Mary, Province of North America, May 15, 1984,* Sister Marie Gabrielle *(for Reverend Mother General Maria Dolorosa) presiding:*

I know Reverend Mother wants to banish herself to Alaska and not be part of the administration anymore, but I don't think she should do it. None of us knew what was going on. We all thought Jane was annoying and not much fun, but we didn't think she was crazy. Except maybe Kat—Sister Anselm—and that was different. Kat said something to me once and I didn't believe it. If you'd known Jane, you wouldn't have believed it either. I thought Kat was just getting spooky, and of course she didn't like Jane. None of us did.

I was right behind Sister Anselm when she hit the tower room and I came in right after, and it was the strangest thing I've ever seen. I don't think anyone could have predicted it. Certainly not from quiet little Jane. There was this rope and all this blood. Jane had a knife and Annie was pulling at it, I think trying to get it away from her. Sometimes it looked like Jane was trying to kill somebody with it, Annie, or maybe Kat. It was very confusing.

5

From a statement made by Anne Fairchild Bliss *to* Det. Lt. R. F. Delaney, *November 7, 1983, Northton Municipal Hall, Northton, Connecticut:*

It never occurred to me to wonder why she had a knife. Maybe she wanted to cut the rope. She had a knife. She was holding it when I first saw her.

From a statement made by Sister Mary Anselm *to the General Chapter of Inquiry, Agnus Dei, Motherhouse, Society of Mary, Province of North America, May 17, 1984,* Sister Marie Gabrielle *(for Reverend Mother General Maria Dolorosa) presiding:*

The knife was the only thing that surprised me. It was a kitchen knife. One of the ones they keep for cutting un-cooked meat. And she was swinging it wildly. Martha—Sister Beatrice—said when she first came in she thought Jane was trying to kill Annie, and I suppose sometimes it looked that way.

From "News of the Week," Publishers Weekly, *December 20, 1985:*

CARROLL AND STRAND TO PUBLISH NOVEL BY NORTHTON NUN SUICIDE WITNESS

John Harror, senior trade book editor for Carroll and Strand, had announced the signing of *Nuns,* a first novel by Annie Fairchild Bliss, based on last year's sensational Galloway suicide case. Bliss was a postulant in the Society of Mary during Galloway's tenure there and testified in both the police and Church inquiries into the incident. She is reported to have been one of four people actually on the scene at the time of Galloways death.

Harrow, who acquired the book as a complete manu-script, says Carroll and Strand plan to publish it as their lead title for fall '86. Agent Janice Rothman obtained an advance of $275,000 for author Bliss, and Caroll and Strand have announced plans to auction reprint with a $425,000 floor sometime in March.

8

Conversation on North Lawn, Agnus Dei, January 8, 1986:

SISTER ANSELM: David Marsh sent it. It's from some publishing magazine.

Sister Marie Lucienne (née Miriam Bender): That can't be serious.

Sister Anselm: Of course it's serious. Janice Rothman is David's agent.

Sister Marie Lucienne: A complete manuscript? She must have written the idiotic thing in six weeks.

Sister Anselm: Nobody's saying it's Hemingway, Lucienne.

Sister Marie Lucienne: I wonder what she *said.*

E P I L O G U E :
P A R T   T W O

Agnus Dei, August 26, 1986

1

Someone, a benefactor of the Order, Kat was sure, had given them a window-unit air conditioner for the library. Old Bonaventure cranked the thing up every morning after chapel and let it go full blast until evening recreation, keeping the thermostat at colder than cold. Nobody minded. Even the light cotton of summer habit was too much when it covered everything but your hands and your face. Sometimes the top of Kat's head sweated. It was one of those things, like finding out your face was a different shape than anything you'd ever imagined it to be, that constituted the surprises of going traditional.

"Going traditional" was this week's euphemism for shaving your head. Kat had never understood why, since the practice was optional, it had to be called by the term the people who didn't choose it found most comfortable.

She let herself into the library and behind the catalogue desk. She put her mail down on the green felt blotter. A letter from Constance, probably the wedding invitation. A letter from her mother, postmarked Cullen, Maine, home of a particularly expensive "substance-abuse clinic." An otherwise blank envelope with "Sister Mary Anselm, S.M.S." in the upper right-hand corner, which probably contained formal notice of her September assignment to the New York mission. The problem with the mail you received in a convent was that it almost never managed to surprise you.

She took a stack of books from the retrieval cart and headed for the far stacks, at what was really the front of the room. The windows there looked out on South Yard and the drive, on Northton and the hill. She was going to miss it, no matter how much she liked New York.

"Letter from Constance," she told Martha (Beatrice, she berated herself, *Beatrice*). She dropped the books she was carrying on the table. "I think it's the wedding invitation."

"Are you going to ask permission to go?"

"Why not? The Order is concerned to keep close and cordial relations—"

"Stop quoting," Martha said.

Kat sat down and started to sort books alphabetically by author, which was the only way Agnus Dei filed books. The Dewey Decimal System, apparently, was a Protestant plot. She felt one of those nagging tugs that were the trace of a nicotine craving and tried to work harder, to bury the desire in activity. It didn't work. She would always be addicted to nicotine. Fortunately, so long as they let her wander around in full habit, she'd probably be too embarrassed to go back to smoking.

"Kat?" Martha said. Her voice sounded strangled.

"Anselm," Kat said, not looking up.

"*Sister*," Martha said.

Kat turned, unthinking, inattentive. Then her eyes caught

327

the flash of emerald green coming up the path through South Yard, and she froze.

"Dear God in Heaven," she said. "Annie Bliss."

"Exactly," Martha said.

"Annie Bliss," Kat said again. Then she broke out laughing. "Annie Bliss in a five-hundred-dollar dress."

2

The girl who answered the door was a novice, one of the little Italian girls, not someone she had known well, or at all. Sister Maria Aftonia. Annie couldn't remember her baptismal name. Whatever it was, it had been the name of a cipher, and this girl was no longer a cipher. She fussed.

"I don't know what the rules are in a case like this," she said. "We've never had alumnae come back except at receptions and of course—"

Annie cut her off. "Only postulants, novices, and professed Sisters past the anteroom," she said. She didn't know if it was true. Vatican II had made a hash of everything. She headed across the reception room to the "Victorian corner," a tight little niche with scrolled chairs and minuscule coffee tables and illogical curves of wall that cut off her view of almost everything. Almost. There were always the windows, looking onto South Yard.

She took the largest of the wingbacks and sat down with her hands in her lap and her feet on the floor. Then she realized what she was doing, and crossed her legs at the knee. She felt wrong—wrong to be back at Agnus Dei, wrong to be walking around in all this green silk and driving that little silver car she'd parked at the foot of the steps. Sometimes she wondered if she was ever going to get used to it. Sometimes she wondered if she was ever going to get a full night's sleep again.

Agnus Dei was a weight, a boulder she was carrying on her head. She had felt it beginning to crush her as soon as she pulled into the drive.

She looked Maria Antonia square in the eye (always meet life head on, her shrink was fond of saying) and said, "I'd like to ask Reverend Mother's permission to see Kat—to see Sister Anselm."

"You don't have to ask anyone's permission," Maria Antonia said. "You're on the list.'

"All right," Annie said. "I'd like to see Sister Anselm. If she's free."

"Would you like some iced tea while you wait?" Maria Antonia said.

3

At the last minute, Kat took the copy of Annie's book David had sent her (an "uncorrected proof," as he put it) and stuffed it into her pocket. It was worn and ragged. Everyone from Reverend Mother to Angela Louise, home for the summer from a teaching apostolate in Missouri, had read it twice. Kat had a vague idea that if things went right, she should ask Annie to autograph it. Just to show she didn't mind. That nobody minded. That nobody wanted Annie to disappear or pretend she'd never existed.

What every last one of them wanted was for *Jane* to disappear. Into a black hole.

She wanted to ask Annie: Have you been able to stop thinking about it? Do you wake up in the night with it? Have you been able to make a life?

Or did Jane win this one after all?

4

The first thing Annie thought when she saw Kat was that she'd never doubted Kat would be a nun. She watched the small-boned figure float toward her in gray habit and white novice's veil and all-concealing wimple and realized she'd never *seen* Kat in a postulant's dress. In her mind, Kat had always been a woman in traditional habit, a nun incarnate.

"Annie?" Kat stopped just short of Annie's chair. Annie smiled at her tentatively.

"She went to get some iced tea," Annie said. "The little girl—"

"Maria Antonia. Do you remember her?"

"No."

"Angela Martucci. She was my prie-dieu partner. She

329

never said a word until we hit the senior novitiate, and then you couldn't shut her up."

"I got your invitation," Annie said. "To your profession. And Martha and Miriam's, I guess. I don't even know how many made it through."

"Seven," Kat said.

"Seven."

Annie went to the windows and looked out over the long slope of South Yard to the fieldstone wall. To the left were the shuttered windows of West Wing, where Kat must have spent the year before this one. Annie wondered what that was like: worse, because of the silence and restrictions of enclosure; or better, because in West Wing you would be cut off from any sight of North Tower, any reminder of . . . things. Things. She really shouldn't have come. She was getting her first headache in two and a half years.

She leaned forward and pressed her face to the broad windowpane. "Did you know my brother was in jail?"

"I'm sorry," Kat said. "For something serious?"

"David got him a job with one of those companies he has stock in. I think they make cement. They made Stephen a salesman and then they caught him rigging figures or something and then they prosecuted. They gave him six months with three suspended. My mother sat in the courtroom the whole time Stephen was pleading guilty and she . . . acted like my mother. Which she doesn't actually do a lot anymore."

"We've all read your book," Kat said gently. "Everybody in the house. Reverend Mother wants Vanessa Redgrave to play her in the movie."

Annie scratched her fingernail against the glass, for something to do. "It's not very well written," she said.

"I don't think you spent a great deal of time writing it."

"No," Annie said. "No, I didn't. David sat me down at the typewriter and my . . . my psychiatrist said it wouldn't be a bad idea, and I tried to make it sound like the books I like, and then David looked at what I'd done and went over it the best he could, and then the next thing I knew . . . the next thing I knew, I had a great deal of money."

330

"There's nothing wrong with that," Kat said. "You always wanted that."

"Yes, yes that's true. I always wanted that."

"Annie—"

"Please," Annie said. She could feel the tears pushing out of her and the boulder on her head. She couldn't make herself turn around. She didn't want to see Kat's face. She didn't want to see anything of Agnus Dei, not anything at all. "Please," she said again. "Just tell me one thing. Who killed Jane Galloway, you or me?"

5

Somewhere, someone was riding a mini-tractor through the dead heat of summer. It sounded like a wasp trapped in glass, angry and frantic.

Annie was pressed against the window, balled up into a vertical but convincing mock of the fetal position. How long had those muscles been so tight? How long had Annie been so tight, so defensively closed, so frightened? Kat tilted her head forward, letting her jutting veil close out the world. That was what the veil was for, to cut off peripheral vision, to serve as an aid to Custody of the Eyes, to force a nun to look at God and only at God. And Who was God? According to her last retreat master, the God you could see was the Christ in every man.

In her dreams, the blood flowed endlessly, the knife was sharp and sticky in her hand. It cut a thin red line into her palm.

She looked up at the massed armor that was Annie's back and said, "I did."

6

It was like melting. Annie turned away from the window and looked at Kat, Sister Anselm now, straight and calm and eternal in that ancient habit.

"You're not lying to me?"

"There's no reason to lie," Kat said. "It wasn't willful. No one wanted her to die."

"*I* wanted her to die," Annie said. "I *hated* her. I was

331

standing up there, looking at that noose, and then I turned and there she was and it was like I'd had a hood over my eyes for months. I'd been walking around kicking myself for not being as perfect as she was, and all the time she'd been picking at me, pushing me, trying to get me to . . . she set up the whole thing. She wanted to see me dead."

"She was disturbed."

"I read the papers," Annie said. "My shrink was big on that. On not avoiding it. I read about the marks they found on her. Child abuse. And instead of feeling sorry for her, I was glad, Kat, I was—"

"Sshh," Kat said. "Stop it."

"I talk to my priest about it. I talk to my shrink about it. I even talk to David about it. It doesn't go away."

"Don't worry about it so much," Kat said. "Ask God's grace and let Him give it to you."

"I just didn't want to have been the one who killed her," Annie said. "It was like, if I killed her I could never get back from it. Back to the Church, I guess. Back to somewhere I could think I was a good person. Do you know what I mean?"

"I think so."

Annie sighed. She didn't mind looking at Agnus Dei now. She didn't even mind remembering it was beautiful. She just didn't want to be reminded very long.

"You know," she said, "sometimes I realize it's been two and a half years, and I'm still not making any sense."

7

She was coming back up the steps after seeing Annie to her car when Martha came up to her, her eyes too wide and dark in the white of veil and wimple.

"I was bringing the tea," Martha said. "And then I heard you."

"Sister." Kat bowed slightly.

"I was there, Sister. I was right behind you. You could not possibly have killed Jane Galloway."

The mini-tractor was running again. It still sounded angry. Kat looked down the drive at Annie's car making its way to the gate, a silver bullet, a magic weapon against werewolves and vampires and monsters of all kinds. From her point of view, material possessions were an ineffective defense, in this world or the next. From Annie's point of view, they probably did quite well. She brushed past Martha and headed for the open front door, sending up a short prayer for rain.

"Sister," Martha said again.

Kat stopped on the top step and looked back. "What difference does it make?" she said.

Martha blinked. "But I saw you," she said. "Jane was dead and you were only halfway to her."

"What difference does it make?" Kat said again. "There is no sin where there is no intention to sin."

Martha wavered. "But if Annie killed Jane Galloway," she started.

"Telling her would accomplish nothing," Kat said. She looked down the drive again and saw Annie's car picking up speed on the Old Northton Road. Annie in a little silver bullet of a car and a five-hundred-dollar dress. Agnus Dei, that had come off better than anybody expected in Annie's flagrantly ungrammatical chronicle of sex and sin and death. Agnus Dei was a building on a plot of land and a name on a letterhead, that was all. It was a manifestation of Christ in the world only so long as *they* were manifestations of Christ in the world, every second of their lives, act by act, word by word, intention by intention. She had added her belief in that—in the necessity of that—to the things she had believed when she first came through these doors.

She wanted to take Martha's hand and say: being a nun is more than being called "Sister" and having old ladies try to give you their seat on the bus. Being a nun is even more than working overtime to see the face of God. Being a nun is being a manifestation of Christ in the world.

Martha was still staring at her. Kat shrugged. "Why kill her," she said, "if I don't have to?"

"She said she wanted to kill Jane."

"She never had the faintest idea what she was doing."

"But," Martha said.

Above them, the bells started ringing the noon Angelus. There were bells in North Tower again. Reverend Mother had had them put up right after the Chapter of Inquiry closed.

Kat went into the foyer and crossed the reception room, taking the shortcut to chapel. She could feel the heavy weight of the fifteen-decade olivewood rosary banging against the side of her leg, the weight of Annie's novel in one pocket and her devotions book in the other. She said her rosary in chapel these days.

Then she made novenas, for Annie and David.

LONDON-PARIS-BROOKFIELD, CONNECTICUT
January 1984—October 1985

A NOTE

About three quarters of the way through the writing of this book, I opened a copy of *Time* magazine and got a surprise—there, in the religion section, was a picture of *real nuns*. Habits—modified, but no shorter than calf length, and with headdresses that completely concealed the hair. A regular convent chapel, complete with Sisters in look-alike ranks.

There are, of course, a number of Orders of "real nuns" (i.e., nuns as most of us grew up thinking of nuns) still operating in the United States. They even have an organization of their own, to promote traditional convent life in a country that doesn't seem to have much use for it anymore. To read magazines and newspapers, however, especially in the last few years, is to get the impression that they, and the way of life they represent, have become extinct.

It is possible that the "new nuns" have it right, and the traditionals are fighting a losing battle. I hope not. In working on this novel, I spent almost two years researching post–Vatican II traditional Orders, their problems and their ideals. I think there is a lot to be said for their point of view, and I hope I made that clear.

I would like to thank, now, the nuns who taught me English and biology and mathematics, and in doing so taught me the value of total commitment; the girls I went to school with who later entered Orders, who showed me that a radical response to God could be coupled with common sense and generosity and openness to people and ideas and everyday life; and everyone, in and out of the American Roman Catholic community, who offered the insights and information that make this book more complete than it otherwise would have been.

Thanks, too, to my husband, Bill DeAndrea, who read every page of this book as it came out of the typewriter, through endless drafts, and complained only once in a while —and who made dinner and made me eat when I worked too late, and who got up to keep me company when I had to run off somewhere and didn't want to drive alone, and who kept the home fires burning when I had to be in New York.

I want to thank my sister-in-law, Joan Berry Papazoglou, who was pressed into reading this at different points to determine where I was "boring." Her comments were invaluable.

Thank you, too, to Sandra Manilla, who kept my life in shape during the first year of writing, and let me park myself on her couch whenever I was going crazy from having spent too long a time closed in by the four walls of my office—the last she has done not just for this book, but for my entire career, and listened to my complaints besides.

To Meredith Bernstein, my agent, for unfailing enthusiasm, which always showed up just when I had decided I should never have got myself into this long a project to begin with, and probably didn't know what I was doing.

And to all the people at Crown: Betty Prashker, my editor, for good advice and even better insights; David Groff, for a brilliant line edit without which this would be a much poorer book; and Amoy Allen, for kindnesses too numerous to mention.

ABOUT THE
AUTHOR

ORANIA PAPAZOGLOU was educated in Catholic schools in Connecticut and was graduated from Vassar College. She has published two other novels. SWEET, SAVAGE DEATH and WICKED LOVING MURDER. She lives with her husband, mystery writer William L. DeAndrea, in Brookfield, Connecticut, and in Europe.